LEGACY
of the
Highlands

HARRIET SCHULTZ

Legacy of the Highlands
Copyright © 2011 by Harriet Schultz

ISBN-13: 978-1467910538
ISBN-10: 1467910538

Printed in The United States of America

Cover design by Judy Gailen
Book design by Natasha Fondren of the eBook Artisans

WITH THANKS

With thanks to Martha Ives, Judith S. Hellenbrand, Marlene Bloom, Sandra Curcio, Sukey Rosenbaum and Maxine Durst for their advice and constant support.

I'm also grateful to several participants on Scotland's Grampian Life forum, who provided invaluable assistance in the early stages of the book.

To Ed, for always believing

CHAPTER 1

*S*hould he tell her? Maybe, but Will Cameron knew that his wife would worry and that was the last thing he wanted. She looked so comfortable, curled up in an overstuffed chair near the fireplace, as she paged through a prestigious gallery's auction catalog in the fading light of the late winter afternoon.

Will watched her for a few minutes, then forced his attention back to the stack of architectural plans he'd been scrutinizing as he lay sprawled on the living room's hardwood floor, but it was no use. How was he supposed to concentrate when his mind was consumed by an ill-defined uneasiness? Besides, he was probably imagining that someone was tailing him. Yet if that were so, why was he suddenly unable to sleep through the night? And why was he on edge every time he left the house? Will knew that he had to tell Alexandra the reason for his anxiety, but it could wait another day.

For now, he'd blame his mood on work. He shoved the pile of blueprints aside with a muttered curse. "Something's wrong with the specifications for Diego's zillion dollar project, but I can't figure out what it is and it's driving me nuts. I'm tempted to run these through the shredder," Will grumbled as he flipped onto his back. "I shouldn't care if that arrogant S.O.B. loses a few million, but I do." He rubbed his eyes and ran a hand through his shaggy, dark brown hair.

"Diego will understand if you need another day or two," Alex said as she turned toward him. "You may not be friends anymore, but he trusts your expertise, especially if you tell him you have some doubts about this." She was worried about him. He'd seemed so stressed recently, and work couldn't be the only cause. But she knew this man well enough to accept that he wouldn't tell her what was really bothering him until he was good and ready.

"Why don't you take a break? I'll start dinner, we can have some wine, and you can look at the plans again later," Alex suggested.

"Yeah, you're right." Will yawned as he eased his strapping body into the down-stuffed cushion of his favorite chair, the mate to the one Alex had just vacated. Food, followed by sex, was just the distraction he needed. "I am kind of hungry," he said with a grin.

"Me too," Alex whispered. She hadn't missed the twinkle in her husband's eyes and guessed that his hunger didn't only involve food. She paused beside him and ran the tip of her tongue up the side of his neck until he shivered. When he reached for her she darted away, but the smile and raised brows she directed at him spoke volumes.

He followed her to the kitchen, pressed his body against her back, and wrapped his arms around her waist. She leaned her head against his solid chest and sighed. "We're not having dinner now, are we?"

"No, we're not," he assured her.

Alex sighed as Will nudged her hair out of the way so that his lips could find the curve between her neck and her shoulder, while his fingers slid under her sweater. His stroke was gentle, but insistent, and when his palms reached her nipples, they were already hard under the bit of lace still covering her skin. With one smooth motion he flicked the obstacle's clasp open and she raised her arms to help him tug the sweater over her head. Alex wanted to feel his warm skin against hers and reached back to strip off his sweatshirt, but his firm grip held her where she was. She understood then that he was intent on taking the lead this time. She closed her eyes and willingly surrendered, eager for the journey.

Will dipped his fingers into the glass Alex had set on the counter. She flinched as he slowly ran a bitingly cold piece of ice around the center of each breast until he turned her toward him and lowered his mouth. The change in temperature as his tongue licked the moisture from her reddened nipples made her gasp, and her hands dug into his hair to keep him precisely where she wanted him to be. When he pulled away, she watched his eyes shimmer with lust as his gaze lingered on her body, now only covered by low-slung jeans. She reached for her zipper, but he quickly covered her hand with his. "No. This is way sexier than being totally naked. Stay like this, at least for a while," he murmured. She reached for his crotch, but he took a step back. "We'll get to that, but for now I want to look at you." Will's voice was hoarse with passion.

"You're torturing me. Let me touch you," she moaned.

"Not yet," he whispered as a lascivious grin lit his flushed face.

"Okay, if you'd rather be a voyeur..." she challenged as her hands rose to her breasts and she caressed herself. Her light green eyes never left his and a minute later his self-control shattered. He scooped her into his arms and headed for their bedroom.

Hours later, completely sated, they napped. They

woke around 11 p.m. craving something sweet and decadent and zeroed in on their favorite ice cream's sticky sweet mix of chocolate, marshmallow and caramel. "Neither of us is going to be able to sleep if we don't have a Ben & Jerry's fix," Will said. "You stay warm in our bed and I'll go to the store. Don't worry about me freezing my ass off in the middle of the night."

"I feel no guilt, *mon amour*. You're the best husband ever. What would I do without you?"

"You'd have to get your own freakin' ice cream," he tossed back and winked. Their lovemaking had relaxed him so well that he'd stopped thinking about the sense of dread that had become his companion.

Alex leaned against the pillows and watched her husband stumble naked around a room that reeked of sex as he tried to find where he'd carelessly tossed his threadbare jeans. She lazily admired the body that she never tired of—broad shoulders, firm butt, long, muscular legs, and a chest sprinkled with silky dark curls that she loved to run her fingers through. Thick lashes framed gold-flecked eyes tinged with blue and green. Those eyes, those eyes. From the moment they met, she knew she'd want to stay lost forever in those eyes.

Alex groaned as the sound of the doorbell yanked her out of the depths of sleep. When it rang again and again, she forced one eye open to squint at the green glow of the bedside clock. It was 3:00 a.m. Will had to have heard the maddening sound too so why didn't he wake up and send whoever it was away? She rolled toward her husband's side of the bed, but instead of the expected warmth of his slumbering body, there was emptiness. "What the..." she mumbled. Her heart began to race in confusion as she sat up and grabbed a robe to cover her nakedness.

She shouted her husband's name as she flicked on lights on her way to the door. Where could he be? Of course! She smiled as she remembered that Will had gallantly offered to walk the few short blocks to their neighborhood's all-night market to satisfy their post-sex craving for ice cream. But he'd left around eleven. He should have been back hours ago. Where the hell was he? Her thoughts were muddled as she raced barefoot across the living room's cold hardwood. Will must have forgotten his key. That had to be it.

His name was on her lips as she opened the door, but her eyes widened when instead of her 6 foot 4 inch husband, she found a uniformed cop who looked about sixteen and a paunchy older man in a dark suit.

"Mrs. Cameron?" the suit asked.

Her mouth refused to form words so she just nodded. She put a hand on the door to steady herself as fear took hold and her stomach did a flip-flop.

"Your husband is William Cameron?"

"Yes," she whispered, then pulled the short silk robe more tightly around her body when she noticed the younger cop checking her out. Something must have happened to Will if the police were there at three in the morning. Her mind raced to come up with an explanation, while she tried to convince herself that she was in the midst of a particularly vivid and terrifying dream.

The older man flashed a badge. "I'm Pete O'Shea, a homicide detective with the Boston Police and this young man is Officer Jim Warren. Is it all right if we come in?"

"My husband isn't here ... I'm not sure," Alex mumbled, but O'Shea hadn't really been asking her permission, and she stepped back as the two men strode into the apartment. The detective grasped her arm and steered her into a chair.

"Find a blanket and a glass of water," he growled at his young partner, then added in a voice that was barely audible, "whiskey would be better."

Alex pulled her body as far as possible into the gray cushions of Will's favorite chair and drew her legs under her. Her heart was pounding and she couldn't expand her lungs to take the deep breath she desperately needed. She lowered her eyes and waited until she could make her voice work. Then her words tumbled out. "Where is Will? Is he hurt? Is that what you came to tell me? What's happened to my husband?"

O'Shea recognized the woman's imminent hysteria and knew it was best to keep this kind of news short and simple. "I'm very sorry to have to say this Mrs. Cameron, but your husband is dead. He was murdered tonight."

"What? What did you say?" Alex's brain couldn't immediately decipher the detective's words and she stared at his deeply lined face. It was a kind face, yet this man with the warm brown eyes had just allowed his mouth to say something monstrous. Her lips parted as she attempted to speak, to question, but her tongue seemed to have been ripped from its roots and she remained silent until a shudder wracked her body and she began to wail, "noooooooo, nooooooo."

"Please go away," she begged as tears streamed down a face that was deathly pale. "He went out for ice cream. I'm sure he'll be home soon. You need to leave."

"I wish that was the case Mrs. Cameron, but I've

seen the body," the detective said. The young cop handed O'Shea the plaid blanket he'd found in the bedroom and the older man threw it over Alex's bare legs, then wrapped her quivering shoulders in a navy blue throw that he'd grabbed from a nearby chair, but she continued to tremble uncontrollably. She tried to take a sip from the glass of water that the rookie put into her hand, but she couldn't swallow. Was she paralyzed like in a dream when you can't run from danger?

"You're lying! Why are you lying?" she shrieked as she pounded the arm of the chair with her fist. She grasped O'Shea's hand and raised her pleading eyes to his weary face, then recoiled as she saw the detective's own sorrow there. "I want Will. I want him to come home." Her words were barely audible.

"Ma'am? Mrs. Cameron? I need to ask you some questions," the detective said after giving her a few minutes to compose herself, but Alex was incapable of acknowledging him. Through the fog that surrounded her brain, she heard him say that Will had been killed just one street away from their luxurious condo in Boston's Back Bay neighborhood. A young couple out walking their dogs discovered his body in an alley when the animals began to howl in alarm.

Police really do say, "Is there someone we should call, ma'am?" after delivering a life-shattering *coupe de grâce*. The only person Alex wanted at that moment was Will, but she whispered her best friend Francie's phone number instead.

Alex was oblivious to the routine questions O'Shea continued to ask. He'd just begun another attempt when Francie pushed past the young cop who'd answered the door and burst into the living room. She wore jeans and a sweatshirt turned inside out. There were slippers on her feet instead of shoes, her dark, curly hair was sleep rumpled and she was panting. "I need a minute to catch my breath. I ran here."

A moment later the diminutive whirlwind known as Francesca Sandburg glared at the detective as she wrapped her arms around Alex and uttered soothing sounds in her friend's ear. "Don't you have a heart? Leave her alone! Stop badgering her!"

"You want whoever did this to be caught, right?" the frustrated detective argued as he paced from one end of the large room to the other. "The first twenty-four hours after a crime are critical and Mrs. Cameron might provide us with the lead that we need to catch the bas ... the person who did this."

"Besides, we need to bring her to Mass General. That's where they took Mr. Cameron. Next of kin must identify the body, ma'am, and then we can connect her with people who are trained to deal with this sort of thing," the young cop added.

"Don't the two of you dare gang up on me," Francie warned. "You won't win. You obviously know who 'the body' is or you wouldn't have come here in the middle of the night to tell Alex that Will is ... is..." Francie's face flushed and her gray eyes filled with tears. She ignored the tissue O'Shea offered and swiped at the wetness with the back of her hand. "You said that you found Will's driver's license in his wallet. His picture is on it. Isn't that enough?"

"No, ma'am. We know this isn't easy, but regulations require a formal identification."

"Fuck the regulations," Francie muttered. "Give me a minute to think, all right?" she snapped knowing the cop was just trying to do his job. She took a breath in an attempt to calm down. "How about this? My husband is Will's lawyer. He can identify him. Or Will's parents can do it. They live near here on Beacon Hill, right on Louisburg Square. Call Anne and John Cameron. You need to notify them about this anyway, right?"

"No!" Alex shrieked, finally connecting to the conversation around her. "If I go with them I can prove that they've made a mistake. The man they found can't be Will. Someone must have stolen his wallet and then that person was murdered. That's why they think it's Will. I know it's not true. I won't let it be."

O'Shea took Francie aside. "Look, I know this is rough, but I've been through this enough times to know that it will help your friend come to grips with the reality of what happened if she sees her husband's body." He didn't wait for an answer. "Get her into some warm clothes. The morgue's kept at about 40 degrees."

"All right, all right," Francie conceded and clutched Alex's hand as she led her to the bedroom where she helped her dazed friend change into jeans and two heavy sweaters for the ride to the hospital in O'Shea's unmarked car.

Alex and Francie had their arms around each other as the detective guided them through the hospital's chaotic emergency department to the deathly hush of the morgue. At his signal, an unsmiling attendant wheeled a gurney toward them. The shape that rested on it was covered in a sheet so white that it gleamed like fresh snow under the room's harsh lights.

"There's no blood on it. I thought there'd be blood," Alex whispered. The smell of disinfectant and other unidentifiable substances made Francie clutch her stomach. The two women tightened their hold on each other, then Francie nodded and the attendant gently lifted a corner of the sheet to reveal Will's expressionless face, his skin devoid of its usual ruddy color.

"Oh God, oh God, oh God. Please, God—no," Alex begged and gripped the table as her knees gave way. The hand that reached toward her dead husband trembled as if she'd had one cup of coffee too many. Will's body had always responded to her touch and she hoped that maybe, just like in a fairy tale, she'd miraculously be able to wake him from his slumber. She brushed a strand of silky dark hair off his forehead and began to stroke his face as she whispered his name over and over, while a stream of tears ran silently down hers.

"He's not going to wake up, is he?" she finally murmured.

"No sweetie, he's not. Maybe we should go," Francie said, but Alex ignored her. "This is all my fault. I told him about a shortcut through that alley. I wanted him to get home faster so we could, we could … it must have been so dark. He should never have gone out for ice cream in the middle of the night. If only he'd stayed in bed … oh, Francie," she sobbed, "I'll never forgive myself."

"Shhh, shhh. You didn't force Will to do anything he didn't want to do. Terrible things just happen sometimes, that's all." Francie wasn't sure that Alex had even heard her.

"His face is so pale and he's cold. Where are his clothes?" She scanned the room without moving, and when she didn't see Will's clothes she told Francie that they had to find a blanket for him. Her friend just nodded. Alex's hand glided from his face to a muscular shoulder and then to his chest. "His heart's not beating! I can't feel his heart!" Her own began to pound as a part of her slowly began to accept what she was seeing. "It's because he's really dead, isn't it?" She wondered how skin that had been blazing hot when they'd made love just hours ago could now be as icy as a statue. Was that even possible? "This is Will's body, but it isn't him. It can't be true Francie, can it?"

Alex continued to stare at her husband's lifeless form. Finally, she gently cradled his face and kissed his forehead, his eyelids and then his lips. She lingered there before she abruptly straightened her shoulders, turned, and resolutely walked away.

"I thought ... I thought ... that ... that ... if I didn't see it, it couldn't be real. That's not so strange, is it?" she stammered before her throat closed again. With a lifetime of Catholic guilt, she assumed that God had taken her thirty-four-year-old husband from her as punishment for some transgression. What mortal sin had she committed to deserve this damnation? Wasn't it enough that He'd already stolen both of her parents? Now the greedy bastard had to have her husband too? Was her love somehow toxic, carrying with it a sentence of death?

CHAPTER 2

No matter how hard Alex tried to keep her brain enveloped in a shroud of protective mist, investigators continued to mine her memory for potential clues in the days following Will's murder. "Do you have any idea why someone would want to kill Mr. Cameron? Did he have any enemies? Was he having an affair? Money troubles? Was he a gambler? How about his family or business associates?"

She was tempted to scream, "He's dead because of me! I wanted some fucking ice cream and he was in a hurry to get back so we could continue to screw our brains out. And I told him about the shortcut through that goddamn alley. That's why he's dead." She wished for a do-over with the same determination she'd had since she'd been a little girl in her attempt to get it, whatever "it" was, right, but death didn't come with do-overs.

"Why don't they just shut up and go away?" she asked Francie's husband, David, as she stalked out of the living room after yet another round of questions. "They're never going to find the murderer anyway."

No witnesses had come forward, although the attack occurred steps away from a street filled with trendy restaurants, sidewalk cafes and designer shops. The police knew that Will had never reached the store. No ice cream container was found at the scene and the convenience store's security camera confirmed that he'd never arrived there. "We've ruled out robbery as a motive because your husband's wallet, watch and wedding ring were untouched. Whoever did this either got spooked and ran before he could take anything, or wanted us to know the killing was deliberate," Detective O'Shea told her. She begged the cop to give her Will's ring and sobbed in frustration when she was told it was being held as evidence.

The only clue to what was starting to seem like the perfect crime was the Scottish dagger, a *sgian dubh*—Gaelic for "black knife,"—found beside Will's body. Kilted Scots traditionally tuck a *sgian dubh* in one of their heavy socks. Legend has it that once the knife is drawn, it must taste blood before it's returned to its sheath, but forensics quickly ruled out this particular knife as the murder weapon. Investigators theorized that the dagger was left as a signature, although a search of international crime databases turned up no murders with the same distinctive marker. The knife itself was the kind that could be found in any shop that sold Scottish souvenirs so there was little chance it could be traced back to its source. But as the only clue, police doggedly pursued it.

"What was your husband's connection to Scotland?"

"We spent a week there as tourists last year," Alex answered in a monotone as she nervously picked at a hangnail. She'd already bitten her nails to stubs, a habit she'd broken as a teenager. The compulsion to do something with her hands was overwhelming and she'd started to crave cigarettes, another habit she'd fought with Will's help. But he was gone so what did it matter? Maybe she could bum a smoke from one of the ever-present cops.

"Why did the two of you go to Scotland? What did you do? Who did you meet? Was it your husband's idea or yours?"

She thought they must be really desperate to try to connect Will's murder to an eventless vacation, but she had no strength to argue and there was that dagger to consider. "We'd spent some time visiting friends in London and on a whim decided to drive up to the Highlands since neither of us had ever been. Will likes—liked—single malt so we stopped at a couple of whiskey distilleries, went to Loch Ness ... we didn't see the monster, " she added sarcastically, "hiked up to the castle in Edinburgh and spent a few days in Inverness. It rained a lot."

"Was there anything, anything at all Mrs. Cameron, that seemed odd or unusual during your visit?"

"No, nothing. I've already told you that Will was excited to discover that Cameron is a Scottish clan name. He bought a few souvenirs. Other than that, it was just a chance for us to get away together."

"Are they ever going to stop asking me about Scotland?" Alex groaned in frustration to Francie after yet another round of questions. "Millions of people visit the damn country and none of them end up murdered because of a stupid vacation."

In a brick townhouse on Beacon Hill's ultra-exclusive Louisburg Square, Will's mother, Anne Cameron, raged at her husband, John.

"You should have warned him! Goddamn it to hell, John, you and your asinine Scottish ancestors. Why didn't you tell him?" she shrieked, hurling the words like razor-sharp spears. Angry red splotches marred her carefully tended porcelain skin and her voice cracked as her airway tightened with grief.

"Anne, Anne," John Cameron whispered, his own

tears blending with hers as he tried to console this woman who he loved desperately, to somehow ease his own grief by comforting her. Repulsed, she shoved him away, her delicate features contorted by anguished fury.

"Please listen to me, Anne. What do I have to do to make you believe me? Tell me and I'll do it," he begged with growing exasperation. He turned his back to her as he propped his hands against the wall, leaned into it and lowered his head. When he spoke again, his tone was calmer. "Don't you know that I would have done anything ... anything, if I had the slightest suspicion that there was danger? I would never have left Will defenseless. He was our child, I've lost my son too."

"You had a choice! But no, you had to continue your cursed father's quest for Scottish independence and turn a blind eye to the risk of being involved with those blasted tartan terrorists. Tell me, John, how could an intelligent man be so stupid?" Anne couldn't even look at the man she'd once loved. The moment they'd been told that a Scottish dagger was found next to Will's body, a white-hot poker tore through her gut. "You have to go to the police and tell them everything."

"You know I can't do that." John collapsed into a chair, braced his elbows on his knees and cradled his head in his palms. He didn't look up when his wife said in a voice softer than a whisper, "I'm just as guilty as you. If only I'd been strong enough to stop you or to warn Will to be careful. And now I'm too frightened to turn you in."

Only an occasional sob broke the hushed silence as each parent dealt with unfathomable sorrow alone. Anne curled her lean body into a ball on their bed and gazed at the logs that blazed in the marble-framed fireplace of their opulent bedroom. She tugged a thick down comforter around her shoulders, but it did nothing to thaw the block of ice where her heart used to be. Blind fury was a new emotion for Anne, and she aimed it directly at her husband and the blood feuds that Scots continued for centuries.

She glanced at the man she'd been married to for thirty-five years, her blue eyes hard as the cobalt they resembled. The cold, deadly malice in her voice shook him.

"You're a fool, John Cameron. My only comfort is knowing that you will burn in the fires of hell for all eternity and that your black soul and our angel son's will never meet."

CHAPTER 3

*H*ours after Will Cameron's murder, four men sat around a scarred wooden table in a seedy Gloucester, Massachusetts, bar that reeked of stale beer and cigarettes. No one in this historic seaport at the tip of Cape Ann, north of Boston, would take note of what seemed to be a group of fishermen out to hoist a late-night beer or three. Their clothing and behavior were unremarkable; their faces bore the weathered complexions of men most at home on the sea.

"So, Jamie lad, is it done?" the oldest of the four asked as he leaned across the table toward a tall, burly young man a year or two out of his teens whose dark eyes flashed like an excited child's after braving a roller coaster for the first time.

"It is, sir." His pimply face flushed as he made an effort not to smile. He was pleased with himself. After months of training, planning, waiting and several missed opportunities, he'd completed the task and earned the respect of his accomplices. His mind, relieved of anxiety, wandered. At first he thought it odd that the stunning relief he'd felt as he watched the life drain from Will Cameron's body reminded him of the release of orgasm. But then he'd remembered the phrase taught to him by the French whore who'd ended his innocence, *le petit mort*—the mindless limbo at the moment of sexual release—and he understood.

"Well then, that's good." The older man's slow and deliberate words yanked Jamie back to the present. The man's speech was laced with a slight accent—Irish? Scots? English? Or something else?

"And the camera? You remembered to use it lad? You weren't tempted to take some of his valuables as a souvenir, were you? This must not look like some ordinary robbery," one of the other men whispered in a voice made hoarse by years of smoke. He nervously stubbed out another cigarette in the overloaded ashtray.

"I did as I was instructed," Jamie said through clenched teeth as he shoved his empty beer bottle into those crowding the middle of the table with enough force to topple half of them. "As for the camera, see for yourselves." He removed a tiny digital camera from his pocket and slid it across the table.

Business concluded, the men relaxed and clinked their bottles in a final toast to a job well done. They'd be paid handsomely for helping this young man lose his virginity, in a manner of speaking. The gory photos of Will Cameron lying in a pool of blood provided all the proof the others would demand. They lingered for a few minutes more, chatting quietly, before setting out into the inky darkness to disperse like wraiths into the chill, foggy night. To anyone watching, it would seem that they were headed for their individual homes and their beds.

The older man's footsteps echoed as he made his way from the bar toward the end of a nearby deserted wharf, satisfied that from there he'd be able to see or hear anyone approach. He stuck his hand in his pocket once more to reassure himself that the camera's proof of Jamie's success was still there. Then he flipped open his cell phone. He hoped that the pea-soup fog that rendered him virtually invisible wouldn't distort the phone's signal. When the connection was made to another phone a continent away, he let out the breath he hadn't realized he was holding.

"Tell me," said the faraway voice. It was a command, not a request.

"'Tis done, and done well." He'd never doubted that they would be successful. Betrayal always came with a price, after all, and John Cameron's treachery carried with it a sentence of death. Not his, mind, but that of his blood so that his time on earth would be a living hell. First his son, and then...

"And the woman? What of her?" the far-off voice interrupted the man's momentary reverie. "Cameron's punishment is to see the death of his line. If this son of his planted his seed before you got to him, the woman must die too."

"Agreed, but we have to be sure she is with child before we act. We don't want more blood, especially a woman's, on our..." He didn't complete the sentence. "Someone's coming," he muttered as his heart began to pound. He quickly stuffed the phone in the pocket of his yellow slicker and wrapped his damp fingers around the handle of a razor-sharp dagger. He pasted the merry expression of the truly drunk on his face and staggered toward the sound of approaching footsteps, his path illuminated by the beam of a flashlight that blinded him as it was raised to his face.

"Evening," said a uniformed cop. "Not exactly a great night for a stroll, eh?"

"Good evening to you, officer. Ah, Christ, I had a bit too much and wanted to walk it off before heading home." He slurred his words and smiled engagingly, showing teeth that would make a dentist grimace. "Wouldn't want the old lady to take a frying pan to me head now, would I?"

"Ah," said the officer with understanding as he returned the smile. "No, we wouldn't want that. Can I give you a lift?" The bars wouldn't close for an hour yet and the area around the docks was quiet. He didn't want the man to topple into the frigid water or be tempted to get behind the wheel of a car.

"That's kind of you officer, but there's no need. It's an easy walk." He wished that the cop would stop blathering and leave him alone. Why do Americans have to be so damn friendly, he thought with disgust, as he struggled to maintain a foolish grin when he really wanted to snarl. Was he going to have to kill this cop who seemed to be memorizing his features? It would be easy enough to slash the whoreson's throat, but such an act would bring on a world of troubles. Besides, he was certain that a dim-witted, small town cop in Gloucester would never connect a boozed up fisherman to a murder in Boston.

"Well, take it easy on the drink," the cop finally responded. "I hope your wife doesn't give you too much trouble."

"It won't be the first time. And a good night to you, sir," he said and began to walk back toward the town. As he increased the distance between himself and the law, he gradually relaxed his grip on the knife.

CHAPTER 4

*T*he day of Will Cameron's funeral should have been bleak, complete with lightning, thunder and howling wind, but it was one of those impossibly brilliant, early spring days that are greeted with joy after a long, dreary New England winter. The bright sun, however, provided little warmth and Alex shivered, as much from frayed nerves as the air's chill. She shaded her eyes to gaze with disgust at the news helicopter that whirred overhead. They were like buzzards circling a carcass, but she knew that the media loves tragedy, especially when it involves high-profile pillars of Boston society like the Camerons.

Will's flower-covered mahogany coffin rested above the grave after its slow trip in the hearse from church. As it was lowered into the ground, Alex had a clear vision of her heart being ripped from her chest. She felt the urge to scream at the top of her lungs, but stifled the impulse by focusing on the aching finger she was deliberately strangling with her rosary beads.

Francie's husband kept his arm wrapped around Alex's waist as if he expected her body to slump to the ground. She was oblivious to the sea of black-clad friends, family, colleagues and curiosity seekers who crowded around the grave until she noticed the strikingly handsome man standing some distance from the throng. Diego Navarro. He was dressed in perfectly tailored black, his eyes hidden behind sunglasses, his body somehow tightly coiled and lithe at the same time. He has some nerve to show up here, Alex thought, as he raised one finger to lower the dark-tinted barrier between them and her eyes met his for an instant.

The gaze of the man who had once been Will's dearest friend never strayed from the young widow. He'd expected Alex to be devastated, but her pallor and weight loss alarmed him. Every protective instinct he had prodded him to pull her into his arms and shield her from further hurt, but he knew that was impossible. After his fight with Will, they'd severed all ties to each other except for a few business interests. That was why Will had been examining the plans for Diego's latest project the day of his death. He wasn't even sure if he should be here now, but how could he stay away? Will was his brother. And Alex? He'd acknowledged long ago that his feelings for her had never been brotherly.

"Did you see Diego? He's over there," Alex whispered to Francie as she tilted her head in his direction.

"My fault. I thought you would want him here … for old time's sake, so I called him. He's pretty broken up…"

"I can see that," Alex murmured, then turned her attention back to Will's open grave as the priest intoned, "Oh God, we commend to you the soul of your servant William Matthew Cameron, that he be received by your holy angels in Paradise and have joy everlasting through Christ our Lord. Amen." A final sprinkle of holy water and it was over. Alex bent to pick up a handful of loose earth and held it tightly for a few moments then brought it to her lips before tossing it into the deep hole where Will would rest for eternity.

"My child," the priest began as he walked toward her, his outstretched hands pale and trembling, milky blue eyes gentle with concern, but she turned her back to him and walked away. She had nothing to say to the priest. Why should she be on good terms with the God he represented, a cruel deity who'd abruptly snatched Will away from his future, their future? She didn't want to hear that it was God's will or that her husband had gone home to be with Jesus. Bullshit! It was all bullshit. They could all go to hell and take their greedy God with them. She had no use for Him. He'd taken her parents and now Will. She felt abandoned, alone and very afraid.

Anne and John Cameron were stunned by their daughter-in-law's snub of the family priest and quickly placed themselves between her and Father Scanlon. "Screw them," Alex whispered to Francie and David as she glared at the senior Camerons. " I don't care what anyone thinks anymore, especially those two uptight people. They have as little use for me as I do for them." Over the years they'd made Alex very aware that they'd expected Will to marry some slack-jawed, prep-schooled debutante, not the daughter of an electrician. It was a relief that she wouldn't have to try to win their affection ever again.

Although their grief should have matched or exceeded hers, Alex saw no outward sign of it. Not a hair was out of place on the blonde head that Anne Cameron leaned toward the priest. Her eyes were dry, of course. Tears would ruin her perfect makeup. The only crack in Anne's serene façade was the chalk-white color of the elegant fingers that held her Chanel bag in a death grip. Will's father stood straight and silent beside her, his strongly boned face tanned as always, his expression vacant. His black hair was stippled with white near the temples, which only enhanced his good looks. He glanced toward Alex and allowed her to see a fleeting glimmer of excruciating pain in the gold-flecked hazel eyes that were so like Will's before he abruptly looked away. Alex watched him reach for his wife's hand, but Anne pushed his arm away and put more distance between them.

If the loss of their child didn't bring them together nothing would, Alex realized, but their behavior wasn't that surprising. The Camerons were going through all the right motions, but seemed as devoid of emotion as ever. She'd never been able to figure out how the loveless coupling of these two cold people had resulted in a warm, passionate man like Will.

Alex mechanically accepted condolences as she walked with Francie and David toward the limo waiting to take them to the Cameron's Beacon Hill townhouse for a reception. "Can you and David find another ride? I need some space to pull myself together." She lifted her sunglasses and saw that the sister she'd never had, the woman who hadn't left her side for a week, was already shaking her head no. "Absolutely not," Francie said. "It's a bad idea for you to be alone … at least not yet. Look, Alex, it's a big car. David and I will sit up front with the driver if you want privacy in the back."

"Francesca," Alex began, deliberately using the form of her friend's name that meant something serious was about to be said. "You've been the best and I love you for staying glued to me this week, but you've got to back off. I need to prove something to myself. Please," she implored. "It's only a ten minute ride, a baby step. Let me do this."

Francie finally nodded and hugged Alex as if to transfuse her with some of her own strength. Alex's eyes scanned the crowd for Diego, and when she didn't spot him she assumed he'd already left. She thought it was odd that he hadn't spoken to her, but at least he thought it important enough to be there. David helped her into the car and shut the door with a solid thunk.

"We'll see you at the Camerons' house," Francie shouted and waved as the limo pulled away. Alex wasn't sure of much at that point, but she'd explode if she had to play the well-mannered, grieving widow much longer. How was she supposed to make small talk with people she didn't even know as they ate their way through the food and drink the Camerons' cook had prepared? She'd been to enough bereavement receptions to know that she was headed to a party, not a somber gathering to mourn the burial of a loved one.

She settled herself and desperately tried to blend into the blackness of the limo's back seat. If she were invisible maybe it wouldn't hurt so much. The constant battle she was waging between acceptance and denial, and the overwhelming urge to somehow exit her body and run away, strained her overburdened resources. Avoidance was an increasingly attractive option. Escape might be the only way to save herself from a complete and permanent breakdown.

As the long black car slowly headed toward the cemetery's gates, Alex's panic increased. Impulsively she leaned toward the driver. "If I asked you to take me to Logan Airport instead of to Beacon Hill, would you do it?"

The driver shrugged and turned to look at her.

"Diego! What the..." she sputtered. "Where's the man who drove me here from the church?"

"He decided to take the rest of the day off. Someone had to steer this giant boat out of the cemetery. Why not me?" When he tossed his sunglasses onto the seat next to him, Alex saw that his eyes were bloodshot and swollen. The forced smile he aimed at her never reached them.

"You've been crying," she said softly.

"And that surprises you?"

"A little. Yes. No. I know that you loved Will. I guess he would have wanted you to be here," she admitted with a sigh.

"And do you? If not, I'll leave."

He had her off balance and she wasn't sure how to behave toward him. "I really don't care what you do and I don't have the strength to argue, so you may as well hang around, at least for the Camerons' little do. Then you can go," she said and shifted her gaze away from him, but not before she saw him flinch at her curt dismissal. Diego didn't say anything and turned his attention back to the procession of limousines headed for Beacon Hill.

Diego Alessandro de León Navarro was Will's oldest friend, the son of a self-made, immensely wealthy Argentine and a sensuous Italian beauty. Both men, as only children of privileged families, became as close as brothers when they'd met at the kind of prep school that exists for the sons of the very rich.

Like many moneyed South Americans, the Navarros used real estate as a safe haven for their assets and maintained homes in Buenos Aires, New York City, Miami and Bariloche, high in Argentina's Andes.

The Cameron family's fortune also reached into the stratosphere, but their New England reserve dictated a lifestyle of less flamboyant, quiet wealth than the Navarros.

The brick townhouse on Boston's Beacon Hill where Will had grown up was among the city's most exclusive properties, but it whispered wealth instead of shouting it.

Will had been amused when Diego quickly exchanged the threadbare jeans he'd preferred in college for custom-made shirts and bespoke suits that skimmed his body. The last time Alex had seen him, a platinum watch that tracked three time zones had circled his wrist. His favorite transportation alternated between the family's Gulfstream and his Maserati Spyder, depending on his destination and how quickly he wanted to reach it. Although most of his life had been spent in the U.S., his parents had gifted Diego with an aesthetic in clothing, manners and morals that were sophisticated and European. With the ease of someone who never had to be concerned about money, he'd told his friends that it was no big deal to spend a few hundred every couple of weeks to have his thick, black hair trimmed. Not an extravagance, he'd explained. He simply didn't like the look of a fresh haircut. None of this was affectation or a need to impress; it was simply Diego. He was kind and generous and as Will's best friend, he'd been part of their extended family until the friendship had abruptly ended a year ago. Alex still suspected that Will's explanation for the sudden rift was pure fiction. She had no idea why he'd never wanted to tell her the truth.

Alex was out of the limo as soon as Diego steered it to the curb outside the Camerons' tall, red brick house. She ran up the steps as if there were no place she'd rather be. In reality, she dreaded the next few hours, but she wanted to be with Diego even less.

She noticed the music the minute she entered the house. Bloody hell, they've got jazz on the sound system. Their son's dead and they're throwing a freakin' party. She told herself she'd have to tolerate an hour of chitchat with people she barely knew, offers of food and drink and comments like, "How perfectly awful. Call me dear ... we'll do lunch." But the urge to flee became too hard to fight and she began to search for Diego, although she wasn't sure what she wanted from him. She assumed that he'd followed her into the Camerons' house, so it was odd not to spot him circulating through the jovial crowd, charming the pants off some easily-impressed female. She wouldn't be surprised if the notorious womanizer had already hooked up with someone and left.

She found Anne and John who gave her what passed for a hug as she quickly made her excuses—a migraine that would only respond to serious medication and sleep. Her father-in-law insisted on escorting her to the door and would have seen her into one of the waiting limos, but he was cornered by a group of friends so Alex made her way out alone. She forced air into her lungs as she stood outside the house shivering in chilly, late afternoon air that carried the scent of wood smoke from nearby chimneys. As she approached one of the waiting limos she heard the Camerons' front door shut and suddenly Diego was there. The suit jacket he wrapped her in still held his body's warmth. She mumbled her thanks.

"*Preciosa*," his deep voice rumbled his pet name for her near her ear. "Are we never to speak again?" Alex heard the endearment and wasn't sure how to react. Will had once told her that Diego had warned him that she was a precious gem that many men—himself included—would be tempted to steal. The nickname stuck.

"I have to get out of here. I have to get away." Her voice was tinged with hysteria as she turned toward him. Repressing her emotions all day had finally gotten to her, and as her knees turned to jelly and her heart began to race, she knew that she was on the verge of a major anxiety attack.

"Tell me where you want to go. I'll take you." Strong arms embraced her and she reluctantly leaned her head against the reassuring warmth of his solid chest. For the moment she'd allow herself to pretend that Will hadn't hated this man. She needed his strength.

The driver of one of the waiting limos understood the unspoken command in Diego's expression and dashed to open the car's door for them. Once settled, Diego gathered her to him. She was still trembling and he had to fight the urge to pull her onto his lap and wrap her in his arms.

"Where to, sir?" the driver wanted to know.

"Alex? The man wants to know where you want to go," Diego whispered as if speaking to a child.

"I don't know," she murmured. "You decide." The eyes that met his were bloodshot and filled with tears.

"Take us to Logan," he instructed as he gently dabbed the wetness from her face with a handkerchief. It was warm inside the car, but she was still shivering and her indecisiveness alarmed him as much as her appearance. The intense need to protect this woman overwhelmed him. Will had been part of him for most of his life. Diego was sure that the man he still thought of as his best friend would want him to take care of his widow and he would do it. He was also sure that as soon as Alex was stronger she'd zero in on what he'd done to end a lifelong friendship. Once he'd explained, perhaps she'd deign to thank him politely for his help and then walk—no, run—out of his life, but he wasn't going to worry about that now.

Alex didn't contradict Diego's instructions to the driver. Maybe it was paranoid and totally illogical, but she had to get out of Boston. If Will—her beautiful, kind-hearted Will—could have his life snuffed out in the city of his birth, then she wanted no part of it. And it hurt too much to spend even one more night in the bed they'd shared, surrounded by a zillion reminders of their life together. She didn't give a damn whether she was doing the right thing anymore. Escape meant survival. And despite an initial longing to join Will in death, Alex knew that somehow she'd survive. What amazed her was who was helping her to do that.

Diego loosened his hold on her to tug his phone from his pants pocket. The momentary separation made her miss his body's warmth and she was relieved when his arm came around her shoulders again. He pressed one of the phone's numbers. "I'm on my way to the airport. How soon can you be ready to take off? Good. No, not Buenos Aires. File a flight plan to Miami. We'll be there soon."

"Florida?" Alex raised an eyebrow.

"Yeah, Florida. My family has a house there and from the way you're trembling, I thought some sun might help."

She nodded.

"I'm worried about you Alex. It's not like you to let someone else, especially me, seize control."

"I know, but I'm not the same woman I was a week ago." She didn't want to justify her behavior to him or anyone so she changed the subject. "Can I also assume that we're not flying commercial?"

"That would be correct. There's a bed onboard so you can get some sleep. You look like you haven't done much of that," he said and resisted the desire to stroke the dark circles under light green eyes that always reminded him of celadon. He was grateful that Alex seemed to be oblivious to the internal battle being waged inches away from her.

"Where did you fly in from?"

"I was halfway around the world holding meetings about a project in Abu Dhabi when I heard about Will. My plan was to go on to Buenos Aires from here and then return to the Middle East after the funeral, so the plane's been standing by, but we'll head to Miami instead."

"Okay." She wondered why he'd circled half the globe for the funeral of someone he no longer cared about. "This Middle East project, is it the same one that Will was looking over for you? He thought something was wrong, but didn't know what. He was working on it the same day..." She wept softly as she remembered the way Will had shoved the plans aside minutes before he began to make love to her.

As they approached the airport she asked Diego to call Francie. "Can you let her know that I'm okay? I don't want her to think I jumped into the Charles."

"Of course. Anything else?"

"No. I think that's it," she sighed and realized that for the first time in a week she felt safe.

CHAPTER 5

*T*he Gulfstream jolted as it touched down in Miami, startling Alex into wakefulness. She rubbed her eyes and wondered how smart it had been to make her escape with Diego. Then again, he'd served as a means to an end. She'd wanted out of Boston and she'd accomplished that. It wasn't like her to use people, but she wasn't the same woman she'd been a week ago.

As they made their way through the airport, the bright colors of vacationers made her feel like a crow among parrots in her funereal black clothing. The designer suit's narrow pencil skirt and fitted jacket that had looked so chic in chilly Boston that morning was now a wrinkled mess. She shrugged out of her jacket and dragged it by one finger. The terminal was warm, as if the air conditioning was on low. Sweat began to trickle down her back and between her breasts, gluing the black silk of her blouse to her body. Her pantyhose clung to her legs like plastic wrap. It annoyed her that Diego still looked cool, perfectly tailored, and as confident as ever as he strode beside her, navigating them through the airport's organized chaos.

Once past the security barriers, Alex watched with envy as friends and family greeted arriving passengers with hugs and smiles. She had no family to meet her, here or anywhere. Family—what a loaded word! It implied so much — warmth, love, acceptance, security; all that she'd craved since her parents died in an alcohol-fueled car crash as they'd sped toward Manhattan on a snowy night, late for a Broadway show. She and Will would have built their own family when the time was right. But the fates, or God, or whatever was in charge of human destiny, obviously had something else in mind. Alex's natural optimism had shifted into pessimism so deep that the only future she could envision contained no promise of joy.

She prayed that her inner core, the steel that only her husband had recognized in her, would somehow get her through the next days and weeks. She'd stopped thinking in terms of months or years. A future without Will was terrifying. One day at a time would have to do for now.

Diego led her out of the terminal to a black Mercedes with dark tinted windows. When Alex caught sight of her reflection in the car's mirror-like finish, she grimaced. Florida's humidity was already frizzing her hair and she irritably tucked it behind her ears. What was left of her makeup was melting. Her appearance was one of the few things still within her control and now that had been taken from her also. "The hell with it," she mumbled.

"Welcome home, *Señor* Navarro," the cheerful driver said as he opened the car's door for them. Diego shook the man's hand and introduced Alex.

"Miguel, this is Mrs. Cameron." The man nodded to her.

"Welcome, *Señora*. I hope your stay in Miami will be pleasant."

"Thank you." She hoped the expression on her face was a smile and not a grimace. Despite a brief nap on the plane, she was as cranky as an overtired two-year-old. All she wanted to do was strip off her clothes, shower and crawl into bed. She was grateful that Diego didn't try to make conversation.

After snaking its way through Miami traffic, the car slowed to cross a narrow bridge and was waved through a gated security checkpoint. Minutes later, they arrived at Diego's home. Alex looked out the window in time to notice the discreet brass plaque on a stone pillar next to the driveway that read "Villa Recoleta." Ornate wrought-iron gates slid open at the touch of a button on the car's dashboard. Ground lights illuminated lush landscaping and the villa beyond. The house—was it pink?—had the look of Mexico or Tuscany, which made sense since Diego's mother was Italian and his father, Spanish. The beauty of the place took her breath away and helped to improve her mood a tiny bit.

The Mercedes glided to a stop in front of a pair of enormous, intricately-carved wooden doors. Diego extended a hand to help her from the back seat as a man emerged from the house. He stood with erect military bearing, impeccably clad in a dark navy suit, starched white shirt and charcoal gray tie. The suit's fine tailoring did little to disguise the muscles that were apparent beneath his clothes. Alex wouldn't have been surprised to see him salute his returning master.

"Welcome to the Villa Recoleta, Mrs. Cameron," he said formally. Then he grinned at Diego and the two greeted each other as only men can by pounding each other on the back. Diego introduced him as Serge, but didn't elaborate. She assumed the tall, blond man was a butler or some other household employee. He had a slight accent that she couldn't place. Eastern European?

German? Didn't matter. Fatigue was making it hard for her to think clearly.

An olive-skinned, fortyish woman hurried toward the door and hugged Diego, then excitedly said, "Welcome, welcome, *Señora* Cameron. I am Luisa. I will do everything I can to help you feel at home." A radiant smile reinforced her words and her dark eyes twinkled with a mixture of kindness and delight. Alex liked her immediately.

"Are you hungry? The cook prepared a light supper as soon as we heard you were on your way. I am sure this has been a difficult day for both of you." Alex didn't know how to answer. She felt like she was a character trapped in an endless play, only she didn't have a script. Was it just this morning that Will had been buried?

Diego saw her confusion and jumped in. "I think you should show Alex to her room, Luisa, and perhaps send a tray up. I'll find something to eat in the kitchen."

The woman nodded. "Of course, *Señor* Diego, as you wish. Come with me, *Señora*." She wrapped her forearm around Alex's in the European fashion, patted her hand maternally, and opened a pair of French doors that led to a large inner courtyard which they crossed to reach the opposite wing of the house. Diego didn't take his eyes off Alex and only turned away when he could no longer see her.

Alex paused to admire her surroundings. Trickling fountains, a profusion of flowering plants, shade trees and columned loggia formed the sheltered heart of the villa. She could hear chirping birds and the thrum of insects. "This is beautiful," she murmured.

"Yes, it is lovely, *Señora*. This way." Luisa led them through another set of French doors, past a casual sitting room to a grand staircase, which they climbed to the second floor.

Luisa opened one of the doors along the wide corridor. The elegant simplicity of the room's butter yellow walls, soft lighting and delicate four-poster bed draped in a gauzy fabric suited Alex's need for calm. She crossed the room to step onto its balcony, drawn by the sound of the ocean. The air was still warm, but with a cooling night breeze. She inhaled the salty scent of the sea and began to unwind.

"Shall I close the doors and draw the drapes so the light doesn't awaken you in the morning?" Luisa inquired, then waited patiently as Alex explored her surroundings.

"Yes ... please. I love the sound of the ocean, but I need to sleep. I haven't had much rest in the last week," she explained, but the dark circles under her reddened eyes made that statement unnecessary.

Luisa nodded. "I understand. *Señor* Navarro told me about your loss. *Lo siento*," she said and squeezed Alex's hands in sympathy before she closed the balcony doors and drew the drapes. Silence filled the large space except for the subtle hum of central air conditioning. "The television and sound system are in that cabinet and you'll find an assortment of novels and magazines near the bed. There is nightwear in the closet and also some swimsuits for tomorrow. They're all new, so choose whichever you like. Toiletries are in your bathroom and the tub is filling," she said and paused for breath. "If you need anything else, *Señora*, you only have to ask. The Navarros believe *mi casa es su casa*, so please consider the Villa Recoleta your home," Luisa concluded as she stood in the doorway. Alex sensed that the woman was reluctant to leave her alone.

"Thank you, Luisa, I'll be fine after I get some sleep,"

Alex said, comforted by the woman's sincere concern. "You've been very kind. Thank you. And please call me Alex."

"It would be my pleasure. I will have your supper brought up. *Buenas noches*, sleep well."

Alex peeled off her clothes and pulled her hair into a ponytail. She sighed with pleasure as she lowered herself into the bath's scented water and silently blessed the Navarros for choosing a tub large enough to accommodate her long legs. Luisa had lit a few candles and their subtle perfume filled the air. "Bliss," Alex murmured, and allowed the water to soothe her.

Clean, dry and wrapped in a powder blue silk robe, Alex put her hand to her stomach as it growled and realized she was hungry for the first time since she'd forced down a piece of dry toast along with a mug of strong coffee early that morning. One of the household staff had left a tray in the bedroom's sitting area while she'd bathed and she hungrily dug into a salad dotted with goat cheese. There were slices of juicy pineapple and papaya, assorted cheeses, crusty bread, a glass of wine, sparkling water and chocolate chip cookies, still warm and fragrant from the oven. Luisa would quickly learn that chocolate was her houseguest's favorite comfort food. Alex reached for a second cookie as she leaned back and sighed. Maybe leaving Boston with Diego hadn't been so crazy after all. It might make perfect sense to avoid reality in his family's luxurious oasis for as long as possible.

Whoever delivered supper had also turned down the bed and whisked away the clothes she'd carelessly dropped on the floor. She dragged her body across the room, tossed off the robe, and sank into the kind of dreamless sleep that had eluded her without Will next to her, his warm, naked body spooned against hers, the two of them slumbering as one. She'd always felt safe in his arms, as if nothing bad could happen so long as he held her.

When she finally woke the following afternoon, she tried to shake off the residual grogginess of too much sleep. She shielded her eyes as she opened the drapes to let light fill the room. One glimpse of the sun glinting off the ocean's sparkling blue water turned the decision of what to do for the rest of the day into a no brainer. She considered each of the swimsuits in the closet and finally pulled on a dark blue bikini that exposed more flesh than she liked, especially with Diego around, but it would have to do.

She found the kitchen, introduced herself to Isabel, the Navarros' cook, and helped herself to coffee and a sweet roll. "The house is so quiet. Is Diego still asleep?"

"No, *Señora. Señor* Navarro left the house early this morning. When I asked if he would return for lunch, he said he had business to attend to and wasn't sure when he would be back."

For some reason Isabel's news upset her, until she realized that it would be easier without Diego around to hover over her like some guard dog. She brushed a few crumbs from her lap, thanked Isabel for breakfast and headed to the beach.

Alex felt her body gradually unwind as she lay on the warm sand, her tense muscles relaxing under the sun's relentless heat. Her creamy, freckled skin burned easily, so she only allowed herself an hour in the sun before reluctantly trudging away from the ocean toward the sheltering palms that formed a natural border between the house and the beach.

Alex felt a little better in this tropical environment, far from Boston and all that happened there. But that fragile peace shattered with the sudden ringing of her cell phone. It was Detective O'Shea with yet another routine question about her vacation in Scotland with Will.

She ended the call as quickly as she could, but it had rattled her. Despair, that was as difficult to control as a riptide, pulled her under, gasping for breath, no matter how hard she fought against it.

She recognized the start of an anxiety attack and reached into her bag for a small pillbox. Sometimes the little orange pills prescribed after Will's death smoothed out the bumps, other times not. She popped one into her mouth and as she waited for the drug to kick in, she closed her eyes and concentrated on the feel of the sand as it trickled through her fingers and the sound of palm fronds rattling gently in the breeze.

She put her hand on her chest, relieved that her heart's anxious racing had resumed its normal rhythm. Relaxed, she was able to capture an image of a happier time. As she drifted into a drugged sleep, her last conscious thought was of her trip to Scotland with Will.

CHAPTER 6

*T*hey were Highlanders!" Will had exclaimed with boyish enthusiasm when he'd come across an impressive display on Clan Cameron at a museum in Inverness. "Now I know why I like single malt whiskey so much. It's hereditary!" He burst out laughing at the absurdity of this statement.

His hazel eyes twinkled as he'd wrapped his arms around Alex and pressed his lips to her temple. She loved the ebullience and joy with which Will had always approached life. His good-natured, boyish charm was a big part of his attraction, but it was his unselfconscious masculinity that had sealed the deal for her.

They'd decided to visit Scotland on a whim after spending a couple of weeks in London with a former partner of Will and Diego's. The three men had become wealthy enough to never have to work again when they sold their interest in a Venezuelan oil exploration company after Diego's father got wind of President Chavez's plan to nationalize the industry. Will had never wanted to coast on his family's money, and the timely buyout gave him the independence to return to architecture, his first love.

While in London, a Scotsman at their friend's local pub heard them talk about their planned trip and urged them to visit an Inverness gift shop owned by his uncle. "Mr. Mackinnon's gruff, aye, but he will treat ye fairly, especially if you give him regards from Ewen. That's me," he'd grinned. "He's a Scot through to the bone. You won't find any tartans made in China in his shop!"

They'd taken Ewen's advice and found that Mackinnons' carried the usual Highland paraphernalia—kilts, plaid scarves, broadswords, dirks, sweaters and even bagpipes. Since discovering his Cameron roots, Will had enthusiastically embraced his clan's tartan. Alex wasn't surprised, therefore, when he'd zeroed in on a treasure chest covered in his family's red, green and yellow plaid. It was trimmed in dark brown leather and closed with an ornate brass hasp. Will had insisted that it would make the perfect place for a boy to keep his toy soldiers. His words had made Alex's heart clench in a flash of pain and guilt. He'd love to have a son, she thought. She'd been able to become pregnant easily enough, but it seemed as if her body didn't want to carry a baby to term. They'd already lost two and they were unsure if they would try a third time or eventually adopt. But there, in a small Scottish shop, as she'd watched her husband's face glow with unsuppressed glee, she'd realized the boy Will had been referring to was himself, and not some longed-for offspring.

He'd placed the box on the counter along with a book on Highland history, a volume about Clan Cameron, and a set of coasters adorned with a sheaf of five arrows pointed toward the Gaelic words *Aonaibh Ri Cheile*—the Cameron family crest and motto.

The shop's aged proprietor hadn't seemed surprised by his choices. Many Scots had dispersed—some willingly, others not—to America during the centuries of hardship that followed Bonnie Prince Charlie's failed 1745 rising against the English. Many of those émigrés' descendents visited the Highlands in search of their roots.

The shopkeeper had raised his bushy gray eyebrows inquisitively as he'd examined Will's selections, rang them up and placed them in a bag. "So you're Scots, aye? And a Cameron too I would guess."

"That's right, I am. Can you tell me what the words on these coasters mean?"

"Ah, to be sure. Well, it's the Gaelic, you see, and they translate into but one word in English — 'unite'," said the shopkeeper as he'd glanced toward Alex. "And is your lady Scottish too?"

"Well, yes. My father was a MacBain," Alex had replied. She bristled that the shopkeeper had directed a question about her to Will as if she couldn't speak for herself.

"Ah. MacBain and Cameron. A good match," the old man nodded.

"Why?" Will and Alex had asked in unison. He had their full attention.

"Well, now," the proprietor spoke with the musical lilt and slow cadence of a Celtic storyteller. "It would not do for a Cameron to be marrying a Macintosh for instance. There was bad blood between those clans for hundreds of years. Nor would it be seemly for a Cameron to wed an English lass, for the Camerons were Jacobites, ye ken, and bravely fought for the Bonnie Prince in the '45." He'd leaned closer to Will. "In fact your ancestor, Archie Cameron, was the last of the Jacobites to be hanged in London — at Tyburn Prison in 1753, I think it was."

"Hanged? I'm related to someone who was hanged?" Will had responded with incredulity, his voice tinged with excitement.

"Aye lad, he was and without a trial. But ye've chosen

well, Mr. Cameron. Yer woman is descended from Jacobites too. Gillies Mor MacBain's sword brought down fourteen of the English at Culloden before he himself was killed. So yer missus is not simply a Scottish beauty with those lovely green eyes and reddish hair—ach, yer a lucky lad—she's the blood kin of bonnie fighters."

Alex had had enough of history and told Will, "I think I'll browse a bit more and leave the family history lesson to you," but Will was so engrossed in the man's tales that he'd scarcely noticed that she'd walked away.

The shopkeeper finally introduced himself as James Mackinnon, which reminded Will to mention that a Scottish acquaintance named Ewen had recommended the shop and sent regards. "Ah, so ye've met Ewen? He's a good lad and I'll have to thank him for sending you and your beautiful wife my way." Then he'd leaned his elbows on the counter and studied Will intently as he resumed the lesson on Scottish history as it applied to Clan Cameron.

"Ye should know that another of yer clans-men—John Cameron it was—signed our Declaration of Arbroath back in 1320."

"That's my father's name!" Will had no idea what Arbroath was, but acted suitably impressed. The propri-etor's interest in Will seemed to escalate with the men-tion of John's name.

"It's very likely that you and your Da are descended from that very John Cameron. Do ye recall your grandda's name?"

"Of course. My grandfather was John Cameron too. What's the Declaration of Arbroath?" Will had asked. The hook was firmly planted in his mouth and now all this walking encyclopedia of Scottish history had to do was reel him in.

Alex couldn't help but overhear the men's conversation

in the small, deserted shop and groaned, sure that Will's question would set Mackinnon off on yet another tangent. It was already late afternoon. She was cold, her feet were wet from a sudden downpour, and she wanted to get back to the cozy bed and breakfast that was their temporary home. Will, however, showed no sign of impatience and continued to listen attentively. She sighed and began to paw through a pile of cashmere sweaters.

"Our Arbroath document is similar to America's Declaration of Independence. In fact, it's said that your Thomas Jefferson drew inspiration from it for the one he helped draw up for the colonies." The jowly man seemed to enjoy instructing an obviously fascinated American about Scottish history. "Basically, this letter, signed by clan chieftains at Arbroath—your John Cameron was one as I said—asked His Holiness Pope John XXII to persuade the English to leave Scotland in peace. We dinna like the English here, lad, but no matter how many of them we killed, they kept coming back." He'd winked conspiratorially at Will as he leaned closer and lowered his voice. "We still doona like them, but we canna kill them any more." He'd shrugged and sighed, then continued his story. "The vicious devils didn't want peace. They only wanted to conquer us, rape our women, steal our lands and banish our culture and they succeeded. They have our land, our culture is fast disappearing and they still rape us, only now in a more civilized, economic way by taking the lion's share of Scotland's North Sea oil revenue and taxing our blessed whiskey to death. Ah, but you're not interested in an old man's rants," he'd finally mumbled.

"Look here lad," he'd said, directing a gnarled, arthritic finger at a portion of the document. "See what they asked the Pope?"

"May it please you to admonish and exhort the King of the English, who ought to be satisfied with what belongs to him ... to leave us Scots in peace, to live in this poor little Scotland ... and covet nothing but our own."

"What happened then?" was all Mackinnon's normally articulate audience of one had been able to say.

"Unfortunately, Pope John took eight years to finally act. Many of us still believe that the English have no right to Scotland. We should be a free and independent nation. Why it's unnatural to be united with your sworn enemy!" His face reddened with fury as his voice rose. "D'ye ken that I must carry a passport that says I'm British? I'm a citizen of Scotland, by Christ!" Mackinnon shook his head in disgust. "I spit on them for stealing my country!"

"Jeez, what a story," Will had said.

"Sadly, 'tis not a tale, lad, and I apologize for going off like that and taking up so much of your time, but ye seemed interested." He'd reached below the counter then and tucked a rolled-up paper in the bag with the rest of Will's purchases.

"You're a good lad and because ye've indulged a lonely old man, I've given you a wee gift. Take this copy of the Declaration of Arbroath home and read it. You must show it to your Da, too. It's shameful that he didn't share your clan's glorious history with you so you wouldn't need to be instructed by a stranger. Tell him what you've learned here today and show this paper to him. And let him know it's sent with the compliments of James Mackinnon for raising a fine, braw son. Do ye promise lad? Do I have your word?"

"I'll do it. Of course I will. Thank you Mr.

Mackinnon." Will extended his hand to the old man who grasped it tightly in both of his.

"No need for thanks lad. The pleasure's all mine. It's always good to welcome home a fellow Scot. If you'll be so kind as to leave your address in the States, I can post a catalog to you from time to time."

"Why not?" Will had obligingly provided the information Mackinnon requested.

Alex placed two cashmere sweaters—one in a heathery blue for Will and another for her in a shade of amber that reminded her of whiskey—on the counter. The wily shopkeeper added them to their tab.

As he did so, Alex eyed a couple of weathered, wooden plaques on the wall behind him: "Twelve Highlanders and a bagpipe make a rebellion," read one; "If ye canna bite, dinna show your teeth," the other. Interesting philosophy, she'd mused. Package in hand, they'd thanked him, he'd thanked them, and they'd left.

"That was—gosh, interesting is an understatement Alex. It was awesome. It was almost like that guy was expecting us so he could teach me about my family's connection to Scotland. Or do you think he pulls that same act on everyone to get them to buy more stuff?"

"Could be." Alex had assumed the man's friendly patter and exaggerated Scottish brogue had as much to do with entertaining himself on an off-season, rainy afternoon in his empty shop as it did with any real curiosity about their ancestry.

As soon as Alex and Will were out of sight, Mackinnon locked the door and placed a "closed" sign in the shop's window. He carefully folded the paper with Will's address on it and tucked it into his pants pocket as he headed to the cramped back room he used as an office. He dialed a number on the black rotary phone that sat on his desk. The thing still worked and, as a thrifty Scot, he wouldn't replace it until it was beyond repair.

"Himself walked into my shop today," Mackinnon had said with satisfaction. The others had thought him daft when he'd assured them that the son of John Cameron would show up there one day and now they'd have to eat their words. He didn't speak again until the person he'd called paused for breath. "Aye, I'm certain this lad is Cameron's son. I said I'm certain, didn't I?" Mackinnon had responded irritably. "Why he's the spit of the photo we have. He said he's from Boston and brought regards from Ewen. What more do ye need? Yes, yes, I gave him the paper and told him to give it to his Da. He promised he would and I believe him." Mackinnon continued to listen, nodding occasionally. "Aye, of course it can be arranged. The usual place?"

As Will and Alex walked back to their B & B, he'd draped an arm across her shoulders and began to stroke her neck. His touch was light, but it made her skin tingle. And while her stomach said otherwise, she no longer wanted food and she certainly didn't want to discuss Scottish history. What she'd desperately wanted at that moment was the man who exuded ... exuded ... maleness from every pore in his body.

She'd shifted her head and her lips met his ear. "I keep visualizing you in a kilt, galloping across a field on a beautiful black stallion, racing to get home to me."

"Was I wearing anything under that kilt?" Will

murmured, picking up on her fantasy and making it his own. His lips spread into a mischievous grin as he lowered his head to give her earlobe a gentle bite.

"Everyone knows that a real Scot never wears anything under a kilt, and I'm pretty sure that the bulge in your jeans would be a lot happier if you had a kilt on. Why, I'd be able to reach right under and..." she teased.

"God, Alex, have mercy or I may have to drag you into an alley and tear your clothes off." Then he shook his head. "Christ, I sound like one of my barbaric ancestors. I'm sorry."

"No need for an apology, my love. The idea has its appeal, but I think we better wait until we get back to our room."

Their suite in the ancient stone manor house that was now a bed and breakfast contained an immense four-poster bed and a fireplace, which the landlady thoughtfully left laid. Will struck a match and the kindling caught. His boyish playfulness had completely vanished, replaced by a more adult need. His eyes had met Alex's and she went to him, slowly skimmed her palms down his arms and grasped his hands. They knew each other well enough to realize that this kind of desire wouldn't be satisfied by tender lovemaking or an everyday quickie — it could only be relieved by slow, sweaty, no-holds-barred, breathless, unbridled lust. That they still desired each other — they were not newlyweds after all — with such intense passion surprised and thrilled them.

"We should get out of these wet clothes and warm up in the shower," Will had murmured hoarsely as his arms came around her waist. He nuzzled her ear while he began to tease the bare skin beneath her shirt.

"Mmmm, a hot shower is one of your more brilliant ideas." She fleetingly regretted that the soap would wash away his body's muskiness—an aphrodisiac in her already aroused state—but she knew the water's delicious warmth would feel great on her chilled skin. They'd quickly stripped off their clothes and as Will began to soap her body, Alex knew there wasn't a chance in hell that she'd be cold again that night. He'd quickly washed himself, then passed the soap to her as he turned away. "Do my back, okay?"

She worked the heather-scented bar into a creamy lather, then slid her hands over the long muscles of his beautifully formed back. She'd closed her eyes as her hands continued their downward journey until her hands cupped his firm ass. He could have posed for Michelangelo's David, she'd thought dreamily, but this wasn't cold marble under her hands. Will held his breath, waiting, as Alex's fingers slid ever so slowly toward the cleft between his cheeks, but before she reached her goal he'd suddenly turned and grasped her wrist, breaking the spell.

"If you keep doing thaaaat," he'd dragged the word out quietly, "I'm going to come right now and I don't want to do that until later, much later." He'd bent to kiss her and her mouth opened to welcome him. His erection brushed her thigh as he'd deepened the kiss while his fingers tormented her, working their magic as they moved in lazy circles. They'd only begun and Will was already driving her mad. Alex was beyond restraint and started to wrap her legs around his waist when he abruptly drew away, his breath ragged as he tried to regain control. "I want you. Oh, Christ, I want you, but not quickly. I want to tease you and make you scream."

"I'm ready to scream now," she'd moaned.

"Me too, but we've got all night."

The sun's glare woke them just a few hours after they'd exhausted themselves.

"Shhh ... go back to sleep," Alex had mumbled as Will stirred.

"Can't. Gotta pee. Then I need food," he'd whispered groggily as he untangled his limbs from hers.

She'd yawned loudly and opened one eye to watch him walk across the room. The desire his naked body provoked was set aside as her empty stomach growled.

The previous night's activity had made them grateful for the bounty of Scottish breakfasts. Their cheerful hostess may have been old enough to be Will's granny, but that hadn't stopped her from flirting with him each time she'd pop out of the kitchen to the breakfast room with another course.

"You're a big, braw lad," she'd commented, taken by his size, good looks and easy charm. "And ye have the hearty appetite of a Highlander, Mr. Cameron ... if ye don't mind me saying so," she'd added, with a wink and a slight curtsy. "Eat up, eat up. I enjoy a man who knows how to satisfy his hunger," she'd said as she aimed a knowing glance at Alex.

It was obvious that the name Cameron meant something in this part of the world, and Will had lapped it up. "I bet our hostess was visualizing you in a kilt the same way I did," Alex teased as they'd walked off their breakfast and he'd laughed. "Maybe I'll have to buy one," he'd grinned, "so we can play Highlander and ravished lass when we get home."

CHAPTER 7

*A*lex fought to keep her eyes closed. She knew that once they opened she'd have to face the grim reality that she was alone on a beach in Florida and not in the Highlands with Will. The drugged dream — or vision or whatever it was — made her believe she'd somehow lived their Inverness vacation all over again. Her impulse was to try to conjure the mirage back, but it was already dusk and a chill had replaced the day's heat. She wrapped a large towel around her goose bump-studded arms and hurried up the lighted path to the sanctuary of the house.

"*Un momento por favor, Señora* Cameron," Luisa called as Alex headed for the stairs.

"Your friend, *Señora* Francie, phoned today. She said you are to call her as soon as you returned. The *Señora* said she was very worried about you, but I assured her that you are well. You looked so peaceful resting on the beach that I didn't want to disturb you," Luisa explained. "But first you must eat. The cook told me that you ate little today."

Oh, come on, Alex thought irritably. The drugged dream about making love with her dead husband had left her in a horrible mood and she wanted Luisa to leave her the hell alone. But the woman was simply being a good hostess, so she made herself bury her own emotions and tried to be a polite, appreciative guest.

"Okay, fine, I'll eat," she answered petulantly. "Has Diego had dinner yet?"

"Did he not tell you? *Ay, Díos mío*, that boy," she said shaking her head. "He left this morning and we're never sure when he'll return."

"That sounds like Diego. I guess I was still asleep when he left so he couldn't say good-bye. Don't worry about it. Can I have dinner in the courtyard?"

"*Seguro, Señora.*" said Luisa. "Of course you may eat wherever you wish. Would fish and a salad please you? Some wine?"

"That sounds fine, thank you," she answered distractedly as she crossed the large kitchen, its intricate tile work and rustic stone floor another reflection of the Navarros' heritage.

Alex felt safe in the verdant oasis of the villa's courtyard as if its walls could protect her from the outside world. Will's murder was so irrational that she had trouble believing that she wouldn't be the killer's next prey. Maybe that was the real reason she'd left Boston, but she wasn't ready to examine her motives yet, so she tucked that thought away in the corner of her mind where she stored her other fears.

She decided to sit at one of the small tables scattered around the courtyard. They reminded her of those outside Paris cafés, just large enough for a coffee or an aperitif. "*Señor* Diego often chooses to dine at this table also when no one else is in residence," Luisa commented as she served Alex's dinner.

"I'm not surprised. Diego likes beautiful things and this is a gorgeous spot. And Luisa ... I was rude to you before. I'm sorry."

"There is nothing to forgive, but I thank you for apologizing. There are many who think nothing of treating an employee rudely. I already know you're not like that," the older woman said. "Enjoy your dinner, *Señora*."

The sautéed snapper was simply prepared and delicious, and the accompanying wine had that hint of sweetness that she preferred. She'd never understood the appeal of dry wines. Will's parents had been appalled when she expressed her dislike for brut Champagne in favor of the less expensive, but sweeter, extra dry. Her mother-in-law haughtily informed her that Dom Pérignon, the only Champagne the senior Camerons ever served, doesn't even produce an extra dry.

"She's used to Asti Spumante or beer," she'd once overheard Anne Cameron hiss to one of her stick-thin friends as they'd twittered hysterically at Alex's expense. She'd been very aware that Will's mother was ashamed of Alex's middle class pedigree, but not enough to hide it—as if she could—from her equally stuck-up girlfriends.

As Alex fractured the crisp caramel atop the *créme brûlée* dessert, she wracked her brain about the one clue the police had found—the *sgian dubh*. Will's murder must be connected to their vacation in Scotland. It had to be. Why else was the Scottish dagger left beside his body? It was supposed to mean something, send some kind of message—unless it was a diversion intended to lead investigators on a fool's errand. But damned if she knew what it was. There had to be a link, there had to be, but any connection eluded her. Even more disturbing, the police had come up empty after interviewing the owner of the bed and breakfast where they'd stayed and that gift shop owner, Mackinnon. Without witnesses or evidence, the trail was already cold.

The medical examiner concluded that Will had quickly lost consciousness after his jugular was pierced with expert precision. The choice of weapon — a knife instead of a gun — implied that the attack was personal and that the assailant had enough confidence to get close enough to complete the job swiftly and silently.

Forensics surmised that the Scottish dagger — whose blade was too narrow and free from any trace of blood residue — wasn't used to inflict the deep, fatal wound. If the murderer had slashed Will's throat, it would have been more difficult to determine the weapon's precise size. Detective O'Shea had explained that many knives, unless they're very thick, make the same size cut when used in a slashing motion. But Will's neck hadn't been slashed. He'd been stabbed, the blade entering the side of his neck point first, which left a clear impression of the knife's dimensions. Because of the upward angle of the wound, police were also sure that Will was attacked from behind and that the killer was a couple of inches shorter than he or had crouched. Will was strong and very fit, but he'd had no chance to react or defend himself and probably never even saw his attacker. If he'd fought there would have been scrapes, bruises or some trace of skin, hair or fiber beneath his nails, but there were none. Everything came up blank. No bloody footprints, no fingerprints, no DNA except Will's, no witnesses, no murder weapon, no anything.

Frustrated, she concentrated on something she could control. Something basic. She had to shop for clothes, shoes, makeup, and everything else she would have brought with her if she'd known she was going to end up in Miami after the funeral. People like Diego kept clothing in each of their homes so he hadn't considered that she'd arrive in Florida with only the clothes she was wearing. So ... she'd go shopping tomorrow. That small decision took care of how to fill one day, which was how she now lived her life. She scraped up the last of the rich dessert then climbed the stairs to her room to return Francie's call.

"*Ciao*, Francesca." Alex smiled as she pictured her best friend pacing like a caged tigress, a bundle of nervous energy until she could relax and lose herself in conversation.

"Alexandra MacBain Cameron! What kind of friend has someone else—and Diego Navarro yet!—leave a voicemail that she's on her way to Florida and then doesn't call for twenty-four hours? Are you crazy? No, don't answer that. I guess you're allowed to be a little bit nuts. What's going on? Talk to me. Are you all right?"

"Well, if you'll be quiet for a minute..." Alex replied. She didn't like being put on the defensive, but if the situation were reversed she knew she'd be grilling Francie too.

"Okay, okay. When I'm worried, I can get a little hysterical. I'm sorry, but you were so upset and..."

"I'm fine. Or I'm as fine as I can be," Alex interrupted.

"I was kind of shocked that you'd left with Diego."

"Yeah, me too, but he knew exactly what I needed and made it happen. And you know what? A part of me was sure that he would. Diego's always been a take charge kind of guy."

"So how's it going?" Francie probed.

"Fine, actually. He was gone when I woke up today, off on some business trip I think. When he gets back he and I will have to talk. It was Will who was furious with him after all, and so I went along with it. I never heard his side of what happened between them, so who knows, maybe we can work things out and put it all behind us. I don't have the energy for feuds."

"So when are you coming home?" Francie asked in her no bullshit fashion. Subtlety was not her style.

"Who knows? It's going to be a long time before I'm ready to face reality and besides, I feel safe here."

After a brief pause Francie changed the subject. "You'll never guess who called this morning."

"I give up. Who?" Alex was tired and wasn't in any mood for games.

"Will's father! Can you believe it?"

"You're kidding!"

"I wish. John Cameron actually said he was worried about you because you'd left their house with a migraine and then didn't answer your phone. He asked where you were and of course I played dumb, but I'm pretty sure he knew I was lying"

Alex began to pace restlessly. She opened the French doors to the balcony and inhaled the salty air. It helped. She'd never been comfortable with her in-laws and without Will as a buffer she didn't expect to have much to do with them anymore. "Did John say anything else?"

"No, but he sounded kind of weird ... almost jumpy ... not Mr. Suave at all."

"He probably wanted to tell me I've been excommunicated from the high and mighty Cameron family and I have to move out of the condo. You remember they bought it for us as a wedding gift, right?"

"Cut it out, Alex. What would people say if they did something so despicable to their recently widowed daughter-in-law?

"I shouldn't have let Will go out that night."

"Stop that! So you had fabulous sex and you BOTH wanted ice cream. So Will, being a great guy, offered to get it. I know you're going to whine, 'I told him to go through the alley,' but shit, Alex, we know that man only listened to you if he damn well wanted to. It was his decision, not yours."

"Are you done?"

"No, I'm not. You could not have kept it from happening. You're not God, Alex. You don't control the universe. It just is," Francie said, her voice softening.

"I know ... I know." She wiped her runny nose and the tears that began to drip from her chin during Francie's tirade. "It's easier if I have someone to be mad at, to blame, you know? And since it looks like this guy is never going to be caught ... I guess I'm it."

"Come home, sweetie. Maybe if you get back to a normal routine it'll help. You could go back to work or start a business or something to occupy that sharp mind of yours. I know you don't have to work, but..."

"I'll think about it and believe me, I know I'm lucky not to have to worry about money, but bottom line? I don't want to come back yet. I'm in a very luxurious, secure cocoon and I think I'll stay a while."

"Define 'a while'."

"Maybe a week ... maybe even a month. I don't know. By the way, I'm very grateful that David stays in touch with the police. O'Shea called today with a routine question and it freaked me out."

"David says the cops are surprised that the Camerons haven't used their influence to apply pressure on the investigators. O'Shea is going to talk to Will's parents again."

"Does he think they have something to do with it?"

"David didn't get that impression, just that in a high

profile case like this O'Shea expected the brass to lean on him to solve it quickly. Will's parents couldn't be covering up something, could they?"

"No, of course not. They adored him, but it's odd that John isn't on the phone with the Mayor or even the Governor every day. He has access. I wonder why he doesn't use it. But enough about my in-laws." Alex rubbed her eyes and yawned. " Look, France, I'm wiped out and I've got a big day of shopping ahead of me. This time I'm not exaggerating when I say that I've got nothing to wear!"

"Retail therapy is almost as effective as drugs or chocolate so give your AmEx a good workout. Sleep well, sweetie … and call me!"

"Don't worry. I will. Give my love to David, and tell him to give you a big hug and a smoochy kiss from me. Bye."

David had been listening to Francie's side of the conversation and was now watching his wife intently from their canopied bed in a room bedecked with enough frou-frou floral prints to double as a Laura Ashley shop. She raised both palms in a gesture of bewilderment and shook her head from side to side.

"I don't know what's going on with her. She still blames herself for what happened. You saw what a mess she was and now … she says the change of scenery was good for her and she wants to stay in Miami indefinitely. This isn't like Alex. She's usually so strong and rational."

David wasn't going to offer his opinion on this subject without an invitation.

After a few minutes of silence, Francie raised her eyes

to him. "Aren't you going to say anything? I'm worried about her. She wouldn't do anything stupid like hurt herself, would she?" Alex's hasty departure and her guilt about Will's death, combined with John Cameron's sudden interest in her, were troubling.

"No. Alex isn't the suicide type, she's a survivor," said David. "Maybe it was smart for her to start the healing process in a place she doesn't associate with Will." He paused, took a breath and dove into the deep end. "Don't jump down my throat, but sometimes I think she's right to believe that she's partly responsible for what happened to Will."

"What!" Francie snapped, hands on hips and an edge in her voice.

"Well," he began then hesitated.

"David, you better tell me what you mean if you expect to get any sleep tonight."

"Okay. I've walked from their apartment to that market with Will lots of times. He never went through that alley. He never even considered it. He always stuck to the street. He liked to watch the people. I think she's right that she put the idea about the shortcut in his head that night. No guy is going to take his time when he knows his woman is naked and waiting for him at home."

Francie seemed uncharacteristically calm as she sat down in an overstuffed chair across the room from him and drew her legs up. She rested her chin on her knees, concentrating. When she looked up, her large gray eyes met his.

"Maybe you're both right," she finally said. "If someone wanted to kill him — and even the police have hinted that this was a well-planned execution — they would have found a way to do it. If it didn't happen in that alley, it would have been someplace else. So," she concluded with her own brand of logic, "it wasn't Alex's fault. Like I told her, it just happened. There was no way to prevent it."

"Yeah, that's true," David conceded. "Hey, you didn't tell me that John Cameron called. What was that about?"

"Oh! In all of the craziness I forgot. He wanted to know how to get in touch with Alex. He said he'd left messages on her machine and on her cell and she hadn't called him back. And not only that, he said Anne had been leaving messages for her too! Imagine — the in-laws from hell are finally showing concern for her. I told him that she'd gone away for a while. I couldn't tell him where she was unless I asked her first, right? So ... anyway, I said I'd pass along a message if I heard from her. That's all."

"Maybe Will's murder was like electro-shock therapy for them and they've undergone a personality change," David offered and then stretched as his mouth opened in a giant yawn. "It's late, Francie. We could both use some rest. Come to bed."

He held his arms out to her and she tossed her nightgown to the floor as she climbed in next to him.

CHAPTER 8

Anne Cameron glared at her husband's back as she hurried to keep up with his long stride. "John, slow down," she gasped, winded by the pace he set. His apparent indifference only increased her anger.

"John!" she shouted in a tone that he couldn't ignore. "Please!"

He decreased his gait and allowed her to catch up as they left Beacon Hill and crossed into the Common.

"Sorry," he said, "I didn't realize."

Aside from those few words, neither of them spoke. They'd aged since Will's murder. Lines marred the fine skin around Anne's mouth and it wasn't drifting mascara that caused the dark crescents below her eyes. John's usual tan had been replaced by splotchy, ashen skin. He wore rumpled khakis and a blue oxford shirt that needed laundering. Beautifully tailored designer slacks now bagged on Anne, reflecting unnecessary weight loss. Her black cashmere sweater had a few small stains on the front and looked no different on her skeletal frame than it would have on a hanger. The flawless veneer they'd always presented to the world had cracked the day after the very public funeral and no longer mattered.

An hour earlier John had shouted for Anne as he'd left his study after ending a lengthy phone call, one he'd been expecting with dread since the night Will died.

"What do you want?" Anne had said coldly in response to his shouts.

"Get your coat and we'll walk over to the Common."

She'd never responded well to commands, but he'd piqued her curiosity. John's news could only be about Will. They no longer spoke to each other unless it was about the investigation into their son's murder.

Anne used to easily cram shopping, the gym, lunch, some tennis, and an evening charity gala into one day with energy to spare. But that was before. Now she was constantly tired, so she was happy when John stopped so she could rest on one of the Public Garden's benches. He motioned to the space beside him, but she sat at the opposite end. The bench overlooked the pond where Boston's fanciful swan boats would soon resume their seasonal glide over the water. Will had loved coming here as a child. The routine was always the same. First, a ride on a swan-shaped boat, then a visit to the eight brass ducklings commemorating Make Way for Ducklings, where Will's quacks would grow progressively louder as he neared the mama duck. They'd laugh when the ice cream cone they'd bought him would cover his hands in stickiness as they wended their way up Beacon Hill to Louisburg Square and home. They'd been a happy family—once upon a time.

"What was so important that you had to drag me out here?" Anne pulled herself back to the present and turned impatiently toward her husband. "Do you know why our son was murdered or who did it?"

"No. His murder had to be deliberate or the bastards would have taken his wallet, but for the life of me I still have no idea why someone would want to kill our boy and neither do the police. Good Christ, it still doesn't make any sense." He reached for Anne's hand, but she yanked it away. "Don't touch me," she snapped.

If she'd slapped his face he could have dealt with it. Her indifference hurt worse than any physical pain and he tried to compose himself, to swallow the lump in his throat, before he began again, more gently this time. "You hate me now, I know that, but I'll always be grateful that you kept my secret. Maybe I should have told the detectives everything, but I have to believe that this horror isn't connected to my activities. I want you to know that I've got someone I trust looking into it. And I pray to God every day that I'm in no way to blame because I couldn't live with myself." John's voice cracked and he gazed straight ahead, focused on nothing, as tears welled up.

Anne didn't reply. Nothing John said could shake her belief that Will's death was connected to the money John quietly funneled to a group dedicated to independent nationhood for Scotland. What he did was illegal so they couldn't tell the police, but Anne was tempted, so tempted. John had been upset when some of the group's members began to advocate violence in their quest to finally win freedom from England. But his political activities bored her. That bullshit about hindsight was right. She should have paid attention to her husband's clandestine meetings and quiet phone conversations.

She'd always assumed his secrecy involved a mistress. Would that it were so simple. John was always discreet with his women, as she was with her lovers. Anne knew that John would never bed a woman who wanted anything from him but sex and perhaps money. He'd never tolerate one who imagined she could ever take Anne's place, who would harm his family and his position.

"We have to talk to Alex," John began. "She may know something—or have something—that she shouldn't. If Will was assassinated, the same people who did it could come after her next." He turned toward Anne. "Look at me Anne. I beg you. Can't you see that I'm bleeding, that my pain is as deep as yours?" He needed absolution, and the only person who could give that to him was a woman who wouldn't even look at him.

"You'll never make me believe that the Scottish dagger placed next to Will wasn't a calling card, some message for you," she snarled as her eyes flashed in his direction.

"That's being looked into. It doesn't seem to have anything to do with me, but it may be connected to a man named Mackinnon. He's that shopkeeper Will and Alex met when they were in Scotland. You know, he's the guy who gave Will that rolled up parchment to give it to me."

"How do you know this? Who gave you this information and don't you dare lie to me," Anne hissed as she jumped to her feet.

"You can't repeat this to anyone, even the police."

"Someday I'm going to explode and all of your little secrets will spill out."

"That's a chance I have to take." John leaned toward her although there was no one nearby to overhear him. "Our English friends, Nina and Tom Addison, are agents for British intelligence. They've been very helpful."

Anne's eyebrows rose in surprise. "Nina and Tom? But they're..." she paused, unsure of how to complete the thought. "I never would have guessed."

John continued as if he hadn't heard her. "Because of the *sgian dubh* and my own involvement with the cause, I asked Tom to quietly check into Will's murder. The only thing he's come up with so far is this connection to Mackinnon. It might not mean anything, but I promise you I won't stop until we have answers." His final plea, "so you'll stop blaming me" was unspoken.

CHAPTER 9

*A*lex poured coffee into a large mug as she nibbled the crisp edges of one of the sweet Argentine croissants called *medialunas* that the Navarros' cook baked each morning. She'd slept well after last night's talk with Francie and she was glad to feel a bit more human. But should she? Was it too soon to start to feel a tiny bit normal? Then she pushed this internal conflict aside to be examined later. First things first she ordered herself.

"I need to go shopping today," Alex announced as she put her cup in the sink before the ever-attentive Luisa could do it for her.

"Of course, of course," the housekeeper replied, shaking her head. "I knew that you arrived with no luggage…"

Alex cut her off mid-sentence. "Don't worry about it. Can I use one of the cars? And I hope it's all right if I borrow some jeans and a T-shirt from Mrs. Navarro since I don't think a swimsuit is appropriate for the mall, even in Florida."

"I will have the car brought around in about an hour. That should give us time to find some clothes for you in *Señora* Navarro's closet. Miguel will take you wherever you want to go. You're not familiar with Miami and they drive like crazy people here."

"Tell Miguel I don't need him to take me anywhere. I'm from Boston so I'm used to crazy drivers."

"Please, *Señora*, allow us to spoil you. I insist."

"Fine," Alex shrugged, bowing to Luisa's determination. The staff was under orders from Diego to protect his guest, but Luisa recognized that under her grief Alex was an independent woman. She wasn't surprised that Alex balked at Diego's very masculine need to take care of her.

A half hour later, Alex checked herself out in the mirror. The black pants that would have been a perfect length on Giovanna Navarro were capris on her longer legs, but at least she'd found something simple in Diego's mother's somewhat flamboyant, colorful wardrobe. It would be good to wear her own things and she looked forward to buying everything from underwear to makeup.

Luisa instructed Miguel to take their guest to the Bal Harbour Shops, an open-air mall with Saks, Neiman's and smaller stores ranging from Prada to the Gap. "I'm sure you can find whatever you need there," Luisa assured her as she gave Alex's hand a reassuring squeeze.

A few minutes after the elegant vehicle began to crawl up congested Collins Avenue, past South Beach's Art Deco trendiness, mega-hotels, and innumerable white, high-rise condos that crowded every inch of beachfront space, Miguel's cell phone chirped. Alex understood enough of his rapid Spanish to know that he was talking to Diego and wasn't surprised when Miguel passed the phone to her. The handsome Argentine was still her strongest link to Will, despite the lingering unease about the men's estrangement.

"Diego," was all she managed to utter before her composure cracked.

"Shhh, hush, please don't cry," he crooned. "God, I'm so far away. I feel helpless."

Alex hadn't realized how lonely she was for a familiar

face until that moment, but she pulled herself together. "You, Diego Navarro, are the least helpless man I know," she said then quickly changed the subject. "How come no one knows where you are or when you're coming back to Miami?"

"I'm not used to giving my schedule to the household staff, but I should have left a note for you. Can you forgive me for being so thoughtless?"

"You whisked me out of Boston, so I'll give you a pass this time. Where are you anyway?"

"I flew back to Abu Dhabi. We're in the final stages of negotiations for a complicated project here and my guess is that I won't be able to get away for another few weeks at least. Will you still be there when I get back? Do you need anything?"

"I need clothes, but I'm going to take care of that today and as for your question, I don't expect to leave for a while. The house and staff are wonderful, but can you please tell Luisa that I'm not an invalid? She wouldn't even let me drive myself to the mall today. I'm sitting in the back of your chauffer-driven Mercedes as if I'm too far gone to be trusted with one of your cars."

"I'm afraid that's my fault. I may be halfway around the world, but I feel responsible for you. And before you start to argue, I know damn well it's not politically correct to be chivalrous, but it's how I am. You've always known that, so indulge me a little."

Alex groaned, but she was also grinning. "I know that you mean well even if you are an alpha-male control freak."

"I disagree, but we can talk about that when I get back. Meanwhile rest, get some sun, and let Luisa take care of you until you're strong again. I'll be there as soon as I can. Take care of yourself ... please."

"Nothing's going to happen to me. And you be careful too."

Diego's face was grim as he ended the call and ran his hands through his hair. The hotel's luxurious suite was fit for a sultan, but it felt like a cage to him. He'd stretched out on the bed in the middle of their conversation and wasn't surprised that just the sound of Alex's voice had made him hard. He needed a woman badly, but he only desired one, and he couldn't have her. Alex was right; he was a control freak. He should have asked his father to take over their company's negotiations to build a resort in the oil rich country, but oh, no. He'd stubbornly insisted that he had to see it through.

Witnessing Alex's grief made him ache and he was determined to shield her from anything else that could hurt her, including himself. He wanted his hands on her, but that was the last thing she needed to deal with while she was so vulnerable. He promised himself that he wouldn't seduce her, only he wasn't absolutely sure that he could trust himself. If it ever happened, it would have to be her decision. He was powerless and he didn't like it. He didn't like it one bit.

Alex had no heart for shopping—as clear an indicator of her mental state as any since shopping always had the same therapeutic effect on her as meditation did for others. It took just an hour in Saks to buy everything she'd need for an indefinite stay. She had another two hours to kill before Miguel would return for her, so she wandered into the mall.

As she passed a hair salon, she impulsively decided

to get her shoulder-length hair cut. One of the shop's top stylists had a cancellation and fifteen minutes later as she fidgeted in his chair she declared, "cut it," then covered her face so she wouldn't have to watch the dance of scissors and razor. An hour later, she couldn't wipe the grin off her face when she saw the result. "I love it. Thanks." she said with relief, then headed toward the mall's exit to meet Diego's driver.

"Are there more shops you would like to visit?" Miguel inquired as he stowed her shopping bags in the trunk.

"No, thanks, I'm exhausted." She might fool herself into thinking she was emerging from the cavernous pit of grief, but the few hours at the mall made her feel like she'd run a marathon. She needed a nap and was anxious to get back to the villa.

"Your hair, *Señora! ¡Qué bonita!*" Luisa said approvingly as Alex pirouetted in front of her, delighted that a change she'd feared had turned out so well.

"I'm happy you like it. I do too," she said as she bit into one of the gooey chocolate chip cookies the cook had baked especially for her.

"It pleases me to see you smile, *Señora*," Luisa said. "It makes me sad to see one so young and so beautiful in such obvious pain."

Alex didn't want to wallow in sorrow so she quickly changed the subject. The cookie's sugar had already hit her bloodstream and ramped up her energy. "I spoke to Diego! He called on the car phone."

"I'm glad that he found you. He called here first and I told him Miguel had taken you shopping," she said as she poured a glass of milk to accompany Alex's second cookie. "He's a dear man and he cares for you."

"I know he has a good heart, but the situation with us is a bit complicated."

The older woman noticed the lightning fast change in Alex's expression. Something Diego had done clearly upset her. "I respect your privacy, *Señora*, but if you ever want to talk … I've known Diego since he was a boy and I remember your husband from his many visits here during school vacations. If you think I can help, I would be honored if you let me."

"Thank you, Luisa. Diego and I have some things to work out. I'm sure it'll be all right."

"I understand," Luisa replied and gave Alex a gentle hug as she left the room.

As days and then weeks passed, Alex gradually grew stronger. She slept soundly, ate well, swam mindless laps, read, watched movies in the villa's theater and took long walks on the beach. Her freckled skin finally tanned and the sun added glints of gold and copper to her auburn hair. When she looked in the mirror, instead of hollow-eyed pallor, she saw the glow of health. She never wanted to leave this enchanted Shangri-la. She was afraid that when she went home to Boston, she'd fall apart.

She still grieved … a lot. Will's murder was very real to her and there was no pretending that he was alive. But as time passed she became aware that the shape of her grief had changed. There was a gnawing emptiness at her core and she accepted that this void was now a permanent part of her. She missed Will the way she imagined an amputee must miss an arm or a leg. Most of all, she mourned the future they'd never have, the memories they'd never make. She'd have to learn to be content with those she already had.

CHAPTER 10

*A*lex was swimming laps in the pool when she heard loud voices and a commotion coming from the normally tranquil house. Adrenalin surged through her body like an electric current, triggering her heart rate to soar well beyond the soothing, exercise-induced thump-thump of a moment earlier. Fight or flight. Her senses sent up a red alert and for a split second she wondered how long she'd be able to hold her breath if Will's murderer crashed through the door and she had to play dead at the bottom of the pool in order to survive.

Then she saw the reason for the ruckus—Diego.

He emerged from the house and stood at the side of the pool, arms crossed, grinning at her. A moment later he impulsively tore off his shirt, kicked off his shoes, unzipped his pants and dove into the water as cleanly as a sleek seal. He'd stripped quickly, but not before Alex eyed his magnificent body and the tiny black briefs that left nothing to the imagination.

He surfaced beside her and she began to weep as he murmured soft, soothing words in unintelligible Spanish. Would this man's lifelong connection to Will always remind her of what she'd lost and overwhelm her with sadness?

She'd made a decision while he'd been gone. He would have to tell her why he and Will had stopped speaking. She knew their affection for each other wouldn't have allowed the rift to be permanent and was determined not to waste another minute being angry. It had been Will's fight, not hers. She took a couple of shaky breaths and tried to smile as he made a futile attempt to dry her tears with his wet hands. He towed her to the shallow end of the pool and sat next to her on the steps.

"What am I going to do without him Diego?"

"You're a survivor and you'll be fine in time," he said softly and then his face hardened. "No! You'll do more than survive, Alex. Way more. Will would be miserable if you never found happiness again ... and you will, in time, *Preciosa*, in time. I promise."

She almost believed him. His black eyes blazed and he gripped her hands so tightly that she winced. He saw her reaction and quickly raised her fingers to his lips. "I'm sorry," he said as he kissed one hand then the other. "Strong emotions sometimes make me forget my own strength. Forgive me."

She nodded and lowered her head to gaze at the hands that his lips had just touched. Her delicate diamond and emerald wedding band glinted in the sunlight. Diego tipped her chin up with one finger and kept it there so that she couldn't turn away.

"Listen to me, Alex. The passion you and Will shared ... well, it was something rare. We both know that kind of love doesn't die. It will always be with you, even when you fall in love again. My friend Will, the man we both loved, lives on in our hearts and in our heads. He'll always be with us, *amiga mía*."

"I know that, but it's not the same," she whispered. It seemed natural to find herself in his arms and she rested her head on his chest for a moment. Her bare skin felt like satin and Diego's lips itched to explore her neck, so he reluctantly loosened his hold. Friendly affection was one thing. That would be quite another. "Let's dry off, " he said as he effortlessly pulled himself out of the pool before his body's response to her became too difficult to control.

"I'm going to ask Serge to make a couple of mojitos for us. Is that all right?"

"Sure," she replied. "And stop looking at me that way," she added when she noticed Diego checking her out despite the modest competition Speedo she had on. Even so, his gaze made her feel naked.

"I can't help it. You look wonderful and I didn't know what condition I'd find you in. I was afraid ... well ... I was afraid, that's all."

"I'm a little better than when you left. It's going to be a long road, but at least I've begun the journey. Didn't someone say the journey of a thousand miles begins with one step?" she said as she toweled off her dripping hair.

"I think it was Lao Tzu if I remember my Chinese philosophy correctly," he said, fascinated by the way the muscles in her arms flexed as she tried to make her hair's wet spikes behave. "Your hair is different. Shorter, yes?"

"Yeah. I had it cut the day after you left. It's too hot here for long hair. Do you like it?"

"It looks good on you, but I like long hair. If you were my woman and cut your hair I'd be tempted to put you over my knee," he blurted out and had the grace to blush.

Alex stifled a giggle. She knew Diego would never lay a hand on her or any other woman and she was enjoying his obvious discomfort.

"So, Navarro, you'd spank me? And no doubt enjoy it! You idiot," she teased.

"That was really bad, wasn't it? Come," he said, taking her hand. He was happy to see her smile even if the joke was on him. "Serge will bring our drinks to the courtyard."

Alex hadn't seen the mysterious Serge since the night she'd arrived at the villa and she wondered what, precisely, his job was. She doubted that the muscular gentleman's duties were confined to welcoming guests and serving drinks.

"Will there be anything else, sir?" Serge asked deferentially after he delivered a tray of canapés along with their drinks.

"No, but I need to see you in my office later — perhaps in about an hour."

"Very well, sir. "

Alex wouldn't have been surprised to see Serge click his heels before departing.

When he'd gone, she turned to Diego. "What's Serge's real job? He's definitely not a butler."

"Your instincts are good." Diego hesitated before continuing. "Actually, Serge is my bodyguard. My parents insist on it, the same way they equip all their homes with elaborate alarm systems. It may appear excessive, but it makes them feel safe. I'm a grown man, but they still worry that some desperate group will kidnap me for ransom, so Serge travels with me. Since our company has its own security team in Abu Dhabi, Serge stayed here for some well-deserved down time. And if he was doing his job right you weren't aware of it, but I wanted him here to protect you," he added, shrugging his shoulders.

"Protect me? Why? I can't believe you think I need a bodyguard."

"Until we know why Will was murdered and the bastard who did it is caught and punished, I don't know what to think. But while you're here, you're under my protection and that includes Serge."

"It's a little extreme, but I guess I understand. It makes sense that your parents don't want anything to happen to you," she said as she sipped her drink. The Navarros' world was very different from the one she inhabited. Diego's father grew up poor, but had built a vast real estate fortune. And Latin America had a history of being more volatile than Boston. "If the Camerons had been a little more paranoid about Will's safety he might still be alive," she added softly.

Diego nodded and drained his drink. "Maybe, but if someone's determined to get you, they usually will."

"I guess," she answered as she gazed into her glass lost in thought. "Where's Serge from?"

"He's an interesting character. His full name is Sergei Sidovsky. He says he spent his childhood in Russia, then his family emigrated to Israel when he was eleven or twelve. I guess that much is true, but in his world truth has many meanings. He was an agent in Israel's Mossad. My father always insists on the best and there is no better intelligence and security operation anywhere in the world. Now he works for us," he concluded as if it was the most natural thing in the world to have a former elite spy on the family payroll.

"Oh! And I thought he looked so Aryan with his blond hair and blue eyes. I was really wrong. Why the butler charade?"

"I assume it's the cover that my father and he agreed upon. When one's family employs so much staff, it would be hard to know everything about everyone. That sounds horrible, doesn't it? Will always said I was spoiled rotten. He was probably right."

He lowered his head and sighed deeply. When he looked up again, the cloud had passed from his face.

He leaned back and his muscles rippled as he stretched. The towel he'd wrapped around his hips had shifted and barely covered his thighs ... or anything else. Alex knew she was in mourning, but she wasn't blind, and didn't think there was anything wrong with admiring the work of art sitting across the table from her. Diego was extraordinarily handsome, but, unlike Will, he knew it and was very aware of the effect his smoldering eyes, chiseled jaw and full lips had on women. And the body, oh, the body. The man effortlessly exuded charm, sex and a hint of danger, a lethal mix.

Diego was both flattered and disturbed when he felt her eyes on him. He abruptly got to his feet. "I have business to discuss with Serge. You'll have to excuse me."

"Wait! You can't just dismiss me. We need to talk, too. You and I are pretending that everything's fine, but I can't forget that Will was furious with you and then you disappeared from our lives for a year. I never believed his explanation for the fight so I want to hear your version."

The reminder that all wasn't well between them felt like a knife in his belly and Diego turned away so she couldn't see his pain. "I'll tell you whatever you want to know, but not now. Let me take you to dinner tonight. Luisa will want to feed me, but it's time you experienced a little Miami nightlife. I'll reserve a table for us at Norman's. Shall we say eight o'clock?"

"I'll hold you to that promise, but dinner out sounds good. That gives me enough time to soak in the tub and take a nap. Later."

Diego pulled on a T-shirt as he strode to his father's study in a remote corner of the villa. The office was sparsely furnished with only a large mahogany desk, a couple of leather chairs, two phones and a custom-made computer. The place obviously existed for business and nothing else. Serge was already waiting for him so he closed the heavy door that rendered the room soundproof.

Diego sat at the desk while Serge stood. Before he'd left the country, he'd told the bodyguard to learn everything he could about Will's murder. He was accustomed to giving orders and expected them to be carried out. Serge never disappointed him. "What have you got?"

"I put my U.K. contacts on this because of the dagger that was left at the murder scene. The name Cameron is associated with a clandestine independence movement in Scotland called the Group of One Hundred. There's remarkably little current information about this organization or its membership, but I'm working on it. So far your murdered friend has no connection to this group, but my contact heard some chatter about a John Cameron. Of course that's a common name in Scotland, so we need to go deeper to find out if this John Cameron is actually Will's father."

"That son of a bitch. I wouldn't be surprised if he is involved," said Diego with disgust. He pushed his chair back so hard that it crashed to the floor and then he stalked from one end of the room to the other as he clenched and unclenched his fists. "I never liked Will's parents. They're made of ice." He paused to refocus. Serge was used to Diego's volatile temper and calmly awaited instructions.

"Do what you need to do. Pay whomever you need to pay. Beat the shit out of Cameron if it'll help get the information we need. If that *hijo de putana* father of his had anything to do with Will's death he'll be very sorry.

The murdering bastards who did this will pay." Diego seethed with anger as he paced the room. "Not only will I know who did this, but I will also know why. I'll expect daily reports. That's all," he concluded.

"Yes, sir," acknowledged Serge as he pulled the door closed. Lifetime membership in the shadowy netherworld of international espionage gave him advantages that no police force, even Interpol, MI-5 or the CIA, could match. Those connections, combined with Diego's deep pockets, made him sure that the identity of Will's killer wouldn't stay secret for long. What would happen once they found the twisted son of a bitch would be up to Diego.

CHAPTER 11

Alex felt like Cinderella getting ready for the ball. She told herself it was nothing more than a casual dinner with a friend, but she hadn't been to a restaurant since Will's death and she couldn't pretend she wasn't excited. She styled and re-styled her hair and told herself to stop fidgeting as she applied makeup. Although her wardrobe was limited, she tried on and discarded several outfits before finally settling on a narrow white skirt and fitted black tank top. She added silver stiletto sandals that set off her tanned legs and dabbed perfume behind her ears. Will had been dead for less than two months, yet she still had an innate need to look good. What was it that made women seek admiration from men, even those they didn't care about? The instinct probably went back to caveman days, she concluded, and ordered herself to chill and simply enjoy the company of an old friend. When she came downstairs, Diego's reaction to her appearance told her that the effort had been worthwhile.

"You look beautiful," was all he said as he took her hand and waved good-bye to Luisa who'd been watching them like a smug fairy godmother.

"Wow," Alex murmured when she spotted their transportation. Diego's low-slung, silver Maserati Spyder was a radical and welcome change from the staid, chauffeur-driven Mercedes she rode in anytime she'd left the villa.

"I'm glad you like it. I love this car," Diego said as he held the door for her. An instant later the motor roared to life. The noise of its powerful V-8 engine and the sense that she dare not distract Diego from his deft maneuvers all but eliminated conversation. The car's contoured leather seats hugged his body and his eyes never wavered from the road. His driving reflected his personality: skilled, confident and aggressive. "Nice going, Navarro. Maybe you'll let me drive her some-time," she commented as he pulled up in front of the restaurant in Coral Gables. He surprised her when he quirked a brow and grinned. "Maybe."

"*Señor* Navarro, how nice to see you again. It's been too long," said the *maître d'* as he personally escorted them to a table. "Gianni will take care of you this evening," he said, motioning to a waiter who instantly appeared by his side. "If you need anything, please let me know." The restaurant was a favorite of Diego's and based on the reception he'd received, and the discreet nods and smiles from various waiters, he was also a favorite of its staff.

The mouth-watering aromas wafting through the crowded, noisy restaurant from its open kitchen made Alex happy to have her appetite back. When Diego ordered steak, she decided to have the same. He added a variety of wines to complement each course. "They serve Argentine beef here. It's the best," he said with national pride after the waiter and sommelier departed. Then he turned his attention to the 18-year-old Macallan single malt he'd ordered—a taste he'd acquired from Will—as Alex toyed with the delicate stem of her vodka martini's glass. As they waited for their first course to arrive they said nothing, nor did they let their eyes meet, suddenly awkward with each other. Alex crossed her legs first one way, then the other, but couldn't get comfortable.

She cracked first. "We have to talk. I need to know precisely what happened between you and Will," she began after she'd drained her drink. Diego squirmed as her green eyes locked onto his and he signaled for another round. Whatever was coming next might be eased with alcohol. "You were such an important part of Will's life and mine, and suddenly—poof!—you vanished last year. I want to know why."

"No small talk first?" he sighed in resignation. "I guess this isn't going to be the amusing evening I'd hoped for." He slowly buttered a slice of crusty bread and took a bite, stalling for time. "I'm surprised Will didn't tell you why we fought." he finally said.

"Oh, he told me, but I want to hear it from you. He was always honest with me, but my intuition tells me he lied about this. I don't know whether he was protecting me, or you, or himself and now you're the only person who knows the truth."

"It's a long story and I'm afraid it will upset you. I don't want to do that."

"I'm not that fragile," she snapped while she absent-mindedly fingered her wedding ring, a tangible link with Will. He'd handpicked its emeralds because they reminded him of her eyes.

Diego gazed into the amber liquid in his glass as if he'd find an answer there. He tried to maintain a pleasant expression, but Alex had seen his eyes grow cold and his jaw clench. He reached across the table and took both her hands in his. The physical link seemed to ease his tension and he rubbed his thumbs back and forth over her knuckles as he gathered his thoughts.

"Okay. You have a right to know and since there's no one else who can do it, I'll tell you, but not in the middle of a restaurant ... later, when we have privacy. Can't we simply enjoy our meal and talk about inconsequential things? Tension is bad for the digestion." Diego's lips curved into a tentative smile and she watched him rearrange his face into a reflection of the lighter mood he hoped for, yet there was still that unfamiliar hardness in the ebony eyes that rested intently on her face.

"I guess I have no choice since I can't very well force you to talk about something you don't want to," she conceded, and smiled coolly as she withdrew her hands from his grasp.

The strain eased somewhat when the waiter brought their first course. They limited the conversation to innocuous comments about the delicious food, friends they had in common, Diego's parents, Alex's enjoyment of the villa, even politics—anything to avoid talking about Will. They gradually became comfortable with each other again, assisted no doubt by the quantity of alcohol they consumed.

"This has been nice, Diego," Alex admitted once the table had been cleared, "but don't think I'm so drunk that I've forgotten your promise to tell me what went down between you and Will."

"Don't insult me, Alex. I'm a man of my word. I said I would tell you and I'll keep that promise. But first some dessert and coffee," and he motioned to the attentive waiter.

"We'll have the molten chocolate cake with cognac *anglaise*, and two coffees."

"Just one order of cake," Alex said to the waiter, "and two forks, please." She knew she'd want a taste and she didn't want Diego to feed her. It would be too intimate and she sensed he needed clear boundaries. Maybe she did too.

The confection was heaven—gooey, warm and intensely chocolate. Alex rarely ordered dessert, but she was glad Diego had a more hedonistic approach to food. The stimulation of the sugar and caffeine seemed to counteract the effects of the wine and her mind began to clear. After Diego signed the check, she asked him to phone Miguel to pick them up.

"You're in no condition to drive. You remember that my parents died in a car wreck after too much wine, don't you?"

"Of course, and I remember very well what it did to you. I value my life—and my car—too much to ever drive after drinking. And I would never put you in danger." Reassured by the sincerity of his words, she relaxed. They strolled past the small shops near the restaurant as they waited for Miguel. The night was warm and breezy and Alex felt pleasantly relaxed in the company of an old friend. Once more she congratulated herself on the decision to leave Boston. She knew she'd have to go back, but except for Francie and David, she didn't miss the place a bit.

She didn't notice the crack in the pavement until her narrow heel became wedged in it and she stumbled. Diego's arms came around her in an instant and he caught her before she fell.

"Jesus! I could have broken my neck!" She studied the impractical stiletto sandal and the sidewalk crack until her erratic heartbeat quieted. "Good reflexes. Thanks," she said quietly, as their eyes met.

"I told you that no harm would come to you while you're with me and I meant it. You know I'd protect you with my life if needed."

"Isn't that a little melodramatic?" Alex responded, but he ignored her. She bit her tongue before she blurted out that he sounded like a macho egotist and that she could protect herself—or at least she thought she could. The arm that was still around her waist tightened possessively and as his hand drifted toward her hip, she drew away, putting distance between them. Give this man an inch and he takes a mile she thought. Although she was pretty sure that he wouldn't come on to her, this was Diego, after all, and his proximity made her nervous. Will had often joked that seduction came as naturally to his friend as breathing. He might instinctively make a move on her before he realized what he was doing and she wasn't absolutely certain how she would react.

He feared the same. His heart had lurched when she'd stumbled and then did it again as he drew her body against his side. He was relieved that she had the sense to pull away before he did something he'd regret.

With perfect timing, the now-familiar black Mercedes rolled to the curb beside them. Diego waved Miguel back into the car and held the door for Alex. She deliberately slid to the far side of the seat and relaxed when he took his place in the opposite corner. Neither spoke on the short ride back to the villa. They were aware that Diego could no longer avoid talking about the rift with Will. And even if she wasn't absolutely sure that she was ready to hear about it, Alex had to know.

Despite blaming herself for sending Will on the errand that ended his life, Alex had gradually accepted that his murder wasn't of the wrong time, wrong place variety. Someone had marked him for death. But why? And who? On those questions, she still drew an increasingly frustrated blank. She didn't think that Will's fight with Diego had anything to do with it, but whatever happened between them must have been pretty bad if it had ended a friendship that had lasted since they were boys. And she'd never bought the outrageous tale Will had spun for her. She needed the truth and the only person who could provide that now was inches away from her.

"You still up for going through with this tonight?" Diego asked, when they reached the villa.

"Yes, more than ever." She wanted this sword of Damocles out of the way.

He led them through the courtyard and past the pool where he grabbed a couple of oversized towels. They kicked off their shoes and walked barefoot onto the moonlit beach. Diego spread the towels on the sand and they sat for a few moments, settling themselves like mirror images, backs straight, hands wrapped around their knees. Stars filled the sky and there was a gentle breeze off the ocean. Alex inhaled the sea's briny perfume and allowed the sound of the surf to soothe her as it always did. If it were Will beside her, she thought, it would be a perfect night to make love on the deserted beach.

"Where do you want me to begin?" Diego's voice broke through the increasingly erotic images flitting through her mind. Focus, she told herself. She was sure he would tell her the truth. Diego might be many things, but above all he was a man of honor.

"Was this fight building for a while or was it something sudden?"

"The roots of it weren't so new, but what happened … oh, it was definitely sudden," he began. "Your husband betrayed my trust and for me that was unforgivable. When I found out, I guess our testosterone got out of hand and then stubbornness took over. We might have

gotten past this eventually. After all, he was my brother."
He paused and grew quiet.

Alex knew the men had felt as close as brothers, but
this was the second time she'd heard Diego refer to Will
as his brother. She thought it was strange, but didn't
want to interrupt him. After all, she always thought of
Francie as her sister.

A moment passed before he sighed deeply and
continued. "Not only am I furious that my best friend
was murdered, but it kills me that we never had the
chance ... the chance ... I wish ... shit!" His voice
broke and he turned away from her as he began to weep.

Alex was shocked that this paragon of masculinity
was sobbing unashamedly next to her. She wanted to
comfort him, but friend or not, he had hurt the man she
loved. So she turned away as tears ran down Diego's face
and waited for him to compose himself.

"I'm sorry," he whispered after a few minutes. He
took the tissue she handed him and wiped his eyes, blew
his nose and took a steadying breath. "What kind of man
am I, crying like a child? The last thing you need is for
me to fall apart, but reliving that night is harder than I
thought it would be."

"I know, but I still don't understand what happened.
Please tell me," she implored. "Once we put this behind us,
maybe we can figure out why he was killed and who did it."

"You're right, that's the important thing now." He
stood and extended a hand to help her to her feet. "Let's
walk. I can't do this sitting still." They strolled quietly
for a few minutes before he spoke again. "I'm sure you
know the old story about how Will's parents met mine
right after both couples were married."

"Of course. So?"

"My guess is you don't know the whole story."

She wanted him to talk about the reason for the fight with Will, not the oft-told, ancient history of their parents' first meeting. "Okay, fine. Do it your way, as if I have any choice," she grumbled.

"You think this has nothing to do with what happened, but you'll see that it does. Anyway, my parents and Will's were seated across the aisle from each other on their way to Paris from London. My parents had flown there from Buenos Aires, and the Camerons from Boston. The stewardess brought a bottle of champagne to each—this was in first class when there was no such thing as upgrades and you knew that if someone was in first, they belonged there. Well, anyway," he continued smoothly, oblivious to how obnoxiously elitist that remark was, "they discovered that not only had their weddings taken place on the very same day, but they had reservations to honeymoon at the same Paris hotel, the Georges V."

"Yeah, yeah." Alex interrupted. "I wish you'd get to the point. What does this have to do with a fight you and Will had so many years later?" She thought Diego was avoiding the real issue and wanted to get him back on track.

"It has a lot to do with it," he shot back. "If you'd be quiet and listen, you'll find out."

"Okay, okay. Go on," she said, ignoring his obvious irritation.

"So anyway, that's how they met and they became ... I guess you could say 'intimate' friends. They visited each other's homes and ... well ... one thing led to another and, and..."

Alex had never heard Diego stammer before and it frightened her. His tension was making her edgy. "And what?"

He paused as if to gather his courage and blurted out, "About five years ago Will and I found out that his father had slept with my mother and my father had slept with Anne Cameron."

"What? No way! That's awful. How can you say something like that? You're lying!" she shouted, appalled by this twisted fantasy. The Navarros might be sexual creatures, but the Camerons? And especially the glacial Anne Cameron? Impossible!

"Why would I lie about something like this? I was blown away too, but I'm convinced it's the truth. I found some pretty steamy letters from John Cameron to my mother in an old piece of furniture my parents asked me to empty before they gave it to one of the maids. My mother likes to redecorate and our staff benefits. I showed the letters to Will and we figured the rest out."

Alex gasped, unable to form coherent speech.

"Do you want me to continue?"

"You mean there's more?"

"I'm afraid there is. Are you all right?"

"Not really, but you may as well tell me the rest. Surely it can't be worse."

Diego almost said, "That's what you think," but suppressed the urge. "John's last letter referred to the news of my mother's pregnancy. He wrote that he was sure that my father was thrilled that they were expecting a child and he mentioned that Anne was pregnant also. He assured my mother that all would be well, their children would be great friends, and that was it. Once I told Will about the letters, I stopped thinking about them, but your husband ... well, he thought that because of our parents' intimacy, that last letter was strangely worded."

"Did he ask John about it?"

"No. We knew the letters weren't meant for our eyes and we were mature enough to realize that our parents had moved on and we should let their past stay there. I was okay with that, but last year Will decided that both of us needed to have a paternity test. He couldn't get it out of his mind that he might be Ricardo Navarro's son and that John Cameron could be my father. Our mothers gave birth within weeks of each other, so ... anyway, he said that he couldn't live with the uncertainty. He told me that his foundation, his very sense of self, had cracked and only the truth could restore his equilibrium. He had to know who he was. It's obvious that there are lots of similarities between us — our dark hair, the way we both talk fast when we get excited, that we're the exact same height."

"Oh ... my ... God. Holy shit! Wait a minute. Let me digest this." Alex strode toward the water gesticulating like a mad woman. Diego didn't go after her and when she came back she seemed a little calmer. "Let me see if I've got this right. You and Will could be brothers? Like for real? And Will knew this?" Alex's mind was racing, thoughts popping up with the staccato speed of a machine gun's rat-a-tat-tat.

Her eyes darted restlessly from the starlit sky to the expanse of sand and ocean until they finally settled on Diego. He was lying on his back watching her, his head supported by his arms. When their eyes met, he reached for her hand and she curled up next to him. "So is it possible? " she whispered.

"Will thought so. I didn't care. I'm a Navarro. I told Will it didn't matter who'd stuck his cock in my mother, I am my father's son! Jesus, Alex, I'm sorry. I should have found a better way to say that."

"Are you finished or is there more?"

"More. Where was I?" He took a breath, then continued. "Will finally had a DNA test. He lifted some strands from John's hairbrush and the results proved that John is indeed his father. It should have ended there, but that wasn't good enough for your husband. Oh, no. He demanded that I do the same with my father. He kept pushing and pushing and pushing. To shut him up, I finally caved. I told him I'd do it, but that was to get him off my back. I never intended to have the test."

"And you haven't…?"

"No, but someone else made that decision for me. Last year, when we all went to Buenos Aires to visit my parents, Will snuck into my father's bathroom, took some hair from his brush and a sample of mine and sent them to the same lab he'd used."

Alex thought she finally understood. "He didn't tell you he was going to do this, did he?"

"Of course not, the deceitful bastard. He didn't give a shit about what I wanted. I'll never forgive him for that," he whispered as his throat tightened and his eyes filled. "When he told me about it, I went ballistic. I think I hit him first, but it happened so fast that I'm not sure anymore. I wanted to kill him and he was banged up pretty badly, but he broke a couple of my ribs. We never had a chance to make it right. That was the last time I saw him." He covered his face and began to cry softly.

"Hush, hush," Alex finally said as she wiped her own tears away. She rubbed his back and stroked his hair, the way she would have soothed a child. Her mind was reeling from this bombshell and until she had time to absorb all its implications, she'd have to treat it as a fairy tale. It was too grotesque to be anything else.

"I'm glad you told me." She hesitated before asking the next question, but she had to know.

"So ... did he tell you what the test said?" she whispered.

He nodded. "That's probably why I wanted to kill him. My father didn't make my mother pregnant. John Cameron did."

"So you and Will are..."

"Brothers. Yeah, we're really brothers."

They trudged back down the beach toward the villa in silence as each tried to cope with the emotional overload of Diego's revelation. Alex couldn't figure out why Will had done something so despicable to his best friend. If he was worried about his own paternity, well, that was his business. But to deliberately turn Diego's world upside down? To betray someone's trust like that was so uncharacteristic of the man she loved that she'd never understand. Why hadn't he trusted her enough to tell her about this? To explain away his bruises and a cut lip that needed stitches, he'd made up an elaborate story about joining a bar brawl when someone insulted his beloved Red Sox. A few weeks later, when she'd asked him to invite Diego for a visit, he admitted the lie and simply said that Diego had attacked him and he didn't want to talk about it. She was astounded that Will's best friend would beat him so viciously. When she'd pressed him for the reason, Will told her he'd found out that his mother and Diego were having an affair. Will had confronted him and Diego had denied it. They'd traded insults until one of them took a swing at the other. Will swore he'd never speak to Diego again. It was obvious to her that the hurt went way deeper than her husband's external injuries and if Diego had the power to inflict such lasting pain on someone she loved, she would have nothing to do with him either. And now she was left to wonder if Will would have ever told her the truth. Maybe eventually, but they'd run out of time.

Instead of going inside when they reached the villa, they collapsed onto chaises near the pool, reluctant to be alone. Diego quickly closed his eyes, but Alex knew he was awake. The man next to her had laid his soul bare, so how could she not give him the same honesty? She began to tell him Will's version of their fight.

In the middle of her story, Diego's eyes flew open and he bolted upright. "Will told you that I slept with his mother? Me? Holy shit, couldn't he come up with anything better than that? Drunk or sober, no one would believe that even someone with my overactive libido could ever lay a hand on that cold bitch's skinny body. His first story, the one about the Red Sox bar fight—now that was pure Will and something you and I know could've happened. He loved that team." His smile didn't quite reach his eyes as he recalled how fanatical Will was about the Red Sox.

"The thing about you and Anne was pretty hard to believe, but he stuck to it so I accepted it as the truth eventually" replied Alex. "I couldn't imagine that even a letch like you would have sex with—how did you say it?—a cold, skinny bitch like her." She made a face that looked like she'd sucked on the sourest lemon as she imagined the unlikely pairing, then shook it off. "I've seen the women you date. They're all exquisite, not bony old hags. I mean, look at you. It's obvious you can get any woman you want."

"I can have any woman, Alex?" Diego taunted, one dark eyebrow raised in amusement as he turned toward her. "Even you?"

She knew he was trying to lighten the mood and decided to play along. She could use a little levity herself. "Down, boy," she laughed and gave him a good-natured shove. "Maybe the thought crossed my mind once or twice when I was young and naïve and we all used to hang out together in college," she admitted, "but you never seemed interested in me that way. And then things got serious with Will and ... well ... you were smart enough not to test your charm on me after that."

The moonlit night, raw emotions and exhaustion must have overridden Alex's internal editor and she'd revealed thoughts that should have remained unspoken. He was looking at her in a way that made her uncomfortable, as if she were a particularly delicious dessert. Uh oh. Testosterone alert, she cautioned herself and willed her mouth to stay shut. The ball was back in his court and she waited to see if he'd lob a return.

"Since we're being honest, I'd be a fool not to want you and I've never been accused of being a fool." He sounded angry, but a moment later his tone became wistful. "I've thought about what it would be like with us ... but even back then, I knew that sex with you would be more than a casual fuck, so I didn't try."

"Hmmm ... you know that the f-word is one of my favorite expletives, but as a synonym for sex it's kind of nasty, don't you think?"

"I actually meant it as a compliment. Let me explain," he said amused by her reaction. "I'm sure you know women who have sex just for kicks, but for others it's an expression of feeling. The Alex I know wouldn't want a one night stand, a casual 'fuck'—although if I've read you wrong … I'm sure it would be a most enjoyable night for us both." He aimed a devastating smile at her.

"And all this time I assumed I wasn't your type." She glanced at him then quickly looked away, afraid to make eye contact. What was wrong with her? Why was she toying with this man? Jesus, Alex, she told herself, stop sending mixed signals before things get even more out of hand.

"Do you want me to tell you that you're desirable? Well, you are." Out of patience, he hurled the words at her to make it clear they'd passed the point of wordplay and were moving into the minefield of verbal foreplay. It was up to him to end it. He'd already become aroused twice that night and if he had another erection she was going to wind up naked under him. "I want you, but long ago Will made it clear to me and any other male that looked your way that you were his and off limits. To me, Mrs. Cameron, you are still off limits. I may be many things, but I won't dishonor my brother by taking advantage of his wife, a woman who's obviously still in shock and not behaving like herself."

Diego's jaw clenched and his face flushed with anger. Alex knew that flirting with him was like waving red in front of a bull and then expecting the taunt to be ignored. She had to stop. "I'm sorry. I'm so sorry. I've embarrassed both of us and insulted you, which is the last thing I want to do. Your friendship is too important to me. You're right, Diego, I'm not myself. I don't know if it's tiredness or the wine or something else…"

Diego didn't look at her as he strode back onto the beach, stopping where incoming waves lapped the shore. Alex watched him pick up stones and angrily fling them into the sea while she tried to figure out why she was amping up the electricity between them. She needed to explain it to herself as well as to him.

"We have to finish this," she said when she caught up with him. His hands were on his hips, his expression cold and unreadable when he turned to face her. "Well?" he asked impatiently.

"I'm not sure who I am anymore. Can you understand that? Part of me is missing and I don't know how to be!" Tears threatened, but she was determined to get the words out. He took a step toward her. "Don't!" She raised a hand to stop him from coming closer. "You know how Will was, how we were together. He was playful and we flirted like mad all the time. Maybe acting that way with you is a way for me to try to seem normal, like nothing's different, although I'm very aware that you're not Will." She took a shaky breath before continuing. "And … dammit, I miss his body. It would feel really good to be held by a strong pair of arms right now, but I'm sane enough to know that it's Will's body that I want, not someone else's, even yours."

Diego nodded. He didn't say anything until they returned to the lighted path to the villa.

"It's late and we're both exhausted. I'll see you at breakfast and maybe we can go for a run." He squeezed her hand and pressed a soft kiss to her forehead. "Sleep well, *Preciosa*."

"And you, Diego," she replied.

Still wide awake hours later, Diego stared at the bedroom ceiling as if he could find an answer there. Friendship and responsibility be damned. The woman had no idea what it cost him not to pull her to the sand and make love to her. The conflicted emotions he'd forced himself to bury years ago as he'd watched his best friend and Alex exchange vows had been resurrected, and he wasn't sure he could suppress them or even wanted to. He hoped he'd convinced her to stop toying with him. Christ, he'd never even kissed—really kissed—her and he couldn't get that image out of his head. If he were smart, he'd fly back to Abu Dhabi or home to Buenos Aires and put a continent between them. But she said she needed him and he was a man of honor. She was his brother's widow. He wouldn't abandon her.

CHAPTER 12

*A*fter just a couple of hours of restless sleep Diego headed out for an early morning run. The mindlessness of hard exercise always helped him work through a problem and he had a lot to sort out. He was flattered by Alex's flirtatiousness, but he had to believe she was only taking her feminine muscles out for a test drive, to see if her battery still held enough charge to rev a trusted male's engine. She'd pushed his tachometer's RPMs near the red zone and it took tremendous discipline to throttle back. But if she wanted to play it that way, if that somehow helped her confidence, he'd go along ... but only to a point.

He was drenched with sweat by the time he pushed thoughts of Alex aside and shifted his focus to Will. He was sure — more than sure, one hundred percent certain — that Serge would find the murderer, and once that happened the rage that was building inside him like a volcano would have a chance to erupt. Diego had little doubt that he'd want to kill the monster with his own hands, but not until the bastard spilled the reason for the murder and who was behind it. He didn't trust the American justice system to mete out adequate punishment. A smart lawyer could come up with some minor technicality and the murderer could be acquitted, free to live his life while Will's was over. This killer would pay. He'd make sure of it.

Later that morning he and Alex sipped coffee in companionable silence in the villa's courtyard. Showered, and refreshed by his run, Diego intently scanned The Wall Street Journal while Alex flipped through the glossy pages of the latest Ocean Drive magazine. They were at ease again, the previous night's tension gone until Alex abruptly put the magazine down.

"I need a big favor."

"Of course, anything, or at least anything within my power." Diego raised one eyebrow, but continued to read the newspaper.

"I'm ready to go home. Do you think your pilot can fly me up to Boston today or tomorrow or should I make a reservation?"

"Are you sure that's what you want?" he said as he leaned toward her to study her face. She looked very different from the shattered woman that he'd brought to Miami. She glowed with health, but he also knew that she was still emotionally fragile.

"Am I sure? Maybe yes, maybe no. But it's time to face reality and my reality is Boston, not Miami."

"Fine. I'll come too," he answered matter-of-factly and stood. He'd expected that once she felt ready to break free of the villa's protective cocoon, she'd fly away like any beautiful butterfly, but he didn't think he was ready to let her go.

"Why would you do that?"

"Why not?" he said as he stretched and yawned loudly. "Look, Alex, I'll always regret that Will and I didn't get things right before he died, but I have to live with that. The least I can do now is to help you. I don't want to think of you walking into that house by yourself."

"But I won't be alone. I have Francie and David." Damn him, she'd been so sure she was ready to be on her own and now Diego was planting tiny seeds of doubt where her resolve had been.

"I know Francesca's a great comfort to you, but she has her work and her own life with David. And as dependable as David is, he's not Will's brother ... and I am, whether I wanted to know it or not. We're family. He'd expect me to watch out for you. If the situation were reversed, he would do the same for me."

"You obviously have this very masculine compulsion to protect me and I'm grateful, but I need you to accept that I can't keep leaning on other people or I'll never be able to stand on my own two feet again. I think I'm ready and I have to try."

"Let me come along ... just as your safety net. Your place is big enough that you'll hardly know I'm there."

Diego's determination and strength were comforting, but the implication that she couldn't take care of herself was pissing her off.

"How about this. I'll go home by myself. You can call me every day, or even twice a day, if that will make you feel better. I swear that at the first sign that I can't handle it, I'll tell you and you can ride to my rescue." She aimed a captivating smile in his direction.

Diego had engaged in enough negotiations to know when he was outgunned. "You win," he finally said. He ran a hand through his already tousled hair in a way that Alex noticed was so like Will and turned his back to her as he texted his pilot. "The plane can be ready in a few hours. Does that suit you?"

"That's perfect. Thanks."

"You know, life was a lot simpler for men when women weren't so damn independent," he grumbled and left the room.

Three months after Alex had fled Boston, the Navarro jet brought her back to the starting point. The pilot had radioed ahead for a car, which was waiting on the tarmac when the Gulfstream touched down. Traveling Navarro-style was painless and the limo pulled to the curb in front of her Commonwealth Avenue condo in record time.

The trees on the wide boulevard that had been bare skeletons when she'd left Boston in early April were alive again and everything was in bloom. Hot pink azaleas had emerged after winter's bleakness and joggers vied with bicyclists for supremacy of the road, taking advantage of summer's long daylight hours. She knew that a few streets away, the Charles would be dotted with sailboats and Harvard crews racing their sculls.

As she walked up the familiar steps to her spacious apartment on the top floor of a stately mansion that had been converted to condos, she wondered why she'd let her pride reject Diego's offer to come with her. Then she reminded herself that she was strong, she could do this. All she had to do was put her key in the lock and turn it as she'd done countless times. How hard could that be? Key in lock, clockwise twist, customary click, open sesame. The door swung open and silence rushed toward her. She paused, unsure of herself. Then she took a deep breath and crossed the threshold.

The apartment smelled musty from being closed up for months. She should have had the cleaning service come in, but there'd been no time. So she opened the windows and hit every light switch as she walked from room to room becoming reacquainted with the home she'd known so well. She saved the master bedroom for last. Its door was still closed as it had been since the night Will died. Her last memory of that room was watching him cover his naked body in faded jeans and a sweatshirt as she lay on their bed admiring him, sated from their lovemaking.

She told herself that she had to open this door too if she was ever to move on. It was time. She took a steadying breath and turned the doorknob. The room looked as neat and impersonal as one in a hotel. Someone, probably Francie, had straightened the place up, damn her. She'd fantasized about spending her first night at home in a bed that still held Will's scent, but the rumpled sheets from that long ago night were gone. Like so many others, that choice had also been taken from her.

She ran to the closet, desperate to see if his clothes were still there. They were, and his belongings drew her to them the same way she'd been drawn to the man who'd owned them. She tenderly ran her fingers over each of his shirts and could almost visualize him wearing them. Finally, she slid a light blue one with frayed cuffs off a hanger and pressed the soft fabric to her face. It was only cloth, but it had touched Will's skin and not just his scent, but his very essence was woven into it. His spirit would always remain in this room, the last place they'd been together.

As she prepared for bed, she fished one of his unwashed T-shirts out of the hamper, pulled it on and buried herself under the covers. Depleted, she quickly fell asleep and dreamed that she was wrapped in her husband's strong arms.

The instant she woke the next morning, Alex realized she was starting a day totally and absolutely alone for the first time since Will died. Francie had stayed with her until the funeral and then Luisa and Diego had taken over. Her chest tightened and her heart began to pound as an adrenalin overload pumped into her bloodstream. She imagined the walls closing in and her lungs cried out for air. She tried to convince herself that she wasn't going to die, but it didn't work. The crippling panic attacks that began in the days following Will's murder had gradually disappeared in Florida. She'd thought they were gone for good. She grabbed the phone and hit Francie on the speed dial with trembling fingers. "Please be there, please be there," she murmured.

"Alex? Is that really you? You're in Boston?"

"Yeah. I'm having a panic attack. My heart's racing, my hands are shaking, I can't breathe and I think I'm going to throw up."

"I'm not going to tell you to relax, but I'm headed out the door on my way to you. Let's keep talking and maybe you can try to calm down."

"I can't ... I can't." She tried sitting first on a chair then the floor, but she felt like she was going to jump out of her skin so she paced from one side of the apartment to the other. She was out of breath and her voice was tinged with hysteria as she gasped, "God, I can't breathe!"

"Alex, you know what this is and you know it'll pass. You're not going to die. Now listen to me. Listen! Do you know where your tranquilizers are? Good. Take one, then get one of those paper bags the doctor gave you."

Alex didn't say anything and Francie was alarmed by her friend's labored breathing, but then she heard a paper bag crinkling as Alex slowly breathed in and out, and she knew the hyperventilation would taper off.

"You're doing fine, you're going to be okay," Francie said as calmly as she could although the intensity of this episode scared her silly.

"I hate this! I was fine in Florida and I was sure these damn panic attacks were gone. Oh, God, Francie. I don't know if I can do this."

"Of course you can, but you shouldn't expect to do it all by yourself. You're strong, but there's only one Wonder Woman and she's that Linda what's-her-name actress chick from the TV show we used to watch as kids." Then she switched gears. "Isn't Diego there? Didn't he come back with you?"

"No, he's still in Florida. I convinced him I'd be fine and he believed me. Jeez, men can be so dense. Doesn't he understand that I see Will everywhere I look? His shaving stuff's in the bathroom, his towel is still on its hook, his dirty clothes are in the hamper. What am I supposed to do?"

Only Alex could answer that question so Francie switched the focus to another subject. "Talk to me about Diego. Remember how we used to think he looked like a hot, hunky pirate? I only saw him for a few minutes at the funeral, but he still looked gorgeous and a little bit dangerous."

"Gorgeous? That's a serious understatement," Alex's voice became more animated as the terror retreated. "That man is beyond hot and he is most definitely dangerous. Even the way he moves is a combination of threat and seduction. On top of that he's kind and thoughtful and isn't too macho to let me see him cry. Put it all together and you've got a lethal combination. I wouldn't admit this to anyone but you, but for the past few days I couldn't stop myself from flirting with him! His phero-mones must be really potent. Watch out, married lady! No one is immune."

"I hear you. I'm sure he'll show up in Boston at some point," said Francie in a tone that betrayed none of her anger. She wanted to break Diego's stupid neck. How could he have let their friend return alone to the home she'd shared with Will? And judging by the way Alex described him, it sounded like he'd tried to seduce her too. He'd supplied Francie with regular updates on Alex's condition and he'd promised that when she decided to come home, he'd be with her. If Alex had been able to convince him that she was fine, maybe she should go directly to Hollywood to pick up her Oscar.

"I'm crossing Commonwealth and should be in front of your door in a minute. Look out the window and buzz me in when I get there, okay?"

"You're the best, Francie. Have I told you that lately?"

"No. But as that hokey song goes, 'that's what friends are for.' Hey, I'm here but after speed walking I am so not schlepping up three flights of stairs. I'm gonna wait for the elevator," she grumbled, feigning irritation, but was relieved that she didn't need to call 911 for her friend.

The women threw themselves into each other's arms and held on tight. Then Francie stepped back, took both of Alex's ice-cold hands in hers and quickly assessed her friend's condition.

"You look terrific! You're so tan! And your hair! It's gorgeous. I wasn't sure I'd like it short, but I love it," Francie exclaimed before choking up with emotion. "I was so worried about you," she said as she playfully tousled Alex's spikey hair.

"It's wonderful to see you. I missed you soooo much."

"Me too, Alex. I know I gave you grief about staying away so long, but seeing you now I guess you were right. It would have been too hard to tackle the apartment and everything else right away. You look like you're more together ... are you really?

"Yeah, despite today's major anxiety attack I think I am. I mean there are still times when I cry and have trouble sleeping and can't even force chocolate down my throat, but that feeling of being broken is slowly going away. The sadness never really leaves and it probably never will, but it's changed. You know how when you start a new workout your muscles hurt so much you can barely move, but you force yourself to do it anyway? Eventually your muscles adapt and one day the pain isn't so bad. I'm taking baby steps, but something inside feels different I guess."

"You don't know how relieved I am to hear that," said Francie as she hugged Alex again.

"I am too, France. Believe me, I am too." They sat quietly for a while, comfortable with the silence as only friends with a shared history can be.

When the two women met as twelve-year-olds, Alex had already spent a month in friendless misery after the MacBain family moved from working class Buffalo to Mamaroneck, a New York City suburb. No one had bothered to consult her. She was simply told that her father could earn more as an electrician in wealthy Westchester County than in economically depressed upstate New York and that was that.

The business prospered in tandem with a local building boom and almost overnight the family had money for things that had been unaffordable, like braces. That's how Alex met Francie. They'd bonded over a shared hate for metallic smiles and a mutual crush on the rock star handsome orthodontist whose work tortured their fragile adolescent egos, then guided each other through pimples and teenage heartbreak. When Alex met Will, she told her best friend that she'd found the man she was going to marry.

A few years later, Francie had helped her survive the unimaginable when her father's sleek new Jaguar crashed into a concrete overpass on a snowy February night as he and her mother sped toward Manhattan, late for a Broadway show. It wasn't a huge surprise to Alex that her parents' mangled bodies had blood alcohol levels well beyond the legal limit. A taste for fine wine was one of the byproducts of the senior MacBains' success, as well as the sense of invincibility that had left their only child parentless at twenty-three.

"So now that you're back, will one of your baby steps be a call to Will's parents?" Francie wondered.

"God, no. Well … maybe. I can't stand them, but Will was their kid and I'm sure they'd like to have some of his things."

"And you have to find out why his father was so anxious to get in touch with you. Even if you're not curious, I am. Just do it when you feel less vulnerable. And vodka can't hurt. Maybe a little chocolate too," she said and they began to laugh.

Francie's personality was as bubbly as champagne and lifted Alex's mood better than any pharmaceutical. They sprawled on the floor, cushioned by the overstuffed pearl gray pillows that they pulled off the couch and nibbled their way through a bowlful of peanut m & ms.

"Where are all the yellow ones?" whined Francie eyeing Alex accusingly. "Did you pick them out already?"

"Ummm, yeah." Alex grinned at her friend. "Diego's pilot brought a couple of bags on board for me and I started to eat them on the flight up. You know I always eat m & ms color by color, first the yellow, then the red, the green, the blue, the orange and last, but not least, the brown ones." She hated when the company began to make special bags at Christmas in red and green since it was no fun to finish half the package in one color before starting on the other.

"I've always loved this apartment," Francie said dreamily. "Will's parents may have their faults, but they did okay when they bought this place for the two of you."

"Yeah, it is pretty nice," Alex agreed. She loved the high ceiling with its ornate crown molding and the view of Commonwealth Avenue from the front bay windows. The place owed its character to its first life as an elegant mansion before being converted to three large condos.

She was bursting to tell Francie the news that Will and Diego were brothers, but she didn't know if he wanted to keep that private. She'd always wonder how Will would have reacted if the DNA test had turned out differently and Ricardo Navarro had been his biological father and not John Cameron.

"So now what?" probed Francie interrupting her thoughts. "You know David and I will help you with anything you need to do."

"Thanks. I know that." Alex stood and stretched her arms toward the ceiling before lowering herself back to the floor in a lotus position. Watching her, Francie groaned, "Shit, my legs are too short to ever get them to do that."

"But they get you where you want to go, don't they?" Alex grinned, giving Francie the same response she always had since they were fourteen and Alex had shot up six inches to 5'10" while Francie's height froze at 5'2".

"A minute ago you asked, 'now what?' With my life on hold for a few months, there's so much to do I'm not even sure where to begin. I'll have to write a zillion thank you notes for donations people made in Will's memory. And I've got to figure out what to do with all of his stuff, but I can't face that yet. It would make it too final, ya know?" As she spoke, her fingers twisted the sparkling band on her left hand. "And then there are all the details to settle about Will's estate." Her eyes began to burn as she fought back tears.

"It's good that David's your lawyer. He's organized all of that for you and he said it's no big deal. You've been through a horrible time, sweetie, and I think you're doing great," Francie said encouragingly.

Tears began to fall in response to her friend's kindness. "No sympathy, please. I can't take it."

"I understand. How about this? You can procrastinate about your to-do list for one more day, but right now you're going to shower and get dressed and then we'll walk over to the Prudential Center for some major retail therapy. We always have so much fun playing with the makeup at Sephora!"

Alex was lost in a daydream and didn't answer. She was still running her fingers over her wedding band.

"Anybody home?" Francie said as she tapped gently on her friend's head.

"Sorry, I tuned out for a minute. Yeah, shopping would be great. Let's spend lots of money at the Pru."

With Alex out of earshot in the shower, Francie

called Diego, but his phone went to voicemail. "You get your lying, sorry ass up here as soon as you can. I don't care what Alex told you, she shouldn't be here by herself."

He returned the call within seconds, panic in his voice. "What's wrong? What happened?"

"For starters, she had a major anxiety attack this morning. I thought I'd have to call 911. You and I knew how hard this was going to be so why aren't you here with her? You promised me you'd do that."

"Is she okay?" he said ignoring Francie's diatribe. His only concern was Alex.

"Yes, for now. She's in the shower so I can't talk long. I don't want her to know that you and I have been keeping tabs on her, but you really need to be here, at least for a few days. She's already stressing out about going through Will's stuff and seeing the in-laws from hell again and…"

"She plans to see the Camerons?" He had his own questions for John Cameron since Serge had come across more evidence linking Will's father to the radical Scottish independence group. He didn't want Alex to be anywhere near that man. Until he was satisfied that John had nothing to do with Will's murder, Alex could be a target too. Francie was right. He was an idiot to send her to Boston alone and unprotected.

"I can be there this evening. I'll tell her I had a business meeting in New York and decided to pay her a quick visit. She won't believe me of course, but I won't tell her you called me. I'm sorry I dropped the ball."

"Good. I'm going to tell David to meet us here for drinks and then we'll all go out for dinner around seven. Try to make it." She didn't wait for his response before ending the call and muttering, "bastard."

The phone rang as Alex poured wine for Francie and David that evening.

"*Preciosa*," Diego murmured and Alex imagined him smiling as he used the nickname he'd given her years ago.

"And hi to you, too," she replied, the smile in her voice mirroring the grin on her face. "It's Diego," she whispered to Francie.

"Hi, Diego!" Francie shouted loudly enough for him to hear.

"Is that Francie with you? Tell her I say 'hi' back."

"I will and you give Luisa my love. I miss her," said Alex as she pictured the villa. "Are you sipping a mojito in the courtyard?"

"No, I'm actually in a car and the driver says we're about five minutes away from your house."

"What! You're here?" She felt lighter than she had in the past twenty-four hours. It had been so much harder to come home than she'd expected.

"I had to fly up to New York for an unexpected meeting and when I got back on the plane I realized I could be in Boston for dinner. I hope you haven't eaten yet."

Francie and David exchanged a knowing look as they watched Alex throw herself into Diego's arms. When she turned toward them again her face was flushed. As he released her, he tenderly cupped the side of her face with one hand to study her. "Let me look at you." His expression became serious as he recalled Francie's description of Alex's crippling anxiety attack that morning.

"What do you mean, 'let me look at you?' I'm the same person you said good-bye to twenty-four hours ago." His obvious concern and her reaction to him made her uncomfortable in front of their audience and she removed his hand from her face.

"My turn," Francie said. She stood on her toes to hug him and planted a passionate kiss on his mouth. Then under the cover of protests from her husband and Alex's laughter she whispered, "thanks for getting here so fast," then added loudly, "God, Diego, you're yummy! I didn't think it was possible for you to get even better looking, but you have." Coming from another woman, he might have been embarrassed, but Francie said the words with her arm once more wrapped around her man's waist. David offered a firm handshake, which turned into a back slapping male embrace.

"Good to see you again," he said to Diego. "It's been too long, but keep your hands off my wife!"

Diego raised his own hands in surrender. "You have my word, but you're a lucky man to have a woman who kisses like that," Diego teased as he winked at Francie.

"How long can you stay?" Alex interrupted.

"A few days if that's okay with you. I'll call the Ritz to reserve a suite."

"Don't be ridiculous. I have a couple of perfectly good guest rooms. How do you think I'd feel if you went to a hotel after you opened your home to me?

"Well…" he hesitated, "if you're sure."

"I am. It's settled."

After a few glasses of wine, Alex reminded them that they hadn't eaten. "I know you're a white tablecloth, impeccable service kind of guy," she said turning her attention to Diego, "but it would be fun to go to Quincy Market and graze through the food stalls there. Is that okay?"

"It's been years, but that place is fine. Are you sure you wouldn't prefer going someplace quiet, with waiters?"

"What? You don't want to serve yourself? God, you are spoiled!" Alex teased.

"I didn't say that ... I just offered ... *Díos mío*, Alex, give me a break! We Navarros may be used to servants, but I'm far from helpless. I had to carry my own tray when I lived in the dorm that first year of college, didn't I?"

David interrupted their playful repartee. "Can we go? I'm starving. We can ride in on the T," he said as he wrapped his arm possessively around his wife's waist.

"Or we can take a taxi," Diego smoothly countered. "I haven't been on a subway in years and I'm not sure whether I want to be squashed against a bunch of strangers' sweaty bodies. Now if it was the damp body of a certain beautiful woman..." he said leering at Alex. The smile he was hoping for appeared on her face.

"Stop it!" Alex grinned and pushed him away.

"I'm kidding! Quincy Market sounds great. By all means let's ride the T."

Alex was amused by Diego's ability to enjoy himself in an atmosphere so different from the chic restaurant he'd taken her to in Miami. They sat on benches at a long wooden table under the historic building's rotunda and began their meal with thick clam chowder. It was the one course all of them could agree on. They then went their separate ways with instructions to buy four of whatever each wanted. Alex bought pizza, David chose lobster rolls and Francie found a stall with spanokopita and dolmades. "I love Greek food," she gushed as she set the overloaded tray on the table.

Diego was gone so long that Alex began to worry. "I'm going to look for him. He must be lost." But as she rose from her seat, she spotted him carrying a tray with a self-satisfied smile on his face.

"I found fish tacos! In Boston! There's this tiny shack in Baja where they make the best ones, but I tasted these and they're surprisingly good," he exclaimed. Alex dabbed a blob of white sauce from his lip and was startled to realize that her first instinct had been to lick it off his face. She hoped no one noticed the blush she was sure was there.

"Dig in," David suggested unnecessarily.

By the time they'd finished every last morsel of the eclectic international feast, they were groaning and clutching their stomachs.

"I think we'd better walk this off," Alex finally said as she barely stifled a burp. "This was fun. Will used to love this place," she said as they left the market. Diego draped his arm around her and she leaned her head on his shoulder. Francie took her friend's hand and squeezed it reassuringly. Their silent support was comforting and she was able to think about Will minus the usual crippling sadness. Could it be possible to talk about him and feel pleasure? Maybe Diego was right, and Will would want her to be happy again. She liked to think that he was watching them and cheering her on. The image made her smile.

"Should we head back to my place for coffee or a drink?" Alex suggested. "We were so busy stuffing our faces back there that we hardly had a chance to talk," she said, and couldn't resist adding, "unless you want to stop at Emack and Bolio's for ice cream. They have a flavor called Serious Chocolate Addiction that's…"

"Shut up, Alex, or I'll throw up. I'm dangerously stuffed and I feel nauseous," Francie groaned. "Did I really eat pizza, chowder, tacos, spanokopita and lobster?"

"Killjoy. Fine, no ice cream," she conceded playfully.

Christ, she felt good and she was having fun. Will was dead and she was enjoying herself without feeling guilty ... or disloyal.

They walked toward the Haymarket T station, but continued past it. The night was clear and a breeze off the Atlantic had cooled the summer day's heat. "May I borrow your husband for a few minutes?" Diego asked Francie as they strolled away from downtown.

"Sure, but I want him back," she quipped.

"Of course," Diego said as he and David increased their pace.

"What's up? What don't you want the women to hear?" David asked.

"Alex told me that you've stayed in touch with the authorities and they're no closer to solving Will's murder than they were right after it happened. I want you to know that I've got people looking into it and I'm certain that it won't take long for us to find out who did this. I know you're a lawyer, so I won't go into the details, but I can assure you that Will's death will be avenged."

"I guessed as much since you're not the kind of guy who stays on the sidelines as a spectator. But for both our sakes I'm going to forget that we've had this conversation. As an officer of the court I can't know anything about what you might do, but as Will's friend I'm relieved to hear that someone will get to the bottom of this. I'm sure that makes Alex happy too."

"She doesn't know. When the time is right, I'll tell her."

"Good. If you do anything that could get you arrested, don't tell me about it, but also know that if I can help in any way, ask."

"Thanks, but like you said, it's best if you maintain your distance."

"I will. But my offer stands."

"You're a good man. We should join the ladies. If they ask, all I wanted was your opinion on a legal matter."

They headed up Beacon Street and along the Common. The beauty and peace of the Public Garden looked so inviting that Alex suggested they cut through it on the way back to Commonwealth Avenue. As soon as she spotted a bench, she raced to it, sat, kicked off her shoes and ran her feet over the cool, slightly damp grass. "Aah," she sighed with pleasure. The strappy sandals were killing her feet and she cursed herself for choosing fashion over comfort, but she hadn't expected a hike.

"I'm so happy to be with the three people I care most about," she said as she became aware of the peace she felt for the second time that evening.

"Do you think you can walk the rest of the way, madam, or shall I carry you?" teased Diego.

"You're not serious."

"I am," he replied and scooped her into his arms as if she weighed nothing.

A part of her wanted to demand that he put her down, while another reveled in his strength and wanted to cling to him. Her nose picked up the spicy scent of his cologne. Will never wore cologne. This wasn't Will. "Put me down! Put me down now!" she shrieked as Francie and David cracked up.

Diego reluctantly lowered her before he embarrassed himself. His physical reaction to her was no longer in his control and he sensed that Alex had been very aware of his body no matter what she'd said.

He was right. Alex couldn't blame her racing heart on anxiety — not this time. To cover her reaction, she bent down to stuff a small piece of tissue between the start of a blister and one of the sandal's straps and they continued on their way.

Blissfully barefoot on the kitchen's cool tile floor, Alex made coffee while Francie gathered mugs and filled a small pitcher with milk.

"So, is there anything you want to tell me about you and the gorgeous *Señor* Navarro?" The flush that crept up Alex's face was answer enough.

"Me and Diego? Are you crazy?" she erupted.

"Not crazy, sweetie, observant," Francie commented softly as she reached for a bag of cookies.

"Nothing's going on, so drop it. Just drop it." Alex bristled as she stalked out of the kitchen, then did an about face a moment later. "Forgot something," she mumbled as she picked up the coffee tray to bring to the living room where Diego and David sat in front of the TV, companionably watching the Yankees score two runs to tie the Red Sox four all.

"Help yourselves," she said, but the men were too engrossed in the game to hear. She shrugged, tossed a cushion onto the floor and stretched out. Why in hell would Francie think something was going on with her and Diego? She was just flirting for chrissakes. It didn't mean they were having sex. And if that's all it was, why was she so defensive?

"Hey! We were watching that," David said to his wife when she joined them in the living room and turned off the TV.

"Why do you have to torture yourselves watching the Sox?" Francie asked. "You know what will happen. They'll be ahead until the eighth inning and then pow!

They start playing like our nephew's Little League team and blow it. Besides, we're here to talk, not zone out in front of the tube."

She poured coffee then cuddled next to David. She rested her hand on his thigh as he absentmindedly twisted one of her curls around a finger and watched it spring back into place when he let go. No one spoke. They sipped coffee and munched on the chocolate chip cookies Alex always stocked for those times when she thought she'd die if she couldn't have something sweet.

She looked from one face to another. Not only was this normally talkative group silent, they weren't even making eye contact with her. Their behavior was pissing her off big time. "What? What's going on? You people are freaking me out. If you're worried that I'll break if we talk about Will or even his effing parents, I can assure you I won't. But I can't stand this silence. Please, someone, talk!" she commanded looking directly at Diego.

"All right, okay, I'll start." His back straightened as he shifted from a TV-watching slouch to perch on the edge of the sofa. "Alex and I are going to Scotland, and we need to leave soon." He continued before anyone had time to react. "But first, you and I," he said, his dark eyes fixed on Alex, "will have a long talk with John Cameron."

All hell broke loose as if Diego had said that he and Alex were going to run naked through the street. Francie jumped to her feet. David grabbed her hand and tried to pull her back down. "Let go of me," she hissed and shook free of his grip. Alex was on her feet, too, and soon Diego and David joined them.

"Darling, Francie," Diego said condescendingly, which only irritated her more. "If you give me a chance to explain, you'll see that if we have any hope of tracking down Will's killer it's perfectly logical that Alex and I have to go to Scotland. Serge is sure Will's death is connected to that country. The *sgian dubh* left beside his body means something. We all know that. And the police here are clueless. Come on!" he railed, but was wise enough to close his mouth when Francie approached him hands on hips, eyes flashing with anger.

"First of all, Mister Navarro, Alex is still a wreck and today, after she had a huge panic attack, we made a list of the things she has to do in Boston. In Boston, Diego, not Scotland! And who the hell is Serge, some goon you hired? Who do you think you are, fucking James Bond? No way are you going to take my best friend traipsing around the world to find a murderer. You'll get yourselves killed and I won't allow it!"

"She's right you know," added David. "Alex should stay in Boston. Going to Scotland now to track a criminal is crazy. Let the authorities do it." He sent a silent apology to Diego. After what he'd told him, David knew he had to cover his ass.

Alex was steaming as she clapped her hands to get their attention. "Stop it! Just stop it! Sit down and shut up. All of you!" To her surprise, they quieted and sat. "Am I invisible? Why do any of you have the audacity, the arrogance, the chutzpah to think you can decide what I will or will not do?" She glared first at Francie and her husband and then at Diego. "Since I finally have your attention, I'll tell you what I've decided. And don't say anything until I've finished." She knew it would require all their strength to follow that last request, but she hoped that her three friends recognized glimmerings of the spunky Alex they used to know. She threw another of the sofa cushions to the floor and gracefully lowered herself onto it, facing them.

"I've already told you that I need to start doing things for myself. You're my best friends in the whole world and I love you, but I need to prove to myself that I can be strong again. Will wouldn't want me to remain a blob of Jell-O and neither do I. Okay so far?" They nodded their agreement.

"First, I agree with him," she pointed at Diego. "I have to see John Cameron and find out what the hell he wants from me. I can do this alone, but I'd prefer that you come along. Will you?"

"Of course, *Preciosa*. Anything, you know that," he said softly. Because of what Serge had told him about John's possible connection to the Scottish nationalists, he had questions for Will's father too.

"And I still have to go through Will's things."

"I can help you do that," Francie volunteered.

"Thanks, but that's something I want to do myself."

"Okay ... fine. I guessed you would say that," she muttered and slumped into her seat. "But if you change your mind..."

"Great. Next, I want an update from the police. They seem to have forgotten about Will and I want to know if they have any new leads."

"As your lawyer, I've been checking with them regularly and they haven't forgotten, but there's still nothing new so you can skip that one. I'll stay on it," added David.

"Good. I can always count on you, can't I?" she smiled warmly at him. Diego felt a pang of jealousy, but let it go. "And that makes me more certain about the next item on my to-do list. Diego's right. In about a week or so, he and I should leave for Scotland and see what we can turn up there. Will's murder is connected to the week we spent in the Highlands. I know it. And since Serge is already there, we'll be safe. He's Diego's bodyguard," she added for Francie and David's benefit. "And he's no goon. He was with Mossad." To Francie, whose grandparents had survived the Holocaust, Israel's agents were the gold standard.

CHAPTER 13

*A*lex shivered and pulled the covers up over her shoulders, but a familiar scent—which, in her Pavlovian response, meant 'wake up'—tickled her nostrils. A moment later, her groggy brain registered that the aroma teasing her senses was coffee. She forced her eyes open, ridiculously buoyed by the familiar smell and the sound of footsteps in another room. For the briefest moment, she thought she'd had an extremely vivid, horrific nightmare and that, as usual, Will had woken up first and made coffee. It only took an instant for that comforting image to shatter. It wasn't Will; the footsteps belonged to Diego.

She dragged herself to the shower and let the steaming water soothe her tight shoulders. It was going to be strange to share this space with another man, however temporarily, but she couldn't very well ask Diego to leave, not after he'd been such a generous host. On the other hand, a Boston apartment, even one as large as hers, wasn't a luxury villa, and they'd be in closer contact here.

Although Diego had assured her that he'd never come on to her, she was aware that the promise was becoming harder for him to keep. The strong embrace he'd wrapped her in when he'd arrived the night before, the way he touched her whenever the opportunity presented itself, and the more frequent use of his pet name for her were all signs that she couldn't ignore. And she wasn't immune to him either. Her physical reaction whenever he was near made her question her own will-power. There was unmistakable electricity between them and each knew the other felt it. These feelings shamed her, yet what could be more natural than to want the solid comfort of a man's body? She didn't want sex necessarily. What she craved was skin-to-skin contact, although it was a given that sex would be the price she'd have to pay. It would be up to her to decide whether that price was too high.

By the time Alex finished her shower and padded barefoot to the kitchen, Diego was gone. She spotted a note next to the coffeepot and was amused that he knew her well enough to realize it would be her first stop. Caffeine fix in hand, she sat at the table and opened the folded sheet of paper.

"Alessandra" it began. Diego's mother always called her that—Italian for Alexandra—and she wondered why he had, then she continued to read. "I have to take care of some business today. I know you're surrounded by memories and I don't want to intrude on your privacy. I'll be back by 6:00. Let me choose the restaurant tonight ... one that takes reservations and has waiters." His attempt at humor made her smile, probably the response he'd intended. "I hope today isn't too difficult. If you need me for anything at all, you can always reach me on my mobile." It was signed with a flourish, "Yours, Diego."

A few streets away, Diego stood at the window of his Ritz Carlton suite gazing at the tranquil greenery of Boston Common directly across Arlington Street from the luxury hotel. He'd been working since early morning and the sleeves of his fitted white shirt were rolled up to just below the elbow, revealing deeply tanned, muscular forearms sprinkled with silky black hair. He'd abandoned his necktie hours earlier and the shirt's collar was open. He slowly ran his knuckles over his eyebrows to massage away the tension in his forehead while he gazed at the park, hoping some of its calm would transfer itself to him, but he couldn't get his mind off Alex.

He wasn't sure whether it had been wise to leave her by herself, but she had his mobile number and she hadn't called so she must be okay. She insisted that she was strong and although he knew it wasn't true yet, he vowed to do everything in his power to help build her confidence even though that conflicted with his equally strong need to protect her. He told himself that if she were to move on with her life, she'd have to have absolute belief that she was strong again, so for now he'd hold back. When she was ready to start the next phase of her life, he had no doubt that it would be with him.

He forced thoughts of Alex aside to focus on everything Serge had told him when he'd reported in from London a few hours earlier. He was making progress, but it was a slow and tedious business. "This is like peeling back the layers of an onion. You've got to be patient," he'd reminded Diego although they both knew that admirable trait wasn't one that Diego possessed. The former Mossad agent's intelligence sources in the U.K. had confirmed that Will's father was part of a covert Scottish nationalist group. For Alex's sake, Diego hoped that John Cameron wasn't even remotely involved in his son's death, although it was starting to look bad.

Serge's contacts told him there'd been chatter about

schisms in Scotland's oldest and most secretive independence movement. Some of its members, frustrated by the
snail's pace of the mainstream Scottish National Party's
political efforts, were determined to win Scotland's freedom from England by any means, including violence.
His sources confirmed John Cameron's tie not only to
this Group of One Hundred, but also to a man named
Mackinnon, the same one Alex remembered meeting
when she and Will were in Scotland. Serge told Diego
that he would check into the man's well-established retail
business in Inverness to see if it was a front for the group.

"Mackinnon's son was convicted of conspiracy to
commit terrorism and is serving a long jail term," Serge
told his employer. "Evidently he was involved in building bombs to use in I.R.A.-type terrorist attacks. His
group came pretty close to detonating them in London.
I imagine the senior Mackinnon's not a happy man, and
his connection to John Cameron and Alex is of interest."
He assured Diego that he'd check it out.

Diego poured himself a whiskey and began to pace
as he tried to tie the various threads together. While
he and Alex were in Miami, he'd pushed her to recall
every detail about the week she and Will had spent in
Scotland. He wasn't surprised that the Mackinnon that
Serge said was connected to Will's father was the same
man Alex had told him about. She'd remembered that
they'd gone into a gift shop in Inverness and its proprietor had talked Will's ear off about his family's history.
The man had asked a lot of questions and then gave Will
a replica of some old document to pass along to John,
but she didn't know if Will had ever followed through.

"Was there a reason that you and Will went to
that particular store?" Diego probed. "There must be

a lot of gift shops to choose from in a touristy city like Inverness." Diego had probed.

"We'd met some guy in our favorite London pub, a Scot ... I'm pretty sure that his name was Ewen ... and when he heard we were going to Scotland, he suggested that we go to this store since the owner was a friend and wouldn't rip us off."

Diego had passed the information along to Serge who agreed that Alex and Will might have been set up. He said he'd try to track down this Ewen character.

Serge effortlessly slipped into the role of a well-bred English barrister to visit the upscale Mayfair pub where Alex recalled meeting Ewen. The former spy was clothed in a Savile Row suit, hand-sewn leather shoes and completed the metamorphosis with an expensive black umbrella carried like a proper Londoner. He impressed the barman with his generous tips and the after-work regulars with his skill at darts and his knowledge of English football. They took no notice when he began to slip some questions about Scottish politics and the elusive Ewen into their comfortable male banter.

"Oh, that bloke's been gone for a while," recalled the barman as he expertly built another Guinness for Serge. "I remember your Ewen because we don't get many Scots in here. This one was pleasant enough when he was sober, but he'd shoot off his mouth whenever he'd had a bit too much. Liked to drink the expensive stuff—single malt whiskey, I recall."

"Shoot off his mouth?" Serge replied, urging the publican to elaborate as he took a sip of the dark brew.

"Oh, he'd go on about how the Scots were oppressed

and exploited by us English pigs, that we'd stolen their country and now we were robbing them of their oil. That talk may be fine in Scotland, but here in London it's none too smart. I'd toss him out for his own safety when he got like that. First it was the troubles with the Irish and now it looks like the Scots may be up to the same business. Ah, well." He shook his head in resignation as he wiped the bar with a clean white cloth then smoothly filled orders for other patrons before resuming his conversation with Serge. "A posh Mayfair pub like this isn't the place for brawlers. My clientele won't have that and neither will I. Talk is that this Ewen went off to America. The last time he was in — it was about two, maybe three months ago, I seem to recall — he had another Scot with him ... a strapping young lad, but Ewen did all the talking. He blathered about the two of them having some job in the States, but he didn't say what it was they'd be doing. Personally, I was glad to see him go. He was trouble, he was."

He slid another Guinness across the bar to Serge, its creamy head forming a perfect dome atop the black liquid. "Might I ask what your interest is in this man? Is he in trouble with the law? Or is it that he's heir to a huge fortune left to him by one of your posh clients?" the barman asked, grinning at this improbability.

"I wish I could tell you, but it's to do with a legal matter. Confidentiality, you know. Might anyone else have some idea as to his whereabouts?" asked Serge.

"I'll ask the gents then, shall I?" the barman said genially as he moved toward a small group of regulars. "Ned, John, Charles — a question, gentlemen, if you please. Our barrister friend is trying to find that big Scot who was fond of shooting off his mouth. You know the one. Have any of you seen him recently or do you recall what he was to do in America?"

"Nah," came the chorus of responses.

"He did boast that he'd have enough of the ready to buy a round for the bar when he got back. I wouldn't forget a promise like that," recalled Charles.

"Right, Charlie! So we can add liar and braggart to our Ewen's list of less than admirable traits," added Ned.

"He's gone and good riddance I say," commented John as he waited for the barman to draw his pint of bitter. Glass in hand, he moved closer to Serge, casually leaned his elbows on the bar and slowly sipped his drink. He ran a hand through his copper-color hair and turned toward Serge.

"Not many Scots in London," he began softly, "but you might try a pub called the William Wallace over in Marylebone. It's near the Baker Street tube stop. That's where I'd look for this Ewen if I had a mind to."

Serge morphed into a Scot on holiday to visit the Wallace pub that evening, but no one there seemed to know Ewen. The man had obviously left London. It was time for him to move on too.

He spent the next couple of days gathering the tools of his trade from a few trusted former associates, then loaded it all into a rental car and headed to Scotland. Everything he'd learned so far led back to James Mackinnon and his Inverness gift shop. It was time to pay the man a visit.

CHAPTER 14

*J*ohn Cameron was panting and dripping with sweat as he neared the top of the Empire State Building's 1,860 steps on his home gym's StairMaster when the doorbell rang. Anne was still asleep and the housekeeper had left for her weekly trip to the local farmers' market. There was no one there to see who was at the door but him. He grabbed a plush white towel and wiped the sweat from his face as he took the stairs two at a time.

When he opened the door, a stocky deliveryman was ambling back to a van, double-parked outside the Cameron's red brick townhouse.

"Wait!" John shouted and the man stopped and reversed direction. "Sorry it took me so long to answer the door."

The messenger grunted a reply as he thrust a manila envelope into John's hand along with a clipboard and pen. "Sign theyah," he said, his speech tinged with a thick South Boston accent.

John scrawled his name, grabbed a bill from the tip dish on the hall table, and handed it to the messenger.

"Tanks," the man said, a grin spreading across his pock-marked face as he noticed the bill was a five and not the usual single. Some people didn't tip him at all. He'd be happy to make more deliveries to this ritzy Louisburg Square address.

John brushed aside the desire to resume his short-circuited workout or shower, and instead headed directly to the wood-paneled library on the townhouse's second floor. The room was a masculine oasis with floor-to-ceiling bookcases, worn leather furniture, a faded Oriental rug, and lighting designed for reading. He felt at peace in this quiet space, where Anne never ventured and the scent of sweet tobacco smoke lingered. The ritual of filling one of his many pipes with fragrant brown leaves, tamping it all down, and finally igniting it always helped him to relax. Anne and the housekeeper thought it was a filthy habit, but he didn't care. A man could do what he wanted in his home and this house was very much his. Camerons had lived in it for generations. Some day it would have been Will's. He closed the door and turned the latch to ensure that he wouldn't be disturbed, then settled his tall frame in a well-worn, brown leather chair, lifted his feet to the matching ottoman, and laid the envelope on his lap.

Minutes passed as he drummed his fingers nervously on the innocent-looking packet. He knew who'd sent the envelope by its distinctive seal, but this was the first dispatch he'd received since Will's death and this particular missive filled him with dread. He didn't have to open it to know he was fucked. He'd prayed they'd never find out what he'd done, or if they knew they would let it go. He'd been deluding himself and he knew that once he slit open this envelope his life would be irrevocably changed. He'd been expecting something—he wasn't sure what—that would clarify, explain … either ease his guilt or send him to purgatory. He turned the envelope this way and that as if he could divine its contents simply through touch. He was sweating, nauseous, breathless, and his heart was racing. He almost wished for the massive coronary that his anxiety mimicked. A quick death, yes, that would be best. But his body didn't cooperate.

When he could no longer stand it, he broke the flap's archaic wax seal and half expected the thing to blow him to bits. He set his shoulders and tried to prepare himself for whatever was inside. His fingers shook as he frantically flipped through the envelope's meager contents and then he froze, unable to tear his eyes away from a photo of Will, his son, his baby boy, lying on the ground, sightless eyes open wide, staring at nothing. Blood was pooled around his head. "HE DIED FOR YOUR SINS!" was scrawled across the photo in bold, black letters, large enough for a blind man to see. Will was dead because of him. It was true.

He fell to his knees and the agonized scream that emerged from the depths of his soul sounded inhuman to his ears. He blindly seized the nearest object—a heavy crystal ashtray—and hurled it across the room, but the damn thing was too solid to break. He wanted to smash something or someone, to tear himself limb from limb, to hear the sound of glass or even bone shatter. He scanned the room, desperate to find some outlet for his raging anguish and began to pull books from the shelves and fling them wildly in every direction.

Then his eyes zeroed in on the portrait of his father above the mantel. "You bastard," he growled. "This is your fault! You killed your own grandson! How could you do this to him? How dare you do this to me!" He grabbed the painting and pulled until it came off the wall. He drove his knee through the middle of his father's likeness in a frenzy of madness and grief. Finally, he pounded his fists into the wall until it was stained with the blood of his knuckles. It was only then that he allowed himself to stagger to his chair as grief surpassed his anger. "Oh, God. Oh, God," he wailed over and over until, finally spent, he filled a water glass with whiskey and, as always, chose the easiest course—he drank himself into oblivion.

One floor above, the racket in the library woke Anne from her drug-induced slumber. She lay in bed, half-asleep, and smiled. He'd murdered their son. She'd known it all along and she was glad that now he knew it too. It was all his fault.

CHAPTER 15

When Alex woke to the smell of coffee and bacon on Diego's second day as her houseguest, she didn't make the mistake of thinking that it was Will puttering in the kitchen.

"Good morning, Alessandra," Diego greeted her cheerfully as she shuffled into the sun-filled kitchen while she tightened the sash of her green silk robe. It was the same one she'd thrown on the night the police came to tell her Will was dead.

"Coffee?" Diego asked, raising a dark brow in question.

"Thanks." Her voice wasn't quite ready for full-fledged speech. "You're up early," she mumbled between sips from a large mug of steaming coffee. It would take another few swallows before she'd be fully awake, but her eyes were working fine as she studied the man leaning back against the counter, legs crossed at the ankle. He was wearing shorts, a sweat-soaked black T-shirt and, since he also had on running shoes, she didn't need caffeine to figure out he'd already gone for a run.

"I think I got up around five. I couldn't go back to sleep so I decided to work off the other night's gluttony. The four of us ate like pigs." He patted his flat stomach and grinned.

Ooh, you're so obvious Navarro, she thought, but she wasn't going to be manipulated into commenting on his body. She was all too aware of his muscular thighs and the way the fitted T-shirt hugged his sweaty torso. She battled the all but irresistible impulse to glance at his crotch.

"You made bacon? I didn't know you could cook."

"I can do a lot of things you don't know about," he replied smugly as he used an oven mitt to bring her the plate of bacon and scrambled eggs he'd kept warm in the oven. A basket filled with muffins and scones appeared as if by magic.

"You're going to spoil me. You made incredible coffee and cooked breakfast," she said as she shook her head in amazement.

"Since food prep seems to impress you, I'm tempted to take credit for your meal, but I brought it back from the café down the street. I ate mine there a couple of hours ago. I did, however, put yours on a plate and I made the coffee myself," he said proudly.

"Well at least you're honest and you get points for thoughtfulness. It's delicious." She wanted to tease him about his lack of culinary skill, but instead asked, "Why have you started to call me Alessandra? You've never done it before."

He hesitated for a few moments while he decided how much to reveal. "I think the Italian version of your name suits you. You always smiled when my mother called you that. And when I use *Preciosa*, it seems to make you uncomfortable. If you prefer Alex, tell me." Will had always called her Alex and he wasn't going to admit that he was trying to differentiate himself from Will in her mind. Her husband wasn't the man he'd want her to think about when and if he had the chance to whisper her name in her ear.

"It's not a big deal. I've been Alex for so long that Alessandra sounds strange, but I like it actually. And you're right about *Preciosa*. I understand that you mean it innocently, but to other people it's the kind of name a lover would use."

That was precisely what Diego intended, so he said nothing.

Lover wasn't a word to use in this man's presence so she quickly changed the subject. "Are you up for a meeting with John Cameron today if he's free or do you have other plans?"

"Your wish is my command, madam." He bowed from the waist with a flourish and flashed that devastating grin at her again. "Of course I'll go with you. I already gave you my word. Besides," he paused as if choosing his next words carefully. Alex watched as his grin disappeared and the sparkle left his eyes as his mood abruptly shifted. "I've got a few questions for Mr. Cameron too." He turned and headed toward the guest room. "I need to shower and shave, but I can be ready to leave whenever you are. Call Cameron and let me know what he says."

"Aye, aye, captain," she responded sarcastically, but he didn't notice. She munched on a piece of bacon and hoped the protein-rich breakfast would provide the strength she'd need for the day ahead.

Fueled and caffeinated, Alex knew she couldn't postpone making the phone call any longer and quickly tapped the number for John's office.

"Cameron and Associates," the chirpy receptionist answered. Although a lawyer by profession, Will's father spent most of his time managing the family's investments and overseeing their charitable foundation.

"John Cameron, please."

"May I tell him who's calling?

"It's Alex. Alex Cameron."

"One moment, please. And may I say Mrs. Cameron that I'm so sorry about your husband. We were all very fond of him."

"Thank you."

She listened to some unrecognizable canned classical music during the thirty seconds it took John to pick up.

"Alex! I'm so happy to hear your voice. It's been too long. How are you?"

"I'm fine, John. How're you and Anne?" Crap, what hypocrites we are. He doesn't give a flying fuck about me and I don't care how he and his bitch wife are coping, she thought, but she kept the hostility out of her voice.

"We're all right. Thank you for asking. I assume you're back in Boston? Your friend Francie told us that you'd gone away to ... well, to recuperate, I suppose. We were concerned because you disappeared. We didn't know where you were."

"I'm sorry that you were worried. I should have ... well, but I didn't." Damn it, he wasn't going to make her feel guilty. They'd probably been anxious to know where she was so they wouldn't look clueless when, or if, their friends asked about their son's widow

"I'd like to stop by to see you today. What time would be convenient for you?" she said, bringing an abrupt end to the niceties. She didn't want to give him a chance to say no, and his response indicated he was as eager for this meeting as she was.

"Tell me what time works for you and I'll clear my schedule. Shall we meet for lunch or a drink or do you want to come here to the office?"

"How about the bar at the Ritz Carlton at about two?"

"The Ritz it is. I'm looking forward to it."

You are? You won't be when I'm through with you, she thought cynically.

"Fine, see you then. Oh, and John? I'm bringing Diego Navarro with me." Alex ended the call before he could respond.

Francie the fashionista had persuaded Alex to rev up her wardrobe during one of their therapeutic shopping marathons. As she dressed for the dreaded meeting with her father-in-law, she was grateful to have accepted her friend's advice. The obscenely expensive purple silk designer blouse she'd bought at Neiman's with its deep V neck, ruched bodice, raw edges, fitted sleeves and pleated French cuffs was exactly the sophisticated look she wanted. It was chic and feminine, but with cutting-edge style that was definitely not proper Bostonian pearls and cashmere. She paired it with well-cut black trousers and kidskin stiletto pumps. Diamond stud earrings and her wedding band were her only jewelry. She used styling gel to emphasize her hair's deliberately disheveled look and applied subtle makeup. She felt like an actress slipping into character.

"Holy Mary Mother of God," exclaimed Diego when he saw the results of her efforts. He lapsed into rapid Spanish as he rose from the sofa and slowly looked her over from head to toe.

"May I say, Mrs. Cameron, you are spectacular? You take my breath away."

"You may, sir." Delighted, she twirled and made an exaggerated curtsy. "Does your reaction mean that I usually look ordinary?"

"Ah, fishing for compliments, are we?" he teased and then fixed his coal dark eyes on her. "No, you could never look 'just ordinary.' But today, in those clothes, you would turn heads in any city in the world. John Cameron will fall face first into his martini or whatever it is he's drinking these days."

"So you don't think it's too much? I really like it, but I don't exactly feel like myself in this outfit. Francie made me buy it." Why on earth did she need so much reassurance, she wondered, and then answered her own question—because she was jittery about the meeting and wasn't comfortable as a *femme fatale*.

"If Francesca is responsible for that outfit, remind me to thank her." He glanced at his watch. "We should go. I want to arrive first so that we can choose our seats at the table. In any confrontation—and that's exactly what this is—position is everything."

His confidence was reassuring, but the butterflies in her stomach had butterflies. Diego gripped her elbow to steady her as they walked toward the Mercedes limo that was waiting for them at the curb. "I guess these heels are higher than I'm used to. It would be awful if I toppled down my own front steps," she laughed nervously.

She didn't notice the weathered face of a panhandler weaving his way toward them, but Diego noted his approach. The man's eyes were surprisingly clear and focused on them. Diego sensed danger and wanted to get Alex into the car quickly, but she had other ideas. As he was about to help her into the limo, she paused to study him. "I've been so focused on how I look for this meeting that I've paid no attention to you," she said, as she stood in the middle of the sidewalk admiring the charcoal gray trousers that rode low on his hips and the sharp contrast between his immaculate ivory shirt and a fitted black blazer. He'd skipped a necktie and left the top button of his shirt unfastened. She liked that he was tall — the same height as Will.

"You look pretty snazzy yourself, *Señor* Navarro," she commented as she ducked into the car. Her compliment brought an uncharacteristic blush to Diego's cheeks and he mumbled his thanks as he self-consciously shot his cuffs.

"Why did you hire a car? The hotel's so close that we could have walked."

"I guessed correctly that you weren't going to wear your running shoes and besides, I wanted us to arrive in style. Is that so terrible?"

"No, but it's a bit extravagant, don't you think? Will would never have…"

"I'm not Will," he snapped.

"I know," she said almost to herself.

When the driver pulled up in front of the Ritz less than five minutes later, the doorman not only helped them from the car, but also greeted Diego by name.

"Good afternoon, Mr. Navarro," he said, touching a finger to his hat in salute.

"Why does the staff know you on sight?" Alex asked as they entered the lobby and her heels clicked across the marble floor. She was oblivious to the admiring looks directed their way until Diego possessively put his arm around her waist. "You're attracting a lot of attention. We're surrounded by hungry lions and you're the prey."

"Don't try to change the subject. Why does the staff of this hotel know you?" She had no right to question him like some jealous girlfriend, but she couldn't stop.

"Why the interrogation? I rented a suite here. You need your space and I require privacy for my business affairs."

Alex didn't want to argue and decided to back off. "Of course. I know you have other things to do besides baby-sit me, but you don't have to hide it from me either, okay?"

"Agreed. It was foolish not to tell you. Can we please stop sniping at each other? We're on the same side."

She nodded her agreement yet couldn't help wondering whether Diego used the suite for more than business and was upset at the thought that he might need this private place to make love with some woman. She knew that Diego Navarro wasn't the kind of man who could stay celibate for long. His sex life was none of her business, yet if that were true, then why did the idea of it bother her?

The luxury hotel's bar was reminiscent of an exclusive gentlemen's club complete with wood paneling, fire-places, brass sconces, and paintings of hunting dogs. Diego had reserved a corner table away from the distraction of the windows facing the Public Garden. Schooled by Serge to never leave his back exposed, he instinctively seated himself facing the door with a wall behind him. Alex sat to his right. When the waiter approached, Diego told him they would wait for their guest to arrive before ordering. This wasn't a tactic, Alex realized, but a reflection of his upbringing. Exquisite manners were second nature to him.

"Are we waging psychological warfare here?" she asked Diego, amused by his preparation for battle.

"It can't hurt. I want a chance to study him before he puts on his public face. Don't acknowledge him until he reaches our table."

Alex thought he'd seen too many spy movies, but

didn't say anything. A few minutes later, Diego squeezed her hand as John entered and began to scan the room. Alex automatically began to lift a hand in greeting, but Diego held it down.

"Wait. Let him find us," he hissed. His breath was hot on her neck, yet she shivered. Diego's tension was contagious and it made her stomach lurch. Maybe it hadn't been so smart to bring him to this meeting. Then John spotted them and plodded toward the table.

The change in his appearance was startling. Maybe the man had a heart after all, Alex thought. Gone was the fit, handsome man John had been at Will's funeral three short months ago. This person seemed devoid of energy. He was gaunt, the collar of his shirt too big, and the first sign of sagging jowls made him look suddenly old. His eyes no longer sparkled, but they crinkled at the corners when he broke into a broad smile as he spotted his daughter-in-law.

"Alex," he said and extended both hands toward her. "It's been too long. You're as beautiful as ever." His greeting was proper, but lacked warmth and she responded in kind. Cancel previous thought. No heart, at least not for me, she told herself. He walked around the table to Diego, who rose, and the men stiffly shook hands. No hugs or slaps on the back for these two.

"It's wonderful to see you, son."

"Sir," said Diego stiffly, but he seemed oblivious to John's use of that particular word or more likely chose to ignore it. Alex couldn't and her heart leapt into her throat. Son. Until John uttered that word, she'd never considered that Diego was seated across the table from his biological father. She wondered if John even remembered screwing Giovanna Navarro thirty-four years ago and whether he ever gave any thought to the paternity of the two boys born nine months later.

"So nice of you to join us," John said in response to Diego's formal greeting.

Alex saw Diego's eyes harden and his jaw tense as the hand that had been holding hers clenched into a fist under the table. She knew him well enough to realize that he would resent how John was attempting to turn this get-together into his party, his idea, yet he was able to smoothly respond, "Thank you, sir. I'm glad to be here, too."

"You've known me long enough to drop the 'sir,' young man. Call me John. And why aren't you two drinking? Where's our waiter?" John was clearly usurping Diego's role as host again. She gently pried his closed fist open and felt him relax.

"Alex and I waited for you to arrive, of course. And now that you're here…" Diego gave an imperceptible nod to the waiter who appeared at his elbow as if by magic. Score one for the charming Argentine.

It was fascinating to watch these two bulls snorting and pawing the earth as they each sized up their opponent to determine a strategy before locking horns in battle. The level of testosterone was so potent it was palpable. Alex hoped the hostility wouldn't escalate beyond an occasional snarl. She needed a drink badly and turned to the waiter.

"Madam?" he asked.

"I'll have a cobalt cosmopolitan, heavy on the vodka please."

"Cobalt?" asked Diego conversationally, the hard edge momentarily gone from his voice.

"Yeah. They add blue Curaçao to the standard cosmo so it's a beautiful azure. And you know I'm a sucker for drinks in stemmed glasses."

The waiter then turned to John. "And for you, sir?"

"No fancy drinks for me. Double vodka on the rocks. Make it Grey Goose. What are you drinking Navarro?" he asked, a little too loudly.

"In memory of Will," Diego said pointedly as his eyes bored into John's, "I'll have Macallan, the 18-year-old if you have it, or else the 12 will do. Neat, water on the side, please. And you can put this on my account."

"Of course, Mr. Navarro. Will there be anything else?" asked the waiter. No one answered, so he turned toward the bar to put in the order.

John's gaze swept the room while they waited silently for their drinks. When he turned his attention back to their table, the defiant glare Diego had aimed at him instantly shifted into a more amiable expression.

The man is a chameleon, Alex thought, observing Diego with fascination. She knew he could be tender or even show vulnerability, but he was also able to mask his emotions well enough to scare her. The smile he turned toward John Cameron betrayed none of the rage that seethed below the surface, but she could feel it as his fingers found hers. His hand felt familiar — like Will's, she realized — but Diego's grasp was much stronger and lacked Will's gentleness. She wiggled her fingers to loosen his grip and saw a look of surprise on his face as he let go. She guessed he hadn't even realized his hand, conveniently hidden by the tablecloth, had sought hers as if seeking an anchor.

Will's father seemed oblivious to the tension at their table or maybe he was already too loaded to notice. He downed the double vodka like water, then signaled the waiter for another. It only took a few minutes to run out of polite small talk.

"I'm curious about something, John," Alex said in an abrupt segue from questions about the health of Diego's parents, her stay in Miami and the Red Sox. "Why were you so anxious to find me? What was so urgent that you had to leave messages for me with Francie?"

"Frankly, Alex, I'm surprised that you didn't return my calls. That was rude, and you've always had good manners," he said curtly.

"I had other things on my mind," she bristled. "What did you want from me?"

"Anne and I were simply concerned about our son's wife, especially when you disappeared so suddenly. I don't see anything unusual about that," he replied in all innocence.

"Let's be honest, John. We both know that you and Anne never approved of our marriage. We all played our parts because of Will. But he's gone. Why would you care about me now? I don't buy it."

"You're wrong, Alex. Anne and I love you like a daughter…"

"Oh, cut the crap!" she snapped as anger overcame her determination to be civil. She leaned toward him. "I said we don't have to be polite anymore and I meant it so you can turn off the charm. I'll ask you again and I'd like an honest answer this time. What was so important that you had to track me down?"

Diego was pleased by the apparent return of Alex's spirit, but he jumped in anyway. "Tell her, Cameron," he ordered in a tone used by a man who expects to be obeyed.

The older man fixed his eyes on the table and swirled the ice in his glass with his index finger. The confident bearing that was as much a part of him as his patrician nose collapsed bit by bit into slumped surrender.

"All right ... all right. There's a lot to explain, but not here. Not in a public place." His speech was slurred.

"Fine." Diego pushed back his chair and rose to his feet. "We can continue this upstairs in my suite. And don't worry," he added snidely, as he put a hand on John's arm to steady him, "it has a bar."

CHAPTER 16

The elevator whisked them to the fifteenth floor and Diego led the way to his spacious corner suite. The room's mahogany tables, brass accessories and tasseled yellow silk drapes were better suited to an older person, but the hotel was near Alex's house and met Diego's needs if not his taste.

John stood at the large windows, apparently transfixed by the view of the Public Garden until his eyes shifted left toward Beacon Hill and home. "I've lived in Boston all my life and this is the first time I've been in one of this hotel's rooms," he mused.

Alex was about to ask which hotels he'd frequented with his lady friends, but controlled the impulse to taunt him. She didn't like the nasty woman who'd occupied her body the minute she'd spotted John. She even felt a little sorry for him because of the obvious pleasure Diego took in playing cat to John's mouse.

"Make yourselves at home," said Diego, extending his arm toward a yellow damask sofa. "Can I get anyone a drink? Something to eat?"

"No, thanks. I've had more than enough already, although coffee might be good," John said as he rubbed his face briskly with his hands.

"I'll ring for it. You too, Alex?" Diego asked, quirking an eyebrow in her direction.

"Sure, why not?" She was relieved that both men seemed less combative for the moment and that they'd chosen coffee. More alcohol would have amped up the hostility again.

Less than two minutes later there was a knock at the door and a white-gloved, uniformed butler entered.

"Good afternoon, Mr. Navarro," he said.

"Hello, Henry," replied Diego.

The man placed the coffee service on the parlor table, then quickly moved to the room's bar to set out ice and a variety of soft drinks.

"Shall I pour?" he asked.

"No, we'll take care of it. Thank you, Henry."

"Ring if you or your guests require anything else, Mr. Navarro," he said as he left the suite.

"Your own butler. I'm impressed," Alex commented.

"Comes with the room," replied Diego with a shrug. It was obvious that he took such amenities for granted. He poured coffee into two delicate cups and served each of them before filling his own.

She liked watching Diego play the perfect host because she knew that the ruthless side of his personality would return before long, especially if it turned out that John was somehow connected to Will's death. The way Diego was behaving made her believe that Serge must have told him something that implicated John and she was irritated that he'd decided not to confide in her.

No one spoke until John slowly raised his head and fixed his bloodshot eyes directly on Alex. He struggled to take a deep breath and ran a trembling hand through his salt-and-pepper hair. His right eyelid twitched and he rubbed it irritably.

"Alex, you know that I loved Will more than words can say," he paused, waiting for a response.

"Of course."

"You know that I'd never do anything to hurt him, right?" Another pause.

"Yes," she finally replied softly, afraid of what was coming next. She waited patiently for him to continue. So did Diego, showing remarkable restraint — for him. It was obvious that what John was about to tell them was important, something that couldn't be taken back once it was uttered.

He fidgeted nervously with the alligator strap of his wristwatch then jingled the change in his pocket. Diego and Alex remained silent. Tears filled John's eyes and ran down his face as he shook his head from side to side and moaned softly.

"Act like a man, you pathetic son of a bitch!" Diego shouted as he abruptly rose from his chair and stalked around the room like a caged animal before turning to face John. "I have no more patience for you, old man. Do you know anything about Will's murder? Do you?" He grabbed John by the lapels and pulled him to his feet. He didn't resist and was like a rag doll in the younger man's grip. Their faces were mere inches apart.

"Tell me Cameron. Now!" Diego's voice carried enough menace to raise goose bumps on Alex's arms. After another minute of silence John's lips moved, but no sound emerged.

"What? What did you say?" Alex asked.

"Yes! Whatever you're thinking is right! Yes! He's dead because of me! I killed my son!" he shouted before his knees buckled and he collapsed onto the couch. "It should have been me. I was the one who betrayed them, why didn't they kill me?" he whimpered.

His words triggered an earthquake in the precarious

wall Alex had begun to assemble around her sorrow. As it tumbled brick by brick, her strength dissolved like ice in a blast furnace.

Diego didn't move. He only nodded as if John's admission confirmed something he already knew. He looked from John to Alex and back again. His arm pulsed with the need to smash John's face, but Alex looked like she'd been sucker punched in the stomach. One glance at her made his choice simple — she needed him and he'd vowed to take care of her. He pressed her trembling body to his as if a human tourniquet could staunch her pain and mend the jagged hole that had reopened in her heart.

"I can't stand that you're hurting again," he murmured as he kissed her hair and stroked her back. His body infused her with warmth, but scant comfort. In addition to the shock of John's admission, she was furious with the man who was holding her for not preparing her for what he seemed to know was coming.

John continued to ramble and Alex tried to listen through a scrim that shifted from solid to transparent and back again, so that only a word here or there made its way to her ears. How was she supposed to deal with this? The urge to escape that had hit her the day of Will's funeral returned full force, but she was too drained to move.

"It's my fault. Anne was right. She hates me and wants me dead and so should you. I never should have … why did I … oh, Christ," he babbled.

Diego let go of Alex and walked purposefully to the bar where he poured whiskey into two glasses. He handed one to her and kept one for himself.

"Drink it, Alessandra."

"I don't like whiskey."

"Drink it!" he said in a 'don't argue with me' tone that she recognized although he'd never directed it toward her before. He strode to the bedroom and returned with a down comforter that he wrapped around her. Her silk blouse provided little warmth and Diego was too agitated to stay still, so the blanket and Scotch would have to supply the heat his body had given her a minute ago.

Alex sipped the strong amber liquid and watched the two men warily—one straining with the effort to contain his seething rage, the other slumped in defeat before the first blow landed.

"Stop muttering. Precisely how were you involved in Will's murder?" Diego spat the words.

"They said I betrayed them, broke a blood vow. They sent me a letter that said Will was the first, that no one in my family was safe, even Alex. And the pictures! Oh, the awful pictures. I don't know why they killed him instead of me. It makes no sense. It should have been me, but they said I'd suffer more this way."

"What vow are you talking about? What letter? What pictures? And who is this 'they' you keep mentioning? Goddamn it Cameron, pull yourself together and tell us what you know! What—did—you—do?"

Alex could see that the tenuous grip Diego had on his temper was fraying. If he decided to throw John through the window she'd do nothing to stop him, but not before he told them everything he knew about Will's murder. She watched as Diego breathed deeply to calm himself as he removed his cufflinks and carefully rolled his shirtsleeves to just below the elbow. His muscular forearms twitched with tension.

"I'll only ask you one more time," Diego hissed

menacingly as he tipped John's chin up with one finger, forcing the older man to look at him. When John simply shook his head from side to side, Diego lost his fragile hold on rational thought.

"*¡No tienes cojones! ¡Qué maldito puta mierda!*" His anger erupted into a torrent of Spanish expletives. His full lips narrowed as he bared his teeth like a wild animal poised to attack. The spacious suite suddenly seemed too small to contain the emotions swirling within its walls.

Alex understood the gist of Diego's swearing and wasn't alarmed until the last, uttered slowly, deliberately and with icy menace: "*Voy a matarle.*" I'm going to kill you.

John shrank back and watched Diego warily. Even if he didn't understand the words, the threat was clear. Alex's nostrils picked up the unpleasant tang of her father-in-law's sweat. Deodorant's not working, she thought nonsensically.

"*Cálmate, Diego. No vale la pena. Cálmate ... por favor. Te suplico.*" Alex hoped that by using Spanish to beg him to calm down, she might get through to him before he acted. She wanted to go to him, but feared that John might bolt if she left his side. She'd have to hope that Diego would exhaust himself and behave rationally once the whirlwind swirling through him abated. The curses now centered on John's mother and graphic sex acts done to her and by her, but they were uttered less vehemently.

When Diego's tirade began, Alex had put her arm around John's shaking shoulders to gentle him, as if he were a skittish horse. It took a Herculean effort for her to embrace this man, but she would deal with Satan himself if it pointed them toward Will's murderer. A moment later, she abruptly pushed him away, kicked off her shoes and began her own pacing. He would have to fend for himself like everyone else. She whirled toward him and glared. "You! Don't move!" Her face flushed as anger surged through her.

Diego watched her warily as she pivoted to face him. "And you, you son of a bitch, you sit down too. And stop that fucking cursing." Diego's mouth opened, but he didn't move. "Now!" she snapped. He wasn't used to taking orders and certainly not from a woman. His dark eyes sparked with anger, but he sullenly obeyed. He grabbed a mahogany chair from the dining room table with one hand and swung it around as if it weighed nothing. He straddled the chair and lowered his forehead onto his arms where they rested atop the chair's back. Alex couldn't see his face, only the heavy curtain of black hair that fell forward as he bowed his head.

"You both listen to me and listen good," she began, furious that two grown men were behaving like little boys. "We are not leaving this room until each of you tells me everything that you know—or suspect—about Will's death. The lies and secrets end here. I don't care if we stay here for a week." Tears of anger and frustration welled in her eyes. She turned toward the window and hugged herself, hoping to hide what these two macho oafs would surely interpret as weakness.

"Alessandra," began Diego.

"Don't you Alessandra me! Shut up! Just shut up, you condescending jerk," she replied irritably, brushing tears away. The suite seemed to have everything but a box of tissues, so she brusquely grabbed the handkerchief Diego offered.

"As simply as you can, tell me what you had to do with Will's murder," Alex asked John after she composed herself and once again joined him on the sofa.

"I'll try Alex. I'm sorry that I've upset you." He patted her hand, but she pulled it away.

"Apology accepted. Go on."

He began to speak haltingly in a flat voice as his trembling hands absentmindedly rubbed his thighs.

"Okay ... it all began in Scotland centuries ago. I thought I could finally end it, that Will wouldn't have to know, that he wouldn't have to inherit the burden that my father handed to me, as his father passed it to him."

The face he turned toward Alex was ashen and he stretched his hands toward her, palms up, like a supplicant. As he reached for her she recoiled.

"All I wanted was to protect my son. Is that a sin? I didn't want him to know about our family's involvement and then the two of you had to go to that damn store in Inverness. Why there, why that place? And after, once Will brought back the paper that raving lunatic gave him, that Declaration of Arbroath, there was no stopping it. Even then I didn't warn him. God forgive me, I didn't warn him."

"I don't understand. What should you have warned Will about?" Alex leaned toward him and grasped him by the shoulders so he'd have to look at her. "What does the gift shop in Inverness have to do with this?"

Diego continued to rest his head on his forearms, but Alex saw his body stiffen as he listened to John's incoherent account. She frowned wondering how much of this he already knew and how long it would be before he exploded again.

"I'm sorry if I'm not being clear. My brain is a bit addled," John conceded and his body sagged. "Is there more coffee?"

Diego silently refilled John's cup and resumed his head down position.

"Go on," Alex urged, "you were talking about that man Mackinnon and the paper he gave Will." She sensed that a curtain was about to rise in a theater and she had no idea what the play was about.

John's eyes had a faraway look and he began his tale as if in a trance.

"I was playing outside our house—the same one I live in now—when I was a little boy, maybe five or six years old. It was a cold autumn day and I was jumping into piles of leaves that our gardener had raked up. I liked the way they crunched and the pungent smell when he would set the piles on fire. Sometimes he'd even let me strike the match. Anyway, my father called me to come inside. He was quite strict and I thought he was going to punish me for interfering with the man's work. I can't remember the gardener's name. Isn't that strange?"

Alex hoped he wasn't headed off on a tangent, but he brought himself back to the story.

"Anyway, my father took my hand and brought me into the library. We called it a den in those days. No one was allowed in that room without my father's invitation. There were logs blazing in the fireplace and I could see two cups of hot chocolate and some cookies on the table near his chair, so I figured he wasn't mad at me. I always liked that room, still do," he mused, "except now I wrecked it."

He sighed deeply before he continued. "You remember my father, don't you Alex? His name was John, like me. All of the first-born boys in my family were named John. But I wanted something different for my son, so I named him William, for William Wallace. You know, the Scottish hero from Braveheart—the Mel Gibson character with the blue war paint."

When he looked at her expectantly, Alex simply nodded. The John Cameron who was spinning this tale was a stranger. She wondered if he'd allowed Will to see this side of himself.

"You knew him, my father, didn't you Navarro?" he said, turning toward Diego.

"Yes. I met him once or twice when I was very young." Diego seemed pensive as well, but he was as anxious as Alex to find out what John's fairy tale had to do with Will's murder. "You were saying you were in your father's library..." Diego's words guided John back to his narrative the way a sleepwalker might be led back to bed.

"Oh, yes. Right," John's eyes glazed as he slipped back into the past.

"We sipped our cocoa for a while, but my father didn't say anything to me. Finally, he added a log to the fire and sat facing me. He had a very deep voice, the kind that could rumble like thunder or lull you to sleep. Between the fire's warmth, the cocoa and his voice, I remember wondering if I was still awake since it was like listening to a bedtime story. Obviously I wasn't asleep, because I remember every single word he said ... I don't think he ever read stories to me."

"Is it all right if I walk around?" John asked Diego, finally relinquishing control to the younger, more powerful man. "Of course," Diego answered quietly. "What did your father say to you?"

"I was too young to understand a lot of it, but every couple of years or so, he'd repeat the same story to be sure it was ingrained in my mind. He said it began in

14th century Scotland. One of my ancestors and other clan chiefs gathered at a place called Arbroath to write an appeal to the Pope, asking him to help Scotland gain her freedom from England. They didn't actually talk to the Pope. They sent a long letter, kind of like a petition, with all of their wax seals affixed to it."

"I've heard of that letter." The memory transported Alex back to the touristy shop where Will had spent an hour being schooled in Scottish history by the store's busybody proprietor. "Will was blown away to find out that someone named John Cameron signed it. He thought it was a coincidence, but I remember that he told the shopkeeper that you have the same name."

"Coincidence? No, that was no coincidence. There's been a John Cameron in my family for centuries and the one who signed that old document was my grandfather many times removed. Every firstborn Cameron male since then has taken the same blood oath." He shrugged and looked directly at Alex. "Now do you understand? When the two of you came back to Boston from Scotland, Will was furious that I'd robbed him of his heritage. Some heritage. I never wanted him to be a part of it," he said, bitterness hardening his voice. "He told me that Mackinnon gave him something to show me and had even asked for your address. He probably wanted to confirm that he had the right Cameron."

"Yeah," she said, frowning at the memory as she leaned back and closed her eyes. "Will was fascinated by the old guy's stories. He couldn't figure out why you'd never told him that he was descended from Highlanders." She forced herself to stay focused on the present and not get lost in the memory of how that discovery had made Will excited in other ways. But she couldn't stop a fleeting vision of her hands sliding over her husband's wet, soapy nakedness. She wanted to go with the daydream, to drift back to the feel of his body on hers after their encounter with Mackinnon. "Will," she sighed, not realizing she'd spoken his name aloud. Diego shot a puzzled look at her, but John evidently didn't notice anything and went on with his story.

"When Will gave me that copy of the Declaration of Arbroath, he repeated Mackinnon's words verbatim to me as instructed: 'Your Da will want to see it, too. Promise me you'll show it to him.'"

Alex was dumbfounded by John's ability to mimic a Scottish burr and then instantly switch back to normal speech. "That particular document wasn't just a reminder of the blood vow I'd taken. It was a clear message, but I didn't realize it until it was too late. I never told Will about our family history or my connection to Mackinnon and the others so he couldn't protect himself. Goddamn it, he was a man and I treated him like a child and it cost him his life." His voice dropped to a whisper, "Anne kept trying to get me to tell him everything, but I was too stubborn or too naive. I should have listened to her."

John reached for his now-cold cup of coffee, evidently satisfied that his story was finished.

Diego ignored him and turned to Alex. "Do you understand what this has to do with Will's murder?"

"Only a little. I mean it has something to do with the Camerons and Mackinnon and some oath. But no, not really. Not yet," she shrugged.

"I don't get it either. Cameron. Cameron!" he raised his voice until John looked up. "What does a reproduction of a seven hundred-year-old document have to do with you? And what promise did you make to this Mackinnon character? What's this blood vow you keep mentioning?" Diego already knew the answers to some of his questions, but he needed John to connect the dots.

"What? Were you talking to me?" said John stupidly.

Jeez, had the man suffered brain damage from all the booze he'd consumed, Alex wondered as she studied him in disbelief. He'd always been articulate and intelligent and had been coherent until a moment ago. Why couldn't he explain this?

"I'm sorry, I seem to be having trouble making myself clear."

"Damn right," mumbled Diego.

If Alex's impulse was to beat John to a bloody pulp, she was sure that it was costing Diego plenty to restrain himself.

"Do you think a five-minute break might help you gather your thoughts?" Diego asked politely. He would force himself to be patient with this man even if it killed him.

John raked his hands through his hair. "Good idea. Got any aspirin? My head's killing me." Diego nodded and pointed toward the bathroom.

"I knew it! The bastard is connected to Will's murder and I bet he can even tell us whose hand held the knife." Diego's eyes flashed with the primal thrill of a hunter with easy prey in his sights until his gaze shifted to Alex. Her mascara was smudged, there were stripes on her cheeks where tears had washed makeup away, and she'd chewed off her lipstick.

"You look like hell," he said as his tone softened and concern filled his eyes. This gentle, compassionate Diego was as comforting to her as his savage, bloodthirsty side was frightening. Her feelings for him were as inconsistent as his behavior toward her, so when he wrapped her in his arms and pressed his lips to her cheek she surprised herself by returning his embrace. And that's when John walked out of the bathroom.

"So that's how it is," he crowed, grinning smugly as he took a step toward them. "Already making time with your best friend's widow, eh, Navarro? Not that I'm surprised—like father, like son," he taunted, his voice dripping with venom. "Can't you Latin Don Juans keep it in your pants?"

Diego flew at him. He'd been waiting for a reason to hit the older man and there was no holding him back. John's insult, not only to his honor, but also to Alex's and his parents', gave him *carte blanche* to wreak the violence he'd craved. The two men tumbled to the floor with a thud.

"Stop it! Cut it out!" Alex screamed but they ignored her. She had to stop them before John was badly hurt or they'd never find out why Will was killed and who did it. She scanned the room for a weapon, grabbed the silver ice bucket, and dumped its remaining cubes and freezing water over the two panting men as they wrestled. Stunned, they both looked up at her.

"Will you behave or do I have to kick both your asses?" Alex glared at both men and knew she had to seize control if she were ever to hear the rest of John's story. "Mr. Navarro," she began, her voice cold and filled with contempt as she confronted him. Diego had the grace to look embarrassed. "Please leave us alone. Go for a run or hit the gym or I don't care what until you work off some adrenalin and can control yourself." He opened his mouth to protest. "No! Don't say a word, not even one. Go. I'll be fine, won't I John?" The other combatant was still on the floor, breathing heavily, but nodded his agreement. She knew Will would have been amused by this scene and could almost hear his laughter. Alex didn't believe in ghosts, but—just then—she was sure her husband's was there.

CHAPTER 17

James Mackinnon placed a "closed" sign in his shop's front window, locked up and drove out of Inverness, heading east on the A96. He hated to lose a day's income, but there was no one he trusted to mind the store and today's meeting in Elgin was important.

The others would come from Craigellachie, in the heart of the Speyside whiskey region; Aviemore, a ski and hiking destination in the Cairngorm Mountains; and remote Boddam, bordering the North Sea at Scotland's craggy, easternmost point. Each participant could make the round trip by car in a day. Their absence would arouse no suspicion.

Mackinnon's belly was comfortably full from his usual breakfast of porridge, a fried egg, and a thick slice of bread slathered in orange marmalade, washed down by two cups of tea with milk. As a widower for the past ten years, he was used to cooking for himself. It pleased him to eat what he wanted when he wanted, not like other helpless old men who had to pay good coin to some woman to prepare their food based on her tastes and her schedule, not theirs.

Although it was summer, Mackinnon switched on the car's heater to remove the overcast day's damp chill. He tapped the radio's "on" button, but BBC Scotland held no interest for him so he switched to a Gaelic language station.

He smiled broadly as he recalled how proud he was of his grandson. Their people in America had provided him with a detailed description of the braw way the lad had carried out the task he'd so diligently trained for. His Jamie had expertly murdered John Cameron's beloved son and he'd even had the wits about him to leave the *sgian dubh* beside the body and photograph his work. The contact in ... Gloucester was it? ... swore there were no witnesses, but to be safe Mackinnon had sent young Jamie to a friend's sheep farm in the far north, near remote John O'Groats, where he'd work for the next year. It was no sin to take extra precautions to keep your kin from harm, was it?

It took twenty years for Mackinnon to reach the upper echelon of the Group of One Hundred, the ancient alliance that took its name from a portion of the 1320 Declaration of Arbroath:

> *"For as long as but a hundred of us remain alive, never will we on any condition be brought under English rule. It is in truth not for glory, nor riches, nor honours that we are fighting, but for freedom, for that alone, which no honest man gives up but with life itself."*

The organization's present-day members were all direct descendents of the document's original signers. Every one of them, including that traitor John Cameron, had taken a blood oath to fight for Scotland's nationhood and to never reveal the identity of the other ninety-nine members.

Over the centuries, the One Hundred's methods had

often been brutally violent, but in modern times they employed intellect and money instead of broadswords. Throughout history bloodshed had rarely advanced the goal of a sovereign Scotland and was now forbidden. But the group's unity had fractured in recent years, mired in conflict over how to achieve their objective peacefully. Some, including Mackinnon, argued that the political process embraced by the group was agonizingly slow and that less civilized tactics must not be ruled out. The vast majority of its members, however, continued to work for independence within a political framework. After all, they argued, Scotland had her own Parliament again. That was progress, wasn't it? They seemed blind to the fact that real power still rested in London, despite the occasional crumbs the English would toss to the Nationalists. Mackinnon was convinced that Westminster would never willingly remove the yoke from Scotland's neck and set her free.

Today's meeting of the splinter group in Elgin would remain a secret to all but the three who, like Mackinnon, were en route and one other who couldn't attend. The remaining ninety-five members would never tolerate his thirst for vengeance and would cast him and his out for spilling blood in their name. Easy for them, he reasoned. It was his son, not theirs, who rotted in prison because of John Cameron's treachery.

Mackinnon never understood why the majority of Scots kowtowed to a foreign oppressor, which is how he viewed England. Sheep, the lot of them, he thought derisively. He'd cheered when *Sinn Féin* President Gerry Adams declared that he would never enter the chamber of Parliament in London because "it's a foreign parliament and I am an Irish person." And I'm a Scot, by God, yet I've got English pounds in my pocket and my passport says I'm British, Mackinnon thought with disgust.

He rolled the car's window down a few miles east of Inverness and spat as he passed the turnoff to the Culloden Battlefield—which he still called by its old name, Drommossie Moor. "I curse you, Charles Edward Stuart, and damn you, Butcher Cumberland!" Mackinnon shouted into the wind as strands of his white hair blew into his watery blue eyes. It was a ritual begun as a boy, imitating the actions of his Da who'd told him how the Bonnie Prince's ego and incompetence as a military leader led to the savage slaughter of the starving and exhausted—but always courageous—Highland clans on that very spot in April 1746. His Mackinnon ancestors fought in the midst of the front lines, and only three escaped with their lives.

As for the Duke of Cumberland, well, what could a man say about Cumberland? Mackinnon spat again, more forcefully this time, then rolled up the old car's window. Cumberland had been the worst kind of sadist, an English General who wasn't satisfied to just win the doomed battle that ended the Jacobite Rising of '45. Oh, no. After the victory, he'd ordered the massacre of survivors, even the wounded. His troops brutalized, raped, pillaged and burned, leaving women and children to starve. Tartans were banned along with bagpipes, weapons, the Gaelic language and all things Highlanders held dear, effectively ending the clan system.

If it had happened today, Mackinnon mused, it would have been condemned by the world as ethnic cleansing or genocide. And if my folk had won, if only they had won, he thought, I'd no be on my way to a meeting to plot murder and plan for the day Scotland finally rids herself of England's greed and domination. In his dreams, he sometimes visualized his homeland actually breaking away from its geographical tether, to float free, strong and independent once more.

Ah, my bonnie Scotland, he sighed. More than a thousand years have passed and we still fight the same enemy. So many dead, may their souls rest in peace. He crossed himself then lit a cigarette as he reached the outskirts of Elgin.

Mackinnon yanked up the hood of his dark green windbreaker as he walked from the car park toward what remained of Elgin's ancient cathedral. He had no interest in the books and postcards displayed in the ticket office and dug in his pocket for the £3.30 admission charged by Historic Scotland.

He resented paying good money to visit a ruined church, but reasoned that the coin was needed to help preserve his beloved country's past. This rationale disappeared in a flash as he shifted blame for the ticket price to the English. If they weren't stealing the profits from Scotland's North Sea oil, the country's museums and historic sights wouldn't need to sell tickets — at least not to Scots. He didn't give a damn how much tourists paid here or for the trinkets they bought in his shop. When Scotland was free ... the phrase entered his mind unbidden, a welcome obsession.

He walked purposefully down what was once the center aisle of the cathedral, past the resting places of knights and bishops entombed more than eight hundred years earlier. The elements had worn away the nave's stone floor and his shoes squeaked as he walked over wet grass toward the shelter of the octagonal chamber house where he was to meet the others.

"Whose daft idea was it to gather in this ice cold place?" groaned Ian Lindsay the instant Mackinnon entered the gray stone hall.

"We could have done our business in a pub or at least at a cozy teashop, couldn't we have?" added John Malcolm. "My feet are fair frozen. A cuppa and a scone would be good about now."

"Christ, you lads sound like a bunch of yammering women," Mackinnon shot back. "And what have you to say, young Duncan? What's your complaint?"

The man he called young Duncan was no less than forty, but the other men had been friends of his dead father, so to them Duncan Buchanan would always be a lad.

"No complaints about the place, but what age must a man reach before you stop attaching 'young' to his name?" Duncan asked peevishly.

Their good-natured laughter echoed off the building's stone walls and elaborate vaulted ceiling. Mackinnon leaned against one of the massive columns that supported the structure.

"Maybe this will help," he said, grinning as he pulled a flask from his pocket. "I know it will ease the ache in my old bones."

"Is it whiskey?" young Duncan asked hopefully.

"Aye, 'tis. And what else would I bring for refreshment, a fizzy drink? Of course it's whiskey," he said as he unscrewed the cap and raised the silver flask to his mouth before passing it to the next man.

"I hope Michael arrives soon so we can begin. Why

didn't he ride down with you?" John Malcolm asked Mackinnon. "We've never held a meeting without him."

"He sends apologies and thinks me capable to act in his stead," said Mackinnon somewhat peevishly. "One of Michael's bairns tumbled out of a tree this morning and apparently broke his arm, so Michael's off to hospital with the wee laddie. He didn't want us to delay on his account, so I'll fill him in when I return to Inverness."

The other men nodded their understanding, but there was some throat clearing to cover their grumbling. They'd have to be satisfied that nothing they discussed this day would be carried out without Michael's okay. Mackinnon ran on emotion; Michael Graham tempered his ruthlessness with intellect.

"Now to business," said Mackinnon, pleased to be in charge for once. "Ian, close those doors so we have some privacy. We'll have fair warning if some tourist comes along."

Mackinnon paused until he was certain he had their attention. "I'm pleased to report that the police in Boston are still befuddled by the action we carried out and likely always will be. Nothing leads back to my Jamie. We're in the clear, lads."

"And what of Cameron?" Ian asked.

"Michael sent John Cameron a clear message that his treachery was responsible for his son's execution. But we've no worries from him. Our man in Boston reports he's behaved like the coward he is. His Da, God rest his soul, would be ashamed to have sired this particular Cameron. He's not a man, or mayhap I should say he's nay a Scotsman. Life in America makes men soft. I wager he's the first Cameron who can't even lift a broadsword, let alone wield one. He's taken to the bottle like a babe to his mam's breast." The others harumphed their agreement.

"Perhaps we shouldn't be so certain of that," cautioned Ian. "'Tis said that a Scot doesn't fight until he sees his own blood. The sight of his only son's blood could give a man like Cameron a thirst to spill ours."

"Not to worry lad, not to worry. Here, have another nip to calm your nerves." Mackinnon extended the flask to Ian.

"So it's all settled then?" asked John Malcolm as he pulled his cardigan sweater tightly around his lanky frame, unsure if the chill came from the room's damp or from the icy coldness of James Mackinnon's words. Malcolm had been the only one to argue against Will Cameron's murder. The lad was an innocent after all, but he had been out-voted.

"It's not quite settled, no," responded Mackinnon. "Michael has received reports from America that trouble may come from a friend of the dead lad's, a man called Diego Navarro. The two were like brothers I'm told. This Navarro has money and power and the ear of the lad's widow. The lass is descended from Gillies Mor MacBain who struck down fourteen of the English single-handed at Culloden before the whoresons ran him through with a blade. Do ye know of him?" Mackinnon asked his attentive cohorts, who responded with muttered "nays."

"Christ, have ye no interest in our history?" he said with disgust. "They were fierce and bonnie fighters, the MacBains. Why, that clan stood shoulder to shoulder with my own people on Culloden's front lines. I just canna abide harm coming to the lass and I told Michael so, but he has someone keeping an eye on the bonnie Alexandra on the chance she carries a Cameron in her belly."

"Aye, James. That makes sense," said Buchanan. "With young Cameron gone, that clan is finished and John Cameron knows it. But it's still useful for him to believe his son's wife is in danger, no?"

"Right. There's no need to ease the devil's mind or his guilt, but killing a lass is…" Mackinnon scratched his head as he searched for a word. "Well … it's different, is all. But Cameron must understand that no one betrays us. No one! Like all of us, he took the blood oath and must abide by it — or his must die."

CHAPTER 18

*D*iego was stunned that Alex had actually thrown him out of his own suite. What amazed him even more was that he'd obeyed her order to get lost. He'd stormed into the bedroom and when he emerged in shorts and a T-shirt, he'd muttered another Spanish curse and left. Alex had the power to make him crazy, yet he suspected that her brand of persuasion would work on John better than his. Whether she'd be able to handle whatever Cameron revealed worried him, and he was sorry to have put her in that position. He vowed to find a way to make it up to her.

Alex had no doubt that Diego was hurt, and more than a little offended, that she'd ordered him to get out, but she wasn't going to worry about the state of his oversized ego. The wreck of a man in front of her was more important, for the moment at least.

She stood with her arms crossed, facing John. "It's just you and me now and I need you to tell me the rest. You owe me that," she coaxed and braced herself for what might come. Minus the volcano known as Diego, John seemed more composed—a good sign.

"All right. I'm sorry that I'm having so much trouble explaining all of this and I apologize for implying that you were having an affair with Navarro. There's some history between our families and it was a gut reaction. I know you wouldn't get involved with a man like him. What do you want to know?" All of the fight had gone out of him and he was acting more like the confident man he'd been before Will's death.

Alex hadn't missed John's reference to the Navarros, but she let it go. Her fingers were ice cold and she leaned forward to wrap her hands around the coffee pot, but it wasn't warm so she rewrapped herself in the comforter from Diego's bed.

"You told us that your father was involved in some Scottish organization. Can we go back to that?" She wanted to hear more about Mackinnon, but guessed that a chronological telling would be easiest for John. She was less sure than Diego that John was in any way responsible for Will's murder. The Camerons might appear to be heartless, but Alex knew how much they'd loved their son. They would never put their only child in harm's way. Will had once told her they'd never even spanked him.

John took a couple of deep breaths, removed his blazer, and loosened his silver and navy striped necktie. He carefully rolled up the sleeves of his dress shirt just as Diego had done earlier. Alex was freezing, but the two men obviously had some internal source of heat. He rubbed his hands over his face and then, with a faraway look in his eyes, resumed his tale.

"I already told you that my ancestor, John Cameron, was a clan chief and one of the signatories of the Declaration of Arbroath. To Scots that means he's something like George Washington, Thomas Jefferson, Benjamin Franklin—at least that's what my father drilled into me. Naturally this ancestor became my hero,

especially since I had the same name. My fate, I guess."
He shrugged, then continued without a prompt from
Alex. "My father filled my head with glorious, heroic
tales of Clan Cameron, how generations of my family
fought for Scotland's freedom, and how it was my duty
to carry on this fight."

Alex was exhausted, her head ached, and she was
anxious for him to get to the point. Her coffee was cold,
but she gulped it anyway, hoping its caffeine might ease
the pain behind her eyes. She knew she had to be patient
with John, but it was increasingly difficult. "John, I don't
need to know all the history. Let's focus on the present
and why you think you caused Will's murder."

John pulled his chair closer. She couldn't look away
from the intense expression in his gold-flecked hazel
eyes; nor did she want to. He filled his lungs, exhaled
forcefully, and began.

"I'm a member of a secret organization called the
Group of One Hundred. Our name comes from a phrase
in the Declaration of Arbroath," he said.

"You mean that bit about never giving up as long as
a hundred are still alive?"

"Yes. We've tried to win Scotland's freedom for centuries, sometimes openly and with our blood, but more
often covertly," he paused and sighed deeply.

"So are you ... a spy or some kind of terrorist?" she
stammered. The very idea was ludicrous, but it seemed
John Cameron had a lot of secrets.

"Nothing so glamorous. In recent times, the
Camerons' only responsibility was to raise money to
finance the struggle. When my father died, that job
passed to me. It's important to blur the trail of finan-
cial support that comes from what are best described as

'questionable' sources. I know how to do that. It may sound sleazy, but it's done more often than anyone realizes. I'm not a spy and I'm certainly not a terrorist, but money laundering is illegal. I could wind up in prison."

"Oh!" she gasped.

"Some of our support comes from countries and radical groups that take great delight in anything that hurts England. They have no interest in an independent Scotland, of course, but they want us to succeed in order to weaken the British government and to humiliate it."

"This is like a James Bond movie," Alex said, astonished to discover that John Cameron was a money launderer and involved in anti-British conspiracies. Her head was spinning, but she closed her eyes and forced herself to concentrate. Diego would expect her to repeat all of this to him. Would he be as shocked as she was or might John's shady side appeal to him? She wouldn't be surprised if Diego even respected him as a kindred spirit.

"I know it sounds crazy, but I saw myself as part of an ancient struggle for freedom. My father did an excellent job of brainwashing me with stories about the oppression and brutality of the English." He bent his head and his voice dropped, "I was convinced that our cause was just. I still am. I simply couldn't live with some of a few of the more fanatical members' tactics."

"Did Will know anything about this?" she interrupted. She thought that John might have revealed his involvement once Will became interested in his Scottish roots. But then Will would have told her, wouldn't he?

"No, I never told him about what I did or the family's connection to the group. I didn't want to risk involving Will in any of this," John said, his voice rising. "I'm still angry that my father brought me into it. Honor and duty, he said. Bullshit! This isn't our struggle. So what if we are Camerons? My father thought of himself as more Scottish than American, but I don't." He shrugged and rolled his neck to ease its tension, then he suddenly smiled at her.

"You'll probably be shocked that my father was over-joyed when Will chose you as his bride. 'Blood will out, laddie,' he'd crowed. 'Your son is marrying a Scottish lass, a descendent of Gillies MacBain, a Jacobite hero.' But I was terrified that your father, or even you, might be part of the Group of One Hundred too, and would draw Will in. None of us know who all of the other members are. I eventually spoke to your Dad—God rest his soul—and he said your grandfather told him about the organization, but for the past 200 years the MacBains have had nothing to do with it. I neglected to tell him that I did."

Alex didn't want to be distracted, but this tangent was worth pursuing. "Is that the reason you and Anne never approved of me? I don't understand."

"Alex dear, there's no defense for the inexcusable way we behaved toward you, but we feared your influence over Will. My father had researched your genealogy the way other families might run a Dun & Bradstreet check into a fiancée's finances. For all I knew you could have been recruited into this group without your parents' knowledge. I'd worked so hard to keep Will ignorant of his ties to Scotland and its battles and then when you two went to the Highlands ... well."

"Shit," she muttered. It always came back to that trip. Somehow their innocent vacation had sealed Will's fate and Alex began to understand that the chill she'd felt from her in-laws for so long wasn't merely disdain for her lack of social status, but sheer terror.

"I was sure I'd see an independent Scotland in my lifetime," John continued, "so there was no need for Will to know all of this or to have any obligation to become part of it. The fight would end with my generation. I was so wrong! My son might still be alive if I'd told him to be careful, especially after what I did."

He walked purposefully to the windows overlooking the Common and began to roll the sleeves of his shirt back down to his wrists in preparation to face the outside world again.

"John." Alex's voice seemed to startle him. "I'm not through with you. A minute ago you said that Will might be alive if you'd told him about something you did. What exactly did you do to make someone want to kill him?"

"Oh, right, I'm sorry. Give me a minute." He returned to his seat the way a man might approach the gallows. It took some time for him to resume his explanation.

"The condensed version is I found out that there were a few members of the organization who were buying material to build bombs. I wasn't supposed to know, but because I was involved with the money, I came across proof that they were procuring weapons. When I refused to release the money until I knew what the arms were needed for, they tried to bullshit me until they finally admitted that they were going to carry out terrorist strikes in London. They fancied themselves the Scottish version of the IRA. I was outraged. Friends of mine were killed in the Twin Towers. I couldn't allow other innocent people to be murdered in the name of some cause. I tried to talk them out of it, to convince them that violence made them no better than their despised Butcher

Cumberland when he ordered the slaughter of innocent Scots after the '45. We're so close to a political agreement with Westminster. Something this stupid would ruin our chances of ever again being taken seriously. But they wouldn't listen, said their plans were already in motion and it was too late. I played along and gave them the money, but I had to stop them."

"And…" Alex prodded. She had to know. John's face was flushed with anger, but he spoke very softly as if he didn't want his confession to be overheard.

"I contacted someone I trust in British intelligence and turned everything I knew over to him, including names. Of course I couldn't reveal how I'd come by this information—that would incriminate me—but with the leads I provided, three men were arrested. One of those men is Mackinnon's son. He must have known who Will was when he gave him that Arbroath document to deliver to me as a reminder of my oath—and as a warning. I was stupid to think they wouldn't find out it was me who'd turned them in and even dumber to think they wouldn't retaliate. I thought they'd come after me, if anyone, and if they killed me … well, so be it. But I should have protected my family, and that includes you. That was why I tried to find you after the funeral. I couldn't live with myself if anything happened to you too."

"Me? What do I have to do with it? I may have the Cameron name, but I don't share your blood."

"These aren't rational people. Rational people don't deliberately kill innocents like Will. You must be very careful, Alex."

"So it was a biblical eye for an eye? Your son for Mackinnon's? My God! Was my husband a bit of collateral damage, the victim of an international conspiracy gone bad? Is that what you're telling me?" Her voice was tinged with hysteria and there was roaring in her ears. When John nodded, she jumped up from the couch, but quickly sat again when her body began to sway.

"Put your head between your knees and you'll be all right," he advised on his way out of the suite. She also heard him whisper, "it should have been me," as he closed the door.

She was furious that he'd been stupid enough to involve himself with fanatics in the first place and then to think he could expose them and escape unscathed. He may have wanted to protect Will, but how could a man as clever as John not even consider that his family might somehow pay for his actions? What an idiot! But something else was dancing around the edges of her anger. When she recognized the intruder as pity, she tried to banish it. She didn't want to feel sorry for him, but it was there. Along with the sorrow of losing his son, she knew that John also carried an extra burden—unimaginable guilt.

She'd been running on adrenalin for most of the afternoon and the tank was now below empty. Mission accomplished, she curled her body into a ball on the sofa, pulled the quilt around her shoulders and drifted away.

When she opened her eyes the sun had gone down, taking with it the room's natural light. She hadn't heard Diego come in, but there he was, sitting on the floor with his head resting against the sofa, close to hers. As she stretched, trying to work the kinks out of her shoulders, she lazily ruffled his hair with her fingertips.

"Hey," she said softly.

He turned toward her, concern reflected in his dark eyes. "Are you all right?" he murmured and cupped her face in his warm hands. He was ashamed of his earlier behavior and needed this physical connection with her to feel human again.

"I'm fine, but I'm wiped out. It's dark in here, I must have fallen asleep." They were both whispering, the room's dimness forming an impregnable bubble around them. "When did you get back? Did you see John?"

"I watched him leave the hotel about an hour ago. It's killing me to know that I've got that man's blood in my veins. When I saw him today I was stunned by the rage I felt and I'm surprised that I was able to control myself as long as I did. What I'm using too many words to say is you were right to throw me out. I was useless to you and I'm so very sorry that you had to do this alone."

"It's okay," she murmured as she studied his face. The earlier anger was gone and she only saw tenderness in his gaze as he continued to stroke her face. If she were a cat, she'd purr. His touch was strong and warm and felt so good and she needed ... so much. She brought one of his hands toward her mouth and slowly kissed its palm. She was pretty sure that he was offering something, but he'd made it clear that it would be her choice.

Her lips were soft and lingered long enough for him to understand that she wouldn't be kissing him like that unless she wanted more. He stood and headed toward the bedroom.

"Where are you going?" she mumbled, confused. Had she read him wrong? There was that honor thing of his. Maybe he couldn't stop thinking of her as Will's wife. Or did he expect her to follow him?

"I remember that a long, hot soak calms you, so I'm going to fill the tub. Is that all right?"

"More than all right," and she smiled as she visualized sinking into the deep tub, the water's heat seeping into her bones.

"It'll take a while to fill," he said as he perched on the edge of the sofa and drew her pliant body to a sitting position. The soft light coming through the partially open bedroom door allowed her to see the question in his eyes. The decision was hers. It always had been. She wrapped her arms around Diego's broad back and drew him closer until their bodies made contact. It felt right somehow.

Diego's kiss was tentative and his hands quivered as he cradled her face. His full lips opened a bit, testing her response. She ran her hands through his thick hair and down his arms, afraid that if she didn't hold him he'd disappear and the moment she'd been simultaneously dreading and hoping for would be gone. I'm not cheating on Will, she rationalized. It's just sex, a physical need like food or air or sleep. He smelled of sweat, peppermint and spicy cologne, and it was surprisingly easy to surrender to her body's desire once she made up her mind.

Will was on Diego's mind as well. The woman he was hoping to make love with was his brother's wife. But Will was dead and he … well, he was very alive and he'd wanted this woman for a very long time. Miraculously, it seemed that she finally wanted him too. He scooped her into his arms and carried her to the softly lit bathroom.

With the uncharacteristic shyness of a virgin, she kept her eyes closed as he slowly unbuttoned her blouse and lowered the zipper of her pants. Some modesty vanished with the sigh that escaped her lips as he slipped a bra strap off one shoulder and replaced it with his mouth.

In her last moment of lucidity, she told herself that she'd better be fully committed to whatever was to come. Could she really do this? The instant she felt Diego's warm breath on her shoulder, she had her answer. No turning back, she realized, as his mouth crumbled the last vestige of her control. She shivered as he ran his tongue up her neck and nipped an earlobe before resuming the soft kisses that were already driving her mad.

The room was steamy and fragrant from the bath water and Alex wasn't sure whether she wanted to let go of Diego long enough to immerse herself in the tub. But he seemed to know what he was doing, and he was doing it so well, that she gladly relinquished control. There goes the bra, she thought dreamily as he deftly unhooked that bit of lavender lace and continued to nuzzle her neck. Oops, no more panties. He ran his hands slowly down her hips and his fingers stroked the small of her back, massaging away the day's tension. She rested her head against his chest and inhaled his musky scent. Christ, she loved how men smelled. They reluctantly loosened their hold on each other and she slowly lowered herself into the tub. As the water's heat enveloped her, she sighed with pleasure and closed her eyes. When she opened them, Diego was seated on the edge of the tub.

"You're so beautiful." His voice was husky and filled with emotion. His obvious appreciation made her less self-conscious about her nakedness and his gaze, smoldering with desire, intensified her arousal.

"You're not so bad yourself," she replied and blushed. She waited, expecting him to strip and join her in the big tub, then watched, mesmerized, as he pulled the black T-shirt over his head and flung it across the room. His chest was a marvel, its well-defined muscles lightly covered with silky black hair. She wanted to feel that chest against her breasts, but he resisted when she tried to pull him into the water.

He wanted to ravish her, to feel and taste every inch of her body, but he held himself back. He'd fantasized about this moment for years—never expecting it to come and conflicted that it had—and he planned to savor it. He also knew she might regain her sanity at any moment and pull away, so he forced his own need into that part of his mind where his iron will resided.

"Patience, Alessandra, patience," he said softly. "I only took off my shirt so it wouldn't get wet while I wash you."

"Wash me?" she said as a slow grin lit her face.

"Mmm hmm," was his smug reply.

A small gold crucifix dangled from his neck and she was transfixed by the tuft of black hair beneath the arm he stretched toward a cake of perfumed soap. She couldn't tear her eyes away from his body as he rubbed the soap against a washcloth until it was covered in foam. Then he took her hand in his and began to run the slippery cloth up her arm.

"Ohhhhh," was all she managed to say as she melted into a puddle of sensation.

The washcloth continued its journey, circled her neck and slid down the other arm. He leaned her body forward to wash her back, then brought the cloth around and rubbed it gently first around one breast, then the other, and finally across her nipples. I'm going to scream, she thought, but lay back and allowed him to continue. He followed the same procedure with her legs, pausing to kiss each toe and run his tongue along her foot's arch. His mouth was on her foot, but the signal was telegraphed to another part of her body.

"You're driving me crazy," she moaned.

"Shall I stop?" he whispered and their eyes met and locked. There was a taunting smile in his gaze.

"Nooooo…" she slowly shook her head from side to side. "Do more. Please do more." He slowly slid the washcloth to the top of her thighs, then let it sink into the water as his skilled fingers began to caress her. Pleasure built and built until her body tensed before spasming against his hand.

It was hard to look at him when she finally opened her eyes. She was a bit mortified to respond to his touch so quickly, but she had a healthy sex drive and it had been a long time. Plus, Diego was obviously a gifted lover.

"I moaned, didn't I," she said.

"Yeah, you did," Diego grinned as he wrapped her in a thick terrycloth robe. Their eyes never left each other as his arms slid underneath the robe and circled her waist. He was surprised to realize that if she weren't willing to give him any more than this, he'd be satisfied. Disappointed, extremely frustrated, but definitely satisfied. He wanted to give this woman pleasure. His own could wait until she was ready for him.

"You said I had to be patient, but I want you … now," she whispered breathlessly in his ear. Goose bumps rose on his skin as she ran her hands over his chest and became the aggressor. She pressed her mouth to his until his lips parted to welcome her invading tongue and met it with his own.

Somehow, they made it to the bed. Diego tossed aside the blanket with one hand and the two of them tumbled, only marginally aware of finally being on a flat surface. Alex didn't know when he'd shed his shorts, or she her robe, but those barriers were gone and nothing hindered the exploration of each other's bodies they'd craved, but refused to yield to, until this moment. Hard muscle met soft skin. Lips touched, tongues tasted. Hands teased, stroked and finally demanded.

Diego's mouth made her world spin out of control for a second time and she heard his groan as he finally buried himself in her with one thrust. She instinctively wrapped her legs around his waist to draw him more deeply into her body and their hips moved rhythmically as the two of them became one.

Before she lost herself again in sensation, she silently said a brief prayer, asking Will to understand. She wasn't being unfaithful, but she needed the touch of another human being at that moment as much as she needed to breathe. The fact that both she and Diego loved Will, and would never do anything to hurt him, made her hope they'd have his blessing.

CHAPTER 19

"F" ucking, lousy Scottish weather," Serge muttered as a wind-driven summer deluge soaked his jeans. The heavy denim whipped around his legs like sails in a gale as he made his way across the bridge over Inverness's River Ness, headed for the gift shop owned by James Mackinnon. He fought to keep his Yankees' baseball cap atop his head with one hand while the other gripped the collar of his jacket to keep the rain from running down his neck. From mid-span he could see the red sandstone of Inverness Castle atop a hill overlooking the river and hoped he'd have a chance to explore it.

He'd enjoyed the scenic drive from London to the Highlands and added Scotland to the growing list of places he would visit as a tourist someday. His travel, as Diego's bodyguard, rarely included the luxury of time to roam aimlessly for his own pleasure. Today, drenched and chilled, his fantasy destination was a no brainer—any island in the South Pacific.

Only a few pedestrians braved the squall with Serge. Scots may be hardy people, but they're not fools. Those who didn't have to venture out wisely remained indoors. He briefly considered returning to his hotel, but Diego would be pissed if he wasted a day, so he'd have to make the best of it. Besides, he had a soldier's discipline and would never abandon a mission simply because of something as trivial as weather. He could even turn it to his advantage. He'd hoped to observe Mackinnon undetected, when the man's shop was crowded with tourists, but on a miserable day like this he'd be able to have the same kind of uninterrupted exchange with him that Will and Alex had during their visit.

When he'd checked into the four-star Palace Hotel that morning, he methodically swept his room for bugs and only relaxed when he'd found two ways to exit that space and the building quickly. He also installed a miniature motion-activated camera that would record anyone entering his room while he was out.

Instead of continuing to use the identity of the barrister he'd been in London, Sergei Ivan Sidovsky transformed himself into Steve Spencer, American businessman. Careless slips were more easily avoided with an alias that started with the same sound as his real name. Passport, credit cards, driver's license, return plane ticket and even half-used American toiletries obtained from a contact in London supported the metamorphosis. Only Diego knew that he was in Inverness and the name he'd adopted. His painstaking caution might seem excessive, but his years as a Mossad field operative taught him that one tiny, seemingly insignificant mistake could cost him his life.

Despite the downpour, habit and training made Serge take a circuitous route to ensure he wasn't followed. As he neared Mackinnon's shop on the High Street he ducked into a doorway to mop the rainwater off his face. When he spotted the sign for a small shopping center across the street, he decided it might be a good place to dry off. He was chilled to the bone; it wouldn't hurt to take five minutes to warm himself with some hot tea.

As he wandered through the quaint mini-mall looking for a teashop, he zeroed in on a store selling replicas of historic weapons. Its window had an intriguing display of brutal armament that Scots had used in their own defense, and Serge marveled at the upper body strength ancient clansmen needed to slash and thrust the five-foot-long, double-edged claymores they'd wielded in combat. He'd used many weapons in his time, but none so massive as this broadsword.

"Do you know where can I get something hot to drink?" he finally asked a passerby, annoyed that he'd been distracted.

"You'll be wanting the wee teashop just past the chemist's. It's nay so easy to find, but if ye go straight on you'll no miss it."

Serge ordered a scone and tea—black, without milk—from the bored waitress. He dumped two heaping spoons of sugar into the hot liquid and uttered a satisfied "ah," as he embraced its warmth. He was the only customer in the inviting little shop and the girl who'd served him was happy to chat.

"I can tell that you're a Yank. Where in America are you from, if you don't mind my asking?"

"No problem. I'm from Florida," he replied, slipping into character like a chameleon. He aimed a friendly grin at her.

"That's grand." She returned his smile and cocked her head. "You wouldn't want to take me home with you when you return there, would you? " She added that she'd finished school, hated her job, hated living with her parents and most of all she hated Scotland's climate. "Does the sun always shine in Florida? Are you at the beach every day? Is it as beautiful as it looks in photos?"

Serge was amused by the girl's bubbly enthusiasm and he liked how her gray-green eyes sparkled. He also couldn't ignore the way the fuzzy pink sweater she wore clung to her remarkable chest. If she were ten years older, he'd be tempted to give her a trip to Florida and she'd give him ... well, forget that. However, he was flattered that she was interested enough to flirt with him.

"Tell me, what brings you to Inverness? Have you come on holiday?" She refilled his cup and added a couple of shortbread cookies to the plate where his scone had been minutes earlier. "Me ma says I'm terribly cheeky, but I'm curious about people, which is the one thing about this job that pleases me. Ach, look at me blethering on and you wanting a quiet cup of tea."

Serge laughed. Americans were friendly and he was now Steve Spencer, American, so he'd be friendly. He tousled his wet, blond hair to help it dry and directed his light blue eyes at her. "I don't mind at all. I had business in London and decided to take a few days to see a bit of your beautiful country."

"And what sort of work do you do? Oh, my. There I go again, asking questions that are none of my business and I've yet to introduce myself. I'm Mairi. Mairi Graham." She laughed and extended a hand to him, which he grasped and held a second longer than would be expected.

"Steve Spencer," he said, never taking his eyes off her. She flushed as she openly checked out Serge's tanned face, so very unlike the pasty complexions of her fellow

Scots. She'd be disillusioned to find out that his Florida tan had been expertly sprayed on his entire body before he'd left London.

"I own a chain of gift shops and I came over to visit one of my suppliers in England. I've never been to Scotland, so I thought I'd check the place out. I like to wander around touristy stores in other places to see if I can steal any of their ideas. Not nice, but that's business," he shrugged and smiled, feigning embarrassment. "Are there any stores like that nearby? I've just arrived and haven't had time to look for any yet," he lied. Serge hadn't intended to fish, but the girl had started the conversation and he wasn't one to miss an opportunity. Besides, he wasn't anxious to venture outside quite yet now that he was warm and his jeans had started to dry.

"Oh, you mean tourist shops, aye?"

Serge nodded.

"Well, then. Lots of tourists visit Inverness as they travel around the Highlands so of course there are stores hereabouts that sell things to them. One of the best is nearby, on the next street in fact. It's called Mackinnon's. That's the one I'd recommend."

Bingo, thought Serge. "Great! I'll start with that one. Shall I tell the owner that you sent me? I know how businesses sometimes help each other out by sending customers their way."

"Oh, no, it's not like that. First off, this isn't my shop. I work here is all. But you can tell Uncle Jamie—er, I mean Mr. Mackinnon—hello from Mairi. He's not my real uncle you see, but he's known me since I was a wee lass. The Mackinnons and my family go way back. We've lived here forever," she said and rolled her eyes dramatically to show how unexciting she found this kind of stability.

"Thanks for your help. I'll be sure to give him your regards." He chose his next words carefully. "What's your uncle like?" He leaned back and crossed his long legs at the ankle to indicate he was in no hurry to leave.

Mairi wasn't a star student in school, but one thing she knew was people. She tilted her head to the side as she studied Serge. He was beautifully built, not fleshy like so many other American tourists. She'd noticed his body the minute he walked into the shop. Unlike clumsy boys her own age, this man would know what to do to please a woman. Serge sensed that she was appraising him like a prize stallion.

"Some would say Uncle Jamie's dour and no very friendly, which is not the best way for a shopkeeper to be, but the one thing that can get him talking is Scottish history. He's brilliant on that subject and once he starts in on it, it's fair impossible to get him to stop. That's how I'd do it if I were you, as a way to warm him up before you start to ask any questions about his business."

Serge watched the girl appreciatively as she moved around the teashop, wiping tables that were already spotless with a damp cloth. Christ, he'd been without a woman for too long if he was lusting after a teenager.

Mairi interrupted his thoughts. "Maybe you could tell him you've got Scottish ancestors. You don't do you?"

"I don't think your uncle would believe that I've got a drop of Scottish blood in my veins, not with this face. My family's lived in Florida for generations. I don't know where we came from before that."

As he held up his part of the conversation, Serge considered how to best use Mairi's familiarity with the Mackinnons. He might have to overlook their age difference after all and take her to bed. Women were always chattier when naked and well-satisfied.

"I'm glad we met, Mairi." Serge never took his eyes off hers as he extended his hand for a friendly handshake. When she put her small hand in his, he wrapped his other one around it and, like before, didn't release her immediately. "This has been very, very nice, but I have to go." He shot a boyish grin at her as he pulled on his still damp jacket and paid the check with a ten-pound note. The chatty girl was speechless when he told her to keep the change.

Serge was sure that Mairi found him attractive. She obviously thirsted for a life beyond the Highlands and he could fulfill any dream she had thanks to his employer's proclivity to spend money freely to get what he wanted. And Diego Navarro wanted Will's murderer. In all the years he'd worked for Diego, Serge had never seen the man so focused on anything—aside from the hungry way he looked at Will Cameron's widow.

"Bye," Serge said and waved to Mairi as he left the shop. She stood in the doorway watching until he was out of sight, and then sighed with regret as she reached in her apron pocket for her mobile phone.

"Is that you, Uncle Jamie? Aye, it's Mairi. Yes, I'm well. I rang to let you know that you're about to have an interesting visitor…"

CHAPTER 20

*A*lex stretched lazily and yawned, then turned onto her stomach and tried to go back to sleep. A moment later her eyes flew open and her mind began to race, replaying in stunning detail what Diego and she had done.

What got into me, she wondered, but one glance at the naked man sprawled on his back beside her was answer enough. Oh, yeah, Diego did. A smile tickled her lips in appreciation of the play on words before her mouth reversed into a scowl. Shit! This was wrong—very, very, very wrong. But like many things that are wrong, it had felt so good. She needed to think about it, dissect it, and figure out what to do, but that didn't mean her eyes couldn't roam up and down his magnificent body in a way they never could if he were awake.

It was no surprise that Diego was a terrific lover, but Alex hadn't expected his passion to come with the tenderness of soft kisses, gentle hands and questioning, soulful eyes. She was prepared to feel like she'd been fucked; what scared her was the realization that he'd made love to her. The last time that happened was … was. A solitary tear slid down her cheek. She hadn't felt this sated, weak-limbed and cherished since the night Will had left their bed to buy ice cream only to wind up dead. And here she was, naked with another man only a few short months later! What's wrong with me, she wondered. On the other hand, maybe what happened was a sign of something being right, incontrovertible proof that she hadn't died along with Will. The devil and angel that she thought had retired their debates inside her Catholic conscience were at it again and she couldn't decide which one to root for. She needed to talk to Francie.

"I wish I could see inside that pretty head of yours. Your face has worn so many expressions in the last five minutes that I can't tell whether you're happy or sad or angry or something else altogether." Diego was leaning on an elbow, his head on his hand as he watched her mental gymnastics.

"Oh, you're up," she said stupidly.

"It seems that way," he responded lazily as both sets of eyes traveled to the obvious evidence that his body was indeed up and awake. Yet instead of sliding into her as he wanted to, he yanked the sheet up to cover their nakedness. "I'm sorry, Alex. I promised myself that I wouldn't seduce you. The last thing I want is to add to your pain. It won't happen again."

"You arrogant, cocky son of a bitch!" she shouted, as guilt shifted to anger. The sheet fell from her shoulders exposing her breasts as she sat up and turned toward him, but she was beyond modesty. "Do you think I had nothing to do with this? It was me who wanted this and it was me who made it happen. Me, Diego, not you! You were merely the instrument I used for my pleasure, not the other way around. This is the twenty-first century and I can choose a lover and then seduce him. So if you feel guilty take your conscience to the confessional. *Ego te absolvo*. Having sex with you may not have been the smartest thing to do, but I brought this on. And, goddamn it, I enjoyed it!"

Could it get any better, Diego thought with delight. She wasn't just capable of more passion than he'd dared to imagine, but he never knew what she would say or do next and that intrigued him. Too many beautiful women were boring, but not this one. He smiled broadly at her. "I'm glad you enjoyed our lovemaking, but no matter what you want to believe, Alessandra, it was I who did the seducing."

His gaze shifted to her breasts and Alex flushed as she recalled the sensations he'd awakened as he'd caressed them and the rest of her body with hands and mouth for what seemed like hours. Given another minute, she knew he would reach for her and, God help her, she'd do nothing to stop him.

"Stop looking at me that way!" She grabbed a pillow to cover herself.

"I can't help it. You're a beautiful woman and I'm a man who appreciates beauty." His eyes never left her face as he spoke, but he didn't touch her. "Know this, *Preciosa*. You have my permission to use me whenever you want as your—what did you call it?—your instrument of pleasure." The smug expression he wore as he tossed her own words at her made her furious and her eyes shot daggers at him.

"What?" he asked in all innocence. "Come on, Alex, don't look at me like that. You called me your instrument of pleasure. I kind of like it." With a self-satisfied grin, Diego got out of bed and nonchalantly walked his naked body to the closet to pull on a pair of well-worn jeans.

Commando, Alex observed, but then underwear would spoil the line of the snug denim.

"Truce?" His hair was tousled, there was a day's growth of dark beard on his face, the fly on his jeans was halfway down and then there was that chest. How could she be mad at someone who looked so damn sexy first thing in the morning and who'd made her feel alive again?

"Truce," she conceded.

His stomach growled loudly. "That sound means that I'm starving! Let me get in the shower first and then I'll order up some breakfast," he said. "While we eat you can fill me in on what John told you after you threw me out yesterday. We didn't talk much last night, did we?"

Alex chose to ignore his last remark. "Breakfast sounds good. Go shower," she replied. Diego was right, of course. They had to put whatever this was behind them and focus on finding Will's killer. She wrapped herself in a sheet and walked toward the suite's living room to call Francie. Diego might strut around naked, but she didn't want his eyes on her body the way hers had been on his.

"Shit," she muttered when the call went to voicemail. She'd have to wait to ask her best friend for advice.

"Your turn," Diego said as he emerged from the bathroom with a towel wrapped around his hips as he dried his hair with another. "What do you want for breakfast?"

"A big pot of coffee and I guess I could force down a couple of dozen scrambled eggs. Bacon, too. Crisp. Some fruit. And lots of toast, buttered rye toast. Would blueberry muffins be too much? I'm ravenous."

As the shower washed away the residue of the night's lovemaking, she tried to convince herself that Will would understand, but she also had no doubt that he'd tear Diego limb from limb. Yet for the first time since the murder, she knew, really knew, that she would be okay. Maybe not fine, maybe not great, but definitely okay. Hot sex must be good medicine, she concluded.

By the time she'd dried her hair and dressed in the same outfit she'd worn to the hotel the day before, room service had delivered their food. Nothing smells quite so good to an empty stomach as coffee and bacon and her mouth began to water.

Diego couldn't wipe the smile off his face as he watched her pile food onto her plate. "Beauty, passion, intelligence and a healthy appetite — what more could a man want?"

"You're not so bad yourself, Navarro," she grudgingly admitted as she raised the coffee cup to her lips. "Now can we eat?"

In between bites, Alex filled Diego in on the Cameron family's connection to Scotland's Group of One Hundred, John's money laundering, his misguided effort to protect Will by keeping him ignorant, John's exposure of the splinter group's terrorist plot, the arrest of Mackinnon's son, and the price Will had paid for his father's treachery.

"I'm surprised to say this, because I'd love to blame him," Alex said, as she pushed her plate away and undid the too-tight top button of her pants, "but by saying nothing John was only trying to protect Will. And don't forget that he did save lives by exposing this group's bomb plot. I really believe that if he had any idea of what those fanatics would do to Will, he would have kept quiet and somehow lived with his part in the deaths of hundreds of innocents. He made a stupid mistake and I feel sorry for him. This has destroyed him."

Diego listened patiently to Alex's narrative as he wandered aimlessly around the suite's living room. She was relieved that he seemed to have lost the previous day's seething anger. Unlike Will's steady temperament,

Diego was volatile and could erupt without warning. Alex was curious to see how he'd react to John's story. When he began to speak, his voice was calm enough, but as he got into it Alex could almost see his blood begin to boil.

"I have no pity for him." Diego stated. Alex watched in fascination as he ran a hand through his hair the same way Will used to when he was trying to figure out something difficult or complicated. "Cameron isn't evil," he continued, "but he's a goddamned idiot who was in over his head. What does a smug, rich American like him know about fanatical nationalism and battles for political autonomy? Does he think this Scottish quest for country would be more gentlemanly than what goes on in the Middle East, Northern Ireland or half of Africa? He became a pawn in a high stakes game that he wasn't even aware he was playing and Will paid for his arrogant naiveté with his life. Did Cameron think that by ratting them out, they'd go away and that would be it?" He stopped pacing and brought his fist down on the table hard enough to rattle the breakfast dishes. "My God! How could the man be such a jackass? Will wasn't a little kid and he had a right to known about all of this. It might not have saved his life, but it would have made him cautious enough to stay out of dark alleys."

"Fucking hell," Alex muttered. Would she ever stop blaming herself for telling Will about the shortcut through that alley? Although she'd accepted it intellectually, emotionally she'd never be able to convince herself that if Will's killers hadn't done it there, they would have carried it out someplace else. She sighed deeply.

"What is it? What's wrong?" asked Diego.

"Nothing. Everything. You know."

"Have you left out something that Cameron said?"

If she told Diego that John thought she could be a target too he'd stay glued to her, a knight in shining armor. She was still bewildered that a group of radical Scots might want to harm her, but the threat had to be taken seriously or she could wind up dead too. It galled her to admit it, but she knew that Diego could protect her. The man carried a gun and was an expert marksman. He'd also told her that he often concealed a knife near his ankle. Serge had trained him well, but after last night, she didn't think 24/7 togetherness was the smartest thing for either of them.

"Well?" he interrupted her thoughts.

"Okay, okay," she said irritably. He'd sensed she was holding back and would push until she told him the truth. She had no choice.

"John said there's a teeny, tiny chance that these people might want to retaliate against his entire family. I think that's ridiculous. After all, I'm only a Cameron by marriage and this seems to be a blood feud. But John said he had to warn me. That was why he kept trying to contact me when I was in Miami. My guess is he wants to cover his ass and ease his conscience about not telling Will about all of this."

"And you think that's nothing?" Diego retorted as his face flushed and his fist came down on the table again. "Come on, Alex, you're smarter than that. Think about what we know. One of the men Cameron betrays is Mackinnon's son. When you visit his shop, Mackinnon cozies up to you and Will as soon as he hears the Cameron name. Then this psychopath has Will carry a warning to his father. Now Will is dead. And you think you're not part of this? Don't underestimate these

people like your idiot father-in-law did." Diego walked to
the window and attempted to regain his composure. He
wasn't mad at Alex, but at that imbecile John Cameron
for bringing all of this on. For what seemed like the
thousandth time, he wondered how he could carry the
blood of such a stupid man.

Diego's words shook her. She'd had similar thoughts,
but they hadn't seemed ominous until they came from
his mouth. "Do you really think someone might want to
kill me?" she asked. In the days following Will's murder,
she would have welcomed a swift death, but not now.
Not anymore.

"Yes, Alex. I do," he replied. His tone was gentle
again, but he was worried. He was terrified of losing her.
"When we left your apartment for the Ritz yesterday,
do you remember seeing a bum staggering down the
sidewalk near your house?"

"No. All I could think about was our meeting with
John, but I know who you mean. I've seen him around
the neighborhood a few times since we came back from
Florida. He seems harmless enough. Why?"

"There's something about him that doesn't compute.
He acts drunk, but he doesn't have the vacant look of
someone with a burned-out brain. I'm sure he was watching us. I'll check him out, but until I do I don't want you
to go near him or any other strangers."

She sighed, resigned to the fact that Diego now saw
himself as her protector. If that's what he had to believe,
it was fine with her. But she'd never responded well to
orders and she wasn't going to start now. "Speaking of
home, I'm headed there now. I'll see you later."

Diego blocked the door. "Wait," he said, and
unselfconsciously lowered his jeans to tuck in one of his

infinite supply of perfectly tailored white shirts. Zipped and belted, he said, "I'll walk with you."

"I'll be fine," she replied curtly. "It's a gorgeous, sunny day. Look out the window; there are lots of people on the street so stop stressing out. And besides, I want to see Francie. I've hardly spent any time with her since I got back."

"Seguro, *Preciosa*. Of course," he said, but her rejection stung. "Don't forget we have a lot more to discuss and some decisions to make."

"Yes, I know, but I need a break from all of this international intrigue. I'm on overload and I have to digest it all. Some girl talk will help me feel less wired." What she really wanted was Francie's help in figuring out how to handle what she'd begun to think of as the "Diego Situation." Their relationship had changed. He'd let her see into his soul and she knew she now had the power to hurt him. "We'll do dinner. All right?" she suggested.

"Sure. I've got stuff to do today too. Number one, I need to bring Serge up to speed on everything John said. He's in Inverness and I want to know if he's visited our friend Mackinnon yet. We'll meet up later, and please, Alex, be careful," he said, and drew her into an embrace that wasn't so easy for either of them to end.

CHAPTER 21

*A*t the precise moment that Diego was wondering about his bodyguard's progress, Serge was running his tongue up Mairi Graham's soft thigh.

"Mmmm," was all she managed to say as his mouth hit its mark. This man really did know much, much more about shagging than the local boys, she thought, and then lost the ability to focus on anything other than what the brilliant American was doing to her.

Serge's training enabled him to separate his mind from his body with ease, so while Mairi moaned as he entered her and his hips moved with hers, he analyzed his visit to Mackinnon's souvenir shop. He'd managed to scatter a few tiny voice-activated listening devices around the shop and also stuck a GPS transmitter under the fender of the old man's rust heap of a car to track his movements. He hadn't been able to shake off Mackinnon long enough to plant a motion-activated camera, but for some reason the guy had stuck to him like a leech, jabbering away, as he'd browsed through the crap that somehow appealed to people when they were far from home. The bug and GPS might not reveal anything useful about Mackinnon's connection to Will Cameron's murder, but it was a start. He'd lost the stomach for some of the more efficient, brutal ways he'd used to obtain information in the past, but remained adept at those techniques should they be needed.

When he'd left the store, the girl was waiting for him. The unexpected often meant trouble, but she'd known where he was going when he'd left the teashop so he became alert, but not overly suspicious. Perhaps she'd decided that their age difference wasn't a deal breaker after all.

"I thought you might be wanting some company," she began shyly. "A businessman so far from home and all … it must be lonely for you." Serge, amused, nodded in reply.

"Good, that's grand then," she said and moved closer to him. "So how did it go with Uncle Jamie? Did he share some of his business secrets with you?" she asked coquettishly as she took his arm.

If the girl wanted to take the lead he'd let her and they strolled toward the town center. When their nostrils picked up the spicy aroma of Indian food wafting out of a small takeaway, she asked if he'd like to pick up some food for them to eat in his hotel room.

Serge wasn't about to turn down a blatant offer like that. He was hungry, she was fun, and she might be useful in lots of ways. Minutes later he excused himself to duck into a pub. "Got to use the men's room," he explained sheepishly. "All that tea you poured for me, you know." Once away from Mairi, he called the hotel to arrange for a second room. With all the incriminating equipment in his suite, he couldn't bring her there.

"Oooh! I've never been inside such a posh hotel. I feel like a princess," she said as she took in the view of Inverness Castle from the turreted room's bay windows.

"I'll just freshen up. Is that the loo through there?" she asked and pointed toward the bathroom.

"Yes, but don't take too long. That food smells great and I'm hungry. How about some champagne to go with it?"

"That would be lovely. But there's no need to seduce me, you know. I'm already here," she said and blew a kiss in Serge's direction as she closed the door. She was impressed by the complimentary array of expensive toiletries in the bathroom, and she held the cake of perfumed soap to her nose before using it to wash. The luxurious surroundings and her erotic fantasies kept Mairi from noticing that there were none of Serge's belongings anywhere.

Serge effortlessly shifted his focus away from his visit to Mackinnon's and back to the delicious Mairi writhing beneath him. Mental progress report finished, he relaxed and let himself enjoy her lush body. He wasn't sure whether she'd be useful to him in other ways, but for now the way they were using each other was perfect.

With his appetite for food and sex satisfied and his body refreshed by a brief post-coital nap, Serge yawned contentedly and stretched his long limbs. The bed creaked as he shifted position and Mairi opened her eyes.

"You really are a man, aren't you?" she said sleepily.

"Ah … yeah. I guess I am. Did you doubt it?" he replied with a grin.

"Oh, no. What I mean is, it's different with a man. I've only been with lads me own age. They're so quick like. And you … well. It's different, is all." Her face flushed and she was suddenly a shy eighteen-year-old again.

"I'm glad you enjoyed it. And in case it wasn't obvious, so did I," he said. Masterful lovemaking was as much a part of his bag of tricks as his skill at interrogation, hand-to-hand combat and shifting his identity. "You've hardly told me anything about yourself, Mairi. Do you have brothers, sisters, lots of friends?"

He shifted to a sitting position and pulled her toward him so that her back was against his chest. Her wild mane of russet curls tickled his nose and her heavy breasts rested on the arms he wrapped around her. His hands were tempted to move to her nipples, but he willed them to remain where they were. Duty before pleasure.

"Honestly, there's not much to tell," she said. "I'm the second of five children. We're Catholics and Mam and Da obviously don't believe in birth control. I think they're daft. For years there was always a screaming bairn in smelly nappies." She shook her head, remembering. "I'm not even sure that I want children of me own. Let's see, there's Michael who's named for my father, then me, Matthew, Katie and wee Andrew. As for mates ... well, my best one is gone."

"What do you mean, 'gone'?"

"Just gone, is all. Jamie Mackinnon ... that's Uncle Jamie's grandson ... well ... he and I were born the same year and we've always been like brother and sister. About two months ago, or maybe it's three by now, he said he was off to America, but wouldn't say why and believe me, I tried every way I knew to make him tell. I always know if he's lying, so maybe he thought it better to say nothing than to try to fool me. Anyway, I haven't heard from him since, except for a scribble on a card to say he's back in Scotland and off to work at some sheep farm way up north. It's not like him to not come 'round to say hello. And why would a lad give up a good job in a garage here in Inverness to care for dirty sheep in a wee town like

John O'Groats where he knows no one, tell me that?"

Now this was intriguing, Serge thought, but he only continued to show polite interest. "I'm sure your friend had his reasons for taking off. Could he be in some kind of trouble?"

"Jamie in trouble? Ha! That's daft. Uncle Jamie says the lad just took off one day. It could be that he's upset about his own Da being sent to prison. But when it happened, he seemed all right with it," she said, her brow furrowed. "I'd help him if I knew what to do."

Mairi had unknowingly provided a critical piece of the puzzle and Serge's mind began to analyze how it all fit together. First, Mairi's friend's father, the son of James Mackinnon, the shopkeeper, is arrested. Then this Jamie, the grandson—shit, did they all have to be James or Jamie?—goes to America for some unknown reason, returns and unexpectedly moves to the far north.

"I imagine if my father were in jail I'd be pretty upset and I might start to act weird too," Serge said as moved his hand to her milky thigh. "What did the police want with your friend's father? Did he rob a bank or shoot someone?" he asked with an air of innocent curiosity.

"I didn't see it myself, but people say that soldiers dressed all in black, commandos maybe, came to their house one night and took Jamie's Da away. In his night-clothes, he was! Can you imagine? There was a lot of talk, but even Jamie was flummoxed. A few folk guessed that his Da must be connected to the I.R.A. or some such thing, but the Mackinnons are definitely not Irish so that can't be it. Anyway, there I go blathering on about people you don't even know. Tell me something more about you."

"What do you want to know?"

"Well, for starters, are you married?"

He laughed. "No, I'm not married."

"Hmmm, a handsome man like you should be and I'm surprised. Doesn't really matter anyway. You'll go back to your sunny Florida in a few days and you won't even remember me," she pouted.

"Mairi," he murmured softly, "you underestimate yourself. You're not a woman that a man soon forgets." It was almost too easy to ingratiate himself with someone so trusting and unsophisticated. "Maybe you can visit me. I could send you a ticket."

"What!" She pressed her body against his and covered his face in excited kisses. "You would do that? You'd pay my way to America?"

"Why not? It's no big deal. I can easily afford it and I've got a big house near the beach, so you can enjoy the sun for a few days while I work. Think of it as the Mairi Graham traveling scholarship."

She wrapped her arms around him as if he were a genie that would vanish back into his lamp while she imagined herself in a tiny bikini, her skin baked to a golden tan. "Bloody 'ell! My parents would never allow it. It's one thing to do what I please here in Inverness, but this…"

"They won't guess that there's anything between us. After all, you said I'm about the same age as your father and they'd never think you'd get involved with someone so old. I'm sure we can come up with a good story." He pretended to be deep in thought. "I could tell them I've offered you a job in one of my stores. Do you think that would work?"

"I don't know," she said, her brow furrowed. "I've a better idea. Lots of local girls go to Europe or America to work as nannies and my parents know I've helped raise my younger brothers and sister. I could say you and I struck up a conversation in the teashop and you told me you have young children — and a wife of course — and need someone to help care for them. That might do it."

"Sounds great," agreed Serge. "They'll want to meet me, of course." The Grahams and the Mackinnons were close, she'd said, so her father might know more about the arrest of Mackinnon's son and the grandson's disappearance. He felt a brief twinge of guilt that there would be no trip to Florida for the gullible Mairi, but that was how the game was played. His betrayal would toughen her up and even save her from future heartache.

"I know they'll say yes. I just know it!" She bounced up and down on the bed, unable to stay still. "But for now, I'm expected home. I'll talk to my parents tonight or tomorrow at breakfast," she said enthusiastically as she kissed her way down his body and used her talented mouth to thank him in her own, very satisfying, way. Before Serge allowed himself to surrender to pleasure, he fleetingly thought about all he'd have to report to Diego … but that could wait until later, much later.

CHAPTER 22

*A*lex left the Ritz Carlton and strolled back to her apartment in a daze as she tried to process all that had happened in the past twenty-four hours. Her father-in-law's mind-blowing confession about his role in Will's death had been horrifying enough to send her to bed for a week, but when combined with the night she'd just spent with Diego it was like she'd been hit by a knockout punch. Despite it all, she felt the kind of exhilaration that followed a couple of glasses of champagne.

Back in her apartment, she quickly exchanged the now-wrinkled designer outfit for comfortable jeans and a snug Rolling Stones' T-shirt, hit "play" on her blinking answering machine and stretched out on the couch. She was bubbling with feel-good endorphins and wondered what Francie would say about it all.

My friend's a mind reader, she thought, as she listened to three voicemails from an increasingly impatient Francie demanding to know every detail about the meeting with Will's father. There was also one from John Cameron apologizing for his behavior. But it was the last message, from Francie's husband David, which captured her attention.

"Hi Alex, it's David. Call me at the office." He was her lawyer and she hoped whatever he had to say wouldn't spoil her mood. She decided to get his call out of the way to reassure herself that he only wanted to check in with her.

"Hey David. What's up?" she asked cheerfully.

He skipped their usual banter and got right to the point. "A few months before he died, Will left a letter with me that I was to give to you if you survived him."

"What?" Alex bolted to her feet. Will's estate had been settled quickly and he'd left everything to her — apartment, investments and a very hefty trust fund. Could he have changed something, added something without telling her? She gripped the phone with hands that were suddenly ice cold and forced herself to breathe. "Why did you wait until now? You can't drop something like this on me, David."

"All I can tell you is that he left the timing up to me. It's a letter size envelope, but I have no more idea than you do about what's inside. When Will brought it to me a few months before he was killed, he told me that if he died before you, I was to give you time to recover and then hand this over to you."

"Cut out the lawyer bullshit, David! This is me! Talk to me like a friend, not my lawyer."

"Sometimes I think being a friend's lawyer isn't the smartest thing in the world," he said and paused for a long moment. "Look Alex, the last thing I want to do is to upset you, but I'm bound by law to carry out Will's instructions on this matter. When he brought this to me he seemed pretty upset and was adamant that I not even ask him to explain. His also left a letter for Diego and since he's in town I figured I'd give them to each of you now. If you can come in this afternoon, we can get this settled."

Alex sighed, resigned to whatever was to come. If

she'd been able to handle everything that had happened so far, she'd have to dig down and find the courage to get through this too.

"Fine. I can be at your office at one. You coordinate it with Diego.'"

"Okay. And Alex, try not to worry."

"Yeah, sure, easy for you to say," she muttered sullenly. That blew her plan for a laid-back gossipfest with Francie.

Five minutes after Alex arrived at David's office Diego strode in, shook hands with the lawyer and sat next to her. "Do you know what this is about?" he whispered.

"No. I haven't a clue, only that Will left letters for each of us," she said. His presence calmed her and she welcomed the hand that he wrapped around hers. She wondered if he felt as guilty as she did to have Will reach out to them hours after they'd had sex. It was almost as if he knew.

"You look like two kids who have been sent to the principal's office," said David. Their tension was contagious and he was as curious as they were to finally find out what message Will had left.

"Along with the two envelopes, Will left specific instructions for me. The contents of these envelopes are your property. The decision to reveal what they contain to each other, or to me, is entirely yours. Will asked me to be present in case either of you had any legal questions." He extended the first envelope to Alex. Her hand trembled as she reached for it. He gave the other to Diego.

The sight of Will's familiar scrawl made her eyes fill, but if she cried now she wouldn't be able to see and she had to know what he'd wanted to tell her.

My darling Alex,

Since you're reading this, I guess I'm dead and obviously you're not. I hope that at this moment you're a very old lady with age spots on your wrinkled hands, hands that held mine as I passed from this world into the next. But my guess is that's not the case. It makes no sense and I pray I'm wrong, but I have this feeling that I might die young. If it's an accident or happens some other way and without warning, I hope it comforts you to know that I wasn't alone — you were with me, as always, because you are my heart.

Alex could hear Will's voice and felt him in the room. She was stunned that he'd had a premonition about his own death, but she wasn't surprised that he'd never mentioned this feeling to her. If he had, she would have hovered over him in a way he'd have never tolerated, so he'd kept quiet.

Diego's envelope remained sealed. He and David watched Alex close her eyes and press the letter to her breast, but they remained silent observers. She took a few steadying breaths, sipped some water and continued to read Will's words.

One reason that I'm writing this letter is to tell you I love you one last time in case I wasn't able to say it before I died. If I made you even half as happy as you made me, I know I've done well. You brought more joy to my life than I ever imagined. We always said we would love each other forever and beyond. Those aren't just words, darling Alex. My body may not be able to love you any longer, but my soul is yours for eternity.

And there's something else — something I expect we'll have already gotten past, but as I write this it's still new. I should have told you the truth about why I banished Diego from my life and yours. I'll never understand why I couldn't confide in you. I swear it was the first lie of our marriage and the last, but you have a right to know what happened.

Diego found out that his parents and mine slept with each other before either of us was born. My birthday and Diego's are just weeks apart, so I couldn't get it out of my head that either man could have impregnated either, or both, women. I insisted that Diego and I should have our DNA tested so that we'd know for sure which man had fathered each of us. I don't know why this became so important to me, but it was. The test confirmed that John Cameron is my father. The shocker is that he's Diego's biological father too although Diego is, and always will be, a Navarro regardless of his DNA. He never wanted to know and I should never have told him the results of a test I had done without his knowledge. To say I violated his trust is a huge understatement. He had every right to be furious and never speak to me again. I behaved like a jerk and lost the friendship of a man I'd always thought of as my brother. And then I lied to you. I beg you to forgive me.

So, my beloved, it's time to end this chapter and move on to the next. I know you'll grieve, but you have to let me go. Please don't spend the rest of your life unhappy and alone. We both know that you and I shared something rare. I can't imagine either of us ever finding that kind of love with anyone else, but love comes in many forms. I beg you to find it again because your happiness is, and always has been, my own.

Yours forever and beyond,
Will

Alex's tears flowed with the intensity of a tropical storm. Will was gone, but what they'd had together wasn't. She would always have that. This letter was Will's final gift to her.

"I'm okay … I am … really." She said the words as much to herself as to the two men who'd witnessed her distress. She finally turned her tear-streaked face to Diego." You must be dying to know what's inside your envelope. It's not fair to make you wait any longer."

"I can wait," he said as he dabbed at her tears with a handkerchief.

"Me too," added David. "There's no rush."

"I never thought I'd hear from him again. And what he said was so beautiful … but there's something I need to tell Diego. Privately. Can you excuse us for a minute David?"

"Of course. I'll be down the hall if you need me," he said and left them alone.

Alex didn't say anything until Diego's eyes met hers. "Thank you for telling me the real reason for the fight that you and Will had or this letter would have come as a shock. He wanted to apologize for not being honest with me about the paternity tests. There's probably an apology in your envelope too."

Despite her attempt to reassure him, Diego wasn't sure he wanted to know what Will had to say to him. "Will was my best friend and my brother, but right now I'm not ashamed to admit that I'm scared. The last news he delivered almost killed me," he said, and laughed nervously. There was a sheen of sweat on his forehead. Finally, jaw set in determination, he ripped the envelope open and scanned its contents. Alex watched his expression go from soft to hard until he finally crushed the letter in his fist.

Alex waited for Diego to tell her what the letter said. "Well?" she finally probed, running out of patience. She had no idea what Will could have written to make Diego's body suddenly coil with barely contained fury.

"You guessed right. He wanted to tell me he was sorry for what he'd done, that he knew it was wrong, but did it anyway. He hoped that he and I would have gotten past this while he still lived. He said I'm the brother he always wished for, but he knew I didn't feel the same about him because that meant we shared John Cameron as a father. The dickhead also included a copy of the DNA test as proof of what he'd told me." He spoke with the same deadly calm he'd used when they'd questioned John about Will's murder.

"And?" She knew the man beside her well enough to recognize that there had to be more.

"He asked me to take care of you."

"Oh?" The smugness she would have expected to see on his face was absent and hers flushed with the memory of how well Diego had taken care of her needs the night before. She wondered if Will would have made that same request if he'd known what he'd green-lighted.

"Anything else? Nothing you've told me so far would have made you look like you're ready to kill someone, or at least I don't think so."

Until that moment, his gaze had been fixed on the letter that he still held in his fist. He laid it on his thigh and smoothed the crumpled paper with one hand as he reached for Alex's with the other. "I don't know how to tell you this." He paused to glance at the letter again. She didn't say anything, but raised her eyebrows expectantly to encourage him to continue once he looked up. "Will decided to leave these letters with David because he was sure someone was stalking him. He said that if he died suddenly, he wanted someone to know it wasn't an accident and that he'd trust me to get the bastards if the police didn't."

"So he knew," she said almost to herself. "He had a premonition. Why didn't he go to the police? Or tell me? Why would he keep this to himself? Why, Diego, why?"

"I can't answer that. No one can. We can only guess that he didn't think the threat was real and perhaps he didn't want you to worry. Yet it troubled him enough to write these letters, so…" He lowered his head, ran his hands through his hair and sighed. "Stupid bastard."

Diego irritably glanced at the caller ID when his phone vibrated. "It's my father. I have to take this," then he lapsed into rapid Spanish. The *Castellano* dialect he spoke made it difficult for her to follow the brief conversation, but it was obvious that Diego wasn't happy when the call ended.

"This couldn't happen at a worse time. We should be on our way to Scotland, but I have to go to Argentina for a few days. There was some screw up with the Abu Dhabi contracts and my father ordered me home to fix it. He's the only person who can still tell me what to do," he said with a shrug and extended a hand toward her. "Come with me?"

She was reeling from the discovery of yet another secret Will had kept from her. She glanced at Diego, but couldn't answer him. Everything was suddenly too complicated. She needed to be alone to figure things out.

"Well? Are you coming or not?" he asked impatiently, his hand still reaching for hers.

"To Argentina? No, I can't. I'm sorry Diego."

His body stiffened as if she'd punched him in the gut.

"Diego, wait! Let me explain!" she pleaded, but he was already halfway out the door. He almost knocked David down as he sprinted toward the elevator.

"Can you tell me what's going on?" David asked as he stepped into his office.

"Not now. I've got to talk to Diego … to explain. I'll fill Francie in and she can tell you. I've got to go," she yelled over her shoulder as she ran out of his office, but by the time she reached the street Diego had already vanished.

CHAPTER 23

*S*hit! Goddamn it to hell," Alex muttered and stamped her foot in frustration as she stood outside David's office building. Diego hadn't just disappeared without giving her a chance to explain why she couldn't fly off to Argentina with him, but he wasn't answering his cell phone. That he was bouncing her calls to voicemail added fury to her frustration.

She flagged down a cab and gave the driver Francie's address. When her friend opened the door to her hi-rise apartment, Alex was sufficiently calm to gape in awe at the wisps of silk, satin and lace that covered every surface of the living room. "You have enough underwear here to outfit a high class call girl ring," she said with a grin and felt her mood lift.

"True, but I don't think my husband the lawyer would be thrilled if I ran a brothel. Take a look."

Francesca Sandburg's love for fashion began when she'd outfitted her first doll. As an adult, she'd turned her passion into a lucrative business and clothed a loyal following of entrepreneurs, minor celebrities and creative types who were too busy to shop for themselves, but valued and could afford her quirky, yet impeccable, taste.

Alex zeroed in on a dove gray silk camisole accented by cream-color lace and silk ribbons that tied into bows at each side of the matching bikini panties. One tug on that ribbon and … she wasn't surprised when the fingers untying the ribbon in her little fantasy belonged to Diego. The daydream came to an abrupt halt when she spotted the price on the ensemble's Prada tag. "Oh my God Francie! Fifteen hundred dollars for underwear? Who wears this stuff?"

"People with scads of money, of course. The pieces you're salivating over are trimmed with antique lace and sewn by hand," she said with a shrug. "One of my best clients is getting married next month and asked me to find fabulous lingerie for her honeymoon. She's coming over this evening to choose what she likes and price is the last thing she's concerned with."

"Must be nice. I'm so happy that business is good, but I need some advice. The last twenty-four hours have been totally insane and I feel like I'm being tossed around inside a tornado that doesn't want to drop me back to earth."

"Wizard of Oz time, huh? You don't usually go off the deep end about underwear, so I figured when you were ready to talk, you'd let me know. I'll make us some tea," Francie said and took Alex's hand as they walked to the kitchen. "My client's a workaholic and won't get here until at least seven, so I've got three hours free. Are you meeting Diego for dinner or do you want to eat here with me and David?"

"Diego's on his way to Argentina. That's part of what I have to talk to you about." Francie raised her eyebrows, but didn't say anything as she gathered tea things and two bags of cookies—Oreos for her, chocolate chip for Alex.

"Okay. Spill it," Francie said as they settled themselves at the small kitchen table.

"I'm not sure where to begin."

"I'm dying to know why Diego went back to Argentina so suddenly, but start with the meeting the two of you had with Will's father yesterday and we'll take it from there." Francie blew on the hot tea and waited patiently for her friend to stop nervously picking the chocolate chips out of her cookie.

Alex gazed at her friend. She wanted to blurt out that she'd slept with Diego, but that tale would have to wait until she gave Francie a quick summary of John's connection to Will's murder.

"First of all, John's a mess, mentally and physically, which isn't really surprising. It drove us crazy that he just couldn't seem to focus. At one point he and Diego went at it and I was afraid that John would be beaten to death when he was only halfway through his story, so I made Diego leave."

"You what? You made Diego leave? He must have loved that," said Francie as she bit into another Oreo. "So what did Will's father say? I've been dying to know why he was so desperate to find out where you'd gone after the funeral."

"Oh yeah. I forgot that he'd called you. Get this," Alex leaned in and lowered her voice. It still seemed unreal to her, more like a novel than something that actually happened. "John Cameron told us he's part of a secret Scottish independence group. He's their money launderer, for chrissakes, or at least he was."

"What!" Francie exclaimed and almost choked on her tea.

"Can you believe it? But wait, there's more. Evidently, this job is a Cameron family tradition, but one he never bothered to tell Will about. Anyway, he found out that this group was getting ready to plant bombs in London and he turned them in to the cops. These nut jobs found out what he did and decided his disloyalty amounted to high treason. But instead of the death penalty for John, they decided to execute Will. They thought that would be worse. They were right," she whispered, unable to go on.

Alex's usually garrulous friend was speechless. Francie opened her mouth a few times, but no words came out. She frowned as she methodically dipped Oreos into her hot tea and quickly jammed them into her mouth before the soggy mess plopped into the teacup.

"Will was an innocent in all this," Alex continued. "His only crime was being John Cameron's son. I hate the people who did this so much that it scares me. I want to tear their hearts out or boil them in oil or something." She shook her head in an attempt to purge her mind of the various revenge scenarios brewing there.

"They've got to be lunatics," Francie said as she dipped another cookie into her tea and frowned as she nibbled at it. "Did you tell David? Is that why you were at his office today? What about the police? Shouldn't you talk to them?"

"One thing at a time. No, I haven't told David, but you can do it. Diego and I were at his office for something entirely different. Will had left letters with him for both of us. I'll tell you about those later. And no, I'm not going to tell the police about this. John would go to jail and he's already serving a life sentence of indescribable guilt. Besides, the murderer has to be back in Scotland by now. The local police will never have enough evidence to catch him or prove anything." Alex stood and began to pace.

"I still don't understand why John wasn't the one they killed if it's him they were mad at," said Francie. She switched from inhaling cookies to chewing her fingernails.

Alex sighed. "I'm pretty sure John would have

preferred that too. Now he's afraid that they might want to take out his entire family one by one before they get to him. He sent Anne to her sister's in San Francisco. I get the idea she was happy to go and it sounds like she's never going to come back. She despises him, which almost makes the bitch likeable."

"You said they might kill all of John's family. Does that include you?"

"All I know is he wanted to warn me and now Diego's appointed himself my personal bodyguard, although he won't be much help if he's in Buenos Aires. What really worries me is that these animals think they got rid of the last Cameron. They didn't."

Francie pondered the meaning of that statement for a moment. "They didn't? What are you saying? Alex! Are you... ?" she trailed off and glanced at her friend's belly.

"Of course not. You'd be the first to know if I were pregnant."

"Then what... ?"

"Will has a brother. Maybe you should get out the ice cream before you hear this."

"Screw the ice cream. How could he have a brother? You would have known about it. Was he a twin and the Camerons gave one up for adoption?" She paused in her theorizing just long enough to catch her breath. "When did you find out about this brother of Will's? Where is he? Come to think of it, who is he? Why didn't you tell me?"

"Chill, Francie, calm down, but brace yourself. Will's half brother is none other than — are you ready? — Diego Navarro!"

"What? But how... ?" Francie sputtered, more stunned by this than the revelation about John's involvement with terrorists.

Alex still had trouble believing it herself. "The short version is that Ricardo Navarro screwed Anne Cameron." Alex began to laugh as Francie pretended to gag.

"Ewwww, that's disgusting." Francie grimaced.

"Yeah. I prefer not to think about that part of it myself. And, of course, John Cameron slept with Giovanna Navarro, Diego's mother."

"Wait. I'm confused. So Ricardo could be Will's father? Holy crap."

"I wish, but no. Their father is John Cameron. It was all confirmed by a DNA test that my lying sneak of a husband didn't tell me about. I'm so mad at him Francie. I had to hear it from Diego while we were in Florida."

"But how did this finally come out thirty-four years after Will and Diego were born? That's a long time for something, especially this kind of something, to stay a secret."

"It's a long story so here's the condensed version. A few years ago Diego found some letters that made it clear that the Navarros and the Camerons screwed around with each other when they were young. He told Will about it and my husband became obsessed with his paternity and had a DNA test done last year. It proved that John was his father. Diego refused to take the test, but Will went ahead and did his too. When he told Diego that the results showed that John was his father too, they had a huge fight. That's why they stopped having anything to do with each other about a year ago."

"And Will never told you about any of this?"

"No!" Alex's eyes filled with tears of hurt and frustration. Why couldn't Will trust her? Why hadn't he confided in her? She'd never know. The letter he'd left contained an apology, but no explanation to help her understand. "And he kept something else from me too, Fran. In his letter to

Diego he said he thought he was being stalked and that if anything happened to him it wasn't an accident. He asked Diego to find the people who did it if the police don't."

"Wow! I can't believe he didn't talk to you about all of this. Did Will seem different those last months?"

"Not that I noticed, but what does that say about our marriage? I guess it wasn't as perfect as I thought." She brought the cup of tea to her lips and hesitated. "That's not all."

"You mean there's more? No wonder you're a wreck. Spill it."

"I slept with Diego," she whispered and lowered her eyes.

"I knew it!" Francie crowed, a self-satisfied grin lighting her face as she started to dance around the compact kitchen. "The chemistry between the two of you is so damn obvious, especially to someone who knows you the way I do. Did it happen in Miami?"

"No," Alex whispered. "Last night."

"And…"

"And stop acting like this is a good thing. I feel terrible."

"Because…"

"Because I'm ashamed of myself. I cheated on Will! But I needed … I needed…"

"Of course you did," Francie said as she wrapped her arms around Alex. "Don't be so hard on yourself. You've only proved that you're human, that's all. It's okay."

"Is it? Is it really okay for a woman to sleep with her husband's best friend? And now it's even worse because that friend is — what? — my brother-in-law! Oh, God, what am I going to do?"

"Have a cookie," said Francie as she shoved the bag toward Alex. "I'll even share my Oreos."

"A cookie can't solve everything."

"Maybe it can't, but the sugar rush to your brain will help you to think," Francie rationalized. "So was the sex good? Details, I want details."

"Of course it was good. You have Oreo crumbs on your face," Alex said with the first glimmer of a smile.

Francie brushed a hand across her mouth without taking her eyes off Alex. "I've always wondered ... Diego's a gorgeous man and we know he's had a lot of experience, so I wondered ... well, sometimes a man who looks like him thinks that's enough, you know, and that he doesn't have to try really hard ... to please a woman, I mean."

"Stop it! You're not getting a play by play from me. But, so you won't lose any sleep, I'll assure you that Diego's looks pale in comparison to his talent as a lover." Alex's lips curled into the smile of someone who has a delicious secret.

"Alexandra," said Francie accusingly. "If you're going to smile like that, you're going to have to tell me everything."

"No, I'm not. What I need is your advice on where I go from here. Diego's been incredibly generous and kind and patient with me. You know better than anyone how messed up I was when I went to Florida. I began to heal there. Plus, he's determined to find Will's killer and I'm sure he can do it." Her mood darkened and she began to pace. "Remember I told you that I felt like I was caught in a tornado? Now it's more like a centrifuge and I can't find the off switch. Too much is happening too fast and I can't process it. What am I supposed to do?"

"Hmmm, I'm not sure," Francie said as she tapped her scarlet fingernails on the table. Then she leaned forward. "The only way to do this is to use logic. So which should we tackle first? John Cameron, spy; Diego Navarro, Will's brother; or—and this is my favorite—Diego Navarro ... lover!" A huge grin spread across her face.

"You're right. I need to think rationally. Diego told me that he'd called Serge—you know, the former Mossad spy, now bodyguard and ace investigator—this morning to fill him in about John, but he didn't have time to tell me if Serge had found out anything since he's been in Scotland." Alex massaged her brow in an attempt to soothe the dull throbbing that heralded the start of a major headache. She helped herself to a couple of aspirin from Francie's kitchen cabinet.

"Did you and Diego talk about how this changes things between you, you know … after?"

"Not really. We both fell asleep and then we had an argument at breakfast."

"About what?"

"It wasn't a big deal, just which one of us would take credit for being the seducer. Maybe it's stupid, but I didn't want him to think that I had no part in what happened. I wanted it as much as he did and you know Diego—he's got this macho thing going on…"

"And it can be annoying and appealing at the same time, right?"

"Exactly! He can be exasperating and even a little scary, but that same masculinity and confidence are a big part of the attraction. And when you combine that with tenderness and a good heart, well … it's hard to resist. And I trust him." This was the first time Alex analyzed what it was about Diego that drew her to him. "He doesn't have that little boy charm and playfulness that I loved so much about Will, but they definitely share that manly man thing." She suddenly had an "aha!" moment. "That's it! Diego is Will's brother. Whatever chemical thing they share in their genes…"

"Ah, so the similarity is in their jeans, is it?"

Francie taunted and began to laugh hysterically.

"Stop it! You've always had such a dirty mind," she scolded. "As I was saying—whatever chemical thing they share in their g-e-n-e-s must be why I'm attracted to Diego. He reminds me of Will. Will loved him and I loved Will, so Diego sort of has Will's approval. That makes so much sense." Alex leaned back to ponder this twisted logic and, as she did so, a smile slowly spread across her face. Maybe in some strange way this meant she hadn't cheated on Will at all, since it was the part of him that existed in Diego that appealed to her.

"You realize that Diego isn't Will, don't you Alex?" Francie asked as she poured more tea.

"Of course. I haven't gone all mental, but maybe I feel a little less guilty."

"Are you going to sleep with him again?"

Alex frowned then took a deep breath and slowly blew it out as she considered the question. The fear that she'd do precisely that was a big part of why she hadn't gone to Buenos Aires with him. Sex with Diego was great. She'd always had a healthy libido and wasn't going to act like some virgin for the rest of her life. But sex muddied things up and it was way too soon to deal with whatever complications might result from a physical relationship. She couldn't tolerate any more emotional turmoil.

"No, it won't happen again. Now that we've both gotten that curiosity or whatever it was out of the way, we can go back to being great friends."

"You're deluding yourself, dear girl. It's obvious that you're in lust with him and he looks at you like you're a big, juicy steak," Francie said smugly, as she patted Alex's hand. "But you'll have to decide what to do about it on your own. If it were me…"

Chapter 24

*A*n hour after after he'd stormed out of David's office, Diego cleared security at Logan and sprinted to catch the shuttle from Boston to JFK. As he restlessly waited to board, he used his iPhone to snag the last first class seat on an overnight flight from New York to Buenos Aires. He would have been happier if, instead, he were on his way to Scotland with Alex.

His determination to find the killer had escalated the instant he read the letter Will had left for him. "Am I paranoid?" Will had written. "Maybe, but I can't shake the feeling that someone's been following me for at least a month and that my life might end violently. I pray that I'm overreacting. But if anything happens to me, I trust you, my brother, to find the bastard who did it and take care of him." Diego's gut twisted in anger as he read the words again and he knew that payback would be the only way to deal with it. The man who had bled to death, alone, in a dark alley hadn't been some casual acquaintance. That man was his brother, and the blood they shared boiled with outrage.

It was ironic to be happy that Will had gone ahead with the damn DNA test. He wanted the sons of bitches to come after him next. Let them, he thought grimly. When he found whoever had killed his brother, that person would wish that he'd never been born.

● ● ●

Diego envied those passengers in the plane's darkened, first class cabin who were dozing in seats that reclined into something resembling a bed. A sleeping pill would help, but he never took drugs that would affect his mind or reflexes. He irritably readjusted his pillow and curled onto his side, but he couldn't quiet his chaotic thoughts. He slowed his breathing and shifted his focus to Alex and the surprising night they'd spent together. Instead of relieving an itch, the erotic heat between them had left him hungry for more. She'd never convince him that she'd used him for sex and it meant nothing to her. He'd slept with enough women to know—as he'd told her—the difference between making love and fucking. What had occurred between them was lovemaking and he was certain that they'd do it again. Ah, Alessandra, this will be interesting, he thought as he hugged the pillow tighter. Could it finally be happening to him? Could what he felt for this woman be the first stirrings of love? He knew he should be scared shitless, but instead of fear, the thought soothed him and he drifted into a dreamless sleep until he was gently nudged awake by a flight attendant.

"*Buenos días, Señor* Navarro. I'm sorry to wake you, but we'll be arriving in Buenos Aires in an hour. Would you like coffee? Some breakfast?"

He stretched his long limbs, yawned and rubbed the sleep from his eyes.

"Coffee would be fine, thanks, but not for about five minutes. I'd like to wash first," he said groggily, his manners evident even when he wasn't quite awake.

"Of course," she purred. He slitted one eye to watch her hips sway as she walked toward the forward galley on impossibly high heels.

His eyes felt like they had sand in them, his mouth was pasty and his neck was sore. He took the pouch of toiletries provided by the airline and headed for the lavatory to try to make himself human again. He must have succeeded because another flight attendant—this one a shapely blonde—perched one hip on the arm of his seat as he sipped his second cup of coffee.

"Is there anything I can do for you?" she said in a voice filled with the promise of sensual pleasure. Normally Diego would have welcomed the implied invitation and perhaps arranged to spend time with the extremely attractive woman during her layover in Buenos Aires, but he had no interest in her. When the other, equally beautiful stewardess had awakened him earlier, he'd been dreaming about Alex and woke with a throbbing erection. For the first time in his life, the thought of being faithful to one woman held more appeal than terror.

Alex's heart skipped a beat when the phone rang as she got ready for bed. Late night calls had always scared her, even when Will was alive. None of her friends would call near midnight. And there had been a lot of wrong numbers lately with only "private number" displayed on her caller ID. Maybe she'd get rid of this land line and only use her cell.

"Hello?" she said tentatively, convinced that it had to be a wrong number.

"Alessandra…"

Diego's voice was low and husky and she could almost feel his breath on her ear. She sighed and her tension eased.

"I didn't wake you, did I?"

"No. I was about to get into bed, but I'm still up. Where are you?"

"In Buenos Aires, at my parents' house."

"Are you okay? You ran out of David's office so fast and I wanted to explain…"

"Don't worry about it. I was wrong to expect you to drop everything when I could see how Will's letter had affected you. It was selfish, but all I could think about was what I wanted." And I wanted you, he thought.

"So, did you straighten everything out there? You said your father was worried about a contract."

"Yeah. It was a minor problem that I could have taken care of from Boston, but my parents used it to manipulate me into visiting them. I should be angry, but it's good to be with them. My mother always complains that she never sees me. By the way, she sends love to her 'dear Alessandra'. She was disappointed that you didn't come too."

"Another time; I promise. Give her a kiss from me. Your Dad, too."

"What, none for me?"

"That's beneath you, but if it will make you feel better, I'll blow a kiss your way too."

"Mmm, got it." He shifted to a more comfortable position as he remembered how Alex's lips had felt against his. "What are you wearing?"

"Diego!"

"Shall I assume we won't be having phone sex? And you'll probably say no to letting me see you naked on Skype too."

"You're depraved! No phone sex, no naked pictures, *nada. Comprende?*" She'd never let him know that she was enjoying the playful exchange.

"Just as well. I'd be more frustrated than I am already," he said and sighed. "I want my hands on you."

As Alex visualized how his hands had looked on her body and how they'd made her feel she began to doubt her decision to keep their relationship platonic. Before she could respond, Diego changed the subject.

"I had a lot of time to think on the flight down and I realized something."

"Oh? And what's that?" She hoped he wasn't going to say something stupid like he was falling in love with her. She didn't know if she'd ever be ready to hear those words from another man.

"I'm happy to have proof that Will was my brother."

"Good ... that's a really good thing."

"Yeah. And now we better find whoever took him from us. It's a matter of family, of honor. I don't want to put off going to Scotland. Can you be ready in a couple of days?"

"I think so. The only thing on my calendar is a doctor's appointment tomorrow. We can leave any time after that."

"The doctor? Is something wrong? Are you sick?" There was panic in his voice.

"Of course not. It's a routine female thing ... Pap test, you know, the annual works. I made this appointment a long time ago and would have forgotten, but they sent a reminder. No need to worry."

"Good. I couldn't deal with you being sick now."

"I know what you mean. It's like you can take it and take it but if one more thing is added to the pile, bam! It topples, right?"

"True. This is nice ... I've missed you." The words were out of his mouth before he knew he was even thinking them. He wondered if she missed him too, but he wasn't going to ask.

"Do you have any idea when you'll get into Boston?"

"My mother will try to guilt me into staying for a while, but I should be able to leave tomorrow. I'll let you know my plans as soon as they're made."

"Great ... and Diego?" Alex chewed on her bottom lip, hesitant to admit what she'd just recognized.

"Yes?" Diego waited patiently for her to be ready to speak. It was a long pause.

"I'm glad you're coming back."

He breathed a sigh of relief. "Me too. Sleep well, *Preciosa.*"

"And you."

As she left home for the doctor's office, Alex walked past the grimy vagrant Diego had warned her about. He seemed harmless enough, and she was in a good mood, so she greeted him with a cheery, "good morning." He acknowledged it with an unintelligible grunt and shuffled away.

The bright sun felt so good on her face that she decided to walk downtown instead of going underground to the T. Every once in a while she felt uneasy, as if someone were watching her, but when she'd turn to look over her shoulder all she could see were the usual businesspeople, tourists and shoppers crowding the sidewalk. She told herself she was being foolish and, just like Will, she dismissed the warning as nothing more than paranoia.

The OB/GYN's office was in a busy medical building crowded with stressed people on their way to their doctors. She smiled at the well-dressed man who politely stepped aside to allow her to exit the packed elevator at the seventh floor before following her off himself. He waited until she'd turned right, then he went left.

Once Alex disappeared into her doctor's office, the man checked the name on the door then took the stairs back to the lobby, pulled a phone from his pocket and made a call.

"This may be what we've been waiting for. She walked into an obstetrician's office a minute ago. You know, a baby doctor!" he snapped angrily. "Our Alexandra's as slim as ever, but it could be that she carries the Cameron lad's child. If her belly starts to swell, what would you have me do?"

An unemotional voice an ocean away responded as if the conversation were about the weather. "Well now, she and the bairn must have a wee accident I suppose, don't you think?"

Alex's annual check-up was uneventful. She'd known Dr. Higgins for years and the physician greeted her with a hug. "How are you doing? Do you feel all right?"

"How am I supposed to answer that? Yes and no, I guess. I'm better than I was a few months ago, but it's still hard to accept that I'll never see Will again."

"If I can do anything to help, you'll ask, right?"

As the physician examined Alex she asked if she was still taking birth control pills.

"I'd stopped them for a while, but then I started again last month." Alex decided that was all she'd say on the subject. She was glad to be flat on her back, eyes glued to the ceiling, so the doctor wouldn't see the flush that rose from her chest to her face at revealing that she was having sex so soon after Will's death.

"I'll phone in a new prescription. And don't forget to have him wear a condom," was the doctor's only comment.

Alex had no plans for the rest of the day, so she wandered in and out of the designer shops lining Boylston and Newbury Streets. Then, without thinking, she turned off Newbury and headed into the narrow passageway where Will had been killed. She'd managed to put this place out of her mind, but at that moment something that she didn't want to question compelled her to go there.

She stood at the mouth of the alley where Will had taken his last breath and studied it. In daylight, it didn't look at all ominous. A slanted ray of sun made its way past the buildings that lined the space, which smelled faintly of the overflowing garbage cans waiting for pickup. She wrapped her arms around herself and began to slowly walk into the narrow space. She wasn't sure of the precise spot where it had happened, but about halfway through she sensed a change in the air and stopped abruptly to lean against a dirty brick wall.

"Are you here Will? Can you hear me?" she whispered as she slowly lowered herself to the ground. Maybe if she focused hard enough, he would come to her. She squeezed her eyes shut and slowed her breathing. Ridiculous, her logical self argued, but there were moments when she was absolutely sure he was hovering nearby. Fuck logic — she needed to believe in possibilities.

Alex didn't expect to feel more connected to Will in this smelly alley than at home among all his things, yet she did. Maybe his spirit is still hanging around here, maybe his soul can't rest yet, she thought, flashing on movies featuring violent death and spirits lingering between this world and the next ... so she started talking to him, between sobs, as if he were there.

"I miss you, oh God, how I miss you. I don't know how to live without you ... I'm not any good at being alone." She swallowed the lump in her throat, but the real or imagined connection to him was so strong that she forced the words out. She might not have another chance to tell him. "Diego—and yes, he told me he's your brother—is helping me figure out how to live again."

A gentle breeze that carried Will's scent wrapped her in its embrace. Was he trying to tell her that he was all right with whatever this thing was between her and Diego? Or maybe it was simply a ghostly slap in the face.

"You okay, lady? You was talkin' to yourself. You okay?"

Alex was repulsed by the overpowering stench of body odor and blast of whiskey fumes emanating from the rag-clad figure asking about her well-being. Had she fallen asleep and conjured Will's spirit or had he really been there? She wanted to drift back to wherever she'd been.

"Go away! Leave me alone! I'm fine," she shouted, but he didn't move. She thought that it would be bizarre to be attacked in the same place where Will had died, yet somehow she was more annoyed than afraid. "What do you want?" she asked irritably.

The only sign that he'd heard her was a grunt as he retreated a few inches, allowing her to draw clean air into her lungs. When she looked up, she realized that the man resembled the vagrant she'd seen near her house that morning.

"Jeez, lady, I seen ya around an' ya looked sick. Dat's all. I don't want nothin' from ya." He continued to mumble as he staggered away.

"Wait!" she shouted and scrambled to her feet to catch up with him.

"I've seen you near my house. Do you sleep in this alley? Do you know anyone who does? Have you ever seen someone attacked here?" She dug in her purse and extended a twenty toward him, hoping against hope that Will had sent this creature to her for a reason. The police had questioned their own sources among the city's street people, but maybe not this particular one.

"Tanks," he said, pocketing the twenty as he walked away.

"Stop, goddamn it! That money is to buy information. Stand still and talk to me. Please." He paused, but kept his face lowered and gazed blankly at the filthy toes that peeked out from his torn sneakers.

"I don't know nothin' lady. I ain't seen nothin'. I don't know no one. Dat's all your money bought ya. I gotta go."

She grabbed his arm, which was surprisingly solid under the layers of clothing that camouflaged his body. "You're not going anywhere! My husband was murdered! You have to tell me if you know anything about a man being killed here." She could hear the growing hysteria in her voice.

He didn't answer, but instead laid a dirty hand on her belly and raised his eyes to hers. She was stunned and it took a moment for her to back away.

"Did your man plant something in there before dying, I wonder?" His slurred, ungrammatical speech was suddenly clear and precise, with an unmistakable Scottish burr.

"Get your filthy hands off me! Who the hell are you?" Alex balled her fists, consumed by rage. At that moment she was convinced that she could take this man down or die trying. He knew something, was connected somehow. Why else would he have said what he did? He had to be one of them and for some reason he thought she was pregnant with Will's baby. Would they try to kill her now too?

"Wait! Please!" Her shaking hands were no match for the man's strength and he easily twisted out of her grasp and ran. The masquerade was over and she could only watch the obviously sober man, who'd been unable to walk a straight line a minute earlier, sprint out of the alley.

Alex's legs felt like rubber as she jogged toward the street and flagged down a cab to take her to Francie's apartment. She wasn't able to convince herself that his taunt about a possible pregnancy was the rant of a madman.

Francie had a deep belief in all things spiritual and the occult had always fascinated her. In college, the Ouija board and tarot cards accurately predicted too many events for her to discount their legitimacy. Alex accepted her friend's beliefs even if she didn't buy most of it herself.

"You and Will had a very strong connection. What makes you think something like that ends because the body ceases to exist?" Francie asked after Alex told her what had happened in the alley and she'd assured herself that her friend, though thoroughly rattled, was all right. Alex shrugged, but said nothing.

"I wouldn't be at all surprised if Will's spirit hangs around until he's sure you're okay," Francie continued. She had no doubt that the gentle breeze that had carried Will's scent across Alex's face in the alley was his ghost paying a visit.

"You really believe that?"

"You know I do," Francie assured her as Alex leaned forward to clutch her friend's small hand.

"I wish I could be sure he was there," Alex whispered as she tucked a woolen throw tightly around her legs. "Oh, God! I just thought of something. Do you think Will was watching when Diego and I … we … oh, sweet Jesus, that would be awful."

Francie hooted with laughter. "Did you see objects fly around the room or did something try to smother Diego?"

"Stop making fun of me. This is serious."

"I am being serious," Francie nodded and twirled a curl around one finger as she considered all possibilities. "If Will were there—and I think he would be enough of a gentleman that he'd have split and not stayed to watch unless he was kinkier than you've ever told me—he must have been okay with it," she concluded. "Do you want to ask him? I can drag out the Ouija board."

Alex knew Francie was only being half facetious. "No, of course not. You'll push the damn piece around the board until it says it's okay for me to have more sex with Diego. I know you, Francie."

She feigned innocence. "*Moi?*"

"Yes, you! You're a romantic. You see Diego as a knight in shining armor who's going to carry me off into the sunset on his white charger to live happily ever after. But that's the stuff of fairy tales. First of all, it's way too soon. Second, I found Prince Charming once and I'm pretty sure the limit is one per customer. If you think Diego will ever be more to me than a friend, maybe even a friend with benefits, you're going to be very disappointed, Francesca."

"Okay, be that way. Falling for another man doesn't take anything away from what you had with Will—just the opposite, in fact. You two were so terrific together that it makes total sense for you to want to have that again. And if it happens quickly, so what? You'd be an idiot to walk away from happiness based on some arbitrary timetable for grieving and you, Alexandra, are not now, nor have you ever been, a fool. Look at me," she ordered. "If you had a miserable marriage, of course you'd never want that again. But you and Will had a great marriage."

Francie dropped her hands and walked away in disgust as she watched Alex shake her head from side to side. "Do that again, Alexandra MacBain Cameron, and I'm going to wring your neck! You are the most exasperating, stubborn woman! How we stay best friends is a mystery … but I love you even when I think you're being an ass. And you are being an ass!"

"I love you too," Alex said as she hugged her friend. "I've gotta run. Diego gets into Logan soon and I want to pick up something for dinner and finish packing. I'll call you from Scotland."

"You better," she said, and then her tone became serious. "Those people are dangerous. I know you think this Serge person can protect the two of you, but Diego's impulsive and likes to do things his own way. This is real life with real bullets and real blood. It's not a movie. Please be careful."

CHAPTER 25

Serge was edgy. He threw himself into a chair in his hotel room, kicked off his shoes, flipped through a sports magazine, tossed it aside and finally grabbed the remote, but found nothing to watch on TV. He needed action and there could be none until he heard from Diego.

He popped open a beer and examined the uptick in his anxiety level. He recognized the feeling and knew it would be with him until Will Cameron's killer was identified and the mission completed. Heightened senses were required to stay alive in his line of work along with a degree of confidence bordering on arrogance. Detachment figured in there too. He'd known it was time to leave Mossad when his conscience began to interfere with the indifference needed to shield himself from actions he'd witnessed or carried out as an agent. Two years after his retirement, he'd been hired by Ricardo Navarro to ensure Diego's safety and, if necessary, protect him with his own life.

It was a cushy existence and he was well compensated. The senior Navarro would be livid if he ever found out that Serge wasn't glued to Diego. He'd probably be fired if Ricardo learned that it was his son who now gave the orders. Luckily, the willful bastard had a natural affinity for the rigorous training program that Serge had put him through until he was sure that Diego could expertly defend his own body. And he could, but with one major exception—when that body became entangled with a woman's and he allowed his genitals to overrule his common sense. It wouldn't take a genius to figure out that Diego's irresponsible lack of communication for the past twenty-four hours was due to the lovely Alexandra Cameron. What worried him was the risk that particular connection held. From what he'd learned about their adversaries, one possible target remained—Alex—so whenever Diego was with her, the threat extended to him. He knew better than to try to pry Diego away from her, but he had to be sure that his friend was armed and vigilant. Serge knew that his boss wouldn't re-establish contact until he was good and ready.

Since he'd placed the listening devices in Mackinnon's home and business, the man hadn't done anything that tied him to the rebellious offshoot of the Group of One Hundred. He went to his shop, came home, dined with Mairi's family a couple of times, and occasionally drove to the nearby Moray Firth to watch the sun set over the Black Isle. Serge had to consider that the information he'd obtained might be flawed or, with Will dead, the participants had gone to ground to avoid notice. He considered two other possibilities: that they were biding their time to formulate another plan; or, with Mackinnon's son jailed, and revenge carried out against John Cameron for informing the English authorities about the terrorist plot, the splinter group might have disbanded.

Patience often paid off eventually and that morning, as Serge headed to the bathroom to shave, he'd hit "play" to listen to any calls Mackinnon had received overnight. He nicked himself as the old man spoke with someone in Boston who'd obviously been watching Alex. His shoulders tensed as he listened to the man report on Alex's visit to a doctor's office and his theory that she could be pregnant with Will's child. He then heard Mackinnon callously say, "Well now, she and the bairn must have a wee accident I suppose," in answer to the caller's query about how to proceed if, in fact, Alex carried a future Cameron. Serge clenched and unclenched his fists. Diego had to be told and the fucker was ignoring his calls.

CHAPTER 26

*D*iego ran across the tarmac toward the Navarro jet, shouting into his phone to be heard above the whir of a nearby plane's engines. "Alex! Alex, can you hear me? Shit, I can't hear you," he growled and snapped the phone shut. He sprinted up the plane's steps and tried the call again.

"Better," Alex said when she answered, stifling a yawn.

"I'm sorry to wake you, but it's a long flight back to the States and I wanted to get an early start. My pilot says we'll be airborne in about a half hour, which would put us into Boston around seven tonight. I've also arranged for us to fly to Scotland tomorrow."

"Good. I can't stand that the killer thinks he's gotten away with it."

"Trust me, Alex, we'll find him."

"I know. If anyone wants this more than me, it's you."

"I've got a couple of other calls to make before we take off. I'll see you tonight."

"Okay, have a good flight. I'm gonna try to go back to sleep."

He had an instant physical reaction to the thought of waking beside her, but he knew he had to let Alex lead that particular dance or he could lose her. That was one risk he wasn't willing to take, which meant he'd have to fight his natural inclination to take charge.

Scotland tomorrow, Alex mused as she popped bread in the toaster and fried an egg a couple of hours after Diego's early morning call. She tried not to think about the man who'd ended Will's life, but he came to her unbidden in dreams that left her trembling and drenched in sweat. He had to be found and dealt with if she were to ever have peace. She had no idea what form this thirst for vengeance would take, but cutting the killer's heart into little pieces with a cleaver had some appeal. She forced those ugly thoughts away and switched her focus to Diego. Better, much better, she thought and smiled.

About an hour before the Navarro jet was due into Logan, Alex gave a final check to the dinner she'd prepared—a Greek salad was chilling in the refrigerator along with the rotisseried chicken she'd bought on the way home from Francie's. She'd serve it cold, accompanied by white wine, crusty bread and a dessert of strawberries dipped in sour cream and brown sugar—the perfect summer meal. She quickly showered, shaved her legs, pulled on faded jeans and a black tank top and switched off the hair dryer in time to hear the downstairs buzzer. It was Diego.

Excitement bubbled in her veins as she stood at the open door and listened to him running up the stairs to her top floor flat.

"You could have taken the elevator!" she shouted teasingly down the stairwell.

"Too slow," he replied as he wrapped his arms around her, lifted her off the ground and gifted her with a look of such incredible happiness that she couldn't stop herself from grinning foolishly back at him.

"Hi," she finally said.

"Hi," he answered softly and touched his lips gently to hers.

Francie knows me better than I know myself, Alex thought as she drifted into the kiss and the arousal it provoked.

"I promised myself that I would wait, let you decide ... give you time," he whispered into her ear a moment later, "I'm sorry, I couldn't help myself."

"I don't need time. I need you," she replied breathlessly.

Diego's face flushed and his dark eyes sparkled with amusement as they met hers. Alex took his hand and smiled shyly as she led him to the guest room, dinner completely forgotten. She would never make love with another man in the bed she and Will had shared.

"So ... does this mean you want to use me again?" he teased raising one dark eyebrow.

"Oh, shut up," she answered and put an exclamation point on it by tugging his shirt out of his pants to run her hands over his hard, muscled back. His skin was warm, but she felt it quiver.

"You have no idea what you do to me," he murmured hoarsely as she raised her arms to help him slide the flimsy top over her head. Oh, yes, I do, she thought fleetingly as she sank into an abyss of sensation, because you do the same to me.

Damp and sticky from sex and sweat, their bodies were fused to each other and it took some effort to separate. Diego was half-asleep, but one of his fingers repeatedly traced a line from Alex's breast to her waist and back again.

"Stop it!" she grumbled as she shoved his hand away.

"What? What am I doing?" He'd dozed off and seemed genuinely puzzled.

"I'm ticklish and you're torturing me."

Diego turned onto his side and nuzzled her, inhaling her scent. No heavy perfume … a fragrance he couldn't identify, but uniquely hers. He liked it and tightened his hold on her, then reluctantly let go when he remembered his vow to let her lead this particular dance. He propped his head on a couple of pillows and grinned lazily. "Is this our first fight?"

"When we have a fight, Navarro, you'll know it. And wipe that smile off your face."

"Can't I smile at you? I'm happy. When I'm happy, I smile." He reached for her again, but she leapt out of bed.

"Ha!" she taunted. This was fun, but she wasn't ready to let him know that. "I'm going to shower. And in case you're thinking of joining me, the door will be locked. You can use the guest bathroom. Then put some clothes on and meet me in the kitchen. I made dinner."

"*Oui, mon général*, your wish is my command," he said and made a courtly bow which would have looked ridiculous even if he weren't naked. "First you share your body with me and now you offer food. My cup runneth over," he added, as he sauntered toward the bathroom.

His back was to her when she turned to reply and he was already kicking the door shut with his heel. The man's got the most beautiful ass, she observed, then averted her eyes. The last thing she wanted was for Diego Navarro to catch her checking out his body, but it was indeed a thing of wonder.

Once she was sure that he was in the shower, she

grabbed her cell phone. When Francie answered, all Alex said was, "You were right. And it was even better the second time. I love you France. Bye."

CHAPTER 27

"Where the hell are you? Answer the damn phone!" Serge shouted with mounting frustration as he tried Diego's number yet again. The message Diego had left said that he and Alex planned to arrive in Scotland that day. If they were aboard the Navarro Gulfstream, its satellite communications system would have picked up the call, so Diego must be traveling on a jet without that equipment. Or at least he hoped so.

Serge knew his employer well. Diego's father needed the Gulfstream, so he'd chartered a jet for him and Alex. Diego often used his wealth to insulate himself from the hassles endured by the masses. A commercial flight would have required a time-consuming stop in London or Edinburgh to connect to an Inverness flight. More important, private jets were exempt from the stringent, post-9/11 rules against weapons aboard commercial aircraft and Diego was traveling armed.

He was mentally and physically prepared to do battle in Scotland. A slim, yet deadly, knife that he'd learned to wield with the agility of a street fighter was strapped just above his ankle. He'd trained on a life size dummy, although he still wasn't sure that he'd be able to cut a human except in a life or death struggle. A semi-automatic Beretta was holstered beneath his arm, concealed under a roomy, black cotton sweater. He was already an expert marksman when Serge had been hired, but his aim and reflexes were now those of a pro. The bastards had no idea that Cameron blood flowed through another man's veins, a man who was hell-bent on avenging his brother's murder and on safeguarding the woman he'd begun to regard as his.

But for now the warrior rested, his face as placid as a child's. One arm was wrapped possessively around that woman — his woman — as they slept their way across the Atlantic after a night when sleep had been the last thing on their minds.

Beside him, Alex slitted one eye as she slowly emerged from a deep, dreamless slumber. For an instant she was confused to find herself on a plane and not in her own bed. She stirred, but when Diego tried to draw her to him, she pulled away.

"What's wrong?" he mumbled in that half-conscious state between sleep and wakefulness. The man hadn't shaved since leaving Buenos Aires and Alex thought he looked incredibly sexy with a two-day stubble of dark beard.

"My ears popped and woke me up. We're probably almost there." She sat up to see if they were over land, but clouds blocked any view. "Will and I talked about buying small cottage in Scotland one day ... as a hideaway. He loved this place," she trailed off, overwhelmed by memories and conflicting emotions. It felt so wrong to be coming back to Scotland with anyone but Will, let alone a man she'd slept with. Too soon, it's too soon, she told herself for the zillionth time. Despite Francie's assurance that there was no such thing as "too soon" if the right person came along, it still seemed like she was cheating on Will. Yet when she was with Diego it felt right. He was like chocolate to a dieter — hard to resist and definitely delicious, but with an aftertaste of guilt, self-loathing, and a vow to be stronger despite a short supply of will power.

"Alessandra," he said softly. "I shouldn't have brought you here. Of course Scotland is going to trigger memories for you. Will was so excited to learn about his heritage when you visited here." He stroked her back as he spoke, but otherwise kept his distance. "Maybe you should take the plane back to Boston. Serge and I can take care of what has to be done here. You don't have to stay."

"That's ridiculous. Look, Diego, I have as much at stake here as you do and I won't run away from it. Sure it's going to hurt, but a lot of things do these days. I'm staying."

"Good, because the plan I've come up with includes you."

"Plan? What plan?" His arrogance was pissing her off big time. "If you have a plan and I'm part of it, don't you think you should have told me?"

"Yes, of course. I was going talk it over with you last night, but then ... we didn't do much talking, did we?"

"No, we didn't," she conceded and her anger faded, knowing that she was as responsible as he was for how the evening turned out.

The intercom crackled and the pilot addressed Diego. "Sorry to disturb you Mr. Navarro, but we'll be landing in Inverness in about thirty minutes. That gives you fifteen to move around before you and Mrs. Cameron need to buckle your seatbelts."

"Thank you," Diego responded. "Any update on the weather?"

"Sky's overcast, but we're ahead of the storm that's coming in tonight. Temperature is 15° Celsius, 60°

Fahrenheit, a bit cooler than Boston. Local time is 4:30 p.m. Is there anything else, sir?"

"No, that's it. Thanks for a smooth flight. See you on the ground." Diego turned to Alex. "I'll fill you in on my idea after we land. Of course I'll have to run it by Serge, too. There are two bathrooms aft, if you want to freshen up," he said as he rose and extended a hand to help her out of the oversized reclining seat.

"I think I'll stay here," she said and peered out the window again. She wanted to be alone to catch a glimpse of Scotland, but a stubborn cloud cover hid its lochs, glens and mountains and thwarted her chance for a private reunion with the land of her ancestors, the dramatically beautiful land that was now forever tainted by Will's murder.

Diego's mobile phone sounded as the plane taxied to the terminal.

"Thank God," uttered Serge when Diego answered. "Don't you ever check your voicemail? Didn't I teach you to always maintain contact? How am I supposed to protect you if you can't even do something as simple as that?"

Diego's expression hardened, his full lips narrowing in response to Serge's tongue lashing, which was at a decibel level loud enough for Alex to hear. She was surprised when he took it in silence instead of defending himself. Alex suspected that Serge was the only person who could lecture him and get away with it.

"What? What's he saying?" Alex tugged impatiently on Diego's sleeve to get his attention.

He put a finger to his lips to quiet her and focused intently on what the bodyguard was telling him. Diego's brow furrowed and his jaw clenched. Concern filled his eyes as he listened and he wrapped an arm tightly around Alex's shoulders.

Something hard jabbed her side and she lifted his sweater to see if her guess was correct. Before she could see more than the bottom of the holster, Diego irritably tugged the sweater down and glared at her. What the hell was he doing with a gun? As much as she found sadistic pleasure in fantasizing about ways to make Will's murderer suffer, his punishment would have to come from someone more rational than this madman whose combination of Scottish and Sicilian blood predisposed him to violence and vendettas. Once again, Alex was reminded of how little she knew about the man she'd allowed to become her lover.

"What did he tell you? And what the hell are you doing with a gun?" she demanded the moment the call ended.

"We have to go. I'll fill you in on the way."

"Bullshit! I saw that look on your face, Navarro. Tell me what's going on right now or I head back to Boston tonight." She crossed her arms and waited.

"That's exactly what I wanted you to do. I thought you'd be safer in Boston, but I was wrong."

"What do you mean?" she asked, more alarmed by the tension on his face than by his words.

"Serge told me that you were being followed in Boston."

"What? Why would they care about me? I'm a MacBain, not a Cameron."

"Yes, but you slept with a Cameron. Remember you told me you had an appointment with your gynecologist? That kind of doctor also delivers babies, yes? You were followed, and now they think you could be pregnant with Will's child ... the last Cameron."

"That's ridiculous. Do I look pregnant?" Alex asked as she ran a hand over her flat stomach.

"That's not the point! Jesus Christ, woman!" He didn't know whether his anger was driven by worry or frustration that she didn't get it, but he was having a hard time maintaining control. Diego stood over her and gripped the arms of her seat, his face inches away from hers. "Doesn't it tell you something that you were being followed?" he hissed. "Don't you see that they might decide to kill you on the off chance that you've got John Cameron's grandchild in your belly?"

"But I'm not pregnant! I'm not … " her voice trailed off. "No one's going to kill me. If they wanted to, they'd have done it already." His use of the word "belly" jolted her as it brought back the frightening encounter with that man in the alley. She was tempted to tell Diego about it, but he'd lay into her about that too. This was definitely the wrong time to give him a reason to become even more crazed than he was already.

Diego slumped into the seat next to her as they both tried to calm down.

"I don't like that you have a gun," Alex finally said. "Besides, you can't get it through Scottish immigration."

"You can if you have the proper paperwork and I do."

"But isn't it Serge's job to protect you?"

"It is, but he taught me to defend myself and I can, surprisingly well." Diego took her hands in his and used one finger to gently turn her face toward him. He had to make her understand the danger posed by their adversaries. They'd killed at least once and Diego knew they could do it again.

"I have no idea what we're up against here, but please try to trust me. I'll never let anything happen to you," he said as he cupped her face tenderly and whispered, "You've become too important to me."

She heard and nodded, but couldn't, or wouldn't, reply.

"Let's go," he said, breaking the mood as he shifted into action. "We're meeting Serge at his hotel after we pick up our car. I hate driving on the wrong side of the road and I'm going to need you to navigate us through those inane roundabouts they love over here."

"I'll drive," Alex replied. "Don't forget that Will and I spent a lot of time in London, so I'm pretty confident I won't smash into anything." The switch to a mundane topic helped to defuse the tension between them.

"Fine, but a woman behind the wheel and a man in the passenger seat goes against all that is holy," he teased, as a grin spread from his mouth to eyes that sparkled with mischief until he saw that Alex didn't realize he was joking. "Of course you'll drive and I'll do my best to stay calm. I may have more *machísmo* than you'd like, but that doesn't make me a total idiot."

"Yeah, right," she grumbled, but let it drop.

He deferred to her when they chose their rental — a red Mini Cooper, which wasn't just cute, she said, but also the perfect size for Scotland's narrow roads, unlike the muscular SUV he'd wanted.

They reached the hotel easily and found a man Diego recognized as Serge in the lobby bar, but he looked like a stranger to Alex. The transformation in his appearance amazed her. He had a great tan and wore a navy blue Polo shirt, khakis and tasseled loafers with no socks. His military-style short hair had grown out and he could have passed for a more muscular version of Brad Pitt. Serge couldn't have looked more American if he'd been waving the Stars and Stripes.

"What's with the outfit?" Alex asked as Serge led the way to his suite. He'd also lost the accent that had led her to believe that English wasn't his native tongue.

"Oh, this," he said, as he looked down to remind himself of what he was wearing. "The people here think that I'm an American from Florida who's in Scotland on business. I have to look the part." As soon as they were safely in his suite, Serge turned his attention to Diego.

"Did you tell her?" he asked.

"Yes," replied Diego, "she knows."

"And she's okay with what we'll do once we find him?" Serge asked as he paced across the suite's spacious living room. He wanted to finish the job and get the hell back to Florida or wherever Diego was headed next.

Alex glared at them, but they didn't notice. The longer the two men behaved as if she were invisible, the angrier she became. When she couldn't take it any more, she blocked Serge's path and jabbed a finger into his shoulder. "Hey! Can you see me or have I suddenly vanished? The two of you better start to include me in everything. Everything! And stop behaving like I'm some weak damsel in distress."

"She's right," said Diego. "Alex has toughened up since you met her in Miami, although her muscles leave something to be desired," he teased, knowing she'd rise to the bait. He dodged just before her fist connected with his jaw. "Admit it, Alex, you haven't been working out."

"You idiot!" she spat. She was livid, but a part of her liked that Diego noticed that she was growing stronger every day.

"I apologize, Alex," said Serge. "If Diego wants you to be included in our talks, of course you will be."

"Not only that, but she's also part of the plan I've come up with," said Diego.

Serge's eyebrows rose in surprise, then he leaned back in his chair and crossed his arms over his broad chest. "Oh? You have a plan?" Sarcasm dripped from his voice. "Do you think it might be important to hear what I've learned in the last twenty-four hours before you tell us about your ... plan?"

Diego didn't like being second-guessed or patronized. Alex recognized the twitching jaw and icy eyes that signaled the effort he was making to hold his temper and his mouth in check.

"Fine. You're the expert. I defer to you," he said, his speech clipped.

Serge had dealt with Diego's short fuse for years and knew that the storm would pass as quickly as it rose, so he simply proceeded with his report.

"Okay. You both know that one of the listening devices I placed picked up a call to Mackinnon from the man who was tailing you in Boston," he said as he glanced toward Alex for confirmation. She nodded. "They're waiting to see if you're pregnant with your late husband's child. If you are, they plan to kill you. They'll stop at nothing to wipe all traces of John Cameron from the earth."

"Well, I'd better do lots of crunches and watch my diet," Alex joked, but she shivered and felt goose bumps rise on her scalp at the matter-of-fact way Serge spoke about her murder. She and Will had longed for a child for so many years that it was weird to be happy that the regular periods she'd had since he'd died were absolute proof that she wasn't pregnant. And she was on the pill. Nope, definitely not pregnant.

"Alex," Diego said, interrupting her reverie. "Do you remember that vagrant we saw near your house? Remember that I thought there was something off about him? Serge found out that he was one of two men sent to follow you." Diego raked his hair with both hands as he paced from one end of the room to the other. "I told you to watch out for him, didn't I? Christ, I never should have gone to Buenos Aires and left you alone. What if he had…"

"Why are you angry? Nothing happened," Alex shot back, but that was only half true. If this guy were one of them, it was important for Serge to know about her encounter with him. Diego would explode, but that was his problem. She was sure that once she told them, these two men would watch her like hawks. Maybe she should be grateful for that instead of fighting it. She didn't want to die. She cleared her throat and took a deep breath.

"I have something to tell both of you. And Serge, it would probably be a good idea if you get a firm grip on Diego because he's going to flip out." She had their full attention. "One of the men that you just said was following me … well … he and I actually met while you were in Argentina. He seemed harmless enough, just down on his luck."

"What! *¡Dios mío!* Why didn't you tell me about this? What did he say to you?" Diego bolted out of his chair as if a firecracker had gone off under him.

Alex turned her back on both men and gazed out the window at the timeless beauty of Inverness Castle across the river from the hotel. It calmed her until she felt Diego's breath on her neck. I suppose now he's going to strangle me, she thought, but instead his arms came around her waist as he leaned in and whispered, "Don't you know the risk of talking to such a person? I'd never forgive myself if he'd harmed you."

Although the warm strength of his body was

comforting, his compulsion to protect her was maddening and she pulled away. How could he brag to Serge about her strength one minute, then think he had to rescue her the next? She glared at him and shoved him away.

"Do I look hurt? No. Did he do anything to me? No. Well, he did touch my stomach at one point and said something odd, but…"

"He touched you?" Diego interrupted, his face in hers again.

Serge seemed to be enjoying their performance and was patiently waiting for it to end so that he could continue his report.

"Stop interrupting and I'll finish," she hissed. "And stop breathing in my face. You could use a mint or something."

"Okay, okay, I'm sorry. I'm mad at myself, not at you. Go on," Diego said as he silently accepted a mint from Serge. Alex hoped it would keep his mouth busy for a few minutes.

"After I saw the doctor I went to the alley where Will died. I needed to see it. You might think I'm crazy, but I felt Will's presence there. Anyway, I sat on the ground for a while … talking to him … until that same street person came along. He heard me talking to myself and wanted to know if I was okay. Can you imagine? Anyway, I thought he might know someone who'd witnessed Will's murder. I asked if he knew of anyone who slept in that alley or whether he'd heard anything about a man being stabbed there. He mumbled that he didn't know anything and staggered away. I went after him and when I caught up he put a hand on my stomach and said the weirdest thing."

"What?" the two men asked in unison. She finally had Serge's attention as well as Diego's.

She rubbed her head again to try to get rid of the goose bumps that prickled her scalp and took a steadying breath. "I'll never forget his words. He said, very clearly, 'Did your man plant something in there before dying, I wonder?' I wanted to chase him, to ask him what he meant, but he began to run. I knew I was too shaky to catch him so I didn't try. I went straight to Francie's. If they're trying to figure out if I'm pregnant, maybe I should do one of those home pregnancy tests in front of Mackinnon to prove there's no baby for them to worry about." She was dead serious.

"That's not such a crazy idea if it would keep you safe," said Diego. "What do you think?" he asked Serge.

"If your only goal is to protect Mrs. Cameron — and I know that's important to you — her idea could work. These people say they'd prefer not to harm her ... something about her having the blood of some Scottish hero — MacBain, right?"

Alex nodded. "When Will and I were in that man's store, he asked if I was Scottish. I said that my family name is MacBain, and Mackinnon got all excited. He told me my ancestor, some guy named Gillies Mor MacBain, was a hero who killed a lot of English soldiers at the Battle of Culloden."

"Then it seems you're only in danger if they decide that you're pregnant." Serge directed these comments to Alex, then turned to Diego. "I thought my mission was to find the people responsible for the murder and punish them. Has that changed?" To him, this was simply another assignment. If Diego now had a different objective, Serge needed to know.

Alex understood that none of this was personal for Serge. Diego had told her that as a Mossad agent he'd had to kill without being told why. The old Alex would have been horrified, but Will's murder had forced a shift in her sense of right and wrong. Instead of thinking of Serge as a cold-blooded assassin, she began to see him as someone who meted out justice.

Diego's expression softened as he glanced at Alex, but then he turned toward Serge and, like a chameleon, he shifted into the ruthless warrior Alex was starting to recognize. "No. In answer to your question, nothing's changed. If Alex went to Mackinnon now, he'd find out that we know about him and it's those fucking killers we're after. There's no way in hell that I can let them get away with what they did to Will."

"I agree," said Serge. "Right now, they have no idea that we're here or that we know who they are and I want to keep it that way. They suspect that you've left Boston, Alex, but they have no clue that you're in Scotland, so you should be safe for a while at least. And they'd never imagine that there's another male Cameron, and a dangerous one at that." Diego's blood tie to Will had dramatically upped the stakes. "And finally, there's a very chatty young lady who I've..." he hesitated and cleared his throat. Diego had heard all about the voluptuous Mairi Graham and his lips twitched watching Serge try to delicately explain this relationship to Alex. "I suppose you could say the young lady and I are, uh ... close."

Alex noticed Diego's grin and wanted to somehow assure Serge that he could be comfortable around her. "Oh, you mean you're fucking her?" she asked sweetly.

Diego howled with laughter and slapped his startled bodyguard good-naturedly on the back. Serge didn't join their mirth, but simply raised his brows and shook his head from side to side as if they were a couple of playful pups whose antics he had to tolerate until they could control themselves again.

"As I was saying … the young lady's family and the Mackinnons are very close. She even calls the old guy "Uncle" Jamie. Mairi told me that his grandson — young Jamie — is kind of like a brother to her. She said he left for America around the time Will was murdered. When he came back a month or so later, he quit a good job here in Inverness and moved to the far north of Scotland to work as a sheep farmer. She also knows Ewen."

"Who?" asked Alex.

"You know. The man you told us you remembered meeting in London. The one who sent you and Will to Mackinnon's shop."

"Interesting," Alex said. "I'm glad I was able to pull his name out of my brain."

"Yeah, that helped," replied Serge. "Before I came to Scotland, I spent a week in London masquerading as a high class lawyer. I hung out at the Mayfair pub that you and Will went to whenever you'd visit London. The barman remembered Ewen. About a week before the murder, Ewen was in the pub with someone whose description matches Mackinnon's grandson. After a few drinks, they bragged about a job they had in America that would pay handsomely."

"So the evidence all points to this young Jamie person, right?" Alex said.

"Precisely, at least so far," responded Serge. "But we can't act until we're sure."

Diego nodded and tented his hands against his forehead. He slowly rubbed his fingers along his hairline. "We must find this young Jamie." He spat out the name with contempt.

"You seem pretty sure that Mackinnon has no idea that we're on to him. But if your girlfriend is so close to his family, can you trust her?" Alex asked Serge.

"She has no reason to lie to me," he shrugged. "To her I'm a guy she has fun with—one who has enough money to keep her interested and who's dangling a trip to sunny Florida in front of her."

"Ooooh, you're bad," Alex grinned at Serge. Although he wasn't her type, she could imagine a young woman being charmed by his blonde, blue-eyed good looks and his powerful build.

Diego stretched his arms toward the ceiling and yawned loudly. "It's been a long day, *amigo*, and I'm hungry. I noticed a restaurant off the lobby when we checked in. Let's eat and then get some sleep. As for the rest, it can wait until *mañana*."

They were waiting to be seated when a female voice called to someone named Steve.

"Shit," grumbled Serge. "That's Mairi. To her I'm Steve Spencer from Miami and I own a chain of gift shops. You're business associates here on vacation," he instructed quickly as she approached.

The contrast between the girl's creamy skin and hair the color of an Irish Setter was striking. Alex could see why Serge would want to do whatever he was doing with her, even if she had no connection to Mackinnon. The voluptuous girl bubbled with enthusiasm and was obviously happy to see Serge.

"Mairi! Did we have a date?" he asked and slipped his arm around her waist.

"No, Steve, we dinna, but I popped by for a drink

anyway. I hoped I might see you here," she said guile-lessly as her face flushed.

"And you did, so it worked out fine, but your timing isn't so good. I'm about to begin a dinner meeting with some business associates," he said amiably turning toward Diego and Alex. "Mairi Graham, meet Barbara and Rick Sloane. This isn't social or I'd ask you to join us. I'm sorry." He drew her closer and planted a gentle kiss on her temple.

The girl tried, but failed, to mask her disappointment. Alex smiled warmly and extended her hand. "It's nice to meet you Mairi," she said. Diego's smile was dazzling as always. Because Serge introduced them as a married couple, Alex looped her arm though Diego's to better display her wedding ring. The way Mairi was looking at Diego, Alex thought the girl might like to trade Serge in for him.

"Pleased to meet you both," she said and turned back to Serge. "Do all Americans look like film stars or is it just you three?"

They all laughed.

"And are you in the trinket business as well?" She directed this question to Diego. Alex had become invisible.

"No, we're collaborating on another venture," replied Diego smoothly.

"Why don't you two find our table and I'll join you in a minute," Serge suggested. "I want to put Mairi in a taxi to be sure she gets home safely," he said and then hustled Mairi away.

Serge looked grim when he returned. "I had no idea she'd be here. I didn't want her to see the two of you."

"Why not?" Diego asked. "She thinks we're a couple of Americans named Barbara and Rick Sloane. What's the problem?"

"I trust Serge's instincts," Alex said. "If he's upset that she saw us, there must be a good reason."

"These people are sure they got away with murder, which works for us. It will make them sloppy. And although I think Mairi's only connection to them is that of family friend like she says, there's always a chance that she's playing me while I'm doing the same to her. Doubtful, but you never know. It wouldn't be the first time," Serge said thoughtfully as he buttered a warm roll.

"So what are Alex and I supposed to do? Hide in our room?"

"No. I'm thinking that the two of you could be used as bait to draw them out, make them nervous. But we can't blow the element of surprise yet, so it's best if I keep Mairi away from you."

"It wouldn't take a genius to figure out just how you'll do that," said Diego grinning lasciviously as he perused the menu. "I know they eat some sheep's stomach thing called haggis in this country, but what the hell do you suppose neeps and tatties are?"

CHAPTER 28

The sight of the large, white water tower looming over the prison gates made bitter bile rise to James Mackinnon's throat, its foul taste a perfect reflection of his emotions. After only one year inside the walls of Her Majesty's Prison Shotts, his spirited, fun-loving son had become docile, his face pale, his body thin, the sparkle gone from his eyes. Some men took prison life in stride, but his boy was happiest hunting, fishing or hill walking; the regimented confinement of prison life was taking its toll. It would be another few years before his son would even be considered for release.

Twice a month Mackinnon dutifully drove the 170 miles from Inverness to the maximum-security facility south of Glasgow to spend an hour—all the time the fuckers allowed—with his Jamie. These visits were torture for him and reignited his hatred for the man who'd caused his son to be locked up in such a place. Mackinnon's only consolation was that now John Cameron felt even more wretched than he did, and he was glad of it.

Cameron's perfidy had set off a chain of events that ended with Jamie's arrest. Mackinnon himself had faced expulsion from the Group of One Hundred, which long ago banned the use of violence to achieve a free Scotland. They'd made him swear on his son's life that he knew nothing of the plot, and he did as they'd asked. If he'd refused, he and his would have been cast out forever. He would rather die than be the first Mackinnon in 700 years to be expelled from the group and humiliate his clan. Yet he'd willingly risked that very thing once more when he and his friends concluded that Cameron had to pay for his sin. If word of Will Cameron's execution ever reached the group, his brethren wouldn't hesitate to bring the law down on his head. "Fools," he muttered.

He was enraged that his boy Jamie had been vilified as a threat to society, when he should have been hailed as a hero for building a bomb that would have hurt those who continued to regard Scotland as a fiefdom. If the explosion had killed the innocent, well, it was war, wasn't it? The English devils would learn that Scots could be as ruthless as the Irish in the pursuit of freedom.

He'd get some satisfaction from telling his son that their kinsmen had made John Cameron pay for his treachery. He'd not reveal that it had been the hand of his grandson—young Jamie Mackinnon—that plunged the knife into Will Cameron. The lad might be proud of his son's skill and courage, but it would also worry him and prison life came with enough worries. No, for now he'd keep that part of the tale to himself, although it pleased him to see the youngest generation pick up the sword.

The elder Mackinnon was accustomed to the prison's drill. As required, he'd booked his visit in advance. An officer met him on arrival, ticked his name off a list, and he was then subjected to a security search more thorough than those done at airports. Once cleared, he took his place on a hard chair in the unheated, windowless visitors' waiting room until a staff member finally came to fetch him to spend his hour with his son, Jamie. The place reeked of the disinfectant used on its worn, but spotless, floors and he knew the sharp odor would linger in his nostrils on the return trip to the Highlands.

"James Mackinnon," a matron's officious voice boomed, "come with me." Hunched with sadness and fatigue, he followed the woman's stocky figure down a brightly lit corridor. Today's news would do nothing to improve his son's conditions, but he hoped the lad could find some comfort in knowing that the traitor Cameron had finally paid, and paid dearly.

CHAPTER 29

*A*fter the chance encounter with Mairi in the hotel lobby and a quick dinner, Diego and Alex fell into bed, too exhausted to do more than exchange a chaste kiss and sleep.

When she woke the next morning, Diego's naked body was spooned against her back, his hand cupping her breast. He was still soundly asleep and she wondered when in the night they'd sought each other out. His skin was warm and smelled of man and when she felt his arousal she had to fight the urge to turn toward him for some lazy, morning sex. She checked the clock. 8:30 a.m. They'd arranged to meet Serge in his suite for breakfast at nine. Desire would have to wait.

"Wake up. It's late," she whispered to Diego and threw off the covers.

He mumbled something unintelligible as he extended an arm to draw her back against him. "Come here Alex, I'm cold."

"Tempting, but no. We have to meet Serge in thirty minutes. I'll shower first since it takes me longer to get ready."

"You're no fun," he grumbled as he slitted one eye open.

"That's not what you said two nights ago," she teased and quickly turned away before the impulse to run her hands over his chest overwhelmed her. The blanket only covered him to the waist and his biceps flexed as he smiled at her and stretched lazily. She wanted take everything he was offering and reciprocate just as generously. Instead, she told herself what she'd told him — tempting, but no — and ordered herself away from the bed and into the shower.

They polished off the coffee and scones Serge had ordered from room service as they sat near the suite's bay window and watched pedestrians briskly cross the River Ness's bridge to the shops and businesses of the city center. The bright sunshine made the water appear to be studded with silver sequins.

"I still don't like that Mairi saw the two of you," Serge began. "I should have told you to walk away the minute she spotted me so I wouldn't have had to explain who you were." A dust cloud rose when he slammed his fist angrily into the arm of the green velvet sofa. "Shit! I know better than to screw up something so simple."

"What's the problem? You used fake names when you introduced us so she doesn't know who we are," Alex said, but this spy business was more complicated than it looked and if Serge was rattled, than she was too — big time.

"The people who followed you in Boston had to know what you look like and would have emailed pictures of you back here to prove they were doing their job. If Mairi saw those photos on one of her visits to her "uncle's" shop, she'd know I lied when I introduced you as the Sloanes. My cover would be blown."

"But that's a long shot, right? You don't really think she's involved, do you?" Alex asked.

"No," replied Serge. "I watched her face and the only thing I saw was curiosity and the same kind of interest in Diego every female has. So, for the moment, let's assume Mairi's the innocent she seems to be."

"So what now?" asked Diego.

"It's time to rattle their cages. I want the two of you to go to Mackinnon's shop. He'll recognize you right away, Alex — not from your first visit, but because of the surveillance photos, which probably include Diego too. You'll introduce him to Mackinnon as Will's brother and watch the old man's reaction. Ask him to tell your brother-in-law about the family history the same way he did for Will. If I'm reading them right, Diego will be the bait that draws them into our net."

"Oh no you don't," Alex blurted out as her heart began to race from a mix of anger, fear and caffeine. "First of all, why do you think Mackinnon would believe that a man named Diego Navarro could be Will's brother? He's not Diego Cameron, for chrissakes. Give the guy credit for not being a total moron."

"That's why I brought a copy of the DNA test with me," said Diego smugly.

"You're really getting on my nerves, wise ass," she shot back and decided to direct the rest of her comments toward Serge who, after all, wasn't a macho idiot.

"If Mackinnon buys that Diego is John Cameron's son, they'll kill him, just like they murdered Will," she said, her voice cracking. "This is a horrible idea and I won't do it! I'm not going to help you commit suicide," she shrieked. The two men might believe that they could take care of Mackinnon and Company themselves, but it was time for her to get off this thrill ride. Diego would have a bull's eye on his back as soon as Mackinnon found out that he's John's son. No. She wouldn't allow it.

"I know this scares you, but please hear us out before you reject this idea," Diego said.

"Fine, I'll listen. And I'm totally calm. See?" Alex held out a hand that was rock steady. "You were saying... ?" she added sarcastically, with exaggerated patience, but nothing was going to persuade her to change her mind.

"We agree that Mairi's the wild card, but only if she recognized one of us," Diego began. "Serge registered us as Barbara and Rick Sloane so even the hotel staff doesn't know who we are. Nothing is different from before we ran into her last night."

"And what about when we tell Mackinnon who you are? What if Mairi sees us there and then tells him that we're Serge's friends, the Sloanes?" Alex asked.

"That's a lot of what ifs. Serge can keep Mairi busy here. The last thing she'll have on her mind is a visit to her Uncle Jamie's store if he does his job the way I know he can. Right?" he said, turning to Serge who nodded.

"Am I the only rational person here?" Alex's face flushed as her exasperation reached new heights. "If Serge is with Mairi, then the two of us are on our own. Bad idea."

"You think I can't protect us?" Diego lashed out. "I can defend myself—and you—with a gun, a knife or my hands, but it's not going to come to that. Don't forget, Mackinnon's not expecting us and one old man isn't going to take us on during the day in a busy store."

Alex looked toward Serge for confirmation.

"I wouldn't send the two of you off unless I'd already assessed the threat level," Serge began with cool confidence. "And if something unexpected happens, I have total faith in my student. He can definitely take care of himself and you, too. His only flaw, and the one that worries me most," Serge continued looking directly at Diego, "is that he sometimes has trouble maintaining the detachment needed in combat, but maybe that rush of adrenalin works for him."

Diego crouched in front of Alex's chair, but she refused to meet his eyes as he began to speak softly. "Alex, they were able to get to Will because his father never told him about their family's connection to these people. John didn't let Will know that he could be a target." He wrapped his warm hands around her cold fingers and waited patiently until she looked at him. Her eyes were filled with tears, but he ignored them. "The difference is that I'm prepared for them."

"He's right, Alex." Serge sounded so certain, but there were too many unknowns for her to buy into it. It terrified her that Diego was willing to risk his life. She'd never be able to survive another body being lowered into the ground. Was vengeance really that important? After all, nothing they did would bring her husband back.

When she finally looked up, she realized that both men were waiting for her to say something. "You're both wrong. We should go to the police, tell them everything and let them take care of Mackinnon and whoever else is involved. They're professionals; we're not."

"The so-called professionals haven't made an arrest yet. We've dug up most of the evidence and we're going to follow through on it," said Diego. "Maybe we'll bring in the authorities at some point, but not yet."

Alex sighed and began to stretch her neck from side to side as she pushed herself out of the deep chair, then touched her toes. Even that minimal amount of movement made her feel better. "Can we take a break? Maybe a run will help me work off some nerves and then we can try this again."

"Good idea. You two go, but stay alert," Serge warned. He recognized that for now Alex and Diego were each firmly dug into their positions and unlikely to budge. He didn't want to waste any more time as they argued. "I managed to place a bug in Mackinnon's house and haven't listened to the overnights from there yet. I'll do that while you're gone."

After Serge hustled Mairi out of the hotel the night before, she'd directed the taxi driver to drop her off at Mackinnon's cottage instead of at her parents' house. Whenever she was upset, she could count on "Uncle" Jamie for good advice.

Serge's abrupt dismissal had wounded her, but hurt quickly turned to anger at the insulting way he'd treated her. He acted like she was good enough for a shag, but not the sort he'd want for company when he was dining with his fancy friends. Not just that, but she'd been stupid enough to spend her entire paycheck on a new dress to impress him and the dolt hadn't even noticed!

If Steve Spencer thought he could use Mairi Graham and send her away when it suited him, he didn't know her very well. Her Da had told her often enough that she'd cut off her nose to spite her face and that such behavior was childish. Maybe so, but it felt good to retaliate, even if it was she who lost in the end.

Steve's friends had seemed like a nice enough couple. The woman was friendly and the husband was as hand-some as a film star. But then Steve had tossed her out and so she was on her way to Uncle Jamie's instead of spending the evening with her rich American and his posh friends.

Mairi saw with relief that the lights were still on in James Mackinnon's small house. He hardly ever went to bed early, but it was after nine and he was getting old. He answered her knock quickly. "Mairi girl! What a nice surprise. And don't you look lovely tonight. Have you been to a party, lass?"

Her throat tightened and she threw her arms around his neck and sobbed as he drew her inside and onto the front room's shabby, threadbare sofa. "There, there, lass. Has some bloke broken your heart then? Shall I throttle him for ye?"

She nodded, then blew her nose when he handed her his handkerchief.

"You don't know the half of it Uncle Jamie," she said when she regained her composure. "Did Da tell you that I'd met an American who offered me a position as nanny at his house in Florida?"

"Aye, he did mention it. Are we talking about the same man who you sent along to my shop the other day? The rich one with stores all over Florida?

"Aye, that's the one. I forgot that you met him. What did you think of him?"

Mackinnon's bushy, white eyebrows rose and fell with a life of their own as he considered her question. "The man seemed decent enough. There's something about him though—I can't put my finger on it—but it's a feeling that all's not quite as it seems. After my many years in trade I have a canny sense about people and there was something off about this one."

"Da says he doesn't trust any man who'd offer a job to a girl right after meeting her. Why he might even plan to sell me into white slavery! Imagine that. When I brought Steve home, he asked a lot of questions about young Jamie running off to America and then leaving sudden like for John O'Groats. He was even curious about you and why your James is in jail. I thought it was just chat and his way of getting to know the family better, but it was all very strange. I was daft to believe Steve would take me to America. After tonight it looks like I'll forever be stuck here in Scotland." She took a sip of the hot tea Mackinnon had poured for her. "Do you have any biscuits? I could use a sweet."

As he rummaged in the kitchen for the box of cookies, Mackinnon took a quick nip from the bottle he kept on the kitchen counter. He was startled by her mention of both his Jamies—son and grandson. There was no reason for Mairi's American to be interested in them unless ... no, it couldn't be.

"Tell me what's troubling you lass. You may be young, but you're a keen judge of character. You thought this man was all right and now you don't. Did he try some funny business with you?"

"No, it's nothing like that. Maybe it's my fault. I stopped in at his hotel tonight for a pint. We hadn't arranged a meeting or anything, but I'd bought a new dress and..."

"Ah, so you're sweet on the man. He's a bit old for you, isn't he, and he has a wife and bairns back in the States. Mairi, you wouldn't be so foolish as to take up with a married man, would you lass?"

"Ach no, Uncle Jamie. I wanted to see him is all ... to have a chat about the nanny position, you know?" But the pink blush that crawled up her neck to her cheeks was a dead giveaway of her true intentions and it didn't go unnoticed.

"So what happened? Did ye find him?"

"Oh, I did, yes. I caught sight of him on his way to the hotel's restaurant. He was with two Americans—business associates of his he said—and he introduced me, but then he rushed me out of the hotel like he was ashamed to be seen with me. I couldn't join them, he said, because they had to talk about some deal they were working on. So after he tossed me out like rubbish, I came here." She reached for another biscuit and brushed the crumbs from the first off her lap.

"Associates of his you say? I can't imagine that stores in Florida do enough business in Scotland to cause three of them to be over here at the same time," he said, as he rubbed his chin. "I'm surprised there's even one, truth be told."

"They're working on some other venture, not the shops. It was coincidence that they met up, Steve said, as they happened to be in Scotland on holiday. They seemed nice enough, especially the woman. She's beautiful and her husband is a handsome devil."

"Were you told their names?"

"Yes. Let me think for a minute. I remember that hers was Barbara and his..." she chewed her lower lip as she thought. "Oh, I've got it! Barbara and Rick Sloane. That's it. She's tall and slim with auburn hair and she wore the most beautiful emerald and diamond wedding ring. Must have cost a king's ransom. I noticed it because I couldn't help gawking at her handsome husband and she put her arm in his to let me know he was taken. Her eyes are a beautiful light green which is why she's partial to emeralds, I suppose," she said innocently.

"And this devilishly handsome man. What did he look like?"

"You seem awfully curious about a pair of strangers

Uncle Jamie." She raised her eyebrows and waited for an explanation.

"Just making conversation, lass, that's all. And like your Da, I don't quite trust your American so I'm interested in his friends."

"Ah, well then. To answer your question, I thought the man was a film star or at least a model. He's that good looking and his clothes fit like they were made for him. His body was as fine as his face, I don't mind saying." Mairi blushed again as she realized she might have revealed a bit too much to someone who still saw her as a child so she hurried on. "Let's see ... he's tall, a wee bit taller than his wife and has lovely black hair and dark eyes that seemed to be laughing. I can't blame his wife for hanging on to him. I would do the same."

"They sound like a fine pair and I'm sure they would have enjoyed your company," he said and patted her hand paternally. "Do you think you're well enough to go home? I'm old and tired and it's soon to bed for me, but I'll see you safe home first."

Instead of returning to his house after he dropped Mairi off, Mackinnon drove to his shop. He unlocked a battered, black file cabinet in the store's cramped back office and removed a photo of Alexandra Cameron and Diego Navarro strolling arm in arm on a Boston street. He placed the picture on his desk and stared at it. Mairi's description fit these two perfectly. Could it be? And if it was them, why were they in Scotland, especially in the company of the Florida businessman who was so interested in Mairi and asking about young Jamie? Perhaps the American's curiosity about his shop and the Mackinnon family was not so innocent after all.

CHAPTER 30

*S*erge's jaw throbbed as he clenched, then unclenched, his teeth as if he were chewing gum. External signs of inner turmoil were rare in a man trained to compartmentalize his emotions, but he knew his cover was cracking like ice in late winter. "Damn the girl," he muttered as he listened to Mairi Graham give Mackinnon a detailed description of Alex and Diego during her late night chat with the old man.

What angered him most was that there was no one but himself to blame for the fuck up. He should never have been seen in public with Alex and Diego like some amateur. It was his fault that they'd been ID'd by Mackinnon. He'd allowed his dick to overrule his head despite knowing that indulging in a fine piece of ass like Mairi's often led to trouble. That was Diego's style, not his, and he didn't like what that momentary lapse had cost him.

He rolled his shoulders and forced himself to focus as he listened to the recording for the third time. It confirmed that they'd lost their greatest advantage — surprise — and along with it the enemy's cocky carelessness. A quick check of the readout from the tracking device on Mackinnon's car did nothing to ease his mind. In addition to showing the route the man took to drive Mairi home, it also indicated a late night stop at his store.

The two phone calls made by Mackinnon on his office's bugged phone increased Serge's uneasiness.

Mackinnon clearly doubted "Steve Spencer's" identity and may have already ID'd Alex and Diego. The old man's hunch that Barbara and Rick Sloane were really Diego Navarro and Alex Cameron meant they were in deep shit and what had he just done? Sent them for a run ... unprotected. Schmuck! He tore out of the hotel and prayed that they were still on the riverside jogging path he'd suggested.

Early that morning Mackinnon placed a hand-lettered sign in the shop's front window: "Opening at Noon Today." It was his custom to unlock the door at ten, but it was his store and he could open for business whenever he damn well pleased. Instead, after only a few hours of fitful sleep, he sat in his parked car just down the road from the posh hotel Mairi had told him was home to her American friends. He was chilled and hungry for his morning porridge and tea, but he had to see if his gut was right about these people.

His patience was rewarded an hour after his vigil began when an attractive young couple emerged from the hotel in running clothes. Nervous anticipation made his hands tremble as he picked up a pair of binoculars from the passenger seat and lifted them to his eyes. The woman's auburn hair was a bit longer than in the photo he had, but he was sure she was Alexandra Cameron. And there was no mistaking the black haired, handsome devil with her as Will Cameron's South American friend, Diego Navarro. He remembered the warning he'd received about Navarro from their contact in

America—the man is rich, powerful and hot-tempered and therefore a serious threat.

What surprised Mackinnon even more than their presence in Inverness was the passionate kiss the two shared before they began to run. Perhaps they'd done the lass a favor by getting rid of her husband if that's the way it was between her and the dead man's best friend. But what did he expect? It was a well-known fact that American women were fast and loose with their bodies, but it disappointed him that this woman, a Scottish lass descended from the valiant Gillies Mor MacBain, behaved like a common whore as well.

Serge realized it wasn't going to be easy to spot Alex and Diego. Their height usually made them stand out in any crowd, but among Scots—many of whom counted Vikings among their forebears—a 5-foot-10-inch woman and a 6-foot-4-inch man weren't so unusual. He'd covered about two miles along the riverside path before he saw them slowly jogging toward him on their way back to the hotel.

They looked so damn happy that he momentarily regretted that once they listened to Mackinnon's taped conversations that look would vanish. Then he hardened the place where his heart resided—his job was to protect their bodies; their emotions were their business.

Diego smiled and waved when he spotted Serge. "Decided to give your fat ass some exercise?" he teased. Serge ignored the taunt and hugged his friend so he could whisper instructions in Diego's ear.

"Keep smiling and put your arm around Alex. Behave as if nothing's wrong, but get back to the hotel.

Now! Don't ask questions. Just do it." Serge broke the embrace, pounded Diego on the back, and laughed as if they'd just shared a hilarious joke.

Minutes later, in the secure sanctuary of Serge's suite, Diego's back stiffened as he listened to Mairi accurately describe him and Alex to Mackinnon.

"The old fool's definitely on to us. It's time for me to pay him a visit and confirm his suspicions. That's what we pretty much decided anyway," Diego said as Alex sprawled in a chair and guzzled water. She tried not to look worried, but her churning insides indicated otherwise.

"What do you think?" she asked Serge, certain that he'd never allow Diego and Mackinnon in the same room despite their earlier conversation about doing precisely that.

"Before I answer your question, Alex, there's more," Serge said. "The GPS shows that Mackinnon went from Mairi's house to his store instead of going home. He made some calls from there and right now he's sitting in his car outside this hotel. I'm sure he saw the two of you leave for your run and come back with me." He gripped Diego's arm to stop him from walking to the window to check. "No! You know you're an easy target when you stand in a window! He could have you in the crosshairs of a high-powered rifle! Dammit, Diego, I trained you to think defensively. You better tell your memory to retrieve that training and use it." His lecture was delivered in a way that cut off any debate. "I've allowed the two of you a lot of freedom and that's about to end. No arguments," he finished as Diego opened his mouth.

"I was just going to ask," Diego said the words with deliberation, "who Mackinnon called last night and what was said."

Serge hit "play" and they heard the unfamiliar

dialing sounds of Mackinnon's ancient rotary phone before a half-asleep, male voice answered.

"Jamie, lad. Sorry to wake you ... Yes, it's Grandda. Pay careful attention, boyo. You must leave Geordie's farm and you must do it now. Cameron's people are in Scotland and they may know where you are. No, you may not go back to sleep until morning. Do it now and don't argue!" he roared. "Go to the next safe house. Don't even take time to pack a bag. Tell no one — no one at all — where you're going. And lad, keep your mobile phone close. I'll ring you later to see you've arrived safe. God be with you."

Mackinnon didn't wait for his grandson to reply before he ended the call. He knew the young man would follow instructions. He'd killed Cameron's son and the lad knew he could end up in jail just like his Da ... or worse.

"Shit, shit, shit!" Diego said. His face flushed with anger and he ran both hands through his hair as he strode from one end of the room to the other.

"Now what?" Alex asked in a small voice. She moved to the edge of her chair and began to twist the towel she'd used minutes earlier to mop the post-run sweat from her face.

"Before we consider our next move, you need to listen to one more conversation," said Serge.

"Crap. There's more?" Diego said, but Serge had already switched the machine on.

Alex wrapped her arms around herself as the sound of Mackinnon's voice filled the room. Just the thought of the man made her skin crawl and she shuddered in anticipation of hearing his heavy Scottish burr again. But the next voice on the tape wasn't Mackinnon's. It was another half-asleep male who identified himself when he answered the phone as Michael Graham.

"Is that Mairi's father?" Diego was as stunned to hear this name as Serge had been earlier.

Serge nodded and put a finger to his lips. "Shhh. Listen."

"Michael, we've a problem," began Mackinnon.

"Aye?"

"Yes. You know the American that your Mairi's sweet on?

"I do. Has he done something to her, then? I'll kill him if he forced himself on the lass!"

"No, it's naught to do with the lass so you've no need yet to reach for that pistol you keep beneath your bed. She's been a great help in fact. She told me about some associates of the American who have joined him here."

"And what of it? This is why you woke me in the middle of the night?" Michael responded angrily.

"It's who those people are that should worry you—young Cameron's widow and one of the dead lad's friends."

"You're daft, man. That can't be. Where would my Mairi have come across those two anyway?"

"She went to the hotel hoping to see her American and she spotted him and his friends going into the restaurant. But when this Steve Spencer introduced them to your Mairi, he gave them different names. Her description sounded so much like the Cameron woman and Navarro that I went to the shop to look at the photos sent by our man in Boston. It seems a match, but I plan to have a look at the two of them in the morning with me own eyes to be sure."

"Bugger and blast! If it's them, this is bad."

"Aye, 'tis. I've already ordered young Jamie to leave Geordie's for the next safe house."

"You've done well, James. If your hunch is right, we're in for stormy seas. I'll come by the shop at noon. Get some sleep."

Alex's head was spinning. This plan to snare Mackinnon had suddenly sprouted more tentacles than an octopus. She'd stopped believing that they could pull it off, even if she went along with the idea to dangle an armed and dangerous Diego as bait.

"Did you get the impression that Graham was the one giving the orders?" Diego asked Serge.

"I did. Graham steered the conversation and it was he who ended the call. Mackinnon is probably the number two and Graham the mastermind, but when Mairi brought me home so her parents could check me out, her father did a good job convincing me that he's a simple family man who worked hard to support his brood. He seemed bored when I turned the discussion to Scottish politics."

"If he's in charge, that means he's more of a threat to us than Mackinnon, right?" Alex asked.

"Definitely." Serge rubbed a day's growth of stubble on his chin. "Graham apparently gives the orders and Mackinnon sees that they're carried out."

"It seems strange that Will's father never mentioned anyone named Michael Graham when he told me that he'd betrayed these people and turned in Mackinnon's son. I wonder if John even knows him," Alex commented.

"I don't give a shit about Graham or Mackinnon or who John Cameron knows or doesn't know!" Diego said as his lips thinned and his eyes blazed with anger. "What do we do about this grandson? Can we assume from one conversation that he's the murderer? Fucking hell, we have to be sure."

Serge watched Diego pace for a few minutes before responding. "We can't go off half-cocked or we could blow the whole operation. I know you're running out of patience, but can we agree that I'm the professional here?" Serge waited until Diego nodded before continuing. "Everything we know points to the grandson as Will's assassin so we've got to find out where they've stashed him. I'll listen to all of the tapes again and re-examine Mackinnon's movements to see if I interpret them differently with this new information. Your being in Scotland has to have shaken them. And if they're as scared right now as I think they are, there's likely to be more activity and that may draw out the rest of them. Give me twenty-four hours to come up with at least two ways to resolve this and then we'll make a decision. Sound good?"

"I guess we have no choice," Diego conceded grudgingly.

"I want you and Alex to spend a couple of nights in some remote Highland village so I can focus on our options without distractions."

"Excellent idea," Diego agreed a bit too eagerly for Serge's peace of mind.

"This is serious. They know who you are and what both of you look like which makes you easy marks." Serge looked directly at Diego. "Do you hear me? I know you Navarro. Don't do anything that will piss me off."

"Who, me? Piss you off? When have I ever done that?" Diego taunted. "All right, all right. It won't be a hardship to spend a few days in the country, will it Alex?"

"I'd love to get far away from this mess. I can be ready to leave in an hour."

• • •

Serge stood at the window and scanned the area around the hotel's entrance with binoculars capable of spotting a strand of hair two hundred yards away. Mackinnon had left a while ago, but with Diego and Alex's presence no longer a secret, he had to be sure that one of his accomplices hadn't continued the old man's surveillance. It was risky to expose them like this, but the bodyguard was confident that it was too soon for a tail to have been arranged. They'd be safer in the countryside, but until they were out of sight he would remain vigilant.

"Go!" he instructed Diego without turning away from his post once he was sure the area was clear. He kept his eyes on the two of them as Diego tossed two overnight bags in the Mini Cooper and then held the passenger door open for Alex. But the woman didn't get in. Instead she folded her arms and said something to Diego. Serge would have liked to hear what they were saying, but Alex had her back to him so he couldn't read her lips. It was entertaining to watch her challenge Diego's usual role as the dominant partner.

"Give me the keys, Navarro. You said you don't like to drive here ... roundabouts ... wrong side ... remember?"

"That was yesterday. This is now," he stated. Alex didn't have the energy to argue and it didn't seem like this would be a fight she could win. Maybe driving would calm him down and if they got lost, so what? They had no schedule or destination anyway.

Minutes later Diego sped past a sign pointing to the road north. "You missed the turnoff for the motorway. Are you sure you don't want me to drive?"

"I have to make a stop before we leave Inverness."

"Oh?" she said, afraid to hear where that stop would be.

"I should buy a small gift for my parents. And you'll

want to bring something home for Francie. I'm told there's a nice souvenir shop around here somewhere," he said with the innocence of a choirboy.

Alex grabbed the wheel, but Diego righted the car before they careened into a lamppost.

"Are you crazy? Do you want to get us killed?"

"No, but you do! You heard Serge. We're absolutely, positively not going to Mackinnon's or at least I'm not. Stop the car."

"He already knows we're here, so why hide? Come on, Alex. He saw us when we went for a run this morning."

"Diego, this isn't smart. You know it and I know it. What if he has a gun and shoots both of us? Has that possibility even entered your pea brain?"

"You worry too much. Mackinnon isn't going to kill us. When he sees me, he'll be afraid that I'm going to kill him."

"How can you be so sure?"

"Because my reflexes are better than his could ever be," he said as he patted the holster under his arm.

He gave Alex what she recognized as "the look," indicating that nothing and no one could change his mind. So what if an expert had trained him in self-defense, she thought. That wouldn't make what they were about to do any less risky. She could refuse to go along with whatever asinine scheme he'd come up with, but she couldn't let him face Mackinnon alone. "What are you going to do when we get there?"

"I'm not sure yet. We'll improvise. Just follow my lead," he blithely said as he swung the car into a parking space near Mackinnon's store. His eyes met her scowl as he gallantly extended a hand — which she rejected — to help her out of the low-slung car.

"I still think this is idiotic and Serge will be furious. You're the most stubborn, arrogant, foolish, egotistical..." she sputtered. When Diego tried to end her outburst with a kiss, she shoved him away.

"Didn't I tell you in Miami that you're safe with me? I meant that. I only want to play a little game with our friend, nothing more."

It was obvious that one of them was looking forward to the face-off and Alex knew it wasn't her.

The bell jangled as they opened the door to Mackinnon's store and the old man glanced up from the newspaper he'd been reading at his perch behind the counter. If he was surprised to see them, he did a good job of hiding it.

"Good afternoon. And how may I be of help to you today?" Mackinnon asked innocently.

Alex was overwhelmed by an eerie sense of *déjà vu* as her eyes scanned the store she'd last visited with Will. That memory made her as incapable of speech as someone whose tongue has been shot full of Novocain. Diego had no such problem.

"I recently learned that my father is Scottish so I'm trying to find out more about my family," Diego began. "I was told that your store has this area's best collection of books on the various clans. I hope that's true."

Alex regained her focus and reluctantly admired Diego for both his acting and his *cojones*. Besides, there was no stopping him now. Mackinnon was playing his own hand like a world-class poker champ too.

"I'll be happy to help you young man, if you'll tell me your family name. Are you American by any chance?"

"Well, technically, yes, but you probably mean the United States when you say American. I'm from South America. Argentina."

"Well, then, this is a remarkable day. Scots from around the world visit to find their roots, but you, sir, are the first person from your country to grace my wee shop. What did you say your family name is?"

"Our name is Navarro. But that's not the Scottish part."

"Ah, so it's your mother who's Scottish?"

"No. Her people are Sicilian."

"I'm puzzled, young man, truly I am. Didn't you say that your father is Scottish? I'm old and easily confused, but my ears still work fine." He chuckled and raised bushy, gray eyebrows that resembled aging caterpillars resting above each eye.

Diego laughed and shook his head. He leaned toward Mackinnon as if to impart some vital information. "If you think you're confused, imagine how I felt when I found out that my father isn't really my father, but that's a story for another day. The family I want to know more about is named Cameron. It's especially important to me now, because I seem to be the last of our line. Well, except for my so-called father, that is. My brother died recently."

"God rest his soul." Mackinnon said and made the sign of the cross.

I can't believe the fucking hypocrite just crossed himself, Alex seethed and she turned her face away to hide her anger. She rested a hand on Diego's back to prevent him from exploding, but he seemed calm, although he'd shifted his body slightly to put himself between her and Mackinnon.

"Cameron is it, you say?" Mackinnon continued. Despite his composed demeanor, there was a definite tremor in the proprietor's hand as he finally laid the newspaper on the counter. Diego's face reddened as if he was having a hot flash. Alex decided that her tag team partner needed a break before he lost it. It was her turn to climb into the ring whether she wanted to or not.

"Hello again, Mr. Mackinnon," she said, deliberately adopting an unthreatening, girlish voice to offset the quiet menace in Diego's. "I don't expect you to remember me, but my husband and I visited your store almost two years ago. I'm Alexandra Cameron," she said and extended her hand. When he grasped hers, she noticed his was damp.

"I can't say as I recall you or not, but welcome back, Mrs. Cameron. I must say that I'm quite confused so let me be sure I understand. Is this handsome lad who wants to know more about Clan Cameron your husband?" he asked and seemed to be genuinely perplexed.

"Oh, no. This is my brother-in-law, Diego. Will ... my husband ... is dead." The words raised goose bumps on her arms and sent a chill down her spine despite the summer day.

"Ah, so that's the man your ... brother-in-law here made mention of? I'm sorry to hear that, lass. My condolences. Was your man ill?"

"He was murdered. Stabbed to death by some madman." She fought the impulse to jump over the counter and squeeze the man's fat, wobbly neck until his eyes popped. Or she could grab one of the gleaming *sgian dubhs* from the glass display and plunge the blade into his heart. Instead, she smiled and dabbed a tear from her eye. I can give a performance at least as good as his, she thought as she glanced at Diego and saw him casually reach beneath his arm as if to scratch an itch. She hoped he was just assuring himself that the gun holstered there was within easy reach and not that he was getting ready to use it. She had no doubt that he was battling the same murderous impulses as she was and prayed they could maintain their composure.

"My God! Stabbed you say!" the old man exclaimed. "We hear about American violence, but that's terrible. Have the police caught the brute who did this awful thing to your husband?"

Mackinnon said this guilelessly and Alex dug her nails into her palms to keep from screaming. So this is what it's like to be in the presence of pure evil, she thought. She wanted to run away, but couldn't. She touched Diego's arm in an effort to ground herself and he drew her close.

"Are you all right?" he murmured and pressed his lips to her temple.

"Yes … fine," but she remained glued to his side, comforted by his body's strength and its warmth.

"My brother's wife still grieves for him," Diego said, by way of explanation. "To answer your question, some very solid leads are being pursued. You can be sure that the people who murdered my brother will be identified—very soon, in fact—and punished."

Diego leaned toward Mackinnon and quietly hissed the next words. "I believe your countrymen used to draw and quarter their worst criminals—hang them until not quite dead, then undo the noose, lay them out, cut their entrails and beating heart from the body and hack off their head to be displayed in the public square. I understand this kind of punishment. I want the people who killed my brother, my blood, to suffer like that." He said the words with such icy malice that Mackinnon shivered and paled.

"I can see I've upset you. Please accept my apology," Diego said as he patted the old man's hand. "And now

HARRIET SCHULTZ

can you recommend a book for me about the Cameron clan so I can learn about my ancestors?"

"Of course, of course," said Mackinnon, as he quickly pulled a couple of books off his well-stocked shelves and placed them on the counter. He was desperate for a drink and wanted these two out of his shop. "These should provide you with your family's history. And you're welcome to ask me about the Camerons as well," he said as he charged the sale to Diego's credit card.

"I do have one question that won't be answered in those books," Diego said coolly as he fixed his glittering eyes on Mackinnon like a cougar about to spring upon its prey. "Can you tell me what kind of monster could hate my brother enough to end his life? Answer that one for me," said Diego as he turned, clasped Alex's hand and left the shop.

Mackinnon's body was vibrating with fright and it took a few minutes for him to notice that Diego had left the bag of books he'd bought on the counter. He took a long swig and then another from the flask of whiskey he kept under the counter and hoped he'd stop shaking before Michael Graham arrived for the lunch meeting they'd arranged the night before.

CHAPTER 31

*S*on of a bitch! That fucking stupid jackass!" Serge shouted his fury into the suite's emptiness as soon as his headphones picked up the exchange between Mackinnon, Diego and Alex. He fought the impulse to race to his own car, find Diego, and break both of his arms and maybe his legs and then strangle the head-strong prick.

Slowly, slowly, he steered his thoughts back to his original task. Anger clouded the mind and there was no time to indulge his emotions. Perhaps he'd been wrong to teach a man like Diego to defend himself. How was he supposed to protect someone whose courage, confidence and bullheaded determination made him behave like he was invincible?

Since it couldn't be undone, he'd have to devise a way to use Diego's move to their advantage. For the moment there was only silence coming from Mackinnon's and a quick check of the tracker he'd stuck to Diego's car showed it finally heading north out of Inverness. "Thank God," he sighed.

The silence from the shop was suddenly broken when Michael Graham's voice came booming through Serge's earpieces.

"James! James! What happened, man? Are you all right?" Graham shouted. When he'd let himself into the store through the back door, he found that the shop was dark and the front door locked. Mackinnon was on the floor, fast asleep, an empty flask of whiskey beside his snoring body. The old man raised his bleary eyes and smiled foolishly at Michael.

"You're pissed!" exclaimed Graham.

"Aye, I am that. And with good reason," slurred Mackinnon as he sagged to the floor. "Shite! Help me up and you'll soon understand why I needed a wee nip."

Graham dragged a chair across the room and groaned loudly as he hefted the old man's bulk into it. "All right. Out with it," he ordered, "or shall I pour a bucket of ice water down your wrinkled neck to sober you up? You know I'd do it!"

"No, Michael, just leave me be for a minute. I slept off the worst of it," said Mackinnon irritably, but Graham wasn't one to wait when he wanted an answer.

"What happened here? Start talking. Now!" he demanded. Graham's hands were on his hips, his legs spread as he tapped one foot impatiently and glared at the pathetic figure.

The old man scrubbed his trembling hands over his face and concentrated on the day's events. He needed to have his wits about him to be sure Michael understood the threat. When he spoke, his voice was hoarse, his speech hesitant.

"You'll remember a call I made to you, Michael ... oh, I believe it was some two years ago, in which I said, 'You'll never believe who walked into my shop today?' Do ye recall that?"

"Aye, of course I do. You rang me up the day the American Judas's son came to see you."

"Right."

"The lad's dead, so what in hell does that have to do with what happened here today?"

"Patience, Michael. Let me think for a minute. I'm old and tired and a wee bit tight yet and I need to get this right."

Graham was annoyed, but decided to give Mackinnon a chance to gather his thoughts.

"Ah, well," he resumed. "I can say the very same words to you now. 'You'll never believe who walked into my shop today.'"

"What are you babbling about you old fool? You said those words the day Cameron's son came to your shop. The traitorous swine had but the one son and he's dead. Young Jamie showed us a photo of the body after he killed the man and brought back news clippings as proof."

"Yes, the lad did a braw job, but we didn't do our part nearly as well. It turns out Mr. John Cameron spread his seed in more than one garden. The man fathered another son."

Graham's mouth opened, but no words came out.

"It was this second Cameron son who visited my shop today. He was with the dead man's widow." Good Christ, his head hurt. He reached for the flask that Michael had taken from him, but the younger man slapped his hand and tossed the container away with enough force to knock over a display of postcards.

"What exactly did this man say? I want to know every word!"

Mackinnon watched Graham warily. Maybe if he didn't speak of it, it wouldn't be so. But he knew deep in his soul that it was. Michael and the others had to be warned.

"He knows."

"He knows what? Damn it to Christ, what does he know?"

"He knows his brother was murdered and he has a good idea who did it. He said ... he said," the man had trouble getting the sinister words out. "He said he wants to watch those responsible for his kin's death drawn and quartered the way he saw it done to William Wallace in that blasted Braveheart film. You should have seen the way he looked at me, eyes black as coal, shooting fire like some kind of demon." Mackinnon shivered as his voice trailed off.

"Come on, man. Perhaps he has suspicions, but he can't be certain unless you were daft enough to ... to," he sputtered. "You didn't, did you?" Michael grabbed the sweating man by the front of his shirt and pulled him to his feet until they were nose-to-nose. "Did you?" he snarled, shaking Mackinnon hard enough to make his jowls jiggle, an action that helped the older man to completely sober up.

"You'll take your hands off me, Michael Graham, and you'll do so now," he said indignantly. "You may be running this operation, laddie, but I am still your elder."

"I was wrong to lay hands on you, but I must have answers. Start with this man's name."

"He said he's Diego Navarro, the very same rich and powerful friend of the dead lad who we'd been warned about. The one I told you about last night and the one I saw kissing the widow Cameron this morning outside the hotel. He's from South America, he said ... Argentina to be precise."

"And are you so easily fooled that you believe a South American named Navarro is John Cameron's son? Is it just that he said so? Perhaps he was spinning a tale to see how you'd react. Did you think of that, James?"

"If he was lying, the lad should go to Hollywood.

He offered no proof, but neither did I ask for any. I was too befuddled to think."

"It could be that the widow Cameron is more clever than we thought and brought this man here to scare us. Look at the facts. The investigation by the police in America has come to naught so it's natural that the family wants someone to pay for the lad's murder. We understand that need for vengeance. It's what drove us to do what we did to Cameron's son.

"Aye," agreed Mackinnon. "If that gobshite hadn't spilled his guts to the blasted English about the scheme to set off bombs in London, my son would be home with his family instead of in some stinking prison and my grandson wouldn't be a murderer on the run."

"At least you know young Jamie's out of harm's way."

"He's at the next safe house as I told you. After Mairi's visit, I was afraid they might somehow be on to him too, which reminds me … in all of the excitement I almost forgot the original reason for our meeting today and the news I had for you. I tell you Michael, my head's too old for this sort of thing."

"Nay, James. You've had a shock." Graham realized he'd have to go easy with the old man to get the rest of the story.

"Aye, that I have. Two, actually. If you brought lunch, I think I could eat a bit. Let's sit in my office. And grab that bag from the counter. Our visitor obviously cares nothing for money. He paid for his purchases and then left them behind. I think the receipt with his credit card information is in there. Perhaps it will help."

Serge nodded and tried not to feel smug that Mackinnon's

own words provided ironclad proof that the youngest James Mackinnon—grandson of the shopkeeper
and son of the imprisoned bomber—murdered Will
Cameron. Any jury would buy it if illegal wiretaps were
allowed into evidence. He had it on tape, straight from
the old man's mouth.

This indisputable evidence might help Alex overcome her qualms about the three of them acting as judge,
jury and executioner. They had to convince her that their
course of action was justified. Like Diego, Serge knew
that even if the police tracked down the killer, a smart
lawyer might get an acquittal on some technicality.

Their justice would be simple and direct: an eye for
an eye. Mackinnon's careless talk had sealed his grandson's fate. All Serge needed to discover was the location
of the safe house that Mackinnon had mentioned. He
turned his attention back to the voices coming through
his headset.

"When I rang you last night Michael, you'll remember I
told you that your Mairi came by the house because she
felt slighted by that American bloke she fancies, though
he must be close to your age," the older man added.

"She'll not be seeing him again, you can be sure of
that. You said that the lass met some of his friends and
her description made you suspicious enough to look at
our photos of the Cameron woman and Navarro?"

Mackinnon brushed wisps of gray hair off his
forehead and cleared his throat. "Yes, but I had to be
sure so this morning I took it upon myself to sit in my
car outside their posh hotel and who did I see but the
man and woman who turned up in my shop today.

And the shameless way those two behaved makes me believe they're more than friends if you get my drift." He waggled his bushy eyebrows lasciviously.

"You've still got the photos of them, aye? I want a good look at this man who claims to be a Cameron." Graham opened the folder and pulled several pictures from the pile. "Our man in Boston liked to use his camera, I see."

"I suppose it was his way to prove that he did the job we paid for," Mackinnon shrugged. He groaned and stretched his lower back as he stood next to Graham. "This one is the widow Cameron, the bonnie Alexandra," Mackinnon said pointing to a close up of Alex. "And that handsome devil," he said, "is Navarro. Put his next to one of the dead Cameron lad."

They studied the photos of the purported brothers. "Both have the same height and body shape, but I don't see a great resemblance," said Mackinnon finally. "Do you believe they're related, Michael?"

"Maybe so and maybe no. Brothers don't always look alike. What's important is that this Navarro told you he's the dead man's brother and the widow confirmed it. Navarro obviously was letting you know that he plans to avenge the lad's murder whether they share the same blood or not."

"And what if it's true that this man is also John Cameron's son? Then what, Michael?"

"It may not matter. We don't know if Cameron's acknowledged this latest son or has feelings for him. We did away with the son we knew of to punish his father, to rob him of the person he loved most, not just to end his clan. If he has no affection for this Navarro, perhaps the debt is settled. On the other hand, it may be wise to do away with him in case he has a mind to kill us himself or turn us over to the law. The lad clearly issued a challenge, after all. And don't forget that there's still a wee chance that the widow is with child and, if so, that particular Cameron will never see the light of day. Never!"

Mackinnon quaked at hearing the chill in Graham's voice. Although he himself had said the same words when he'd suspected a pregnancy after Alex's visit to a doctor who treats female conditions, he knew it had been just blather. He couldn't condone hurting a woman or an innocent babe, but he didn't know if anyone could stop Michael. The younger man seemed to have no conscience.

"I'm sure I don't need to remind you, Michael, that we gave our word there would be no more violence unless every one of us agreed. We must talk this over with the others. Shall I arrange a meeting at the cathedral in Elgin?"

Graham considered the idea. "There's no time for that. We must act quickly, before this Navarro and the woman leave Scotland. A second murder in Boston would be too risky, so if it's to be done, it must be here. Set up a conference call for..." he glanced at his watch, "about eight tonight. Can you arrange that James?"

"Aye, I've done it before. I'll phone the others. Will you take the call at home?"

"My house is filled with noise and has too many big ears within its walls. I'll come here shortly before eight."

"Fine. I'd best go out front and open up before the constable who walks this street every afternoon comes to check on me. Mackinnon started around the desk when he spotted the bag Diego had left behind. "We should have a look inside, Michael. Who knows, the man's credit card slip may be of some use. " When Mackinnon dumped the books Diego had bought onto the desk, an envelope slid out. "What's this? There's something written on the outside. I'll get my spectacles."

Graham impatiently snatched the envelope from his friend's gnarled fingers. "'If you don't believe me, look inside,' it says. Well, let's have a look, shall we?"

He ripped the envelope and unfolded several sheets of paper. "Jesus, Mary and Joseph, the lad was telling the truth. He is John Cameron's bastard." Graham waved two sheets of paper at Mackinnon. "He left copies of one of those scientific DNA tests and a letter written by Will Cameron that spells it all out in plain English. That's proof enough for me." After a moment's pause, his face reddened and he pounded his fist on the desk. "Damn it to hell! Navarro shares blood with the dead man and something tells me he'll not be satisfied until he spills ours. This changes things."

Serge had but two choices: to act quickly or walk away and let the law deal with the murderer and his accomplices. There was no doubt that his employer would reject the latter, so he had to devise a plan—and fast. He kicked off his shoes and stretched out on the floor. He always did his best thinking while lying on his back, eyes focused trancelike on whatever was directly overhead.

Three potential plans began to take shape. Choice number one would eliminate all of the conspirators and with them any future threat to those he protected. But a pre-emptive strike on five individuals would take time and coordination. It would also require a team of operatives and he didn't want to bring anyone else in on this. Besides, a bloodbath wouldn't go unnoticed and the last thing they needed was to call attention to themselves.

Or they could deliver the incriminating tapes to the police and let the law take care of the entire business. The locals would enjoy taking credit for Serge's work, but neither he nor Diego trusted the legal system to carry out the punishment they had in mind for Will's assassin.

Or … a third possibility began to swirl around the edges of his brain. He couldn't implement it without Diego's okay and he hoped that his unpredictable boss was someplace that had good mobile phone reception.

CHAPTER 32

*T*he radio was blasting through the car's open windows as Diego skillfully guided the Mini Cooper out of Inverness and onto the A9. A breeze that smelled like summer barreled through the car, making Alex's hair dance like a whirling Dervish. After the tense confrontation with Mackinnon, the two of them were content to simply enjoy the scenery, the music and each other's company.

After they'd crossed the graceful span of the Kennock Bridge, Alex lowered the radio's volume, slid her sunglasses atop her head and smiled broadly at Diego. "Life is never dull with you, is it Navarro?" Her innards still bubbled with an adrenalin-fueled high, but for once it was from excitement instead of anxiety.

"Oh, God, I hope not. There's enough time to be bored after I'm dead," he replied as he returned the smile. "The old man was scared shitless, wasn't he?"

"Yeah, he was. His jowls were shaking like a turkey neck. I thought he'd have a heart attack when you told him Will was your brother." They were both giddy and laughed before lapsing into silence as the reality of what they'd done, and why, hit them.

"Serge is going to be pissed," Diego said as they sped past the exit for Tullich Muir and continued north.

"Damn right he will be. We did the one thing he ordered us not to. Are you going to tell him?"

"I won't have to. He already knows."

"He knows? How?" Then she remembered the high tech bugs planted all over the man's shop and nodded slowly as the answer became obvious. "Oh, yeah. He knows and we're in deep doo-doo."

"Piles and piles of it," Diego laughed and then his smile abruptly disappeared. "I had to see that the man responsible for Will's death was only a man, not some mythic figure that I had to fear."

"Do you believe he had the nerve to cross himself and offer me his sympathy? I wanted to strangle him."

Diego grasped her hand and squeezed. "I swear you'll never have to see that man's face again. We've set things in motion and Serge will figure out how to do the rest. He loves a challenge and won't mind what I did once he calms down."

"But aren't you afraid that they'll come after you now that they know you're also John Cameron's son? These people are murderers. I couldn't stand it if anything happened to you," she added in a whisper, her voice cracking with emotion.

Diego took the next turnoff and pulled the car to the side of the road beside a field dotted with grazing sheep. He drew her into his arms and they clung to each other. "Please don't worry, Alex. No one's going to hurt either of us. Shhhh," he soothed as he stroked her hair.

She lifted her hands to his face and saw that the dark eyes that met hers had none of the fiery hardness that had made Mackinnon believe he was dealing with the Devil. She felt as if she could see into his soul. "You're very important to me. You know that, don't you?" she said softly. Diego nodded and tightened his hold on her.

She was sure that he wouldn't rush her, that he

understood that she still grieved and would need a long time to heal before she could ever ... would ever ... but he'd already established a base camp in a small corner of her heart that could become a permanent structure if she let it.

"Come," he finally said. "Let's walk. I remember how much you like sheep and I think I hear one calling your name. Listen. Aaaaa-lex. Aaaaa-lex. Aaaaa-lex."

Diego's sheep impression was absurd enough to wipe away the heavy emotion of the past few minutes. It was a beautiful day, rolling hills carpeted in green surrounded them, and Diego was doing everything he could to make up for putting her through the upsetting confrontation with Mackinnon. Inverness and its high stakes intrigue suddenly seemed very far away.

They held hands as they strolled along the narrow country lane to the sounds of birds chirping and sheep bleating. "It's beautiful here. I'm beginning to understand why Will liked it so much," said Diego as he kicked a small rock out of their path. When he did the same thing again, and yet again, Alex turned to him.

"You miss it, don't you? Soccer, I mean."

"Sometimes ... I guess so," he answered. Diego was a toddler when his foot first met a ball in soccer-crazed Buenos Aires and was a standout by the time he reached college. He was courted by pro teams from around the world, but never considered the sport as a career.

"Any regrets that you didn't become the Argentine David Beckham?"

"Becks? Well it might be fun to be him, but that has more to do with Victoria Beckham than with the game." His words stung although they were accompanied by the kind of grin that indicated he was teasing. But she didn't like it.

"Diego?" she asked tentatively.

"Yes?" he responded, equally cautious.

"Do you think you'll ever tell John that he's your biological father?"

He didn't answer right away. "Probably not. I mean, what's the point? Ricardo Navarro is, and always has been, my father. I don't want a relationship with John and the only emotion I feel for him is hate, although that word is probably too strong. Loathe, despise, even pity are all in there too. If Will hadn't died, I would have been proud to call him my brother even if it meant that John would have had to find out about the DNA test, but now ... no, there's no need for him to ever know."

"Look!" Diego suddenly exclaimed and jogged toward a lamb that was wandering in the middle of the road. "He must have squeezed under the fence."

The small animal gave a plaintive cry and looked at them. "He wants his mother. We have to help him," Alex said, but Diego was already crouching near the lamb trying to lure it with a handful of grass. It took one tentative step toward him and Diego lunged.

"Gotcha!" He wrapped his arms around its spindly legs and buried his nose in soft wool as he picked it up. Alex crooned to the animal and stroked its head just before Diego hefted the struggling creature over the fence.

"I'll never eat rack of lamb again," he said, as they lingered to watch the animal rejoin its mother and begin to nurse. "We better get back to the car. I left my phone there so we could have a few minutes of peace. Serge has probably left a dozen messages by now. It's time to face the firing squad."

Serge's detailed voicemail was brusque. "Listen and obey

for once in your life. I don't think anyone followed you, but you can never be sure so keep your eyes open and guard your back. Find a remote inn and lay low for a couple of days. If anything or anyone seems remotely suspicious, don't investigate. I repeat, you are not to engage. Leave immediately and relocate. Use an alias. No credit cards, cell phones or anything else that can be traced once you're in place. There's an envelope with cash in the glove box, so no ATMs either." He then described the three options to deal with Will's killers. The game was on.

Serge doubted that Mackinnon's people owned the sophisticated equipment needed to track down Diego and Alex, but he never underestimated an adversary. His headstrong charge would follow orders this time, if only to protect the woman he thought he loved. Serge thought Diego was more in lust than in love, but the label the attraction wore was irrelevant. Diego would fight to the death to defend Alex. And he'd increased the odds of that happening when he'd told the enemy that he, like Will, was a Cameron. But for now he would have to put thoughts of them aside and switch his focus to the mission.

Diego's bold move had panicked Graham and Mackinnon into acting rashly. The Argentine was a volatile loose cannon and, even worse, the one person who threatened to connect them to Will's murder. Serge guessed they'd want to dispose of Diego the same way they'd eliminated Will.

The plan the bodyguard formulated and which Diego was likely to okay, reflected the cold, meticulous way he'd carried out black ops as an elite agent. He reviewed how it would play out over and over, considered every potential obstacle, everything that could go wrong, and devised ways to deal with each. Anticipation made him itch for action and he knew he had to calm himself before he proceeded. His most effective weapons were a clear mind and lightning-fast reflexes. He slowed his breathing and began a series of gentle stretches to settle himself, his ritual preparation for combat.

He'd already concluded that only one of the conspirators would die. He also knew how he would do it. As for the others, well … they'd survive if they stayed out of his way. In his previous life, he didn't have the luxury of knowing whether a kill was justified—he'd simply obeyed orders. This was different. It was personal. Diego and his parents were like family and he was fond of Alex. From the moment she'd arrived at the Navarros' Miami villa, he'd witnessed the anguish the senseless murder of her husband caused. And now Diego said he loved her. No, he'd have no problem with this particular kill, although he wouldn't enjoy it. He never did. But neither would he feel any remorse.

Alex studied Diego's face as he listened to Serge's voicemail, but his expression gave nothing away. "Anything I should know?" she asked. It was obvious that something was up and she wasn't sure if she wanted to be told about it. Better to remain ignorant. Knowledge would mean that whatever Serge and Diego had cooked up had her tacit approval and she might not be able to give it.

"No, not really," Diego replied nonchalantly. "He's royally pissed off about our visit to Mackinnon's store and said he'd like to cut out my tongue for telling them that I'm a Cameron. He could do it, too."

"That's a bit harsh. I've become quite fond of your tongue," she said and shifted to hide her blush.

"Yeah, I'm attached to it too, literally and figuratively. Maybe we'll have a chance to give it some use," he added with a slow grin that left no mystery about what he intended. "Serge wants us to stay away from Inverness while he does his work."

"I wouldn't call a few days of exile a harsh punishment. Where will we go?" Alex asked eagerly as Diego turned the key in the ignition, then abruptly cut the engine before they'd moved an inch.

"Christ, my bladder is bursting," he said apologetically. "I should pee before we get back on the motorway. I don't think the sheep will mind, do you?" His eyes sparkled with amusement as he raised her hand to his lips.

"Of course not. Go!" She could use a rest stop herself, but since a woman's requirements were a bit more complicated, she'd wait until they passed a pub. She unfolded the roadmap to figure out where they might go next.

When Diego was sure he couldn't be overheard, he ducked behind a tree and quickly called Serge. There was no answer so he left a message: "Much as I hunger to join you for this little adventure, *amigo*, you're right that my place is with Alex. There's a bible verse that I can't get out of my head, something like: 'Vengeance is mine, sayeth the Lord.' I'll leave this in His hands and yours. Plan number three is my choice too. Do it. Call me when it's finished. *Vaya con Díos*."

He glanced up and down the road before starting back to the car. No one there. He would keep his eye on the rear view mirror to watch for a tail the way Serge had taught him.

"Better?" Alex asked as he snapped his seatbelt closed.

"Much."

"Good. I've found the perfect destination. There's a town called Tain that's not too far from here and it's along Scotland's Whiskey Trail. Would you like to tour the Glenmorangie distillery so you can see how single malts are made?"

"Whatever you want," he replied distractedly. "You navigate."

What an odd reaction from a whiskey aficionado, she thought. If he'd suggested a visit to a chocolate factory, she'd have been bouncing in her seat. Something, probably Serge's message, was making him brood and they rode in silence until she spotted the exit for Tain.

"This is beautiful!" Alex exclaimed as they drove down the town's narrow main street. "It's positively medieval. Can we wander around and maybe find someplace to eat? I really need a ladies' room and I'm starving."

"Food first and then we should find a place to stay. Would you mind if we save the exploring for tomorrow?" he asked as he linked his fingers with hers.

"Sure," she answered and dropped her gaze. Diego's hand looked and felt so right in hers. It shouldn't, but it did. Her heart ached to realize that it was becoming more and more difficult to remember the feel of Will's, a hand she'd held thousands of times.

As they shared a platter of fish and chips, their waiter recommended an inn a half-mile from town. He told them to book a room quickly because the area was a favorite destination for golfers, anglers and hill walkers. When Diego called the hotel, the only vacancy was the honeymoon suite. The landlady told him she'd hold it for an hour.

Rain often appears suddenly in the Highlands and the two of them were dripping wet after a dash from the restaurant to the car and then from the car to the Victorian mansion, cum hotel, which would be their home for the next couple of days.

Alex gave Diego a quizzical look when he registered as John and Laura Matthews. As they climbed the wide staircase to their room, she clutched his arm and forced him to stop. "What's with the names? What haven't you told me?"

"It's just a precaution. Serge doesn't want us to use credit cards or anything that can be traced. He probably thinks everyone's as good at this spy business as he is."

She nodded and began to shiver. "I'm freezing."

"Me too. We'll be warm in a minute," Diego promised as he unlocked the door to their suite.

Alex ran to the bathroom, grabbed a couple of thick towels and tossed one to Diego. "You look like you went for a swim with your clothes on," she said as she watched rainwater drip off him and onto the rug.

"It wouldn't be the first time, but never sober and never in weather like this," he said as he ran the towel over his hair. The fireplace's crackling logs created some heat, but not enough to keep Alex's teeth from chattering.

"We should get out of these clothes and into a hot shower before we both get sick," he said as he headed toward the bathroom.

Alex didn't follow. His words immediately triggered a vivid memory of the rainy day when she and Will had visited Mackinnon's shop. They'd been cold and wet when they'd returned to their B & B and sought the heat of a hot shower and steamy sex. She acknowledged the memory, then tucked it away as she forced herself back to the present. *Déjà vu* be damned. That was then, this is now. Will was gone and she had to go on with her life. But that didn't include getting into a shower with Diego Navarro.

"Well?" he asked and sneezed.

"I'll shower after you … by myself. Toss me a robe and I'll get out of my clothes and sit by the fire."

"Would you like some help?"

She saw the expectant look on his face and blurted, "Don't even think it, smart guy." She caught the snowy white robe he tossed to her and couldn't help noticing that he'd left the bathroom door open as he stripped off his clothes. "Show off," she mumbled. When it was her turn she locked the door securely behind her.

Dry and reasonably warm, they sat cross-legged, facing each other in front of the blazing fire. While she'd showered and dried her hair, Diego had made tea from the supplies Scottish hotels routinely provide their guests. Alex wrapped her hands around the steaming cup and sipped the warm liquid slowly, content until he idly began to stroke her bare calf.

She swatted his hand away, aware that they both wore nothing under their robes and that he could have her naked in a nanosecond if she allowed it. She summoned her flagging will power. "I'm sure that there was more to Serge's message than you've told me. Don't try to deny that the two of you have set something in motion. The sooner you tell me about it, Navarro, the sooner we can do whatever we're going to do in that big canopied bed. Now what did Serge really say and what's he doing while we're here?"

"Ah, Alessandra," he said as he leaned away from her, "you do know how to spoil a mood, but with the incentive you just offered, a man would be a fool not to tell you whatever you want to know." He paused before adding, "and I'm no fool." The smile he gave her carried the warmth of sunshine, although the glow never reached his eyes.

CHAPTER 33

*M*ackinnon would be furious to know that as he keyed numbers into his phone to set up the conference call, he'd provided Serge with the names and locations of all of his co-conspirators, the same men he'd last seen at Elgin Cathedral when he'd informed them that Will Cameron was dead. Ian Lindsay. Duncan Buchanan. John Malcolm.

Serge leaned back in his chair with his hands behind his head, long legs stretched out in front of him. A self-satisfied grin spread across his face as he replayed the tape of Mackinnon's calls to the three men followed by one to Michael Graham to let him know all was arranged. Now we've got all five of you, he thought. The former spy's only disappointment was that they were making it too easy. He thrived on the challenge of a formidable opponent and this contest would only utilize a fraction of his skills.

Their arrogance had made them sloppy so they never considered that their phones might be tapped. Because of that, they'd revealed the coastal location of the newest safe house where the youngest Mackinnon — Will's murderer — was hiding. Serge had all the information he needed to make sure they never harmed anyone again.

He gathered all the incriminating evidence he'd collected and sealed it in a packet to be messengered to a former colleague who now worked for British intelligence.

That agent's team would take credit for the investigation and the arrest of the five men who'd ordered Will Cameron's execution. One name was omitted from the packet. Jamie Mackinnon had already been tried, convicted and sentenced by Serge, Diego and a reluctant Alex.

Duncan Buchanan was the first person Mackinnon notified about the upcoming teleconference so that he could be reassured that his grandson had reached the safe house without incident.

"How goes it Duncan?" Mackinnon asked after confirming Buchanan's availability for that night's discussion.

"All is well, James. Your young Jamie arrived early this morning. He's quiet as a wee mouse and no trouble at all."

"I miss the boy, but I dare not visit. Some troubling developments have made me uneasy about the lad's safety as well as our own. We'll speak of that tonight."

"I guessed that something was amiss when he arrived here at dawn. You wouldn't have sent him away from Geordie's unless someone was on to him. Can you tell me what's amiss?" asked Buchanan.

"Naught definite, but there's cause for concern. Michael will be angry if I say more, so you'll have to wait a few more hours to hear the details. Give young Jamie a kiss from his Grandda," said Mackinnon.

"When I see him."

"Isn't the lad with you?" Mackinnon felt his chest tighten.

"Not at the moment, no. Your grandson decided to go tenting by Boddam or thereabouts for a couple of days, said he wanted to take in the sea air afore it turns cold. He said he might enjoy a hike or two along the nearby cliffs to the Bullers of Buchan or even further along to Slains Castle, you know, the one that inspired that Dracula book."

"I know the one, aye, it's a fearsome ruin right there at the edge of the sea."

"'Tis, and especially in the fog when the narrow path along the cliffs turns to mud and becomes as slippery as a patch of ice. I warned him to take care."

"Don't worry about our Jamie. The lad is fond of the outdoors and has the sure feet of a goat. His Da started him hill walking when he could barely stand. No need to worry, Duncan."

"I won't then," he replied. "But you should also know he's barely said a word since he arrived. He seems to crave solitude and if that's what he needs I'll not intrude."

"Thanks for telling me. I'm grateful," said Mackinnon, scowling as he returned the phone to its cradle. Jamie had always been a cheerful, gregarious boy, so this taciturn behavior weighed on him. If anything happened to the lad it would be on his head. It was he, and no one else, who'd insisted that his grandson was mature enough to plunge a knife into Will Cameron. To his mind it had always been a question of honor, blood for blood. The deed had to be carried out by a Mackinnon. Maybe Jamie had only gone along with it to prove his manhood to his grandfather and now was troubled by regrets. But what was done was done. He'd have a long talk with the lad as soon as it was safe. Mackinnon sighed deeply then unwrapped the cheese sandwich he'd had no stomach for earlier, sniffed it to be sure it hadn't spoiled, then tore hungrily into it.

Mackinnon's anxiety was as contagious as the flu and Duncan Buchanan became infected seconds after the call ended. It only took minutes of agitated pacing for him to come up with the one remedy that would calm his nerves. He headed up a steep flight of stairs to his bedroom and groaned as he got to his knees to stretch an arm under the bed. He breathed a sigh of relief when his fingers grasped the metal box he kept there. He wiped a year's worth of dust off its top, released the lock and removed a handgun and a clip of ammunition. It had been a while since he'd cleaned and oiled the weapon and he hadn't fired it in years, but Mackinnon's call had panicked him. If trouble was on its way he'd have to protect himself, wouldn't he? Perhaps he should warn young Jamie, but warn him of what?

Serge pored over the road maps he'd spread on the floor of the suite, scrutinizing the area around Cruden Bay, Peterhead and Boddam, small towns on the edge of the North Sea where Scotland's right shoulder slopes south. He trusted the accuracy of the large maps more than those on the Internet, but he went to his laptop to verify that the cliffs Duncan Buchanan had mentioned to Mackinnon could cause a credible accidental death.

The rugged granite ledges near the Bullers of Buchan, just south of Duncan Buchanan's safe house in Boddam, seemed ideal. The descriptions, photos and videos posted online by tourists gave him a "you are there" feel for the place. He'd check it out with his own eyes, but for now he was satisfied that the area's geography was similar to Ireland's Cliffs of Moher—maybe not as steep, but certainly as deadly. A British operative had once removed a particularly troublesome member of the IRA by dumping him off those Irish cliffs into the Atlantic Ocean. That body had never washed ashore. In online pictures, it looked like the Scottish coast between Boddam and Cruden Bay had unfenced paths just wide enough to place one foot in front of the other running along steep, knife-edge cliffs high above the North Sea as it thundered into rocky hollows below. Yes, Serge thought, that location seemed ideal.

He checked out an alternate site as well. The ruin of Slains Castle, atop its own dramatic precipice, was a few miles south of the town where the target was supposedly camping, but the castle seemed to be a long way from the nearest car park. He would prefer not to carry an unconscious Jamie Mackinnon farther than he had to, but the literary link to the place appealed to him. If Slains was eerie enough to have served as the inspiration for the Transylvania castle of Bram Stoker's Dracula, then it might do nicely for young Mackinnon's end.

Satisfied, Serge logged off and ran the software that would wipe his hard drive clean so that his research would be impossible to trace. He glanced at his watch; it was 4:30. He'd have a light dinner and get a good night's sleep before heading for the coast. Buchanan had told Mackinnon that the grandson planned to camp out as long as the weather held and the BBC predicted sun for the next few days. This schedule would also give him time to listen in on that night's conference call and fine tune his tactics if need be.

Serge's network of former agents had helped him to obtain the weapons and equipment he might need before he'd left London for Scotland. At that point, he'd had no idea how the kill would be accomplished, but now that his plan was set, he knew he was well-equipped. He sat cross-legged on the floor to methodically check his gear. Then he did it again with his eyes closed until he was sure he could find each object by touch in the dark. Knife. Handgun with scope, silencer and extra ammo. A length of flexible wire long enough to wrap around a neck. Assorted injectable drugs and syringes. Thin lambskin gloves. Mouth operated flashlight. Duck tape. He considered adding a wetsuit to the mix, then decided against it. The sea that battered those cliffs was too treacherous for him to follow Mackinnon into it. If he were overpowered or slipped and fell ... well ... a wetsuit wouldn't save him. All was ready, but he'd obsessively go over it again before he went to bed, another time in the morning, and maybe once more before he left.

After ordering a chicken sandwich and chips from room service, he instructed the front desk to hold all calls. The last thing he wanted to deal with was Mairi Graham, but it seemed she was savvy enough to understand that their brief fling was over. He hadn't heard from the girl since blowing her off when she'd spotted him with Alex and Diego. The only person who had his cell phone number was Diego and he'd been instructed not to call unless he had second thoughts about Serge's assignment.

Serge stripped off his clothes, stretched out on the bed and visualized himself on a beach under Miami's warm sunshine. He had two hours to rest before the conspirators were scheduled to discuss how to handle the not-so-veiled threats Diego had made to Mackinnon and his claim to be John Cameron's son. He hoped that Diego would head back to the Florida villa once they were finished here. Scotland was too fucking cold for a man who'd spent most of his life in Israel.

Alex wrapped her arms around her knees as she sat near the suite's fire and considered what Diego had just told her. Jamie Mackinnon was Will's murderer. Serge had irrefutable proof of his guilt. Diego had spared her the specifics about how the punishment was to be carried out — at her request — but she knew that Mackinnon's grandson would pay for what he'd done with his own life. Her willing complicity in a premeditated murder — deserved or not — revealed a side of herself that she didn't recognize. She wondered if this trait was a legacy of her sword-wielding Scottish ancestors or the brave Celtic warrior women in the captivating tales that her grandmother MacBain loved to spin.

Who was this vengeful woman, she wondered, as she gazed at the fire's flames. Would she be haunted by the execution of Mackinnon's grandson? She'd never seen the young man so perhaps he could remain a nonperson to her. And it might actually give her peace to know that the man who'd killed her husband no longer walked the earth, would never fall in love, have children, be happy … all the things he'd stolen from Will … and her. He'd cold-bloodedly executed the man she loved. Jamie Mackinnon deserved to die. If she were part of a jury, she'd find him guilty and favor the death penalty over life in prison. There was something to this biblical eye for an eye business. And if what was about to take place was truly abhorrent, why was she still so attracted to the man who'd set it in motion?

"You were thinking so loudly that I could almost hear you," Diego said, startling her out of her deliberations. She met his eyes as he crouched in front of her and ran his thumbs over her hands. "What is it? What's troubling you?"

She didn't say anything for a few minutes, unsure if she wanted to hear his answer. "If I asked you to, if I told you I couldn't live with this, would you tell Serge to call it off?"

"No," Diego replied immediately and let go of her hands. She recognized the steely expression of a man whose course is set.

"Why not?" She was wounded by his indifference to her feelings. She irritably pushed her hair out of her eyes and rearranged the robe to cover her legs.

"We've gone over this before," he sighed. "If we hand this monster to the local police, he'd be extradited to Boston where the crime was committed. That's where he'd be tried. You and I both know that it would turn into a media circus and you'd have paparazzi and tabloid reporters in your face whenever you went to the courthouse. The people who did this have enough money from their supporters to hire brilliant lawyers and maybe even buy a juror or two. And Serge's tapes would be inadmissible as evidence since there was no warrant."

He'd been pacing as he presented his case, but then he gentled his voice as he knelt in front of her again. "Please don't ask this of me. We can't risk an acquittal that would free Will's killer on some technicality. Picture yourself in the courtroom when the jury foreman announces, 'We find the defendant not guilty.' How would you feel? Jamie Mackinnon has to pay for Will's murder. My brother had dreams and hopes and plans and assumed he had a future." His voice cracked as he fought back tears. "Dammit, he was your husband, Alex! Your husband!"

Before she could respond, Diego resumed his agitated pacing, gesturing wildly as he mumbled in Spanish. She knew him well enough to realize that the storm raging inside him would have to pass before he became rational again. She'd use the time to figure out how to respond.

He finally crouched in front of her and once more took her hands in his. "Will was my brother. I loved him," he whispered. "I won't be able to live with myself if his death isn't avenged. Can you try to understand?"

"Yes," her voice echoed the softness of his. "You won't find peace until this man is dead."

Diego nodded and Alex watched as he slowly walked away from her. He sighed wearily, collapsed onto the bed and closed his eyes. After a few minutes he raised himself onto one elbow and patted the empty space next to him.

"Come here, Alessandra." It was a request, not a demand, and she didn't hesitate. She'd stopped questioning how a certain expression in his eyes could draw her to him with the irresistible pull of gravity.

Diego wrapped his arms around her, slid his hands down her back and held her, just held her, for a long time. He never wanted to let go of the woman whose feelings and desires were suddenly more important than his own.

His body's heat and the sound of his heartbeat soothed her until she abruptly broke the embrace and turned away.

"Look at me, Alex. Please look at me."

She turned to face him. Her jade gaze never wavered as she met eyes as dark as espresso. She waited until he was ready to speak again.

"I once promised that I would never do anything to hurt you and I meant it. If you ask me to call it off, I will."

She knew what that concession cost him and she buried her face in his neck, inhaling his scent. "You'd do that for me?"

"Yes," he said as he gently stroked her hair. "I don't ever want to cause you pain."

Her decision was instantaneous. "This man robbed

us of someone we both loved and stole Will's future. I've discovered a surprising barbaric streak in myself and that part of me wants the same thing you do. He has to die. But I don't ever want to know how Serge does it. Okay? Promise me. Never."

"I promise," he murmured as he slid the robe from her shoulder and they lost themselves in the healing power of each other's bodies.

Chapter 34

"It's a beautiful evening, isn't it, James?" Michael Graham said cheerfully as he let himself into Mackinnon's darkened shop fifteen minutes before the scheduled 8 p.m. conference call.

"I'm glad one of us is in fine spirits tonight, but what have you got to be so chipper about, Michael?" the old man growled. He shifted and the ancient desk chair creaked under his weight. The cramped office's dim lighting cast shadows over Mackinnon's face as he raised his eyes to give Graham a cursory look. He was feeling his age. He was tired of plots, fearful for his jailed son and fugitive grandson, fed up with the whole damn mess. He wanted to go back to simply blathering about Scotland's shoddy treatment by her English rulers and let things be. Maybe he would sell his shop, buy a simple croft in the Highlands, and live out the rest of his days in peace. The idea had appeal.

"Are you daydreaming man or are you hammered again?" demanded Michael irritably.

"I've had nary a drop since you left. I'm tired is all. You'll remember I had little sleep last night what with your Mairi's visit and then waiting outside that posh hotel for the Americans to show themselves," said a peeved Mackinnon as he grabbed for the Bounty bar stashed in a desk drawer. He hoped the coconut and chocolate confection would provide him with enough energy for the next hour or so. Then he'd want his bed.

"I stopped by that hotel on my way here and was told that the American that Mairi was over the moon about is still there, but his friends—the so-called Sloanes—checked out this afternoon, likely right before they came to see you," said Graham. "I tried to persuade Mairi to pop by to question this Steve Spencer, or who-ever the hell he is, but my daughter is sulking and wants nothing to do with the man, the stubborn bitch. Just like her mother, she is," he snarled.

"How can you call your own daughter and wife such names, Michael?"

"I can if I wish to. They're mine. But that's no mat-ter," he replied, then picked up where he'd left off. "The desk clerk told me he offered to book a hotel for the handsome American couple at their next destination, but they had no idea where they were off to. I should have dropped everything and found a way to pick up their trail. Or, once we knew their identity, one of us should have been watching them. Now we don't know where they are or what they intend to do." Graham restlessly roamed the office, pausing only long enough to study the photos of Alex and Diego as if their images might reveal their whereabouts.

"Aye, well, that's not good, is it?" Mackinnon frowned as he waited for Graham to continue.

"No, it's not, James. This Navarro or bastard son of John Cameron—I don't care what he calls him-self—must be taken care of and soon. From what you said of his visit, he has the determination and money to do us great harm. We need to find him, but damned if I know how to do that," Graham snarled as he stomped from one side of the small office to the other. " Christ, man, how can you work in here? I feel like I'm in a cage. I'll be out front."

"Wait a minute, Michael. Shall I see if the others are ready?" Graham checked his watch, saw that it was two minutes before eight and nodded, his fingers twitching impatiently as he turned his back on the old man and strode into the business's retail space.

Mackinnon punched in the first number. "Is that you Ian? Hold while I bring John and Duncan aboard." Mackinnon continued to press numbers, impressed, despite himself, with the easy efficiency of British Telephone's conferencing set up. Of course it was a Scot, Alexander Graham Bell, who'd invented the telephone in the first place, so obviously the thing was brilliant.

"Good evening gentlemen," said Graham as he lifted the extension and took charge of the meeting. "We have a problem, a big one and I'll come straight to it. Will Cameron wasn't the traitor Cameron's only son."

A chorus of gasps, exclamations and a couple of curses met the revelation that Graham delivered so dispassionately. He ignored their reaction and continued before he was bombarded with questions. "We've learned that Cameron also fathered a bastard, a man named Diego Navarro, who showed up in James' shop today and threatened him. The dead mans's widow was with him and this Navarro hinted that he knew who killed his brother. He also left behind proof that he is precisely who he claims to be. We must decide how to proceed and it must be done quickly. I want to hear what each of you thinks we should do. John Malcolm? What say you?"

"Blast it to hell is what I say," responded John. "I knew things had gone too smoothly. I'm not one to cry over spilt milk, but if ye recall I argued against this murder. It was just a matter of time before this came back to bite us in the arse."

"I didn't ask for a bloody lecture!" Graham snapped. He didn't want the others to know how unnerved he was by Diego's sudden presence, but his irritated response spoke for itself.

"Aye, well … let's see. How we proceed is not a simple question, Michael, is it?" stalled John. "When we met at Elgin Cathedral after the deed was done, James told us that Will Cameron had a formidable friend who we should fear more than the dead lad's father. It's this Diego Navarro isn't it?"

"Aye, 'tis," replied Mackinnon.

"If this man already told the police about us, we'd have been rounded up by now," Duncan Buchanan chimed in. He patted the gun at his side to reassure himself of its presence. "That tells me that he will do whatever he has in mind without involving the law. Did you get the impression, James, that he's capable of violence?"

"Violence of the very worst kind. I felt like I was looking into the face of Satan himself. This man would like nothing better than to dance a jig on my grave, on all of our graves," said Mackinnon who shivered as he recalled Diego's threat to watch with pleasure as one by one they were drawn and quartered.

Ian interrupted. "How can one man, however mighty he may be, do anything to five men — six if we count young Jamie. Be reasonable, man! We're scattered in different parts of the country. I can't believe he knows who all of us are. We've been too careful. I say he's bluffing and we should go on as we were, as if nothing is amiss."

"Ian's right. One man and the Cameron woman pose no danger to us … unless they go to the law with their suspicions," added John Malcolm. "Might they have accomplices here?"

"They may. My Mairi recently met an American businessman here in Inverness. When she saw him with Navarro and the Cameron woman, he used phony names when he introduced them to the girl. Why would someone do that unless he isn't who he says he is and is up to no good? Answer me that, will you," said Graham.

"We need to discover what he means to do so we can protect ourselves," added John.

"I agree. I'll have a chat with this American — Steve Spencer is the name he goes by — and persuade him to tell me how he's connected to Navarro," said Graham.

"And what makes you think he would he talk to you?" asked Ian.

"He may not want to, but he will ... he will," said Graham confidently as he lifted his pants leg to reveal the dagger sheathed above his ankle. "I don't believe there's any immediate danger to us, but we must stay alert. If you've a weapon in your home, even a knife, keep it handy. We'll do another call like this at 7 a.m. tomorrow and I'll want your ideas. By then I'll have had my talk with Mairi's American."

Duncan had more to worry about than the others and wasn't ready to ring off. "Since mine is a safe house, I'm responsible for young Jamie. He's off camping for a few days. Shall I warn him?"

"Let the lad be for now," Michael Graham ordered. "If anything changes, you'll be the first to know."

As soon as he heard Graham boast that he had ways to persuade "Steve Spencer" to talk, Serge coolly gathered the few things he hadn't already loaded in his car. He'd planned to leave for the coast in the morning, but couldn't allow Michael Graham to find him when he came to the hotel to question Mairi's "friend." He was fond of the girl and the generous way she'd shared her luscious body with him, and he didn't want to be forced to kill her father. Mairi would suffer enough when her friend Jamie vanished and her father was arrested.

He had names, dates, addresses—everything the British authorities would need to round up these men and charge them with conspiracy or worse. And he knew just where to find this Jamie Mackinnon. Serge methodically checked the room one last time, then left the hotel through a side door, his immediate objective to get to the murderer's campsite before the young man was ordered to move on. He checked his watch—9 p.m. If he made it to the coast by 1 a.m., he'd have adequate time to scope out the cliffs. He'd then backtrack to Boddam village where he expected to easily find the condemned man asleep on the beach. Nice of the fools to unwittingly provide him with that bit of information and save him a search. He wasn't worried that the conspirators had been warned to remain alert and arm themselves. He'd dealt with much worse.

Michael Graham stormed into the Palace Hotel and took the stairs two at a time to reach the second floor suite occupied by his daughter's American friend. He would have bet his youngest child's life that Steve Spencer wasn't who he pretended to be, so sure was he that the man was a fraud and involved somehow with Cameron's illegitimate son. He reluctantly admired the whoreson's nerve to first work his charm on Mairi and then to have the ballocks to come to their house to sit at his family's table and eat his food! He wouldn't hesitate to use his knife if that's what it took to learn the man's true identity and intentions. And if it turned out that Steve Spencer was exactly who he claimed to be, Michael vowed to beat him bloody anyway for playing fast and loose with his Mairi.

"Room service," Michael announced. No answer. His knock became more insistent. Silence. When he cautiously tried the door, he found it unlocked. He opened it just wide enough to peek inside and saw the vacant room of someone who hasn't simply gone out, but who has left for good.

"Damn it to hell," Michael muttered and tore downstairs to the lobby. He shoved startled guests aside as he cornered the hotel clerk who'd fed him information before.

"The man in 218, is he gone?"

The flustered clerk tapped his computer keys with trembling fingers. "Mr. Spencer hasn't checked out. His last instructions were that he wasn't to be disturbed, but that was this afternoon."

Graham's heart began to pound as if he'd just run a race. Something beyond his control was happening and for the first time since they'd hatched the plan to punish John Cameron by killing his son, Michael Graham was scared. He needed to order the others to go to ground for a bit, starting with Duncan Buchanan who was charged with protecting young Jamie Mackinnon. If the lad was caught and talked ... well, they'd all be dead. Once he did his bit and alerted everyone, Michael would use the phony passport and counterfeit credit cards he had at the ready to disappear without giving a second thought to the family and friends he'd leave behind.

• • •

Few cars were making the late night journey to the coast on the pitch-dark roadway. Although the powerful V8 engine of his rented black Range Rover would have delivered whatever he asked of it, Serge fought the temptation to speed. He still made good time, arriving near the cliffs a little past midnight. Unlike many other operatives, he wasn't superstitious, yet he considered it a good omen that a shroud of coastal fog would obscure his movements.

He avoided the deserted car park at the base of the cliffs south of Boddam and left his vehicle behind a nearby abandoned shack where it wouldn't arouse the curiosity of passers by, especially the law. The rocky precipices were no place for a midnight stroll and the area was most likely patrolled to prevent the kind of accident he was about to cause. He easily found the start of a narrow trail that led uphill. Several "DANGER" signs warned hikers to keep their distance from the perilous cliffs' edge, although the roar of the surf was all the warning any sane person should need.

Serge paused beside each marker to carefully evaluate the terrain and the drop-off as he sought the perfect spot. The coastal fog's moisture provided an assist by turning the narrow footpath along the steep rock face's unfenced rim to mud. He'd already lost his footing once. Luckily he'd landed on his ass and not in the water, but the fall put an exclamation mark on the need for caution. Yeah, he thought with satisfaction, the trail was slippery enough to make an accident not just believable, but inevitable. The place and conditions were better than he'd imagined. And the turbulent sea's deafening roar as it crashed into rocky inlets below would muffle any scream the target might make should he regain consciousness before he hit the water. Assured by his reconnaissance, Serge jogged back to his car and headed north to find his prey.

Duncan Buchanan tossed the television's remote onto a pile of magazines a moment before he shoved the whole mess onto the floor. He patted his pocket for what seemed like the thousandth time, needing the comfort provided by the firearm he'd cleaned and loaded just that morning. He had to do something or the gnawing anxiety since that evening's conference call with Mackinnon, Graham and the others would surely drive him out of his mind.

Despite Michael's orders to let Jamie be, it was only right to warn the lad that something might be amiss, that there could be trouble on the way, especially since they'd learned there was a second Cameron son — a dangerous one with blood in his eye — and he was in Scotland. Screw Michael Graham! He'd gone along with their so-called leader long enough and look where it got him. Scotland was no closer to freedom and he was an accessory to murder. Graham could take his orders and shove them up his arse. It was the middle of the night, but he would find the lad and demand that he return to the relative safety of the house.

He pulled a heavy sweater over his head, added a wind-breaker and shoved his loaded gun into one of the jacket's pockets. He was out of practice, but he'd once been a fair shot and you didn't forget that sort of thing, did you?

"Blast the fog," he uttered irritably as he stepped outside and began to walk, head down, toward the beach.

"Hello there," came a familiar voice out of the mist. "Would that be you, Buchanan?"

"Aye, 'tis. And what are you doing out on a dreadful night like this MacLeod?" he replied, recognizing the voice as William MacLeod, his chattiest near neighbor. He had no time for the man's blether, but his neighbor's next comment froze Buchanan in his tracks.

"I could ask the same of you and I could also ask if your mind has turned to mush. Everyone in the village, including you Duncan, knows that I get by on just a few hours sleep and that I go out walking late each night, rain or shine, winter or summer. And it's rare that I ever see another soul about in weather like this, but you make the third tonight."

"Oh?"

"Aye. Some laddie took sick and his mate had him over his shoulder, carrying him off the beach. Ate bad mussels, he said, and boaked his guts up. I told him to take the poor fellow to hospital as he looked to be unconscious."

Buchanan shuddered as free-floating anxiety gripped him in its vise. Jamie was on the beach. His was the only tent on the sand. Someone had carried Jamie off. He was sure of it. The danger was already here. He wanted to scream, but had to keep his voice calm.

"Did you see them go? Did they drive off in a car, MacLeod?"

"Aye. I heard an engine start and I could just make out the car—it was dark, one of those petrol-eating SUVs, a Land Rover perhaps—as they drove away. The mist made it hard to see, but I'm sure they headed south, toward Cruden Bay and the Bullers, and one would guess to hospital in Aberdeen. Why are you so worried about some stranger with a bad stomach?"

"No reason, but I don't like the thought of someone so sick that they have to be carried is all. I sound like a worry wart old woman," he said and forced a laugh. "Good night to you MacLeod."

"And to you, Duncan."

Buchanan felt like snakes were writhing in his gut. To hell with walking. He had to get to Jamie, and fast. When his temperamental old car's engine turned over on the first try, he let out a sigh of relief. He'd know in minutes if the lad was safe and prayed that his panic was for naught.

As he scanned the rocky shore that passed as a beach, Serge only spotted one tent through the swirling fog. It had to belong to the target, unless Buchanan had disregarded Graham's instructions and already ordered Mackinnon's grandson back to the safety of the house. He'd know soon enough. The weather provided an unexpected assist since it had cleared the area of all but one lone camper. If there were others nearby, they could become innocent victims. The tragic accident Serge planned would become part of a major crime investigation, a situation he had to avoid.

He fully expected Jamie Mackinnon—who was repeatedly described as a "strapping lad" by the old man—to struggle, but that didn't concern him. He was adept at using his hands to overwhelm his quarry and swiftly cause unconsciousness. Serge's body rippled with raw power. He was dressed in body hugging black from head to toe and the small pack strapped to his waist held everything he'd need to do the job quickly. He considered adding a bulletproof vest, then tossed it back in the car. The thing offered minimal protection and he'd never liked the way it restricted his upper body's movement. It wasn't as if some fanatic with a Kalashnikov was lying in wait for him. Mackinnon's weapon of choice was a knife.

The Scot had proven his expertise with a blade the night he'd killed Will Cameron with a swift, jugular-piercing jab to the throat, but he'd be no match for a professional.

Serge flexed his fingers as he pulled on skintight lambskin gloves, placed a tiny flashlight between his teeth and crept stealthily down the beach toward the tent. He crouched beside it to listen for the rhythmic breathing that would indicate its occupant was asleep, but there was only silence. "Crap," he muttered as he snuck inside. The light's narrow beam verified his hunch—empty. He could wait for Mackinnon to return or try to find him. He opted for the latter.

Jamie Mackinnon had downed at least six bottles of beer before he'd stopped counting, but when he finally crawled into his sleeping bag, the oblivion he sought hadn't come. It had been a while since images of the man he'd knifed in Boston had haunted him, and Jamie wondered why Will Cameron had chosen this night to visit. The kill had been easy enough and his conscience was clear so he ordered the spirit to go back where it came from and to leave him be. He left the tent and stumbled to the edge of the sea to empty his beer-filled bladder before it burst. He was struggling to zip his jeans when he felt a tap on the shoulder. He whirled around, mouth open, fists raised.

A drunk and surprised Jamie was no match for Serge. He had the younger man on the ground in an instant and his experienced fingers easily found the sweet spot on his neck that brought about rapid loss of consciousness. He withdrew the loaded syringe from his pack and injected a potent barbiturate cocktail into the young man's body. Jamie Mackinnon would never be aware of anything again. He hoisted the heavy body over his shoulder and carried it to the tent where he tugged a sweater and jacket over the young man's T-shirt and added hiking boots to make a nocturnal cliffside walk look believable. He grunted as he hefted the 200 or so pounds of muscle onto his shoulder again and headed toward the Range Rover for the return trip to the nearby cliffs.

"Hey there! Is something amiss?" came a voice out of the swirling fog, as Buchanan's friend MacLeod spotted the two men.

"Shit, there's always something," Serge muttered to himself, but he reacted instantly. He lowered Jamie to the ground so his hands would be free, although he didn't want to be forced to use them.

"My friend must have eaten some bad mussels. He's been boaking his guts up for hours and I'm taking him home," he shouted toward the disembodied voice in a perfect Scots accent.

"Can I give ye a hand?" inquired the night stroller.

"Nay, no need. I've got it."

"Perhaps you should take your mate to hospital."

Shut up and go about your own bloody business, Serge thought, but said, "Right. Good idea."

"Well then, if you're sure you need no assistance, I'll be on my way."

"Thanks and a good night to you," said Serge as the Good Samaritan bid him the same.

He waited until the sound of footsteps retreated, hoisted Jamie Mackinnon once more, and continued to his car.

Minutes after MacLeod's neighbor finished describing his odd encounter, Buchanan's tires screeched to a halt at the edge of the town beach. He left the headlights on to help him see and ran toward the lone tent that had to be Jamie's.

"Jamie! Jamie!" he shouted breathlessly into the wind as he ran, but there was no answer. Panic hit when he saw that the tent was empty except for a rumpled sleeping bag and a pile of empty bottles. He was wild with dread and cursed everyone who had put him in this situation, including himself, as he retraced his steps to the car. Michael Graham would be furious to not be consulted, but there was no time for that. All he could think of was Jamie and how he'd assured the lad's grandda that the young man would be safe with him.

MacLeod had said the two men, one injured or sick, had headed south in a dark SUV. His old Vauxhall Corsa wasn't fast, but perhaps by some miracle he'd be able to catch up with them. He had no idea of what he'd do if, and when, he did.

Serge left the black Range Rover at the furthest edge of the unlit car park instead of concealing it among the trees that lined the other side of the road. He didn't want to risk being seen by a passerby or worse, a cop on patrol, as he carried Jamie across the narrow road closest to the cliffs.

The hike uphill was more difficult than the unencumbered climb he'd made an hour earlier. He was sweating and breathing heavily, but managed to maintain a steady pace. His equilibrium was thrown off by the heavy body he carried, so he stayed well away from the slippery path at the edge of the cliff. His pants were still muddy from the fall he took on that very path an hour ago. A loss of footing this time could mean death for him as well. He carried a picture of the terrain in his mind and quickly eliminated the Bullers' collapsed sea cave as an option. He had to be sure that the body would wash out to sea and the Bullers' pot-shaped formation might be too enclosed by ledge. There was another spot along the cliff that he'd seen earlier. Two more minutes and he'd be there. He leaned into the wind, trudged a bit farther, and stopped. Without a moment's hesitation, he carefully inched to the edge of the cliff, steadied himself and heaved Jamie Mackinnon into the sea.

Serge lay flat on the ground to recover from the exertion of throwing 200 pounds of dead weight as far as he could. Once he could breathe normally again, he carefully shimmied part way over the edge of the cliff and aimed a powerful flashlight into the rocky crevices below. He had to be sure that the body had landed in the sea and not on some outcropping where the target could wake as the drug wore off and shout for help. All he could make out was the swirling white foam of angry waves crashing into the bluffs below accompanied by the squawking of hundreds of gulls that made their home among the rocks. Satisfied, he stood and made a few sliding footprints in the mud leading from the path to the precipice. Then he reached his gloved hand into a pocket and removed two empty beer bottles with Jamie's fingerprints on them and propped them beside a nearby rock.

Serge was sure that old man Mackinnon would suspect his grandson's death was no accident. He'd also have little trouble figuring out who was responsible, but there would be no way to prove it. If the body washed up and an autopsy was performed — and Serge doubted it would be — the medical examiner would find salt water in the victim's lungs, proof that he was alive and breathing when he hit the water. All traces of the short acting barbiturate mixture Serge had used would have left his system and the extra fine needle would have left no mark. The cause of death would be ruled accidental drowning. He gave the scene a last quick glance and returned to his car by a longer, alternate route to ensure that footsteps that only went one way—up—were left on the muddy path he'd taken while lugging Jamie.

He quickly stowed his equipment and changed into a sweatshirt and jeans in the silent, pitch black parking lot. Diego still believed the hit would take place the following day, so he needed to be told that they had to leave Scotland a day earlier than planned. The Navarro Gulfstream was standing by in London, but Alex and Diego were somewhere in the Highlands and would have to arrange to get to London fast. There was no one in sight, so he decided to make the call before he began the long drive south.

"This better be important." Diego's voice was husky and he was breathless as he put the phone to his ear.

Alex tried to help him maintain the rhythm that had them both on the verge of orgasm, but she could feel his attention shift elsewhere as he listened to the caller. Diego's replies were cryptic, a smattering of "Good. No trouble? Yes, of course," and finally, "I'll do it now."

His mind was obviously no longer on sex when he rolled off her and mumbled his apologies. But one glance told her that he was still semi-erect so she kissed her way down his body to bring him back to life. "Five minutes," she whispered as she straddled him. "Whatever Serge told you to do can wait five minutes."

An hour later, Diego quickly arranged to charter a plane to fly them from Inverness to London. Serge would meet them at the small London City Airport, where Diego's pilot assured him the Navarro jet was fueled and ready to go. Once reunited there, the three of them would head back to Boston.

"Did something go wrong?" Alex asked as she hurriedly pulled on jeans and a woolen turtleneck while Diego, already dressed, threw the rest of their clothes into their bags.

"No. It's all good. Serge had to move sooner than planned. He was listening to our friends tonight and they were trying to decide whether you and I posed any danger to them and what to do about us. Serge is sure they have no idea where we are, but he thought it best to take care of business quickly in case they decided to relocate Will's murderer again. The packet of evidence is already on its way to Serge's friend in MI-5, who promised that all of the conspirators would be in custody by noon tomorrow. Serge is on his way to London. He told me that he found Mackinnon's grandson and..."

"No! Shhhhh," Alex said as she covered his mouth with her fingers. "I don't want to know. I told you I don't ever want to know." She was surprised that she felt nothing, neither relief nor guilt. Maybe those emotions would come later. If she knew the details she'd be able to picture what happened and that could be a problem. It was better to remain ignorant.

Diego opened his arms and she went to him. In a few short months he had become adept at recognizing her needs and fulfilling them. His body was solid and radiated security and comfort into hers. "We better go," he said, reluctantly breaking the embrace to check his watch. It was a few minutes after 3 a.m. "At this time of night the motorway will be deserted and we can make excellent time," he said as he picked up their overnight bags. The comment made Alex's lips twitch, but she didn't say anything. She'd spent enough time racing around with Diego to know that an empty road was irrelevant when he wanted to get someplace in a hurry. But this wasn't the best time for one of their verbal jousting matches.

Serge ended his brief call to Diego, flipped the phone closed and stuffed it in his pocket as he climbed into the Range Rover to begin the journey to London. He turned the key in the ignition and the rugged vehicle's powerful motor roared to life, but an approaching car's headlights made him freeze as he was about to put the 4 x 4 in gear. He waited for the late night traveler to zoom past the spot where he was parked, but instead of passing, the vehicle slowed. Not a tourist then. It had to be a cop on night patrol. He knew better than to run from the police. As anxious as he was to get going, he had no choice but to stay where he was. He got out of the Rover and stood next to it with his hands visible so the cop could see he posed no threat, but he left the motor running and the door ajar.

He'd already changed into jeans and a Miami Dolphins sweatshirt and wedged his gear into the tire well until he could dump it. There'd be no trouble passing for an American tourist. He'd show his U.S. passport and the car rental papers, all in the name of Steven A. Spencer of Florida, and explain that he'd pulled over to rest before continuing the nine-hour drive to London.

The cop would suggest that he check into a hotel and get a good night's sleep. Serge would thank him and agree to find a bed when he reached Aberdeen, less than a half hour away. The whole thing might take five minutes, max, a minor glitch.

Serge never took his eyes off the approaching vehicle as it veered off the road, scanned the car park with its headlights and moved toward him. He cursed the pitch-black night that kept him from clearly seeing the car as it closed in on him.

Cop, Serge thought. Yet every instinct in his body told him to jump into the Rover and get the hell out of there. He'd learned to pay attention to the internal warning system that had saved his life more than once. But if this was a cop—and who else could it be—it would look suspicious for him to suddenly take off. There'd be a chase. And questions. And a delay he couldn't afford. Logic overruled his inner voice.

The car's high beams blinded him. In the split second before his eyes readjusted, the driver leapt out and shrieked hysterically, "Where's Jamie? What have you done with him?" There was the glint of a gun.

Reflex propelled Serge's body into the driver's seat and he threw the SUV into gear before the man's words traveled from ear to brain. His foot hit the gas and he had the Rover moving before he'd even closed its door. Then he felt the unmistakable searing pain of a bullet. The wound didn't matter, survival did. He gunned the engine and tore out of the parking lot, tires squealing, gravel flying, as another bullet or two pinged off the tailgate. He checked the rear view mirror and saw that the other car was no match for his. The shooter would know that too. There'd be no chase.

CHAPTER 35

The waking sun turned the sky over Inverness into a pink, gold and peach masterpiece as the plane Diego chartered taxied to the runway for take off for London. Against the warm glow of dawn, Alex's face was pale and she could barely keep her eyes open.

"Put your head on my shoulder and try to rest, *Preciosa*."

"No, not yet. This country's so beautiful ... but I have to say good-bye to it. I don't ever want to come back here." She gazed out the window as their route took them south, down the Great Glen and over Loch Ness. Then she closed her eyes, overcome by memories of Will, and felt her heart break.

Diego held her hand until she fell asleep. He hoped that the pain that he'd seen in her eyes would be gone when she woke.

Less than two hours later, the jet touched down at the small London City Airport and taxied to the area where the Navarro Gulfsteam was parked. Diego gently kissed Alex's forehead. "Wake up sleeping beauty."

"Are we in London? Have we really left Scotland?" she asked hopefully and felt immense relief when Diego replied, "Yes, thank God."

"Good. I feel like a huge weight is gone."

Minutes later they walked down the steps of one plane and onto the other. The nap had done her good and Alex's mood lifted the minute she stepped aboard. "Is that coffee? Do I smell coffee?" she asked the cabin steward who welcomed them. He brought her a steaming mug as soon as she was seated and then served a breakfast worthy of a four star restaurant.

"I keep forgetting that you really live differently from the rest of us mere mortals," she commented as she dabbed her mouth with a linen napkin and opened the top button of her jeans to relieve the pressure of too much food.

"Yes, I do. Is that a problem?" Diego snapped, then immediately apologized. "I'm sorry. Serge should have been here by now. I'm worried."

"Could he have radioed the pilot? Maybe your mobile isn't working or Serge's can't get a signal," Alex suggested. Diego's anxiety was contagious.

"Maybe. I'll go forward and check."

Diego returned from the cockpit a minute later and exhaled loudly as he collapsed into the cushy leather seat opposite her. "Nothing. Serge assured me it went off without a hitch when he called last night. If anything happened to him…" He wouldn't allow himself to finish the sentence.

Alex got out of her seat and began to massage his shoulders. He groaned as her fingers kneaded away the knots of tension that had become a constant presence since … well … for a long time. Alex scolded herself for being so consumed by her own needs that she hadn't considered the effect all of this was having on him. Diego was tough and he was brave, but even the strongest men crack and need to lean on someone once in a while. She not only owed him her support, she wanted to give it.

"You're very good at that," he said as her thumbs did

their work. "Ever think of opening a massage parlor? You could wear ... nothing?"

"Very funny, Navarro. You had to go for the lewd comment just when I was starting to think that some of your other body parts might want my attention too." She laughed as he tumbled her into his lap.

"Does this mean you've stopped worrying about Serge?" she whispered as she ran her tongue around the edges of his ear, pleased that she was able to distract him.

"No, but maybe there's something we could do to help pass the time. After all, worrying won't bring him here any sooner," he said as he ran a hand up her leg and nuzzled her neck.

"Oh it won't, huh?" Serge teased as he stood leaning against a seatback. "I'm crushed."

Diego forgot that Alex was on his lap and jumped to his feet, toppling her to the floor. When he bent to help her up she yanked his arm hard enough to pull him down beside her and they both began to laugh hysterically to relieve their tension.

"I see nothing's changed," Serge muttered. His shoe squished with each step as he tried to limp around them.

"What's that sound? Why are you limping?" Diego was already on his feet when he spotted the source of the odd sound and the color drained from his face.

"You're bleeding! What happened?"

"It's nothing, just a flesh wound. It bled into my shoe like a son of a bitch, but I think it's okay now."

"How did you get shot? Who did it? You told me everything went fine and that you were on your way to London. What happened?"

"I got careless, ignored my gut. So I took a bullet ... not the first time," he said as if this were an everyday occurrence. "I'm not sure who the shooter was, but he was screaming about Jamie so best guess is it was Duncan Buchanan, the guy with the safe house. Lucky for me the bastard's a lousy shot and drives a piece of shit car. Bullet grazed my ankle before I got the Rover's door closed. The rental people will be pissed."

"Lean on me," Diego snapped as he gripped Serge around the waist and helped him into a seat.

"Stop pushing me around, I'm fine," Serge protested.

"I can see how fine you are bleeding all over the place. Take off your shoe. Alex, get the pilot. He can decide whether we need to call an ambulance."

"I'm not going to any hospital with a gunshot wound. You're smart enough to know what would happen if I did."

"I do," Diego agreed. "Fortunately, my father hired a pilot who was a medic in the Gulf War."

Wound cleaned, closed with butterfly strips and bandaged, Serge allowed Diego and Alex to fuss over him as he reclined in a seat, sipping a third medicinal vodka as the plane sat on the runway, waiting to be cleared for take off.

He'd been through a lot worse and was no stranger to stressful situations, but Alex and Diego weren't. They'd been under intense pressure and had handled it better than he thought they would, so if Alex felt better spoon feeding him and Diego couldn't stop glancing at the bandage to assure himself the wound was closed, he'd go along with it. But he'd be damned if he'd let them put him to bed in the aft cabin like some invalid.

"If you won't use the bed, I will," Alex finally

mumbled in between yawns after Serge's third and final refusal. "I'm so tired I can't think."

The moment the door to the aft cabin closed, Diego moved closer to Serge. "What the hell happened?" He'd always believed that his bodyguard was invincible, an iron man, and because he'd risked his life on Diego's orders, he blamed himself for his friend's injury.

"I told you, everything went off as planned. No one can survive a fall into the sea from the height of those cliffs. Especially when they're unconscious. He's dead. I'm sure of it."

"I know that already! Tell me how you got shot!"

"It was a stupid mistake. It's always a stupid mistake." Serge described the incident in the car park and his misguided assumption that the approaching vehicle was a police car. "It was pitch black, but when the driver started screaming about Jamie, I knew it had to be Buchanan since that was where Mackinnon had sent his grandson."

"How did he even know to look for you? There's no way that they could have found out that we discovered where the son of a bitch was hiding. And if it was Buchanan who followed you to the cliffs, why didn't he use his gun to stop you before Mackinnon went into the sea? I don't get it."

"Neither did I. On the drive down to London I went over everything that happened from the moment I left Inverness. I analyzed every detail over and over and over. It was a good distraction from the pain."

"And?"

"And I came up with nothing solid, just theories. Want my best guess?"

Diego nodded.

"We know that Michael Graham didn't find me when he went to the hotel and that had to have made him suspicious. Don't forget he was sure I'd lied about you and Alex. He's a smart guy, so it wouldn't be a stretch for him to figure out that I wasn't who I said I was. Now, because Buchanan saw me at the cliffs, they know it for sure. Graham must have warned the others and Buchanan came looking for Jamie to ship him off to another safe house. We'll probably never know for sure." Serge cursed under his breath and smashed his fist into the arm of the chair. "I hate loose ends. They always come back to bite you in the ass."

"Let me think about this for a minute." Diego got up to pace, then sat opposite Serge and leaned toward him. "You said you got the tapes to MI-5 and they planned to arrest all of them this morning, right?"

Serge nodded.

"You said Michael Graham might have been worried enough to warn everyone and even order them to disappear. When the cops come to arrest the bastards, are they going to find them gone?" Diego's eyes narrowed and his face reddened as the potential repercussions of this theory hit home.

"It's possible," replied Serge. "Give me a minute to check," he said as he punched numbers into a satellite phone.

Diego listened and watched Serge's face, trying to read his expression until he ended the call.

"It's mostly good."

"Mostly? What does that mean? Tell me exactly what they told you before I wring it out of you," Diego snapped as the anger, guilt and worry that coursed through his body erupted. "Did they get them or not?"

"They got four them around dawn."

"Four? Are you saying that one got away?"

"So it seems."

"Stop being so fucking calm!" Diego exploded. "Was it Buchanan who got away?"

"No, they have him and he won't shut up about a murder on the cliffs, but no one's paying attention to him."

"Then who...?"

"Michael Graham. He's disappeared."

"He's gone? But they'll find him, right? This is the British fucking secret service! How could they screw up and not bring him in? He was the brains of the thing."

"For the reason you just said. He was smart enough to have a contingency plan. Don't forget that he had a lead of several hours from the time he left the hotel until MI-5 broke down his door. If it were me, I'd have a disguise, cash, fake papers and small boat ready to take me to one of the islands or even Ireland. They may never find him."

"Shit. So it's not finished." Diego scrubbed his face with his hands. "There's still a threat to Alex."

"Not just to Alex you idiot!" Serge bellowed. "You're the one they'll be after, not her!" He'd wanted to beat Diego senseless ever since he'd disobeyed explicit orders and went to Mackinnon's store. "Why the hell did you shoot off your mouth about being a Cameron? And leaving the DNA report was really stupid. These people have long memories and aside from Graham still being out there somewhere, none of them will get a life sentence. Hell, they may not even be convicted. This eye for an eye thing could go on indefinitely like some chess game, especially once they tie us to what was done last night. So I can't say that either of you is out of danger. But that's why you keep me around."

Diego lowered his head into his hands as he considered the ramifications of everything Serge had told him. "You're right. I am a fucking moron. So there's a chance... ?" He was afraid to complete the question, but Serge understood.

"A remote one ... but there is, yes."

Diego nodded and sighed deeply. "Have some breakfast before that vodka eats a hole in your stomach and then get some rest." He squeezed Serge's shoulder, then turned and slowly walked to the aft cabin.

They were halfway across the Atlantic when Alex woke and became aware of Diego sleeping next to her. His black hair was tousled and a two-day growth of stubble shadowed his face. There were dark circles under his eyes, the result of 24 hours without sleep. She was tempted to wake him, but decided to check on Serge instead. Her hand had just touched the aft cabin's doorknob when she turned and saw Diego's eyelids flutter as he changed position. Suddenly, she didn't care if he needed to sleep. He could do that later, or tomorrow. Right now, they had to talk.

"You know, I was just thinking..." she began.

Diego knew that any time a woman began a sentence that way it usually meant trouble. He could pretend that he hadn't heard her, but then she'd use some ploy to wake him, so he propped a pillow behind his head, crossed his arms and plunged. "Okay, I'll bite. Is this about what Serge did last night?

"No, that's not it. I'm ashamed to admit it, but I'm really okay with that except that he got hurt doing it. I'm glad he's okay."

"Are you going to tell me what's bothering you or did you wake me up so you'd have company?" he said irritably when she didn't respond.

"I'm not sure what I want to say. It's not about what happened. It's about us," she began.

"Us? What about us?"

She hand combed her hair, stalling for time. She wasn't sure whether she was ready for this particular conversation. It might be better to drop it and just wait and see. She'd been so caught up in grief and adventure and her unexpected feelings for Diego that she hadn't considered, until now, that life would return to whatever her new normal was once the plane landed in Boston. She could hang out with Francie, catch up with other friends, shop, cook, work out, do laundry—all the mundane activities of daily life that had stopped the instant she'd been told Will was dead. Or maybe she'd get a job, open a shop, take art lessons or even learn to tango.

She'd changed since her world had turned into an amusement park thrill ride. Without even realizing it, she no longer needed to plan for every eventuality, and, if things didn't go right, long for a do-over. Events, combined with Diego's impulsiveness and zest for life, had loosened her up.

"Well?" Diego snapped. Alex's behavior wasn't helping his foul mood. He was more shaken than he was ready to admit by Serge's wound and the news about Graham's escape. "If you've got nothing else to say I'm going back to sleep."

"Okay, okay," Alex grumbled, ending her self-analysis. "What I want to know is ... when we get back to the States ... then what?" She studied Diego's face as he considered her question, but his expression gave nothing away. She was afraid that he would go back to partying in exotic places around the globe when he wasn't busy running the Navarros' various enterprises with his father. They'd always be great friends, she was sure of that, but she would also become one more name on the long list of his ex-lovers. Bloody hell.

"You want to know what happens next? I don't have a crystal ball, but my guess is that life is going to be pretty boring for both of us after all of this excitement. But thank God that part is over."

"Over? How can you say that? You told Mackinnon that you're a Cameron! Aren't you worried that they'll decide to kill you or that his people will eventually retaliate for what we did?"

"The man who murdered Will is dead and the men responsible for the vendetta against John Cameron were arrested this morning. It's over, Alex. There's nothing more to fear."

He had to believe that was true—for now at least. She didn't have to know that the threat to them could extend far into the future. Then he remembered that it was John Cameron's over-protectiveness that had contributed to Will's murder and realized he'd have to tell her about Michael Graham's escape … but not today.

"So we're safe, are we? Well, I don't feel safe. Maybe I never will. When someone you love is fine one minute and dead the next, all certainty about life disappears." Her eyes filled with tears as her gaze shifted from his face to her hands and the emerald and diamond ring she still wore on the left.

Diego felt a stab of jealousy and chastised himself for resenting a dead man's hold on her. And not just any man—his brother. Alex would always love Will. He'd either have to accept that or let her go, but the thought of losing her unnerved him. "So is that it? Is that all you wanted to talk about?" Goddamn it, he was wiped out and would have liked more sleep.

"No, not really," she hesitated. "You avoided my question or maybe I wasn't clear. What I want to know is what happens to us, this 'us' that we've begun? Do I go back to whatever my life will be in Boston and you go ... where will you go? To Argentina?"

"Buenos Aires is my home. It's where I was born and our business is based there ... so are my parents."

"Oh," she replied, missing him already.

He'd given the same subject a lot of thought. He'd assumed that what he felt for her was simply physical, but his desire had intensified instead of burning itself out. She was smart, brave, unpredictable, funny, and passionate and he enjoyed every moment he spent with her, even when she exasperated him. And then there was the extraordinary tenderness he felt for her. His heart was no longer just his, and he was determined to win hers. Between him and Serge, they'd be safe from whatever threat the crazy Scots still posed. He'd hire another bodyguard, or two or three, a whole army if necessary. That would piss her off, but too bad.

"I've been thinking too, Alex."

"I can see that," she said and smiled when she realized that he was as unsure of what to say as she had been.

"How old does a man have to be before he buys a house of his own?"

"A house? I don't know," she replied, completely puzzled by Diego's question. "Do you really want an answer?"

"Yes, I do."

"Well, I've been on my own since college, but that's